Aimee's Locket

by

P. L. Parker

This is a work of fiction. Names, characters, places, and incidents either are the product of the author's imagination or are used fictitiously, and any resemblance to actual persons living or dead, business establishments, events, or locales, is entirely coincidental.

Aimee's Locket

Contact Information: info@thewildrosepress.com

Cover Art by *Angela Anderson*

The Wild Rose Press
PO Box 708
Adams Basin, NY 14410-0706
Visit us at www.thewildrosepress.com

Publishing History
First Cactus Rose Edition, 2009
Print ISBN 1-60154-683-1

Published in the United States of America

"Sure you don't want to take me up on my offer?" Jake's teasing was old.

"You wish!" She huffed and stalked out, forgetting to check the hallway first and banged into a boarder walking by. A lascivious leer devoured her, replacing the boarder's previously blank expression.

"Looking for customers?" He smacked his bulbous lips, reminiscent of an overeager suckerfish. "I just might be interested."

Her shoulders drooped in disgust. "You are soooo sickening." She glared at him. "How about you get out of my face before I ream you a new orifice?"

Startled, the man's mouth flew open as he gaped in surprise.

Jake stepped into the hallway and lowered his voice to sound ominous in the ensuing silence. "The *lady* was just returning to her room. I suggest you do the same."

The hapless man barely glanced at his threatening stance before he scurried down the hall. Jake's lips twitched. He couldn't blame him. He'd made the same offer more than once today. But, damn, if she wasn't a feisty piece of woman. At least she hadn't threatened to ream *him* a new orifice—whatever that was.

"Thanks…again! Seems like all I do is thank you for one reason or another." Aimee hesitated, appearing unsure. Her vulnerability stirred deeper feelings in him, making him uncomfortable. "I've had more creepy offers from more creepy men in one day than I've had in my entire lifetime!"

"If you keep running around in your underclothes, it's pretty much what you can expect."

He followed her across the hall. "Stay in there and don't answer the door, and if anyone bothers you—scream. I'll hear it."

She slipped into her room and pivoted, staring up at him. "Why are you helping me?"

Praise for P. L. Parker's work...

FIONA: "She blends a romance to last through eternity, it is absolutely timeless. Impressible, implausible, and elegantly done, this is one story that I don't think I will ever forget!"

~Fallen Angel Reviews (rated 5 angels)

"From the dark, eerie prologue through to the very unexpected ending, FIONA by P. L. Parker is an engaging and eventful account of a life and a timeless love."

~The Long and The Short of It (rated 4 books)

"I have never read a time travel in which the setting was so far back in time, and so it was with great excitement that I started RILEY'S JOURNEY. P. L. Parker did not disappoint!"

~CK2S Kwips and Kritiques (rated 5 cloverleafs)

Dedication

To Ami, who opened the door and held it open,
and to my family and friends
for their understanding, support and forbearance
in reading the same thing over and over again.

Prologue

The large leather-bound book, now worn by time and use, rested on the antique table. Her stomach churning with dread, Sara Reynolds' fingers lightly traced the tooled Oriental lily adorning the cover. If what the old lady said was true, Aimee's life lay within those pages, handwritten by her, and handed down through the generations to be given to her family at just the right moment. But how was that possible?

She gazed across the table at her parents, David and Liz. Motionless, like grief-stricken statues, they waited for her to begin.

With reverent fingers, she opened the musty old journal, jumping as the binding cracked, worried she'd damaged it somehow.

She picked up two dark squares. "Mom, Dad, you have to look at these."

They leaned nearer. Sara held up two old tintype photographs. The first was of a young woman, sitting at a desk, dressed in vintage clothing. The young woman in the first picture was a dead ringer for Aimee, a little older, but with the same wide eyes and full lips. In the second picture, the same woman, older now, reclined on a settee. A handsome man stood next to her, his hand on her shoulder, while seven children of varying ages and sizes ringed the couple—three boys and four girls.

Her mother stared, her face blanching white in the meager light of the study. "She looks just like Aimee. How can that be?"

It had to be a trick—or maybe these were those

old-time photographs that were so popular nowadays. If so, where was Aimee now?

Sara set the pictures aside and leaned over the book, touching the first page, lip reading. The paper was yellowed with age, the writing faded, but it was Aimee's. "It's her handwriting. I'd know it anywhere!"

Her father lunged to his feet, grabbing at the book. "It can't be. The damn book's over a hundred and fifty years old."

She cried out, afraid he would rip it. Her mother stopped him, laying a gentle, restraining hand on his forearm.

"I want to hear what it says," her mother said, mouth pursed with firm resolve. "Whatever it says, I want to hear it."

Sara picked up the book and sat down at the table. "Sit down and I'll read to you."

Her father pounded the table. "I don't want to hear any of this crap."

Liz pushed him away. "Then don't. Leave if you want, but I'm going to listen."

"There's a smiley face in the corner with a note." Sara turned the book peering at the words. "It's from Aimee. She says, 'Jake wrote some notes here and there to tell his side of the story. He thinks it's important. He didn't want you to think he was a lowlife scumbag.' Then she says 'hee hee.'" She paused, glancing up. "I bet Jake's the guy in the picture. Okay," she said, taking a deep breath, "here we go. Page one. My incredible journey started on July 14, 2008."

Chapter One

"Take me with you," Sara coaxed, dancing on tiptoes. "I promise I won't get in the way and your friends won't even know I'm there."

Aimee laughed. "That's what you said last time, and I spent all my time chasing you around."

"You won't today. I promise I'll be good." Sara's young face glistened with hope. "I'll stay right next to you all the time, and I won't say a word."

Aimee pretended to think about it, letting Sara stew while she made her decision. She'd already intended to let Sara go, but it never hurt to let her beg for awhile. She loved Sara as only a big sister could, and even though she was annoying at times, Aimee forgave her. She leaned into the mirror, examining her makeup. Unhurried, she brushed her long hair, pulling it back and tying her favorite sky blue scrunchie around the thick mop. Strawberry gold tendrils sprang free, hanging saucily around her heart-shaped face.

Sara reached over and picked up a puzzle box from Aimee's dresser, examining it from every side, over and over.

"Did you ever figure out how to get this stupid thing open?"

Taking the object from Sara's hands, she unlocked the intricate box and tossed it on the bed. "I've shown you how to do it fifty times, and you still don't have it right."

"Who cares anyway?" Sara sniffed, crinkling her nose. "Not like it's going to matter in fifty years."

"You're just jealous because Dad brought it back

for me and not you." Dad had brought Sara a gift as well, but greedy little Sara always wanted what she had.

"Take me with you." Sara almost danced in her eagerness to be included.

"On one condition."

Sara's face lit up. "Anything! I'll do anything. Just tell me what."

"My room needs dusting, and I don't have time to do it today. Take it or leave it." She knew what the answer would be. Sara'd do anything to be included.

Pouting, lower lip thrust out, Sara's shoulders sagged. "I did it last week."

"Well, okay then. Maybe I'll take you next week." Sighing in fake resignation, she turned around, waiting for Sara's expected response.

"*Okay!* I'll do it, but this is the last time. You'll have to come up with something else next time." Sara ran from Aimee's bedroom, bee-lining to Mom for permission.

Weather in Seattle was iffy even during the hottest parts of the summer, but today looked to be hot. She opened her wardrobe, searching for the perfect outfit. A long brightly-flowered broomstick skirt and matching chemise caught her eye. She wouldn't even have to wear a bra with that one, and the skirt was only semi-transparent. If she got out before Mom caught her, she could forget about wearing a slip as well. The chemise fit like a glove, showing off her tanned shoulders and neck to perfection. Rummaging around in her jewelry box, she donned all of the most expensive pieces—diamond studs given by Mom and Dad as a graduation present, large hoops for the front piercing, several gold chains, numerous gold bracelets and, lastly, all her diamond and sapphire rings. They were her favorites. Every Christmas since she turned fourteen, Mom and Dad had given her another one and, by now, almost every finger glittered. While it might be chancy wearing so much, Pike's Street during the day was usually safe enough, and she had no desire to be there after dark.

Sara ran back in, puffing from exertion. "Mom said I can go if it's okay with you—but we have to be back by three because Mom has that show tonight at the Center, and she wants us to go with her."

A light spritz of her favorite perfume and she was ready. "We'd better be back sooner than that, or you won't get my dusting done before tomorrow."

Sara threw herself on the bed, pummeling a pillow. "You are so mean. Why can't you ever just say 'yes' and leave it at that?"

"Because then I wouldn't get all these boring chores done for free." She laughed, grabbed her purse, and headed out the door with Sara hot on her heels.

Pike's Street Market was alive with tourists and shoppers even this early in the morning. Crowds flowed down the walkways, jostling for space in the limited confines. The scent of a thousand flowers wafted through the covered pathways, mixing with the mouth-watering smells of the food vendors. She squeezed through the crush of bodies, taking pleasure in every jam-packed minute, even while she searched for Sara. Keeping hold of her younger sister was a lesson in futility. Slicker'n snot, she could disappear in the blink of an eye. Threats were useless. She knew by now her big sister was a softie at heart.

Aimee drew in a deep breath. Lilies of every genus bloomed in a riotous display of color—yellows, golds, pinks, and reds—their exotic perfume teasing her senses with flagrant abandon. The perfect blossom was there, she just had to find it. *Eureka!* Handing over the exact cash, she held fast to the delicate flower and stepped into the milling throng.

Sara touched the bloom, her expression puzzled. "Why do you always have to buy just one stupid lily every time we come here?"

"Because they're my favorite. When I have a place of my own, I'm going to plant them in every available space. My yard will be the best smelling on the street."

A new antique shop caught her eye. Dragging Sara behind, she charged in. Antiques were her first love. Her favorite pieces were ivory lockets. She had a prized collection ensconced in a glassed-in case where she could enjoy them every day.

The interior of the shop was small and dark. A friendly faced woman stood at attention near the cash register.

"Hello, girls! What can I do you for?" Her smile and soft voice offered a warm welcome.

Aimee strolled around the shop, missing nothing, and ending in front of the cashier. "I collect ivory lockets. Do you have any right now?"

The woman's gaze traveled the length of her, taking in every detail. As if confirming something to herself, she leaned down and pulled a tray out of the display case. Several ivory lockets nestled in the silk-lined box, but the one the woman picked up and handed to Aimee begged to be purchased. The delicate chain and setting appeared to be real gold. The ivory itself was yellowed with age, and a woman's profile, cut from onyx, rested on the filigree bed. It was so beautiful—and so expensive!

"Uh, I can't afford this." Disappointed, she handed the locket back. *Dang it—she wanted it!*

"Oh, Aimee!" Sara exclaimed, her eyes round with wonder. "It's so perfect."

She agreed, but tuition took every spare penny. The woman again handed the locket to her. "I can give you a better price."

She clutched the locket. "How much?"

"How about three fifty?"

She set the locket back on the tray. "I can't afford that." Taking Sara's arm, she turned to leave.

The woman picked up the locket, dangling it across her hand, "Don't be in such a hurry! How about two hundred, and you promise to buy something else from me next time you're down here?"

Her inner alarm went off. This transaction was just too weird. Why would a shopkeeper drop the price so much?

"Is it stolen or something?"

A shadow passed over the woman's face. "No, nothing like that. Believe me. It belonged to my husband's great-great, whatever great grandmother."

"You have to buy it, Aimee." Sara fingered the clasp. "It's so much prettier than any of the ones you already have."

"Where am I going to get two hundred dollars?"

"Well, how much is in your bank account right now?" Sara just didn't understand the finances of being a college student.

"I can't use that. It's for tuition next fall. Dad'll kill me if I blow it on something like this."

The longer she held the locket, the more it seemed to draw her. She could feel the outline of the black profile and the silky gloss of the old ivory. *She had to have it!*

"Okay. I'll take it!" Turning to Sara, she scowled. "And if you breathe one word to Dad—or Mom—about how much this cost, I'll never talk to you again."

Sara nodded, crossing her heart. "I promise!" She zipped her lips. "Not one word."

The woman's mouth tightened in a slight smile. "I knew the minute you walked in here the locket was for you."

Aimee tilted her head, wondering at her words. She handed the woman her debit card, praying she could earn enough to cover the deficit before Dad noticed. Nothing got by the man. It was her good fortune he was out of town so she had some time to recoup the loss before he got back. Maybe she could borrow a few bucks until payday. The woman handed her the locket wrapped in soft tissue paper and her receipt. Grabbing Sara's hand, she almost ran from the shop, her new treasure clutched in her fist.

Sara stopped, staring through the window. "That woman was weird."

"Yeah! She was kinda. She gave me a really good deal, though." Gripping her sister's skinny shoulders, leaning down nose to nose, she reiterated. "I'm serious. Keep your mouth shut about how much the locket cost. Otherwise, you can just plan on staying home by yourself more often."

"You should put it on. It'd look great!"

"I never wear these things. I just collect them." Still, she was tempted… She unfastened the antique clasp and slipped it on.

"It's perfect." Sara's eyes lit with envy. "Almost like it was made for you."

"Remind me to take it off before we get home." Eagle-eyed Mom would notice it right off.

"Let's go across the street and get a Coke." Sara was always either hungry or thirsty—endearing but irritating. She also had the propensity to try every toilet within flushing distance—not so endearing and really irritating.

As the morning progressed, the chain and locket grew warmer, gathering heat from the sun. Her neck started itching. She scratched, growing pissed. Maybe she'd been scammed and the locket was a Chinese import. Experiencing a brief moment of dizziness, images flashed across her vision. Startled, she stopped, gasping in surprise.

"Your neck's getting all red," Sara pulled on the chain. "Like you're having a reaction or something."

Another wave of dizziness hit her and more images flashed—visions of ladies in old-fashioned dresses, with parasols and bonnets, and men with those funny mustaches and walking canes. She plunked down on the curb, waiting for the dizziness to pass.

"What's the matter?" Sara's concerned face swam before her. "Are you okay? Your face's really white."

"Just dizzy. I should've eaten something earlier." But that didn't explain the weird images.

"Well, let's go get some lunch then. I have some money. Come on, I'll buy." Sara tugged at her arm, trying to pull her up.

She staggered to her feet, feeling lightheaded and nauseated. More of the visions assaulted her, and crying out, she fell.

Sara squeaked in alarm, wringing her hands. "Maybe I should get help."

Passersby stopped, offering to help, but Aimee brushed them away. Self-conscious and confused, she only wanted to go home. "Help me get up again. See if you can find a cab."

"I don't think I should leave you," Sara's voice drifted in and out as she tried to focus. "I think we should go together."

More waves of dizziness washed over her. She could hear Sara screaming and calling her name—then nothingness.

Chapter Two

Aimee flew through the air, hitting the ground with a solid thump. Groaning in pain, she opened her eyes, and then rolled away in panic as a team of horses almost ran her over. The driver cursed, snapping the reins as the wagon careened around her. *The ignorant ass was a maniac*!

"If you roll one more time," an amused voice drawled, "your face'll end up in that pile of horseshit."

Her head tilted to the side. Sure enough, one more roll and she would have landed in a stinking pile of horse poop. Scrambling to her feet, she looked down. Her favorite outfit was covered in black mud. Filth caked her arms and legs, and she could only guess what her face looked like. Rubbing her hands down, she tried to dislodge some of the disgusting sludge, but it stuck like glue.

"If I were you, the next time one of my customers threw me out into the street, I'd make sure I was wearing more than just my petticoat." The amused voice commented again.

"Excuse me?" Turning, she caught sight of the voice's owner.

Kicked-back in a wooden rocker, his feet propped on a railing, the man regarded her from eyes the startling shade of Brazilian aquamarine, rimmed by black lashes so long and thick, she groaned with envy. Tanned by years of exposure to the sun, laugh lines accentuated his firm sensuous lips, while several days' growth of beard shadowed his chiseled jaw. A low-brimmed cowboy hat, tilted back, covered longish jet-black hair.

Jake Marshall leaned back in his chair, studiously admiring the little tart. *She was a tempting little piece!* He scratched his chin. What he couldn't figure out is where she came from. Seemed like she just appeared, rolling in the mud and cussing a blue streak. No matter. He was enjoying the show. His eyes dropped, perusing her from the tips of her feet to the top of her thick mop of curling red-gold hair. Wide eyes the color of old amber flashed sparks, and even the frown she now wore couldn't disguise the perfection of her full lush lips.

Slimmer than he generally liked, the muddied petticoat hid few of her charms—and he'd bet his bottom dollar she had nothing on under the thin chemise. Whores like her didn't usually get this far west. He'd seen some nice ones in the east and even a few in New Orleans, but never here. His groin tightened, reminding him it'd been awhile since he'd last had a woman. He wondered what she'd feel like beneath him as he ground against her, screaming as she climaxed.

He flashed her a wide smile, full of the Marshall charm. "If you're finished with your last customer, I might be interested."

She flipped her hair back, curling her lips in a sneer. "Customer? What customer? And why are you talking to me?"

Sassy, too! He liked sassy! He wondered if her skin tasted like peaches and cream. His mouth watered as his eyes rested on her pert breasts, visualizing his lips suckling the pebbled nipples. He shifted, easing the swelling in the front of his trousers. "Well, the goods you're selling appear to be prime, and I'm not a man to look a gift horse in the mouth."

"I still have no idea what you're talking about, and I could care less, anyway."

"I'll give you double what the last man paid."

Her eyes narrowed to mere slits, her lips tightened. A low chuckle escaped his lips. "Okay, I'll triple his price."

"I told you before, I have no idea what you're talking about." She flipped her mop of hair back. "Quit talking to me you disgusting piece of crap."

Aimee pulled open her clutch bag, flipped open her compact, and peered into the small mirror. *Good grief!* Mud and dirt were smeared all over her face. Thank God she'd stuffed some tissue in the bag before she left. Spitting on the tissue, she scrubbed at the dirt spots. Satisfied she looked somewhat presentable, she added a layer of lip gloss for good measure.

The jerk-off cowboy lounged on the porch, watching her ministrations, lips curling in amusement, his gorgeous blue eyes twinkling. "Only whores use face paint."

"Only creeps bother women who aren't interested!" She snapped the compact shut. "And don't compare me to a *whore*! Have you seen my sister?"

He shrugged, shaking his head. His feet came down off the railing with a thud, spurs jingling "Was she working this part of town with you? If so, I might be interested in you and her both."

Deciding to ignore the creep, she turned away, scanning the street in both directions.

Wooden shops lined a rutted earthen street, muddied by recent rains. Horses and carts were tied to wooden posts while dogs and dirty children chased each other down slatted wooden walkways. *What was she doing here*? It looked nothing like Pike's Street, where she was supposed to be.

"Lady—I said—who's your sister?"

"Sara!" Aimee moved a few feet farther down the street. "Sara—where are you!" Several curious children stopped their play, and a small girl stepped forward.

"I'm Sarah. Who're you?" The child looked to be all of four years old, dirty, clothing torn and frayed, with a mop of unkempt light brown hair trailing down her back.

She bent down, smiling at the small waif. "Well, Sarah, it's nice to meet you, but I was looking for a little bit older girl. Have you seen a girl who looks kind of like me, only shorter?"

The little girl poked a thumb in her mouth, shaking her head no. An older boy ran up, grabbed the little girl's arm, and jerked her away. "We ain't supposed to talk to strangers. Me mum'll beat us if she finds out."

Dragging the little girl behind him, he pulled her into a group of urchins playing in the street.

Women in floor-length, full-skirted dresses and deep bonnets obscuring their faces, scurried along the walkways ignoring the throngs of men who lounged about or stood in groups talking and eyeing the passing crowd. Wagons clogged the streets, pulled by teams of sturdy mules. Whips cracked, drivers cussed, and everywhere she looked, men on horseback rode by, leering as they made eye-contact. Everything looked so real, yet, so bizarre.

"Is there some sort of bicentennial celebration going on?" Why hadn't she heard about it sooner?

He shrugged. "Not that I'm aware of. Just another day."

"Very funny!" She needed to find Sara. It was ridiculous to waste more time with this lowlife scumbag.

"Sara!" she called again and wandered down the street.

He followed for a short distance. "I mean it. You'd better watch where you're going. The good ladies of this town might decide to have you tarred and feathered if you don't cover up."

Aimee whirled, flipping her hair. *She was tired of listening to his shit!* "I didn't ask for your opinion, and, in any event, I don't care what you think."

Stepping onto the covered walkway, she bumped into one of those "good" women. The woman froze, face puckering up, and eyes bugging out. Aimee almost laughed. The woman reminded her of a fat grumpy toad.

"Hussy!" Toad-face pulled her full skirt out of the way, lips pursed in disgust. "Go back where you belong." Head in the air, she sniffed and stalked away.

"Buzz off!" Aimee yelled at her retreating back.

Her single male audience choked, and then burst out laughing. When he stopped laughing, he blurted. "I don't know what 'buzz off' is supposed to mean but I'm guessing it isn't nice."

"Oh, for heaven's sake! Who're you supposed to be anyway? Wyatt Earp? Wild Bill Hickok? Quick Draw McGraw?"

A carved wooden Indian stood in front of a nearby tobacco store. "No, let me guess! I bet you're the Lone Ranger and that's Tonto." She smirked. "You messed up, though. Every other guy I see has either a mustache or a full beard. Your costume doesn't cut it."

Something flickered in his eyes. "Never liked my face covered by a bunch of hair. Too itchy. Besides," he grinned, rubbing a hand across his scruffy chin, "leaves marks on the ladies, both above and below."

Unbidden, several distinct sexual images flashed through her mind.

"Thanks for too much information, Mr. Creepy." *He was so disgusting.* "Quit with the pretense! You've made your point. You're Mr. Big Tough Cowboy and this is the Old West. Fine—I've got the picture! Now tell me how to get back to Pike's Street from here."

Perplexed, the man scratched his cheek. "Name's Jake. Don't know any Pike's Street. Never heard of it. But you can come with me if you want." He arched a dark eyebrow. "I'll pay whatever you want."

She groaned. *He just wouldn't give up.* "Whatever! I'll ask somebody else."

A store opened onto the walkway. She stepped in—only to be chased out by a fat woman wielding a long broomstick and shouting in anger. "And stay out of my store. Go back to the docks where you belong, hussy!"

Hussy? That was the second time in less than ten minutes she'd been called the exact same thing.

"What's wrong with everyone? Good grief!" Stomping her feet, she gave up, deciding to walk to one of the main thoroughfares and find a bus or a cab. She wouldn't find out anything here. If she didn't find Sara soon, Mom was going to kill her—dead!

Her nemesis opened his mouth again. "Better cover up. Otherwise, you're just going to get the same treatment over and over."

"Geez!" She reached into her small handbag, took out a twenty dollar bill and handed it to him. "If it'll make you shut up... Since I can't go in, would you take this money and buy me a scarf or a shawl."

His gorgeous blue eyes flashed with amusement as he stared at the proffered money. "What am I supposed to do with that?"

She ground her teeth. "Are you mentally challenged or just plain stupid? Go in there and buy me something."

He took the money, turning it over and over. "It says here...2008? What kind of game are *you* playing?" His face mirrored his confusion.

"It says 2008 because it *is* 2008! It's legal

tender—like you didn't know that."

"I don't know what calendar you're using, but it isn't 2008—it's 1847—April 16, 1847 to be exact!"

"Oh! For God's sake!" Frustrated, her fists clenched. She wanted to hurt him so bad. "Can we step back into reality and help me out here. I promise I won't tell anyone you slipped out of character for a few minutes. Your secret's safe with me."

"Lady—I don't know who you are or where you think you are, but this is 1847. We're in St. Louis, Missouri, and you can ask whoever you want, but you're going to get the same answer every time."

She stood there, absorbing his words until anger got the better of her. Snatching the money from the creep's hand, she stomped away. He might be better to look at than twenty pounds of chocolate, but he was severely irritating.

"Sara!" she yelled again. *Damn it!* Sara must've wandered too far to hear her. Flipping open her cell phone, she pressed Sara's number. The cell registered "no service." *No service! Great, her battery must be going!* No, it couldn't be that, all her saved stuff came up, and she'd just charged it this morning. *Try again!*

No matter how many times she tried, it was the same result. Disgusted, she stuffed the phone back in her clutch. She'd try again in a few minutes. Must be something blocking the signal.

She rounded a corner, marching fast, looking for a busier route. Horse-drawn wagons of every size and description lined the thoroughfares. Whistles and catcalls dogged her every step. A steady stream of men pestered her with revolting offers and sexual innuendos, while the women glared and turned up their long pointy noses. Children chased her, laughing and throwing things, striking her with dirt clods and even spoiled fruit. *Paybacks are hell!* She hefted a few good-sized clods and managed to deal out some pain before they backed off and ran.

At every corner, she dialed Mom or Sara's phone numbers, but the "no service" messages continued to plague her. She needed someplace higher. At least that's what they did on TV.

The bell tower in the nearby Presbyterian Church was the tallest structure she could see. Entering the cool depths of the sanctuary, she drifted towards the tower stairs, and strolled through the rows of pews, trying to look like she belonged. A few worshipers knelt, lips moving in prayer, but none seemed to notice her.

She stepped into the stairwell and started up the circular staircase. A nail snagged her skirt hem. She lost several minutes trying to free the delicate muslin, gouging her hand in the process. Chest constricted, breathing in labored gasps, sweat pouring from armpits and brow, she made it to the tower door. The climb about killed her. *I'm going to start a regular workout routine the minute I get home.*

She leaned out over the railing, heart pounding in her chest. From high above, the surrounding township was unfamiliar and frightening. No cars, motorcycles, or even bicycles were anywhere, nor could she see any power or phone lines. Holding her breath, hoping against hope, she pressed Sara's number. *No signal.* Try Mom's. *No signal.* Nothing worked.

I must be dreaming.

She crouched down, huddling against the wall. Her heart raced and panic squeezed her chest. No—scared wasn't the right word. *Terrified!* Her mind spun, chaotic thoughts and images raced through her confused brain. Nothing made sense. What screwed up twist of fate landed her in this messed up world? She wanted Mom! She wanted Dad! And she wanted Sara!

Aimee wiped her face. She took a deep breath and stood. Hiding here and whining wasn't doing any good. The only person who could save her was her. She descended from the bell tower, continuing her search. She wandered through parts of town where muscular workers shaped iron into what she could only guess were plows and perhaps other farm implements. A smattering of German, Italian, Spanish, and even some languages she couldn't identify, chattered over the cacophony of sound. In another section of town, Irish brogues were on every lip. She walked for perhaps three hours on dirt-covered roadways, from one part of town to another, always ending up facing vast expanses of open country. The unfamiliar horizon was flat, devoid of the many skyscrapers that cluttered Seattle's skyline.

Frustration pounded at her temples. Where was she? Where was Sara? Why didn't her phone work? There had to be something familiar somewhere. Discouraged, she headed west, jogging towards where she hoped Pike's Market and the ocean would be. She was puffing and winded by the time she made it to the docks.

She stopped, bemused and perplexed. Beyond the piers wasn't the ocean, but a wide slow moving river stretching into the distance. Boats and barges of every kind and nature dipped and rocked on the muddy waters, sails flapping in the wind. Not what she wanted to see. Pissed and growing more pissed, she slammed her hand against a brick wall, gasping as pain raced up her arm. *She hated this frickin' place! She just wanted to go home!*

Seething with activity, the area teemed with dockworkers, French speaking fishermen, and brawny laborers. Scantily clad women waved and gestured from second story windows, yelling obscene invitations to the men below. The dregs of society flocked to these streets, scurrying like rats to a garbage heap.

She'd been through too much. Heartsick, she plunked down on a sagging wooden stoop. Her legs shook with fatigue. The jog across town just about wiped her out. Added to that, she was starving. She scrubbed her hands across her face, surprised when they came away wet. *She was crying!*

In the building behind her, an out-of-tune piano accompanied by an off-key female voice, tinkled with raucous disregard for the ears of the unwitting. A blowsy, middle-aged blonde sidled up. Watermelon breasts strained against the thin cotton of her sweat-stained chemise, threatening to burst from the meager confines. Held aloft by a dirty red satin bustier, the weighty globes jiggled like giant bowls of gelatin.

Her kohl-lined pig eyes roamed over Aimee with contemptuous dislike.

"What man's gonna pay for the likes a you?" She preened, fluffing her filthy blonde locks with dirt-encrusted claws. "Men likes something to hold onto."

Aimee almost gagged as she caught a good whiff of pig woman's offensive personal hygiene. "They must like you a lot."

"That they do." The woman snarled, baring her tobacco-stained snaggle teeth. "So get your fat arse off my stoop and find yer own spot."

"*You* find another place. I was here first, and your stench is messing with my ambiance!"

Eyes narrowed, the woman gasped in outrage, double chin wagging in fury. "Why you little bitch. Oi'll teach you a thing er two."

"Yeah? You and who else?" Good grief. Was she going to have to fight the fat broad? This just wasn't her day.

"Me and meself!" The pugnacious blonde

advanced, fists doubled up, beady eyes bright with malice, and posed to fight.

"Oh—get real!" She stood up. "Keep your stupid spot! Not like anyone wants it—*or you*—anyway."

"And don't come back," the blonde whore screeched, shaking her fist.

Shrugging, Aimee stalked away, stepping into the bustling commotion. Boats and barges were tied up at the docks in large numbers while groups of people bartered and argued with the boatmen. There were even a few of those old-time steamboats tied up, ready to be loaded.

"Wondered where you went," a familiar deep male voice drawled. "But I sorta figured you'd end up here."

Sighing in resignation, she turned. "And why is that?"

"Because it's where all the bawdy houses are—all the whores peddle their wares down here."

"Why you ignorant—I- Am- Not- A- Whore!"

"If that's what you want everyone to believe... My name's Jake, by the way. Jake Marshall." He extended his hand.

Her chin went up as she glared at him. "I'm going to pretend I never encountered you, and you're going to pretend you don't exist and therefore can't bother me anymore." Head high, she strode down the street, only to be stopped as a huge cart laden with farm produce blocked her path.

"Looks like you just can't get away from me." Smirking, he again offered his hand.

Aimee stared at the extended hand. During this long and confusing day, he'd been the only one to offer even a modicum of consideration or concern. Apprehensive and wary, she returned the handshake.

"I suppose Jake is short for Jacob?"

Grinning, he bobbed his head. "My folks are big

Bible thumpers—it's the reason I came west."

He paused, eyebrows lifted. "I didn't hear your name?"

She pulled her hand back. "I didn't give you my name. I believe I read somewhere it wasn't proper for ladies in the Old West to mingle with men of low character."

A shadow passed over his handsome rugged features. "Are you questioning my character?"

"I think you qualify as being an undesirable. You've proven that by your disgusting remarks and crude behavior. I'm sure my Momma would agree."

A pretty brunette, clad in a maroon evening gown cut low enough to display her navel, pushed in front of Aimee. Sinuous, snakelike, she wound her arms around Jake.

"Well, lookee here! If it isn't good ole Jake hisself." Uncaring she had a reluctant audience, the brunette ran her hands over his chest, lingering at the light furring of hair where his flannel shirt gaped open, rubbing small circles while she crooned.

He did have a nice chest, at least the part Aimee could see. Her mouth got the better of her once again. "Well, lookee here, Jake!" She drawled, imitating the strident voice of the brunette to perfection. "Looks like you found the *ideal* date for the evening." *This was the most fun she'd had all day!*

Flushing beet red, his lips twisted in annoyance. She grinned, almost chuckling as the brunette's eyes flared, angry sparks dancing in their depths.

He disentangled himself from the clingy brunette and shoved her away. "I already found my *ideal* date. I just need a price." He waited, gauging her reaction.

"Why you slimy sonofa..." Gritting her teeth, she stomped off. If she stayed, she'd end up in jail for attempted murder, even if it was deserved. He was a jerk from the top of his thick wavy black hair down to his boot clad feet, and she had better things to do than waste her time talking to him.

She got as far as it took for an enormous dockworker to grab her arm and pull her fighting to his hairy chest. "Old Abe could use a good poke from you," he brayed with oafish glee.

Frightened, she lashed out, open-handing his face as she screeched, struggling against his enormous strength. *It was like hitting a concrete wall!* The years of manual labor had left this man rock hard and stronger than a bull. "Get your filthy hands off me before I call the police!"

"Ain't no lawmen down here." He guffawed, spewing spit all over her, his breath reeking of bad teeth and raw onions. "We make our own laws in this part of town."

Clutched tight in his clumsy embrace, his thick, beefy hands roamed over her, sending chills of disgust racing up her spine. The smell of unwashed body combined with fish was overwhelming. She almost retched as he buried his face in the vee of her neck, his greasy hair leaving slime marks across her face.

Scratching and kicking, she gouged, digging her fingers into the brute's eyes, attempting to either blind or cause him serious injury. Roaring in rage, he threw her back, snapping the strap of her chemise as she tumbled free. He wasn't finished. His eyes snapped with fury as he stomped towards her. She screamed, scrambling sideways.

"Hey there, friend," a low voice drawled. "Looks like the little lady isn't interested."

"Mind your own business," the brute growled. "Find another poke."

"Well, I believe this little lady and I had already made plans." Jake reached for her. "Now didn't we already have plans?" he asked with studied insouciance.

"If you was a fixing to poke her, why's she walking away?" The brute stood his ground, his eyes flicking from one to the other.

"Why *were* you walking away?" Jake asked, his attention drawn to the small expanse of breast left visible by the torn material.

She pulled the torn strap back into place and gulped. "I-I—" she stuttered, thinking furiously. "I was just going to check my schedule... to see if I'm available." It was a lame excuse but the best one she had.

He turned his attention to the hulking giant. "Now, see! There's no question about it—the little lady and I were just about to make plans."

"I ain't giving her up. You can wait till we're done." The big brute wasn't about to back down. Sneering at Jake, he reached around to paw at her, again.

"Walk away, friend," Jake's voice dropped, and his eyes narrowed. The big man glanced at Jake's hand resting on the gun slung low on his hip.

"You gonna shoot me over a whore?" He sputtered, incredulous.

"Not my custom, but today, I might make an exception." Jake's tone of voice left no question in her mind he meant what he said.

"I ain't even carrying a gun!" The big man croaked.

"I don't have a problem shooting an unarmed varmint if I need to." He shifted sideways, his fingers tapping the butt of his pistol.

The big man wasn't stupid. He stepped back, a sickly smirk on his too thick lips. "Ain't no whore worth dyin' for."

Jake bared his teeth in a parody of a smile. "You've made a wise decision, my big friend."

The big laborer shot one more scowling look in

her direction and then lumbered off.

Shaken, her stomach roiling, Aimee watched the big brute walk away, fearing he'd change his mind and return.

"Are you paying attention?" Her savior shot her a frown. "If you're not a whore, then you can't wander around down here dressed like that and expect every male in the area to leave you alone."

She clutched the torn bodice. "Thank you. I didn't know what I was going to do."

Apart from her clothing, she hoped she didn't act like a whore. Most of the whores she'd seen were tired and looked old. Her language skills were far above any she'd heard so far. Mom had taught her to carry herself well, and though mud spots covered her clothing, she was somewhat clean. Her lips trembled, unshed tears burned the back of her eyes. She was lost and so confused.

"Where are you going?"

She thought for a few moments. "I don't know. I've walked for hours, and I'm pretty convinced I'm not in Seattle anymore. I don't know what I'm going to do." Night was beginning to darken the sky and the air was cooling down fast.

He heaved an exaggerated sigh. "You might as well come with me. If you stay down here, you'll just attract more attention from men like him."

She glared at him. "Why would going with you be any different?"

"Because I won't force you, but you need to cover up. I don't want to fight every man down here to keep you."

"You don't *have me* to begin with." But her options were slim, bordering on none. At least *he* didn't look at her like every other male did—like she was a cheap piece of merchandise. She revised her thinking. Taking off one of her gold bracelets, she handed it to him.

"Do you think this would buy me anything?"

He took the bracelet, examining it closely. "Looks like real gold. Where'd you get it?"

"It is real gold," she spat. "It cost me a hundred and forty on sale."

"You bought it? A hundred and forty dollars for a bracelet? Where'd you get that kind of money?"

"I earned it." She had some accomplishments she could be proud of. "And not on my back either. I work part-time at Starbuck's, pouring coffee. Decaf mocha, low fat half and half, two lumps of sugar."

"What?" His brow wrinkled

"Never mind." She flipped her hand, dismissing the subject. "The rest of the time I attend college. I should graduate in another year."

Jake's eyes mirrored his disbelief. "No woman attends college. Now I know you're lying."

"I *do* attend college, and I carry very good grades. I'm going to be a social worker and work with abused children after graduation."

His mouth tightened, dimples creasing his cheeks. "Do you plan to work in an orphanage?" He sounded amused and unconvinced.

The conversation was going nowhere. He just couldn't believe she was anything more than a whore.

"Just go buy a coat—*please*." She sighed, tired of arguing. "I'm cold and it's getting late."

He shook his head. "I don't think I can get anywhere close to a hundred and forty for it."

"What do you think it's worth?" She hoped it was enough to at least buy a jacket or something.

He hefted the weight of the bracelet. "I can get you maybe five dollars."

"Five dollars! Are you nuts?" Furious, she reached for the bracelet. He was crazy if he thought she'd give it up for five dollars.

He grinned, sexy and dangerous, dangling the

bracelet in front of her. "Well, you can take my first offer!"

Her hand dropped. She had only her jewelry as bargaining power, but at least that. "Go ahead. Get what you can for it and then buy me a coat or a shawl or something."

"Are you sure?" His brows lifted, the invitation clear.

"Positive. Just get me something."

He shrugged and walked away, motioning for her to follow. "If you stand here, you're just asking for more trouble. Stay with me and keep quiet."

Confused, she ran to keep up. "Why do I have to keep quiet?"

"Because I said so."

She screeched to a halt. "And I'm supposed to do what you tell me? I don't even know you."

He stopped, turning to face her. "That's right, you don't. But at least you know my name."

She'd forgotten that little bit of information. "Oh, yeah, sorry. I'm Aimee Reynolds. From Seattle."

He shoved his hat back. "Seattle? Never heard of it."

He was playing with her again! "Seattle. You know. Almost to Canada—in northern Washington."

Puzzled, he shrugged. "Washington's back east. You've got your directions mixed up."

"You're the one that's confused!" Problem was, he didn't act confused. Bewildered, she reviewed what few bits of historical information she possessed about early Seattle. What was it? Oh, yeah. Settlers set foot in Seattle in 1851.

"What year did you say it was?"

"1847. Why?"

Who knew if Portland even existed in 1847. "Well, my family lives along the Pacific coast, further north than Portland." She hoped Portland existed by now.

"Oh," Jake nodded. "Last I heard, there wasn't much there."

His eyes traveled over her bedraggled form. "I'm surprised you aren't married if that's where you're from. Not many women I hear. You aren't married, are you?"

"No! But I do have a boyfriend—not a steady one—but a boyfriend. Actually, I'm dating several guys right now."

His eyebrows drew together. "So you're not a whore but you have lots of boyfriends?"

"Oh, for Pete's sake! Would you get off the whore thing! I told you I'm not one and I meant it."

"Best get you covered up then—if you're sure."

Her arm lifted. The desire to throw her purse and brain him was so tempting. "Of course, I'm sure. How could I be confused about something like that?" *Like she wouldn't know if she was a whore or not.*

"You seem pretty confused about a lot of things."

She had to give him that one. This had been the most confusing day of her life and it was getting more so by the minute. A niggling fear worked its way into her numbed brain. What if this whole thing was real? What if she wasn't imagining it? *Maybe she'd had a breakdown—and this was her delusion!*

"So how did you get here? First I saw you, you were lying in a puddle of mud. I thought maybe you got kicked out of one of the upper rooms at the boarding house."

The question broke through her reverie and brought back the earlier hours. How had she gotten here? She had been shopping with Sara on Pike's Street, and she'd just bought the locket. Her fingers unconsciously stroked the trinket.

"I don't know. I know you'll think I'm crazy or something, but this morning I was shopping with my sister in Pike's Market in Seattle and it was July 14, 2008."

"You're right," he agreed. "I do think you're crazy! Maybe that's why you're wearing just your crinoline—you escaped from Bedlam."

"Thanks for the vote of confidence." If it wasn't for the fact she had no one else, he'd be the last person she'd ever ask for help.

"Come on." Jake waved her along. "Let's get this over with and figure out what we're going to do with you."

Head down, she tagged along. She didn't want to see the stares that followed them every step of the way. Stopping in front of a tiny shop boasting the grand title of Assayer's Office, Jake turned to her. "Stay right here," he motioned to a rickety wooden chair, "and don't move. I'll be right back."

Aimee sat down, wrapping her arms around her shivering body. It was growing colder by the minute, and she was freezing. She kept her eyes down, watching the booted feet passing by. A few slowed down as they came closer—staring at her, she imagined. The endless minutes ticked by. *Maybe he wasn't coming back. Maybe he took her bracelet and left.* A hand grabbed her shoulder. She jumped, startled.

His face wreathed in a wide smile, dimples creasing his masculine cheeks, Jake grinned. "They gave me seven dollars for the bracelet. Said it was a nice piece. I told him there was a nicer piece out on the porch."

She could just slap him! "You are *soo* disgusting." She snatched the small wad of money from his outstretched hand. A sob welled in her throat. How stupid to feel so distraught over the loss of a silly bracelet, but it'd been one of her favorites, and selling it for less than a portion of what it was worth was depressing.

"Come on," he pulled her up. "I know a nice little place that sells secondhand clothes. We can fix you up there."

They walked for a short distance, ending up in a crowded little shop, clean but dark and dreary. A plump, middle-aged woman stood at the window where a calico cat reclined, watching the roadway. She brightened—a smile of welcome on her haggard face.

"Jake!" she exclaimed. "When did you get back?"

"Yesterday." Grabbing the woman, he kissed her. "How are you?"

"Fair to middlin'." Her faded blue eyes glistened with sadness. "Still miss him, though."

"I know." He rubbed her hand. "We both do."

Turning to Aimee, he introduced the woman. "This is Molly. Molly's husband, Ben, was one of my best friends. We worked together for years. Molly loves me." He grinned, hugging the woman again.

"You silly man," she said, pushing him away and turning to Aimee. "And who is this?" Her eyes grew less warm as she scanned her clothing.

"Just a friend," Jake said. "She's kind of down on her luck. I told her we might be able to get what she needs from you. She only has a few dollars, though."

Molly nodded, looking Aimee over. "I have just the perfect dress for her. Mrs. Abrams dropped off a load yesterday. They look to be about the same size." Shooing Jake out the door, she laughed. "No need to have him here bothering us."

"I don't want him bothering me at all, but I guess that's asking too much."

Molly tsk-tsked. "Jake is the best man you'll ever meet! Don't you go saying bad things about him to me. If I had a son, I'd want him to be just like Jake."

Embarrassed, she glanced at her feet. "I'm sorry. I've just had the worst day, and Jake's been right in the middle of it."

Molly's gaze dropped to the ripped chemise, widening with sympathy.

The room tilted, and Aimee swayed, reeling with exhaustion. She grabbed a chair and held on, trembling, her energy level at rock bottom. She was just so tired. *How'd she get into this mess?*

"Why don't you sit down and have a nice cup of tea while I round up the dress." Motioning her to a small table, Molly deftly poured a hot cup of tea into a waiting cup. "I always keep a pot hot for my customers, makes them feel a little more special," she remarked. "Nothing better than a hot cup of tea to help make things right."

Thankful for the small kindness, Aimee sipped the hot tea. Her stomach rumbled, reminding her she hadn't eaten since this morning. Lunchtime had come and gone, and it had to be after five o'clock by now. Just one more straw on the camel's back.

Molly laughed, her eyes crinkling. "Sounds like you could use some food right along with that tea." Reaching into a nearby cupboard, she brought out a plate of biscuits and handed her one. The biscuit was manna from heaven.

"Thank you so much! I'm absolutely starving."

"I'll have to have a word with Jake. Man should know how to take better care of his woman."

"I'm not his woman!" She choked on the biscuit, wiping her mouth. "He's just helping me out for awhile."

"Say what you like." Molly patted her arm. "Jake wouldn't bring just anyone to me. He must have some feelings for you."

"We just met today, so there's little chance of that. Most of the day, he's just accused me of being a whore or offering me money to do just that."

Molly's mouth tightened. "And are you?"

Startled, she glanced up. "Am I what?"

"Are you a whore?"

Sighing, she sat the cup down and straightened up. "No! I'm not! Contrary to what Jake thinks, I'm not nor have I ever been a whore. My Momma would just die if she heard someone accusing me of that."

"As well she should." Molly disappeared into the back room of the store and bustled back in, her arms laden with clothing. Setting the bundle down, she rummaged through it, exclaiming as she pulled out a flowered-sprigged green dress. "Here it is!"

Motioning for her to stand, Molly held the dress out. "I think this was one of Mrs. Abrams' daughter's dresses." She clucked. "That girl has more clothes than any woman in this whole town—but that's the rich for you! I think the fit will be perfect, and the color is just right with your hair."

She hugged the treasure to her chest. "How much do you want for it?" All she had was the seven dollars from the bracelet and this dress had to cost more than that, even used.

"Is two dollars too much?" Molly asked.

Her mouth gaped open. "*Two dollars*!"

"Well, since you're Jake's friend, I could let you have it for a buck fifty, but that's the lowest I can go."

Her breath expelled. "Sold!" She said before Molly had a chance to change her mind.

"I think I have a corset just your size, and I'll throw in another crinoline for an extra dollar—so two dollars and fifty cents total. How does that sound?"

"Corset? I have to wear a corset?" *Yuk!* Weren't those things gross and uncomfortable, and didn't they cause major health problems? Seems like she read that somewhere once.

Molly looked askance. "Do you want to look like a heathen or one of those loose women down by the docks?"

"Get me the damn corset," she groaned.

Molly's brows drew together in a frown.

Heat flooded her face. "Er...sorry, I meant darn...darn corset. I guess it won't kill me."

"Of course not," Molly said, running her hands down her own ample waistline. "Only loose women go without one, and you don't want people to think you're a loose woman, do you?"

"No—I've had more than my share of that today, so bring it out. I can hardly wait."

By the time Molly sufficiently poked and prodded her into the uncomfortable and confining corset, she was ready to scream. But she couldn't scream because she couldn't inhale enough even to breathe. Several layers of stiff petticoats were draped on and then, almost as an afterthought, the green dress.

Standing back, Molly beamed. "No reason to lace the corset too tight, your waist is so small anyway."

"This is loose?" Aimee gasped. "I feel like a hot dog stuffed into a too small casing."

Shocked, Molly's mouth dropped. "Haven't you ever worn a corset before?"

"No, thank God! Where I come from, no one really cares how small a woman's waist is—usually just how big her breasts are."

"I can't believe that!" Molly exclaimed, her face flushing red in embarrassment. "And you shouldn't talk that way. It isn't proper. Real ladies always wear a corset. It's what sets us apart from the others. Sit down while I fix your hair."

Sitting down was a lesson in creativity. The full skirt and layers of petticoats tangled around her legs, almost causing her to trip. The dang corset was even more uncomfortable, but it did force her to pay attention to her sometimes poor posture. Molly busied herself arranging her hair, parting it down the middle and drawing it back over her ears into a thick bun at the nape of her neck.

Jake's head poked through the door. "Is it safe to come in?"

Molly laughed. "Yes, she's as ready as I can make her. Looks pretty good, too."

A long, drawn out whistle slipped through his firm lips. "Yes, she does."

He winked, appreciation gleaming in his eyes.

Aimee stood up and turned to the mirror. The glass reflected a strange young woman right out of the 1800's. The demure lacy bodice of the dress revealed just enough of her long, graceful neck to be interesting. The full draping sleeves lined with layers of ruching drew full attention to her now almost too tiny waist. The green dress fit her like a glove and was the perfect offset to her red-gold hair.

"I can't believe you're willing to part with this dress for a dollar and a half!"

Molly shrugged. "Mrs. Abrams gives them to me. I used to work cleaning her house, but my knees and hands got too stiff so I had to quit. She likes me so she tries to help when she can."

Aimee's stomach growled again, loud enough to draw Jake's amused attention. "Now I suppose you want me to take you to dinner?"

"Is it proper for an unchaperoned woman to go out to dinner with a single male?"

He grinned. "It is if Molly goes with us."

Delighted, Molly grabbed a wool shawl, at the same time handing a similar one to Aimee. "It still gets pretty cold here at night and you'll need that. Call it a gift."

The café was bustling with customers. Servers hustled back and forth, slapping platters of food on the gingham covered tables. Calling a welcome to Jake and Molly, a short chubby balding man, the owner she assumed, hastened to clear a table and seated them. Plate-sized fried steaks, complete with mashed potatoes, gravy, and beans flavored with bacon grease, magically appeared at almost the same time as they were seated. A bowl of freshly baked biscuits followed along with tall glasses of cold milk. Amazed at the alacrity with which the food was brought out and served, she was at a loss for words.

Beaming from ear to ear, the chubby little man slapped Jake on the back. "When did you get back?"

Choking on a mouthful of food, he coughed. "Rode in yesterday. How you been, Oren?"

"Better than middlin! How long you staying?" The little man pulled out a chair and sat down.

"'Til day after tomorrow. Going out with the Markham party."

The little man nodded. "Heard he was taking another group to Oregon. You scouting for him?"

He set his fork down. "It isn't official yet, but I will. Think I'm going to stay out there this time. I've got some savings and Markham's paying good wages. I can buy a good plot of land and start building."

The little man, Oren, stared at Aimee. "Is this your lady?" He appeared pleased.

Uncomfortable under his perusal, her lip curled. "Not hardly." Adding for good measure, "I do have some taste in men."

Jake gazed at her and then grinned. "Nope. She's just a woman I found on the street."

She gritted her teeth, imagining her hands around his sorry ass throat.

Molly patted her arm. "He didn't find her on the street. We met her outside and invited her to dinner—didn't we, dearie?"

"Yes," she ground out, "that's exactly what happened." Even dressed as she was, Jake was naming her "whore" in front of this kind little man.

Oren stood up. "Better get back to my other customers. Cook made fresh apple pie with clotted cream for dessert—best I've ever tasted. You be sure and have a piece before you go." He turned to Aimee. "It is always a pleasure to enjoy the company of a beautiful woman." He hesitated, bowing with gallant aplomb, then hurried off.

She slapped the table, furious. "If you can't pretend you have any manners, then at least keep your mouth shut."

"Seems to me you drew first blood."

"I did no such thing," she exclaimed, unwilling to admit even the tiniest bit of fault.

"Oren's a good man, and all he wanted to know was whether you were someone special to me, but you made it very clear that you weren't—and if you want my respect, you have to give it first." He picked up his fork and began eating.

Chewing on her lip, thinking it through, she had to admit he was right. She'd thrown the first barb, and he'd returned in kind. It galled her, though.

"I'm sorry," she apologized, choking on the words. "I've just had a very bad day and none of it's your fault. I'm sorry."

Reaching into her small purse, she drew out the remaining money. "How much do I owe for the meal?" she asked, praying she still had enough.

Jake wiped his lips on the cloth napkin and stood up. "Put your money away. You'll need it for a room tonight. I'm staying at the boarding house across the street. I think there's another room available." He tossed down some coins and turned to Molly. "Come on," he said, "I'll walk you home."

"No need." Molly stood up and gathered her shawl. "I moved into the room above my shop last winter." Her eyes glimmered. "I don't feel as alone there." Jake planted a quick kiss on her check as she turned to go.

"I'll come visit you tomorrow." He reached for Aimee's arm. "You ready to go?"

Nodding, she followed him out the door and across the street. It was almost dark now and in this part of town, at least, traffic had lessened as the shops closed for the night.

A sturdy clapboard structure lacking in style or grace, the boarding house's claim to fame was its respectability and clean beds. Jake held the door, waving her in. Candles sputtered in glass sconces, their muted glow dancing across the slatted wood walls. A braided rug hugged the roughhewn floor, bravely hiding the scuff marks of countless booted feet. To the left, a narrow flight of stairs, a ladder really, provided the only access to the second story.

A thin man of indeterminate age, greasy hair parted in the middle and pasted down with some sort of super hair glue, stood at attention behind the front desk. At the first good look, Aimee pressed her lips together, ducking her head to keep from laughing. The proprietor's pox-marked face gleamed in the light of a glass oil lamp, strategically placed near a bulky ledger. Clad in the business attire of the day, his Adam's apple bobbed above a stiffly starched white collar. Gaiters held up his too-long sleeves, and food stains spotted his black vest. In contrast, Jake was the Marlboro Man and he was the epitome of a Currier & Ives print gone bad.

Simpering and fawning, his eyes flickered from Aimee to Jake. "May I help you?" he asked, reaching for a steel nib pen with ink-stained fingers, his reedy voice was laced with pomposity.

Leaning on the desk, Jake motioned to Aimee. "You may. This little lady here needs a room for the night."

"And will you be staying with her?" he asked with artificial concern, his hand poised over the registration book.

"I already have a room, or did you forget." Jake's disgusted look raked over the fawning man.

The proprietor's lips pursed in concentration as he reviewed the entries. "Oh yes. Here you are!"

"Yes," Jake responded wryly. "There I am!"

"And how long will she be staying?" he asked, as though she weren't standing right in front of him.

Jake peered at her, brow furrowed. "How long *will* you be staying?"

"I-I-don't-know," she faltered. "Maybe just tonight."

"Put her down for at least two nights," Jake said. "If she needs to stay longer, we can figure that out later."

Looking down his rather long nose, the proprietor clicked his teeth. "Don't wait too long. We're a busy place. I can't hold a room unless I know she'll be staying. She could end up on the street." He closed the ledger with a slam.

The man-weasel motioned to the stairs. "Her room is the third one on the right. Fresh towels and water have already been provided. Have a good stay."

Without further comment, Jake strode to the stairs and started up. Aimee heaved a sigh and followed.

The upper level was constructed of the same roughhewn wooden slats. Several doors led from the hallway. Jake stopped at the second one on the left.

"If you need anything," he grinned, his eyes sending a heated message. "I'm right across the hall." His eyes roamed over her slim figure, assessing her charms.

"I can't think of a single *little* thing," she quipped, staring at his crotch. "But if I ever do, I'll let you know."

Striding down the hall, she opened the door to her room and stepped in.

"Not exactly the Ritz," she muttered. Oh well, at least she had a place to stay for the night. Anything was better than being out on the street.

Little had been done to make the tiny room homey or welcoming. A single cot, stood against one wall, covered with a hand-sewn quilt. Beneath the small window, a ceramic washbasin with a matching ewer of water sat atop a small washstand. A many-colored braided rug covered a small portion of the floor. In the far corner, a rickety chair completed the stark interior.

She sank down on the bed, drained and exhausted, the sole thought on her mind—undressing and climbing into bed. Ill at ease in the strange surroundings, she rattled the door handle. It didn't have a lock. For whatever security it might have, she braced the small chair under the knob. Dropping her wrap and handbag on the bed, she pulled off the voluminous dress and layers of petticoats. It would take a contortionist to reach the sturdy knot Molly tied in the corset laces. Her numerous attempts to free herself from the treacherous contraption met with frustration.

A night imprisoned in the female torture device was unthinkable. She grabbed the quilt, peeked out to make sure the hallway was clear, and then sprinted across to Jake's door. Tapping softly, she waited for him to answer. When he did, he cracked open the door just enough to look out, his single eye widening in amazement. The door flew open. Dressed only in his unbuttoned trousers, Jake regarded her, suspicion flickering in the depths of his eyes.

She gulped, her eyes drawn to his overt maleness. He really did have a great body, sleek muscular arms, and pecs covered by a slight brush of dark hair continuing down and below the top of his leather trousers, which bulged in a certain area. Jake waved her in, corded muscles danced under his tanned flesh.

"Change your mind?" he asked in a voice roughened by sleep, a sexy smile widening his lips.

Pushing past him in disgust, she presented her corset-clad back to him. "Like *that's* going to happen!" Reaching behind her, she motioned to the lacing. "I can't seem to get this untied, and I refuse to torment myself by wearing it all night."

She felt his fingers working the ties as he chuckled. "First time I've ever undid one of these just because," he said, a hint of slyness in his voice. "Sure you aren't hoping for something else?"

"Totally positive." She looked over her shoulder. "Just get me out of this thing."

As he loosened the laces, the hated contrivance came free. *She had survived*! Scratching with satisfied relief, she turned to him. "Can I ask you something?"

"You can—but I won't promise to answer," he said, as irritating as he could be.

"Sheesh! Are you always so contrary?" *The man was infuriating!*

He rubbed a hand through his thick dark hair. "What do you need?"

"At dinner—you were talking about scouting for some group—Markham—I think you said. What's that all about?"

"I sometimes scout for emigrant trains heading to the Oregon territory. I'm signing on with one. We head west in a few days' time."

"Will you go anywhere near Seattle, Washington?"

"I told you before, I've never heard of Seattle and Washington's east, but if you mean the Oregon territory—yes, we end up there, in the Willamette Valley."

She absorbed the meager information. "How long does the trip take and what does it cost?"

"Takes at least five months—if nothing goes

wrong. It costs way more than you have. Why?"

"Oh…nothing. I just wondered." She turned to leave, lost in thought.

"Sure you don't want to take me up on my offer?" Jake's teasing was old.

"You wish!" She huffed and stalked out, forgetting to check the hallway first and banged into a boarder walking by. A lascivious leer devoured her, replacing the boarder's previously blank expression.

"Looking for customers?" He smacked his bulbous lips, reminiscent of an overeager suckerfish. "I just might be interested."

Her shoulders drooped in disgust. "You are soooo sickening." She glared at him. "How about you get out of my face before I ream you a new orifice?"

Startled, the man's mouth flew open as he gaped in surprise.

Jake stepped into the hallway and lowered his voice to sound ominous in the ensuing silence. "The *lady* was just returning to her room. I suggest you do the same."

The hapless man barely glanced at his threatening stance before he scurried down the hall. Jake's lips twitched. He couldn't blame him. He'd made the same offer more than once today. But, damn, if she wasn't a feisty piece of woman. At least she hadn't threatened to ream *him* a new orifice—whatever that was.

"Thanks…again! Seems like all I do is thank you for one reason or another." Aimee hesitated, appearing unsure. Her vulnerability stirred deeper feelings in him making him uncomfortable. "I've had more creepy offers from more creepy men in one day than I've had in my entire lifetime!"

"If you keep running around in your underclothes, it's pretty much what you can expect."

He followed her across the hall. "Stay in there and don't answer the door, and if anyone bothers you—scream. I'll hear it."

She slipped into her room and pivoted, staring up at him. "Why are you helping me?"

He shrugged. "Guess it's because I'm a gentleman at heart."

"Are you?" she asked. "Are you a gentleman?"

Her unexpected question made him smile. "I can be when I need to."

Surprising, she giggled, her lips curving. "I guess that's an answer!"

Pleased by her sudden warmth and dazed by her smile, Jake was at a momentary loss for words. Chagrined, he turned to leave.

"Jake!" she blurted. "Take me with you!"

He stopped, his gut clenching. *He hadn't seen that coming!*

He waited for her next move, staring at her face, flushed beet red, amber eyes begging.

"Please," she whispered.

The walls closed in, smothering him. He didn't want to hear what he knew she was going to say. He didn't need that kind of complication.

"I have nowhere to go. I don't know anyone, and if you leave, I'll lose the only person who has treated me with kindness since I've been here."

She reached up and took off her diamond earrings. "My parents paid three thousand for these as a graduation present. I'll give you one now and the other when we arrive in Oregon."

He rubbed a hand over his face, giving himself time to think. She was so beautiful, standing there, looking lost and sad. *Damn it!*

He checked the hallway and then pushed her back, stepping into the room. "Even if I wanted to, which I don't know that I do, I can't."

"Why?" Her lips trembled. Tears filled her pleading eyes.

His stomach plummeted. He hated tears. He

didn't know how to deal with them.

"Because this group of emigrants are pretty religious. They wouldn't take kindly to an unchaperoned female traveling with me."

"Even if I'm paying you—like a business deal?" She took his hand and placed one of the studs on his palm. His fist closed instinctively around the gemstone. Holding the gem to eye level, he scrutinized it. *Why was he even considering it? But damn it, he was tempted!*

"Pretty rock." He handed it back and looked away, feeling guilty. He wasn't good at these kinds of things. Taking care of another person didn't fit in his plans. *She* didn't fit in his plans. He liked being alone.

"They're perfect—my parents made sure of that." She repeated her offer. "One stone now and the other when we reach Oregon."

"And I repeat—these people won't allow you to go with me."

"What would it take to get you to take me?" Tears spilled down her silken cheeks. "I'll do anything."

Instinct caused his hand to reach up and cup her face. The texture of her skin felt like satin, soft and smooth. His heart beat sped. She got to him in ways he didn't understand. His thumb stroked the soft contours. "If it was up to me, I'd let you go," he conceded. "But they pay for my services. Maybe if you found a man to marry you, we could figure out something."

"Get married! To just anyone?" Shocked, her eyes glimmered in the lamplight.

His hand dropped. "Best I can come up with. If you're married, they might let you go." *The thought of her with another man tore at his gut. He wanted to kill the bastard!* He gritted his teeth. *She belonged to him.* No other man had the right to touch her.

She drew in a deep breath, blurting out. "Jake, listen to me. I know this is sudden but I don't have any other option. I don't know any other men. Will you marry me—in name only? Once we're in Oregon, I'll give you a divorce, and it'll be like it never happened. You can go on with your life, and you'll have my diamonds to help buy that property you mentioned."

Jake shook his head, heat boiling his guts. "You want me to marry you just so you can get to Oregon?" He didn't know why, but her suggestion sickened him. He'd let her get to him with her tears and her sadness. She'd almost convinced him she was special, but she wasn't. She was just a whore, an expensive one, but a whore.

"I don't have any other choice. I have to get to there and this is my best chance."

"So—you *are* willing to sell yourself—for the right price," he growled, irritated that it bothered him so much.

Her eyes shot amber sparks. "Not selling myself—*I'm* buying *you*. There's a difference."

He raked a gaze over her curves, damning his reaction. Creamy breasts peeked from the cotton camisole, the lace-edged pantalets disguising little of her long slender legs—legs made to wrap around a man. Silky red-gold hair hung in a riot of curls framing skin the color of honey. Slanting golden cat eyes sparkled below dark brows that, at the moment, were raised in fury. Her lips were compressed, waiting for his answer.

"What if I don't want a marriage in name only? What if I want more?"

Her breath expelled in one long sigh. "The deal is," she reiterated, "I pay you to marry me, and then you take me to Oregon. That's it, nothing more."

"And if I say no?"

"Then I'll find someone who will. Surely there's

some man in this town desperate enough to marry me." Her tone reflected her desperation.

"Why do you want to go to Oregon?"

"Because that's where my family is—*or will be,*" she muttered.

Stepping out of her room, Jake hesitated before turning to leave. "I'll let you know in the morning one way or the other. Not a decision I want to make without thinking it through."

"I won't be any trouble," she promised, her eyes shining with hope.

Stomping to his room, Jake threw himself on the bed, pounding the lumpy pillow, trying to get comfortable. Divorce was almost unheard of and the chances of getting one were slim. She was asking for his future, a future he had already planned, full of children and a wife who cared for him—not a loveless existence evidenced by a piece of paper. Walking away would be the best thing he could do for himself, but forgetting her wouldn't be easy. From first sight, he'd been captivated by her liveliness and determination. That she was unbelievably beautiful didn't hurt either. His fingers itched to bury themselves in her long curling strawberry blonde hair, ravage her mouth, and lose himself in her heat.

His loins throbbed. Disgusted, he threw open the window, letting in the night air to cool his fevered skin. She'd offered herself to him. A business deal, she said. But could he handle her nearness and not touch her?

Brushing such thoughts away, he decided to sleep on the matter and make his decision in the cold light of day, away from her disturbing presence.

Chapter Three

Bright and early the next morning, someone rapped at Aimee's door. Holding her breath, expecting the worst, she peeked out. Jake motioned her to follow, stiff and unapproachable, but at least not ignoring her. She breathed a sigh of relief. He hadn't noticed the missing corset. Even if he did, she wasn't going to wear the damn thing.

They stopped at the café of the night before. Early morning diners crowded the small space, talking while they shoveled food, but once again, Oren came to their rescue and seated them. Huge rashers of bacon, eggs, and pancakes were plunked down, along with mugs of piping hot coffee and real cream. *Her plate could have fed both of them and Oren.*

Jake started eating, ignoring her with studied disregard. She fiddled with her napkin, her stomach in knots, wishing he would say something. It wasn't until he finished the last pancake and chewed the last piece of bacon that he acknowledged her presence. Sipping his coffee, he leaned back in his chair, hands resting on his belt.

"Were you serious last night?"

Feeling as though her throat had closed up, she coughed. "Yes," she admitted, awkward and self-conscious. "I was."

"Even about giving up the diamonds?"

She nodded, hope springing anew.

Like a whip uncoiling, he leaned forward, his face inches from hers. "You've got a deal, but on one condition!"

"And that is," she murmured, anxious now.

"I don't want a wife in name only. At least while we're traveling. If you still want a divorce when we get to Oregon, I'll give you one."

Dumbfounded, she couldn't conjure up any words. How could he expect her to act as his wife for five months, a man she'd just met, and then just end the whole thing? *It was ridiculous!*

Hope sank in one short plunge. Anger was her savior. She lashed out. "So, besides paying you, I have to prostitute myself to go with you!"

He shrugged. "That's my deal. If you think you can find a better one, you have my blessing."

"Why are you doing this? Why would you want to sleep with me? You don't want me! And what makes you think I want to sleep with you?"

He laughed, mocking her words. "It's not sleep I'm expecting."

Several diners had stopped eating, blatantly eavesdropping on their conversation. Mortified, heat flooded her face, her voice dropped. "Can we talk about this outside?"

"Suit yourself," he said, standing up and grinning at the gathering.

Humiliated beyond belief, eyes downcast, she headed for the door, amid the snickers and off-color remarks that trickled behind. *He made her so frickin' mad!*

Away from prying eyes, she whirled on him. "Do you always have to be so…so vulgar and disgusting?"

No remorse showed on his lean features. "I thought I was being pretty nice, all things considered."

"You might have considered how your little announcement would affect me."

"Did you," he asked, pointing out her mistake, "consider how your little proposal would affect me?"

"I… I don't understand," she stuttered, confused.

"Marriage is a forever thing, at least where I come from. You offered to pay me to marry you and then, when you're done with me, a divorce. Divorces don't come easy out here and if you take off, I'm still married, but without a wife. I always planned on getting married and having children, but what you offer is a marriage without all the other good things."

She toyed with the locket, finding comfort in its nearness. "But—but if we get a divorce, you can still have all that."

"*If* we get a divorce. The law might decide otherwise."

She sank down onto a nearby bench. "Even if I agreed to your terms, you'd still only have a wife for a few months. What good is that?"

"At least this way, if you have to be a real wife, there's a good chance I'd get a son out of the deal.

"A son!" She gasped, appalled. "Have a child—with *you*?"

"Is that such a terrible thing to consider?" He sounded sad.

Her thoughts whirling in chaotic confusion, she struggled to make sense of the whole thing. What had started as a simple business deal was now turning into a lifetime commitment. *He wanted a son!* She would never leave a child of her own. *Never!*

"What if there isn't a child? What then?"

"Then you're right where you want to be, in Oregon and free of me. I won't expect anything more." The words were said, without emotion, but wrenching all the same. *A baby machine as well as a whore!*

It was still the best choice, but she was beginning to feel like one of those old-time mail-order brides. Taking a deep breath, she relaxed, biding her time and considering her response. No other options presented themselves and time was short. “Okay,” she said, feeling the ax fall. “I accept your terms, but I have one minor change.”

His lips curved, his blue eyes danced. “I bet you do.”

“I want two months to get acquainted before assuming my *wifely* duties. Agreed?”

“One month,” he countered. “And not a day more.”

She sputtered. “Why you sorry piece of...”

“Careful,” he warned, his eyes alight. “You don’t want it down to two weeks, do you?”

Counting to ten, Aimee struggled to find her happy place. Breathing exercises helped calm her wildly thumping heart and helped regain control of the desire to throttle him within an inch of his low-down slimy pond scum life. Gritting her teeth, she glared at him, praying for lightning to strike him where he stood. The sky remained clear.

“All right,” she growled. “One month. Do we have an agreement?”

Jake grinned, white teeth flashing. “We do!”

She stomped towards the hotel, visions of his death by horrendous torture her only solace. Where was one of those serial killers when she needed one?

“You’ll need to buy more things,” he called to her retreating back. “Have Molly outfit you with more clothing and whatever else you women need. Tell her I’ll be by later to pay.” He started down the street, but stopped and turned. “And be ready at three o’clock. We have a preacher to visit.”

“Arrrggghhhhh,” she screeched as he sauntered away. Why didn’t God strike him dead?

Jake waited until he was out of earshot then cursed heatedly. *He was a damn fool!* Part of him never believed she would agree. What had he gotten himself into? He knew she wasn’t cut out for the hardships of the trail. He’d seen her hands. She’d never done a day's hard work in her life. How would she survive out there? What he'd done was saddle himself with another mouth to feed and somebody to worry about. He wasn't ready for that. Her image flashed through his mind—one minute she was soft and pleading, the next she was a firebrand, ready to kick ass. He'd never met a woman who made him so mad or so confused—*at least one he wanted like he wanted her!*

****

Five hours later, Aimee waited, head downcast, beside a clean-shaven and well-dressed Jake in front of the town's foremost preacher. Molly stood next to her, agreeing with amicable good cheer to act as her matron of honor. The preacher's wife, acting as the second witness to the dreadful ordeal, stood on the other side of Jake. Smiling with gracious composure, the preacher opened his Bible and cleared his throat, preparing to begin.

She stole a surreptitious glance around the room, noting the fine wood paneling on the walls, the carved wooden benches, the wall hangings and the preacher's wife—*Oh. My. God!* It was the toad-faced lady of the day before. Wouldn't you just know it. Ducking down, the floppy bonnet obscuring her face, she prayed for a quick end to the proceedings. Wouldn't do for the preacher's wife to recognize her, although she doubted she would make the comparison to the hussy of the day before, gowned as she was today.

The preacher's voice broke through her reverie. "I said, do you take this man to be your lawfully wedded husband?" He peered over his spectacles.

"Oh! Yeah! I mean, I do," she blurted.

Turning to Jake, he repeated the vows. "Do you take this woman to be your lawfully wedded wife?"

He cleared his throat, hesitated and then answered in a firm voice. "I do."

"I now pronounce you man and wife. You may kiss the bride." Beaming, the preacher nodded to Jake.

She tilted her face, her cheek lifted in the direction of Jake's lips, hoping he would take the hint—which he didn't. Not only did he kiss her, but she almost choked as his tongue slipped uninvited into her mouth. Stunned, she jerked back, amazed that he had the temerity to even try such a disgusting trick and in front of the preacher! Jake's laughing eyes danced. A sneaky glance in the preacher's direction confirmed her humiliation.

Gaping at the exhibition before him, the preacher's mouth hung open, his eyes bugging out. At the same time, the preacher's wife got her first good look at Aimee, recognition surfacing in the depths of her toad-popping eyes. Whirling around, Aimee ran from the church, cursing Jake to whatever hell she hoped would materialize in the next few minutes. Things just seemed to go from bad to worse.

Jake, with Molly in tow, hurried out of the church. *The deed was done!* Whether he planned it or not, he was now a husband. Grinning, he listened to Molly's rantings with half an ear.

"Why, I never saw such a thing," Molly's stern voice scolded. "Where are your manners? What were you thinking?"

Jake laughed, the taste of his new bride still on his lips. "I was thinking it was about the best chance I'd get to kiss her for awhile." Taking note of Aimee's stiff form waiting for them across the street, he walked over. "Why'd you run out?"

Red-faced, she snapped. "Why do you think I ran out? Every time I'm around you, you go out of your way to embarrass me."

His eyes narrowed. "I sealed our vows with a kiss—a real kiss, the kind of kiss every man should give his wife on their wedding day." Her mouth tasted like the finest wine, velvety and smooth. *Hell, given the chance, he do it again—and again.*

"It's not like we're really married," she said, lips pursed in a pout.

"We *are* really married, whether you want to admit it or not." He took her arm, pulling her along. *Damn if she didn't get his dander up.* If she'd just act agreeable one time. "And now we're going to have a nice dinner at a nice restaurant, and you're going to act like you're maybe happy about it."

"And if I don't?" she sulked, dragging her feet.

"Then I might have to change our wedding night to an earlier date."

"*You wouldn't dare,*" she cried. "We have an agreement!"

"You're my wife now. The law says I can do pretty much what I want with you."

Wrenching her arm away, she stomped her feet. "I hate you!" she grated through clenched teeth.

Molly caught up, her face sad and concerned. "Jake, that's not the way to talk to your young wife, not if you want her to be happy."

Yeah! But his new bride didn't want that. "Makes no matter if she's happy or not, as she said, we have an agreement. I'll stick to my end as long as she sticks to hers."

He glared, his eyes narrowed to mere slits, waiting for her to make the first move. Molly stood between them, clucking in dismay, wringing her hands and offering words of comfort. Jake's stubbornness subtly relaxed. He hadn't wanted this, but he'd given his word, and he never backed down from a promise. Maybe his new wife just needed some gentling, like a green-broke mare. Bowing, he offered Aimee his arm, acting the gentleman for the moment.

Aimee gazed at the offered arm, considering her

options. She scanned his face, reluctant to admit he had a few good qualities. He offered hope—something she needed right now. Jake was her ticket out of this place and perhaps home, and being on good terms with him would make the whole thing a lot easier. The anger and stiffness drained away. Laying her hand on his proffered arm, she tilted her head. "As you said, we have a bargain. Lead on, Macduff. I'm famished."

Breathing a sigh of relief, Molly turned to go.

"No," Jake stopped her. "This is a celebration. You have to join us, doesn't she, wife?"

"That she does," she said, taking Molly's hand. "I wouldn't have it any other way."

****

Jake chose a high class restaurant, a gathering place for St. Louis's rich and influential. Chandeliers hung from the ceiling, crystals reflecting light in a myriad of colors. Maroon carpets covered the floors, rich in taste and refinement. It was a beautiful oasis in an unbeautiful world.

A host led them to a table, bowing slightly. Jake handed him a tip, remembering his mama's stern admonition about giving too little or too much. He felt awkward, ill at ease—feelings he thought he'd outgrown long ago. It'd been awhile since he'd been in a place like this. He generally kept to places less formal, more to his liking. But this was his wedding dinner, such as it was. He glanced at his new bride. Would she like the place? Would she even care that he'd gone to a lot of trouble to get a reservation?

He seated first Molly and then pulled out a chair for Aimee, smiling into her upturned face. She looked—accepting. Her amber eyes shone as she gazed around the room, her face aglow with pleasure. He heaved a sigh of relief. *She was enjoying it!* He watched as she opened her napkin and placed it across her knees. She held herself well, smiling at the other diners, sipping water. She was comfortable in this environment, like she was born to it. Other than her mouth sometimes, she didn't act like a whore.

She held up her silverware. "Look at these antiques. They're so beautiful."

"They're not antiques, dear." Molly chuckled. "This restaurant is brand new, and I suspect everything in it is new as well."

Jake waved the waiter over and ordered for everyone. Their wedding dinner of prime rib was excellent and the wine flowed freely. By the time they were ready to depart, his pockets were lighter and Aimee was more than just tipsy. He decided a walk to Molly's place in the crisp air would help clear her mind, but it did nothing to stop the giggles bursting from her lips at every little thing. He sighed, rolling his eyes in disgust as she tripped once again on the board walkway, this time falling on her butt, giggling as she sat there.

Molly's lips quirked in amusement. "I think you'd better put her to bed."

He watched Aimee's unsuccessful maneuverings with no small amount of irritation. She struggled valiantly to stand, fighting with the yards of material making up her skirt, along with the layers of petticoats, but she only succeeded in making things worse. She wasn't getting anywhere fast—and neither was he. Resigned, he pulled her up and propped her against a nearby wall. Her unfocused eyes roamed, flicking restlessly, gleaming in the light of the streetlamp. She lurched forward, leaning against him for support.

She poked his brow, pointing at the creases. "Now, Jakey," she slurred, "don't go getting all proper on me." She gazed into his eyes—then belched.

Jake groaned, holding her upright.

She wavered, swaying. "Why haven't I noticed how sexy you are?" She leaned back, smiling like an idiot. "You're not bad for a low-life scumbag."

Jake grimaced.

Molly snorted. "You go get some rest," Molly patted Aimee's arm. Turning to Jake, she hugged him and then stepped into the small shop.

"Come with us to Oregon." His plea was heartfelt.

"Yes, come with us." Aimee hiccupped from her spot by the wall.

Molly shook her head. "Nope! I plan on being buried next to my Ben, not alone in some Godforsaken place I don't belong. This is where I want to be, and this is where I plan to stay."

"Are you sure?" Jake hated leaving her behind. Molly was more to him than just a friend.

"This is my home. You go on, find what you are looking for and make her happy." Molly waved to his bride, who by now was engrossed in studying the intricacies of the lace on her sleeve, crooning a tuneless melody.

Exasperated, he shook his head. "Making her happy would take a better man than me."

"No better man that I know," Molly scoffed. "She's lucky to get you from what I see."

"Yup," Aimee swayed, stumbling sideways. "I'm lucky to have such a wonderful man who married me without knowing who or what I was—or am." Hiccupping again, she offered a lopsided smile.

Molly's laugh echoed from the open doorway. "Looks to me like you've got your hands full, Jake. I'll say goodnight and good luck to you both."

He grappled with the now singing Aimee. She staggered, reeled, and stumbled again. He inhaled, counting to ten, his patience slipping several notches. Dragging her to the hotel and up the steep staircase, he tightened his hold to keep her from falling down and breaking her neck, at least without his help. Earlier, he'd instructed the hotel maids to move her things to his room, seeing no need to pay for the extra cost when she was his wife. As he started into the room, she got a stranglehold on the door jamb, hanging on while he grappled to pull her through.

"Oh, no you don't," she screeched. "This isn't my room."

Boarders banged on the walls, calling for quiet.

The clerk rushed up, a mask of disapproval on his face. "Sir! We don't allow that sort of behavior here."

"We're married," Jake grunted, struggling to loosen her grip. "No business you need to attend to here. Go back to the desk."

The clerk's face flushed. "Well—you're disturbing the other boarders." He flapped his hands. "Do try to be quiet." He scurried back down the hallway.

Breaking her death grip on the door, Jake hauled her in and tossed her on the narrow bed. "Go to sleep!"

She made a half-hearted attempt to roll off the bed. The green pallor of her complexion alerted him in time to grab the washbasin. He held her head while she retched. He'd never been very good around sick people and the rank smell brought bile into his throat. Swallowing the urge to gag, he wiped her face with a wet rag and settled her down in the bed. He picked up the stinking washbasin and carried it into the hallway, his stomach churning in response. Feeling sick himself, he opened the small window, inhaling the fresh air deep into his lungs, waiting for the smell of vomit to clear out.

He gazed at his new bride. She sprawled across the small bed, drooling on the one pillow, her arms and legs flung wide.

Resigned, he dragged the small chair near the bed, sat down, and put his feet up. He'd slept in worse conditions but never guessed it would be like this on his wedding night.

Chapter Four

"Rise and shine!" Jake's cheerful voice roused Aimee from a deep sleep. "Time to get moving."

"Shut up," she groaned. "Can't you see I'm sick?"

"You'll feel better once we're moving." His voice grated in her pounding head. "The steamboat leaves in a few hours, and we need to get loaded."

"You go ahead. Just leave me here to die." She pulled the pillow over her head, trying to drown out his incessant good humor.

He yanked the pillow free. "I said, *get up*. Time to get moving if we want breakfast before we go."

"Don't even say the word," she moaned, her stomach lurching. "Just the thought of food makes me want to puke."

"Nothing left to puke. You did that last night."

"I did!" Mortified, she sat up, blinking in the bright light of morning. "Did I make a mess?"

"Lucky for us, I grabbed the washbasin before you did," he said. "Otherwise, you'd be sleeping in the stuff. The room smelled like shit for quite awhile."

Awareness dawned as the fog cleared from her eyes. "This isn't my room. Why am I in here?"

"No reason to pay for two rooms when we're man and wife." His eyes gleamed with wicked humor.

She crawled from the bed, furious. "We had an agreement. I was supposed to have a month before assuming my wifely duties."

"You seemed to forget it last night."

"I did?" she asked, wondering if he meant what she thought he did. "What did I do?"

He glanced around the small room, ignoring her. *Great! And she was the one berating him for wanting more.*

"Jake," she whispered. "What happened?"

"Nothing much," he grinned, his eyes dancing with wicked glee. "Just normal husband and wife things."

"You absolute scumbag!" she shrieked, reaching for something to throw. "We had an agreement!"

He burst out laughing. "Settle down, wife. Your maidenhood is safe. You got sick, threw up, and passed out. Welcome to wedded life," he added.

Stunned, she gaped at him. "Nothing happened?"

"Other than you throwing up—no. Now as I said before, get ready. We have things to do and not much time."

Mollified, she plopped down on the bed. "Why do you always have to piss me off?" she asked, grumpy and wanting nothing more than to sleep.

"Such a ladylike expression, but no matter. Feel better, don't you?"

Amazing as it seemed, she did. She was still a long ways from good, but quite a bit better than she felt when she first woke up. If she just had a nice cup of coffee…

A fresh basin waited outside the door. Ignoring her, he filled it with water and proceeded to wash up and shave. To keep from staring at his too mouth-watering maleness, she pretended to go through her bags, while surreptitiously watching his every move. Muscles rippled beneath his smooth skin as he tackled the day's growth of beard, handling the straight-edged razor with casual aplomb. She shook herself, feeling like a Peeping Tom.

"Would it be possible to get a bath this morning?"

"Just wash up in the basin," he said, continuing

to shave.

"I asked you if I could get a bath. I know I can wash up, but I want a real bath."

He paused, turning to look at her. "There's a bathhouse out back, but I wouldn't suggest you try that. It's mostly for the male boarders. But if you're sure you want a bath, go down to the desk and see if they'll haul up a tub. Cost you an extra dollar though."

"A whole dollar just for a bath? Doesn't that come with the cost of the room?" She only had a little money left and using some for a bath seemed extravagant, to say the least.

"Nope," he said, turning back to the mirror. "Not in this place. Some of the more expensive places do, but I don't stay in those."

She reconsidered her jewelry. The diamond studs were already promised to Jake but she still had her rings and several bracelets.

"Can you sell this before we go?" she asked, holding out another of her gold bracelets.

"You want to sell more of your trinkets just to have a bath?"

"Yes, I do, silly as it seems, and I'll need more cash for the trip. So, I ask again, can you sell this before we leave." She dangled the bracelet, smiling.

He took the bracelet, examining it for a brief moment. "I think so. Order your bath, and I'll see if I can find a buyer. But be ready when I get back. We're short of time as it is."

Relieved, she grabbed her wrap and rushed out the door before he changed his mind.

Within minutes, a large round tub was delivered to the room, and several maids hurried to fill it with hot water. She undressed and sank down, groaning in delight as the warm water soaked through her aching, alcohol-steeped bones. Not forgetting Jake's warning, she washed all over and hurried to dress.

The small wall mirror was almost too high for her to see, but she was able to wind her mane of hair into a reasonable semblance of a bun and secured it with several of the hairpins Molly used the day before. As usual, small tendrils escaped, framing her face with ringlets. *Not bad for a beginner.* After completing her toilet, she gathered up her belongings, packed them away and sat down, waiting for Jake to return. Almost as soon as she sat down, he stepped through the door, his eyes roving over her freshly clad form. She felt her face heating under his perusal.

"You forgot your corset."

"I didn't forget it. I'm not going to wear it." She stood up, firm in her resolve. Her breasts hadn't sagged yet, and she refused to drag the stupid thing on again.

"Suit yourself. Not me that has to put up with the nasty remarks."

She scowled. "Do you think people will notice?"

He handed her a shawl, grinning wickedly. "Put this on when we're out. No one will if you're covered up, and for myself, I kind of like the view."

Huffing with annoyance, she grabbed the shawl and wrapped it over her shoulders and across her breasts, tying it in back. She felt like an old washerwoman, but it kept her arms free.

He handed her a small wad of cash. "All I could get for your bracelet. Wasn't worth as much as the other one."

She took the cash, counting the bills. The first bracelet had been the more expensive, but five dollars was a pretty paltry return.

They ate breakfast at Oren's café once again and were soon on their way to the docks. A steamship sat in port, solid and unbeautiful, its white paint a dingy gray from the long-term effects of the billowing black smoke. She covered her mouth with a hanky. Inhaling that disgusting soot couldn't be healthy.

She followed Jake to their small cabin. Her lips pursed in exasperation. The cabin had only one narrow berth.

He stored their bags, avoiding her fierce look.

"Where are you going to sleep?" she asked in the sweetest voice she could muster.

"Right here," he patted the bunk. "Right next to you."

"I don't think so," she gritted her teeth. "I have a month, or do I have to keep reminding you."

"You don't have to remind me again. We sleep here together, but I won't touch you, just like I promised."

She searched for her happy place, but it escaped her. "So I'm supposed to believe that you won't touch me even while you're sleeping with me."

"Yup," he grinned. "And I'm trusting you to do the same."

Throwing open the cabin door, she stalked out, head held high. *Never had she met such an irritating man, and now she was married to him!*

Last minute preparations were made and without preamble, the steamboat pulled away, smoke billowing from the stack and streaming behind. Aimee stood on deck, watching the people on the docks wave goodbye, yelling words of encouragement and love to the travelers, their voices growing dim as they faded into the distance. A sob escaped her lips. *No last words of love or encouragement for her.* Fervently, she sent a prayer to God that somehow, someway, she could be returned to her family.

She reached for the locket draped around her neck. Clasping it to her heart, she envisioned her family, wishing with all her might that whatever force had brought her here would send her home again.

"Change your mind?" Jake moved to stand near

the railing.

"A little late, don't you think?" She turned to stare at him. Here was a man who the day before took her to wife, a man she hardly knew. In a different lifetime, she would never have given him the time of day. He was much too sexy and masculine and far too dangerous for her. She liked guys she could boss around—those who moved heaven and earth to please her. He would never let her order him around, it just wouldn't happen.

Jake watched the play of emotions flitting across his wife's face, wondering what thoughts hid beneath the surface. "Do I pass inspection?"

She jumped. "I-I wasn't inspecting. I was wondering how I ended up here, and with you." Her voice sounded sad and discouraged. He shifted, uneasy, afraid she'd start crying again.

"Don't sound so sorry about it. I'm not." He leaned on the rail, watching the banks of the river as the steamboat plowed forward. "I always planned on getting married, maybe not this way, but someday. I plan to keep my wife barefoot and pregnant."

She stiffened, her full lips thinning. "Then you picked the wrong person. I won't be that wife—ever!"

A glimmer of disappointment flashed inside, then vanished. What'd he expect her to say? Their wedding was a farce. A bargain so she'd have a way west. *Bought and paid for—that's about the sum of it.* Whistling tunelessly, he cast a sideways glance at her.

"There's a lot of miles between here and Oregon. We'll see what happens in the meantime." There were a lot of miles ahead, and he *was* her lawful husband. She didn't know it, but he believed in the sanctity of marriage. He hadn't forgotten his Bible-thumping beginnings. Maybe somewhere along the way he could convince her he was more than just a means to an end. He straightened and walked away.

Maybe he could find a card game or some other less prickly entertainment.

Aimee slapped at a bug. Mosquitoes swarmed over the river and rather than be eaten alive, she retreated to the cabin, more alone than she'd ever been before. No Sara to ruin her peace and quiet or mess with her stuff. Stuff that now seemed trivial and unimportant. Disconsolate and depressed, she dumped the contents of her clutch on the bed, passing time as she searched through the paltry collection for anything of value. A twenty dollar bill and three dollars in change—useless unless money hadn't changed in a long time. Car keys but no car. Lip gloss. *Now there's a big help.* Powder-free compact. *She'd meant to buy a new one.* Debit card for a bank that existed a hundred years in the future—*hold onto that one.* Her cell phone—*useless.* And a small tube of hand lotion. She'd have to check on the coins since she already knew the twenty wouldn't fly. Other than her jewelry, the lotion and lip gloss were the only things that might be helpful for survival in the wild, wild West. If nothing else, she'd have kissable lips and soft hands, at least for awhile.

Long hours later, she still waited for Jake, irritated by his disappearance and growing hungry, her stomach rumbled in protest. *I wonder if women are allowed in the dining room by themselves?* Deciding to take a chance, she stepped onto the deck and strolled along the railing. Insects still plagued her but not in the abundance of the earlier swarm. Fiddle music and the sounds of laughter echoed from a doorway near the front of the boat. Viewed through a dirty window, the group of men inside played cards, drinking and smoking, the sweet smell of pipe tobacco drifted from the room. There wasn't a woman in sight anywhere. She opened the door and stepped in. The room grew quiet as every man turned and gawked.

Jake stood up, his eyes flashing. "Go back to the cabin."

"I will not," she spouted with indignant righteousness. "I'm hungry! I want dinner, and you've been gone for hours."

He glanced around the card table. Smirks and jeering looks were on every face and several even dared to laugh.

"Guess we know who wears the britches in your family." One bold dandy sneered, waving a cigar.

Jake threw down his cards, his lips thinning with anger. Looming over the mouthy player, he stated succinctly for all to hear. "I wear the britches in my family, but my *bride* just doesn't want to believe it yet."

Laughter circled the table as more than one head nodded in understanding.

Seething, she searched for a scathing comeback, and when none surfaced, she spun around and stomped away, humiliated again by his inconsideration. She would go eat by herself if need be. She didn't want his company now or ever.

Jake grabbed her arm, whirling her around. "You just made me lose twenty bucks."

Wrenching her arm free, she spat. "I didn't make you lose anything."

Storming away, she went in search of the dining room. *She'd choke before she'd eat with him!* Jake followed her in, pulled out a chair, and motioned for her to sit. Flouncing down, she stared at the table.

"I'm sorry." He sat down, unfolding a napkin. "Time just got away from me. I'm not used to answering to anyone." Smiling, he leaned forward, his lips bare inches from her face. The smell of whiskey and tobacco lingered. On him, it was interesting.

"I don't expect you to answer to me. I just expect

a little attention once in awhile, like at mealtime." Reaching over, she opened her napkin and placed it on her lap. A young male waiter hurried over and placed a large plate of food in front of both of them. Roast beef, mashed potatoes and gravy, green beans and biscuits were the chosen fare, steaming hot from the oven and downright tasty.

"I'll do better," he apologized. "Just give me some time. Who knows, you might even grow to like me."

She nodded, appeased. Stranger things had happened, beginning with her arrival here. She slanted a glance at him. He exuded confidence, a gift she wished she had. Just being near him caused her heart to flutter. She didn't want to feel that way.

Peaceful silence pervaded while they consumed their meal. As they finished eating, Jake wiped his lips and leaned back. "We need to talk."

Her eyes were drawn to his, now warm and inviting. "We need to come to terms with each other or this trip is going to be one big hellhole," he stated.

Several choice wisecracks surfaced, but for once, she controlled the urge to toss them out, instead nodding in agreement.

"We're going to be in pretty close quarters for quite awhile, and we'd better learn to deal with each other or we're going to be in big trouble." Having said his piece, he left it up to her to comment.

"I know," she said. "But I'm still trying to cope with being married and sometimes I feel like you go out of your way to upset me."

"I do sometimes," he agreed, his blue eyes twinkling with amusement. "You need to learn to relax. I promised you a month and until then, I won't bother you other than maybe for a meal and some conversation."

Her face heated. There was still that one month thing to contend with. "I don't suppose you'd change your stance on that one item?"

Resting his forearms on the table, he shook his head. "Nope," he said at last. "We made a deal, and I expect you to honor your end of the bargain."

Rather than start another fruitless argument, she kept quiet. She still had a month to figure something out, and until she did, there was no use in making things any worse than they already were. Exhaling, she stood up. It was time for bed, and she was tired. He followed her out and walked beside her until they reached their cabin.

"Since there's no room for privacy in there," she began. "I'll need a little time to get ready for bed and then you can come in."

Jake's eyes widened in surprise. He nodded, leaning against the railing. "Take your time. I'll wait."

Anxious and miserable, she opened the door and stepped into the cabin. Hurrying to her bags, she searched through and found one of the prim, high-necked flannel nightgowns Molly had included. Tossing off everything but her underwear, she drew the gown over her head, and stepped to the mirror. The long-sleeved voluminous nightgown covered every inch and only her face and neck remained free. Satisfied, she washed her face and jumped into bed, pulling the covers up to her neck.

"You can come in now," she called.

The door opened, and Jake stepped through. His eyes perused the room, coming to rest on her form huddled in the narrow bed. Nonchalantly, he crossed the room, removed his boots and shirt and then lay back. She pulled the covers higher, scrunching into the corner. The bed was not big enough for both of them, and even pressed against the wall, she couldn't prevent their bodies from touching.

"Get over," she grumbled.

He edged over, but not enough to make any

difference. "If I move any farther over here," he growled in return, "I'll fall off."

"Too bad!" Visions of him doing just that swam through her mind. Maybe a little help in that direction would be just the ticket.

"I wouldn't if I were you," he muttered, as though reading her mind.

Hissing, she turned on her side, nose touching the wall. This was just the first of many such nights. She'd better get used to it fast or, as he said, it was going to be one big hellhole. A short time later, soft snores confirmed he'd gone to sleep. Funny how comforting the sound of a man snoring could be. She listened to his snoring long into the night, wondering if she'd made the right choice.

Chapter Five

For two days, the steamboat wound its way up the Missouri River. From there, they traveled overland to Independence where the emigrant train, as Jake referred to it, was camped. Independence, he informed Aimee, was the actual starting point of the long trip to the Oregon Territory.

While he made some last minute preparations, Aimee amused herself for a few hours wandering through the commercial part of town, and to her delight, discovered a small cluttered bookstore. The proprietor, an older dusty-appearing gentleman, pleased by the prospect of a real customer, gave her a rather drawn out tour, pointing out the various tomes of interest. By and large, the books were well used, though several almost new appearing books were interspaced on the shelves. Knowing that she shouldn't, she selected two worn books, *The Abbot* by Walter Scott and *Melmoth the Wanderer* by Charles Maturin, paid for the purchases and hurried out to find Jake.

Crowds of people lined the streets, bartering for goods and equipment, jostling each other in their exuberance. In every corner, wagons were camped, waiting to begin the long journey west. An air of festivity surrounded the activities and as each train left, another formed. Most of the emigrant trains traveled in groups of fifty or so for protection. A leader was chosen from among the travelers and all able-bodied men, and sometimes women, were assigned to guard duty. Since he was planning on staying out West, Jake was outfitted like the rest of the emigrants, his lightweight wagon loaded with the necessities for the trip and to begin his new life at the other end. Few concessions had been made for her comfort, but as he explained, when he'd first planned on making the trip, he'd been single.

Motioning to the wagons of the other emigrants, he curtly mentioned that, of the household items and treasured family heirlooms, only a small portion would reach Oregon. Down the trail, they would unload and leave their possessions, the weight being more than the animals could haul over long distances. The trains following behind would use their discarded personal items and heirlooms as firewood. Aimee stored her few possessions, wrapping her new books in protective coverings. She left the chamber pot in full view, where it would be accessible. When he spied that particular item, Jake turned away, his shoulders shaking suspiciously. Let him laugh. Wouldn't be her with her drawers down when the Indians attacked.

Thinking about Indian attacks and the other dangers they could encounter left her throat dry and palms sweating. History was rife with the large numbers of people who perished on the Oregon Trail. Disease, accidents, famine, and Indian attacks were commonplace. Many of the families had small children, and she glimpsed more than one pregnant woman among the travelers. She counted herself fortunate she wasn't among those so blessed, but if Jake kept to his one-month schedule, she could very well end up that way. *What she wouldn't do for some birth control pills right now.* She'd broached birth control with Molly, but Molly either didn't understand or didn't want to discuss the subject, her face pinking with discomfit. She wouldn't give up yet, someone had to have some answers. If she could just speak to one of those ladies of the evening...

After getting her settled, Jake rode out, asking

her to have supper ready when he got back that evening. She grimaced, weighing the possibilities. She'd had few reasons to cook before, and never over an open campfire, but unless she'd missed something, he didn't have a stove hidden somewhere in the wagon. She'd be the first to admit to incompetence in the culinary arts, but divulging that to Jake wasn't on her agenda. Cooking seemed like a simple chore. She rummaged through the wagon, looking for food. Something ready-made. No help there. Next choice, find someone who could help with the burgeoning task at hand.

Several families were camped nearby, but she decided against approaching the one where a strident-voice woman harangued her husband and three little girls. *Didn't seem to be much point.* A better choice was the one where a middle-aged woman, her husband, and a teen-aged girl were seated near a fire pit, relaxing and conversing. Hesitant about intruding, she waited until they noticed her. They smiled, somewhat wary, but waved her in.

Determined to glean information about the art of cooking under less than perfect circumstances, she introduced herself. "My name is Aimee Reynolds... er...Marshall."

The man leaned over and spat a brown stream of tobacco juice.

She rubbed her hands together, wondering how to explain. "I know this sounds ridiculous," she began, "but I've never cooked a day in my life, and I need your help."

The woman looked surprised while the girl giggled. Humiliated, she hurried to explain. "It was never my job at home to do the cooking, and I don't know the first thing about it, and Jake, er, my husband, wants supper when he gets back."

The older woman nodded. "Expect so."

She held out her hand. "I'm Ardis McAfee, that there is my husband, John, and my daughter, Rose." Rose curtsied. Cute, in an old-fashioned way.

Ardis stood up. A tall gangly woman with the face of an old horse, she nevertheless exuded confidence. Motioning for Aimee to follow, she strode to Jake's wagon and climbed in.

"Looks like you have everything you need," she called. The wagon rocked as she foraged inside. Minutes later, she jumped down, her arms laden with sacks of beans and flour. "First thing we need to do is get these beans washed and cooking. We'll do a big batch and then you'll have plenty for tomorrow."

Content to let Ardis take charge, she stood back, amazed at the speed the older woman accomplished each task. Nothing was done without a purpose.

For the next hour, Ardis and Rose taught her the basics. They pointed out various cooking utensils—items she'd never even guessed were cooking utensils—and how to prepare the simplest of recipes. She retrieved a pencil and paper from her small stash of possessions and took notes, hoping she could decipher her scribbling later on. It took a lot of know-how to cook on the trail, but these two were gracious in their willingness to share their secrets. Sitting nearby and knitting while she watched the process, Ardis scolded her when she made her numerous mistakes, but gave the highest praise when she did something right.

****

Jake rode into camp that evening. Aimee stood by the fire, ladle in hand, sprinkles of flour on her nose. Beans simmered on the open fire and hot biscuits were warming in the pan. Her eyes danced, shining with—mischief? *Wonder what she's up to?*

He swung down off his horse, tied the beast to the wagon, filled a small wash basin, and scrubbed his hands. "Sure smells good."

She waited while he dried, then handed him a plate, her gaze on his face. He sampled the fare, grunting in surprise.

"Is it okay?" She fiddled with her apron, looking anxious.

When he'd asked her earlier to make dinner, she'd looked uncomfortable, and he'd guessed he'd go hungry this evening unless he did the cooking.

He blew on the food. It was hotter'n hell. "Good," he mumbled around a mouthful. The food was good—no, better than good. He made himself comfortable by the fire and dug in, adding seconds before he'd finished firsts. He changed his opinion—*it was damn good!*

She handed him a tin of coffee. "One of the ladies helped me. Her name's Ardis, and her husband is John, and they have a daughter, Rose." She grinned, amber eyes sparkling with mischief. "She's a good teacher but has about as much personality as a peanut."

He choked, coughing up coffee, grinning at the image.

She busied herself cleaning up while he ate and then excused herself to bed.

When they first arrived in camp and she got her first good look at the wagon, she'd rearranged some of the goods and made a spot for a lumpy bed. He slept under the wagon, telling her to do the same, but she insisted too many creepy-crawly things kept residence under there, and she wasn't about to fight for space.

He viewed her exertions with humor. Once they reached the open plains, he'd no doubt she'd change her mind. But she stubbornly refused to budge, insisting she was happy right where she was. He knew better, but let her have her way for the moment.

The area around Independence was a sea of wagons stretching as far as the eye could see. Thousands of settlers flocked, eager to start the long journey to the west. Jake watched the new arrivals with misgivings. Most were farmers, sturdy people with little idea of the hardships they'd encounter.

Part of his job was to get the new arrivals signed up and their supplies checked. Markham was a hard taskmaster and every wagon was expected to have the basics or they'd be left behind. Oxen were the teams of choice, but mules traveled faster, though not nearly as adaptable as the hardier oxen. As a rule, mules were mean and ornery, but he'd purchased his team with an eye to disposition, something the greenhorns didn't know to look for.

He tossed the remains of his coffee into the fire. Better bed down and get some rest. Tomorrow would be a long day. He didn't relish it. Teaching greenhorns got his back up. Why they'd want to come out here without preparing, he didn't know, but they kept coming.

****

Morning came very early. Aimee could hear Jake moving around outside, saddling his horse and building a fire. She jumped up, feeling good for the first time in days. Every day of travel brought her one step closer to home. She climbed out of the wagon, sidestepping as a team of mules were led to a nearby camp.

City born and bred, being near the creatures made her nervous, and grateful she wasn't expected to drive or whatever they called it. Jake's team seemed *nicer,* if that was the word. Even she could tell the difference between his team and some of the others. Only one member of his team caused her real concern, a black mean-eyed tooth-baring devil Jake informed her he named "Jack."

"Because he's a male?" Her innocence showed.

"No," he grinned. "Because he's a jackass! But he's strong and healthy—dumber'n mud, but strong."

Nolan, a son of one of the emigrants, showed up, scruffy hat in hands, his youthful face open and earnest. He scuffed his toe, dipping his head. "I'll be handling the reins for Jake's team. His time's going to be spent scouting for good grazing and watering holes before making camp each day. It's up to me to keep his wagon moving. I plan on doing a real good job." Having said his piece, he turned to go.

"I'm so happy to meet you. You have no idea how scared I am of these guys." She waved at the mules. "I was afraid I was going to get stuck driving or whatever you call it."

"If'n I was doing this all the time, I'd be called a muleskinner." He said, his face turning red.

She offered him a cup of coffee. Hesitant, he accepted and sat down.

Nolan, once he got over his initial shyness, was a chatty fellow and before long, she knew that he was one of six brothers, neither the oldest nor the youngest, he liked to read, and although he had some education, he would most likely go into farming with his father when they reached the Oregon Territory. Younger than Aimee, he seemed more mature, having shouldered a grown man's burden by the time he reached eighteen (or so he said). He was respectful and helpful and only his eyes betrayed the fact he was smitten by her at first sight.

As the days progressed, she made friends with several women besides Ardis and Rose who would also make the trek, spending some time each day getting to know them and gathering bits of information about their families and lives before now. Some viewed the trip with great excitement, while still others voiced bleak concerns about the perils of the long miles ahead, but all held to the promise of a better life at the other end. Aimee viewed the coming venture with great reluctance. The odds of survival, and whether or not she would be one of the lucky ones, were uppermost in her mind. Stories around the campfires were filled with the hardships they would face in the weeks and months to come.

As a whole, they were an industrious and cheerful group. Every evening, without fail, the camp would ring with the music of fiddles, banjos, Jews harps, washboards, spoons, and whatever else could be construed as a musical instrument. Dancing and socializing kept boredom at bay, and she looked forward to relaxing and visiting on the sidelines with the other watchers. On the last evening, Jake searched her out, tugging her from the crowd of watchers and out onto the makeshift dance floor.

"I don't know how to dance like this," she objected, feeling silly, pushing against his chest.

His arms encircled her. "Just relax," he coached, "and follow my lead." Before long, she was gliding to the music, waltzing in the open under the stars, in the arms of a handsome man, inexplicably charmed by the romantic interlude. He guided her through the crowd of dancers, his clean masculine scent teasing her senses as she inhaled. Forgetting all else, she reveled in the moment, delighting in the play of his muscles as he moved to the rhythm of the music with an expertise few men could equal.

"Has anyone ever told you how beautiful you are?" he asked, interrupting her thoughts.

Uncharacteristically shy, she shook her head. Makeup was a thing of the past. How he could think she was beautiful dressed as she was, and face scrubbed squeaky clean, was inconceivable. She'd always taken time with her appearance before now, but the available resources at hand were severely limited. All she had in the way of personal toiletries was the brush Molly gave her, some soap purchased at a dry goods store in Independence, and her treasured tubes of lip gloss and hand lotion.

"You are, you know. I've never seen the combination of eye and hair color you have before. It's unusual and very interesting."

Her face heated from the compliments. His comments were so unlike the Jake she thought she knew. "I look like my mother," she admitted. "But she's so much prettier."

"I don't see how," he said, pulling her closer and whirling faster, spinning around and around the dance floor until she was breathless from exertion.

When the dance ended, he released her, hands lingering, his eyes glowing in the half light of the fire.

"You fit to perfection," he whispered for her ears alone, "almost like you were made for me."

Frozen by his unexpected comment, she searched in vain for a fitting comeback.

"Too bad!" She pulled away. "Dance with somebody else."

The light died in his eyes to be replaced by the closed look he wore around her so much of the time. He turned away, hesitating for one moment. "You won't give an inch, will you?"

"I can't," she said, feeling sad. "My only goal is to reach the Oregon Territory. Until then, I have nothing for you or anyone."

"Who are you?" he muttered.

"I'm Aimee, just like I told you."

"But who or what is Aimee?" he asked, his blue eyes penetrating her reserve. "All I know about you is you suddenly appeared in a puddle of mud, looking like you'd lost your best friend."

"If I told you, you'd think I was crazy. There's just no way to explain what happened."

"Ever?" He looked troubled.

Ever was a long time. If she couldn't find a way home, he deserved some sort of explanation. "I can't really tell you anything, and I'm sorry about that. Someday, if it becomes necessary, I'll tell you everything, but until then, you'll just have to trust that I'm doing what I have to do."

He opened his mouth as if to say something further, then stepped back, disappearing into the dark. A lump formed in her throat. She started to follow him, her heart aching. He was hurt—and she couldn't stand that. It made her sick inside. She buried her face in her hands. *She couldn't be falling for him!* When the time came, she was going home. She wanted her life back. She climbed into the wagon, hating herself for causing him pain.

Chapter Six

The call to "*String Out*" rang through the camp. Aimee jerked awake and sat up. Whips cracked with earsplitting pops. Shrill whistles pierced the air. She struggled out of the bedding and peeked out. Bent over, Jake snapped the harness to the last of his team.

"Why didn't you wake me?"

He glanced up. "Get ready. We leave in ten minutes."

She tore off her nightgown and splashed cold water on her face, shivering in the cool morning air. She ran a quick brush through her hair before tying it back with a length of blue ribbon. She eyed the hated corset. *Who would care when she got home if they knew she refused to wear it?* Mom and Dad wouldn't, and Sara would laugh. She threw on her clothes, tying the shawl across her immodest, unsecured breasts and climbed out of the wagon.

Chaos reigned from all sides. Cussing and cracking whips, the menfolk struggled to get the bad-tempered mules into line. Dogs barked, scurrying from beneath the stomping hoofs. Agitated by the uproar, eyeballs rolling, the animals snapped and kicked, fighting against the reins. Children dashed through the confusion, squealing with excitement as they hurried to finish morning chores.

She grabbed some of yesterday's biscuits, stuffed them with leftover bacon and handed several to Jake.

Wolfing the food, his eyes warmed. "I've got to go help." He wiped a hand across his mouth. "These greenhorns'll never get going if I don't."

He lifted a leg and swung onto his horse. "Nolan'll be here in a few minutes. I'll check by from time to time, but I'll be riding point so might be noon before I do." He kneed the horse and cantered away.

As if by magic, Nolan appeared, mumbled a good morning, and went about loading the wagon. When the last box was stored, he climbed into the wagon box.

The long journey had begun.

Scores of individuals walked alongside their wagons. She chose to do the same, eager for the exercise and wanting to feel a part of the great excursion. Thanks to Ardis, the story had spread about her lack of experience in the cooking department, and most of the emigrants regarded her as pampered and prissy. That slant on her upbringing wasn't far from the truth, but still far below what her beginnings truly were. Yes, she thought, I am pampered compared to these families, but her family hadn't been rich, just comfortable. She'd worked because she wanted to, not because she needed the money. Mom and Dad had always seen to her comfort and expenses, and she'd accepted that without question. Now it seemed selfish and egotistical.

It was amazing the personal information that could be garnered in such a short time. Many of the emigrants came from solid middleclass backgrounds. The journey west was costly and most of the poor weren't able to find the money to make the trip. A good portion had sold everything they owned to head west, leaving little behind to tempt them to stay. Others had parents, sisters, brothers, relations, and friends left behind, promising to send for them at journey's end. For herself, she had only one reason for going west—the chance she'd find the way home.

She fingered the locket. Somehow it was the

catalyst. *She knew it*!

Horrendous clouds of dust, kicked up by the wagons and teams, clogged the air. She tied a kerchief over the lower half of her face to keep from inhaling the grit. By high noon, her new boots, so comfortable at first, had rubbed huge blisters. By day's end, she could only hobble along. Tired, grouchy, and dirty, all she could think of was washing up and going to bed. Anything else seemed too much work.

Jake rode up just about the time she'd finished filling the washbowl.

"I thought you'd have supper ready by now." He swung down. "I could eat my horse."

Her mouth fell open. "I forgot," she stuttered. "I'll get something going." Exhausted, she hobbled to the wagon, aching in every square inch of her body.

Jake watched her, shaking his head. Several times during the day, he'd spied her from a distance, always walking beside the wagon. *Determined little cuss!* A spark of admiration bloomed in his chest. Dirt caked the upper half of her face and a thick layer of dust covered most of her outer clothing. She looked tired and dejected as she attempted to climb into the wagon—ready to drop. Taking pity on the poor misguided city girl, he picked her up and set her down in the wagon.

"Just rest," he said. "I'll fix something."

She crawled onto her makeshift bed, asleep before her head hit the pillow. A few minutes later, he climbed in to check on her. She lay sprawled across the small bed, emitting soft snores, hands flung wide. He studied her for a few minutes, noting the graceful line of her neck and curve of her cheek. Long eyelashes fanned her cheeks, hiding those slanted amber eyes—eyes that flashed with intelligence and fire. Right now, she looked beat to hell.

Sympathizing with her misery, he worked the ugly boots off and then peeled off the sweat-soaked wool stockings. He groaned, cussing under his breath. Her feet were a damn mess, covered with angry looking blisters, oozing and bloodied by the friction of the boots. He didn't know how she'd kept going all day. There wasn't any way she'd be walking tomorrow, or the day after for that matter. Filling a pan with water, he wiped her feet clean, soaping the open sores. Other than moaning and shifting, she snored on. He worked the floppy bonnet from her head, careful not to disturb her slumber. He loosened the long braid, fingering the soft red curls. The wind and sun had burned the upper half of her face beneath the dirt, leaving a white streak below where the kerchief covered. He grinned. She'd be mad as hell about that.

Working with an efficiency of motion, he wiped her face clean, undressed her down to chemise and drawers, and covered her with a robe. His hands lingered, fighting the urge to kiss her—to touch her—everywhere. Cursing himself for his gut reaction to her sweet-smelling skin and soft delicate curves, he jumped down from the wagon. He wanted more than she was willing to give. *Twenty more days and counting*!

Nolan'd lit a fire before heading to his parents' wagon and a pot of coffee was perking. His stomach rumbled. Rather than going to the trouble to fix dinner, he searched through the supplies and found a packet of jerked meat and some of the leftover biscuits. Settling down by the fire, he ate a solitary meal, listening to the laughter and voices from the nearby campfires, yearning for the same.

Chapter Seven

God, she pleaded, *please don't make it time to get up.* Though she tried to ignore them, the sounds of the camp clanged in her brain. Her feet hurt like hell and the thought of another long walk like yesterday made her cringe in agony.

She rolled out of bed, every joint creaking in protest. Her dirty, discarded clothing lay in a pile and rags were wrapped around her tender feet. Her lips tightened. Only one person would've taken the time to make her comfortable. Her first impressions of Jake were taking a hard beating, and now she owed him for that kindness as well.

Disgruntled, she hurried to dress and eased down from the wagon. He was already gone and coffee was warming on the fire. She poured a cup, wishing she'd woke up before he left, at least she could have fixed him something to eat and perhaps thanked him. Her stomach growled. She'd had nothing to eat since about noon the day before. She found the bag of oats and soon had a pot of mush boiling over the campfire. Ladling out a large bowl, she was just lifting a spoonful to her mouth when Jake rode in.

"That smells pretty good," he commented. "Is there enough there for me?"

She hobbled to the fire and filled a big bowl, handing it to him along with a hunk of bread and a cup of coffee.

"Best you ride in the wagon today," he said. "Your feet won't be healed enough to walk very far for a couple of days."

"Thank you, God!"

"What possessed you to keep walking until your feet almost rotted off?"

"Everyone else was!" She sniffed. "I didn't want to look more like a prissy city girl than I already do."

He nodded. "There's more than a few who are in the same condition, not just you. Better let your feet heal, and then walk longer lengths each day till they get hardened up. It's easier for the animals to haul the extra weight now than when we get into rougher territory."

Tossing the last bit of coffee from his mug, he stood up and began packing their goods.

"I can do that," she protested, embarrassed that he would have to do her work as well.

"Tomorrow, maybe," he said.

"You probably think I'm stupid or something, but I'm usually better about taking care of myself."

"I'm not passing judgment." Rummaging through his pack, he handed her a small jar of some sort of cream. "Rub this on your feet off and on today."

Nolan strode up, his eyebrows raised in surprise. "How come you're here so late?"

He glanced up, grinning. "Wanted to spend some time with my new *bride*."

Her chin went up. "How special."

Bending down, bones creaking in protest, she helped him pack the last box. His firm, sensuous lips and his gleaming agate blue eyes drew her attention. His eyes flashed as he closed the gap separating them. Uncomprehending his intent, she gasped as his mouth slanted across hers, lips moving seductively as his tongue slipped between hers, demanding she yield until her lips responded of their own accord. Time stood still as she savored the taste of his kiss, drawn into a swirling morass of feelings heretofore unexplored. He drew back and then planted another quick kiss on her now tingling lips.

"Every minute with you is special." He drew a deep breath, and mounted his horse, spurs jingling.

"Keep her in the wagon today," he instructed Nolan who stood nearby, mouth hanging open, "or I'll whip both of you."

Nolan's red, befuddled face, blanched white. She burst out laughing, covering her confused feelings with her best defense—humor.

"We're seriously scared," she giggled.

His lips twisted in a slight smile. "You should be! After all, haven't you mentioned on more than one occasion that I'm the most low-life and disgusting man you've ever met?"

Face heating, she could only nod. She had mentioned that a time or two.

Nolan fumbled with the reins. "You don't have to worry," he gulped. "If I have to, I'll hogtie her to the wagon."

"See that you do." Jake laughed, white teeth flashing. "But don't let her go until I've had the chance to see it." He wheeled his horse, cantering off, while she searched for something to throw at his retreating back.

Nolan caught her arm just as she was about to let go with a good-sized rock.

"I wouldn't do that if I was you. Jake isn't one to mess with." His face spoke louder than words. He was genuinely concerned about Jake's reaction to her shenanigans.

"Relax, Nolan. It's not like I'd come close to hitting him, but he needs to know who's the boss." She grinned, trying to ease his fears somewhat.

"He's the boss," Nolan croaked. "Leastways, far as I'm concerned, he is."

There wasn't anything she could or would say to change his opinion, and Jake needed to have the emigrants' respect if he were to maintain his leadership position. That she *could* understand.

"You're right," she conceded, "he is the boss and unless we want to be left behind, I suggest we get in the wagon and get going."

Around them, the camp was rapidly clearing out. Their wagon would be one of the ones to the rear of the train today, eating dust the entire time. Notwithstanding that small inconvenience, she was grateful she wouldn't have to walk. Exhilarated by the treat of riding all day, she lay down on her lumpy bed, determined to get some much needed rest. That lasted only a short while. The wagon jolted along the uneven trail, the great wheels rolling over ruts and potholes such that her teeth rattled to the point of breaking.

Crawling over supplies, she dragged herself into the wagon box, holding on as the wagon pitched and swayed. At least her feet were up since her legs weren't long enough to reach the floor, perched as she was on the wagon seat, clinging for dear life to the side rail. The dust didn't seem nearly as bad up here as it was on the ground but it was still thick enough to warrant wearing a kerchief over her lower face. Sunglasses would have been perfect. Were sunglasses invented yet?

****

Each day was a repeat of the day before. Aimee's innate ability to find something interesting in everything broke the monotony. She started a journal, adding bits and pieces of information as events transpired. During the second week on the trail, an older woman died. They buried her in a lonesome grave in the middle of the vastness of the emerging west. Since beginning the journey, the old woman had been confined to her wagon, but she'd insisted on accompanying her family, saying she was strong enough to make the trip. Sadly, that was not the case. As troubling as it was, she knew the old woman's death was only the first. Tears stained her journal as she added the heartrending entry.

Aimee and Jake's contact was left to those short moments during breakfast and then at suppertime. She looked forward to those brief times, her stomach clenching in anticipation when he was near—more alive somehow. They shared a few moments of conversation, but by the time they'd supped and she'd cleaned up the dishes, sleep beckoned and the day would end.

She continued to sleep inside, while he kept to his place under the wagon. They had a comfortable, if somewhat sterile existence, but she was conscious of his piercing eyes following her whenever they were together. He'd not tried to touch her again since that one morning, and she found herself daydreaming about that silly kiss more than once. It was silly, she thought—or maybe not. They had been married for twenty-four days. *Twenty-four days! Oh my God!* Her wedding night loomed nearer. She'd better come up with a plan fast or in six days, she would truly become his wife. Unearthing her cell phone, she flipped it open, just in case a miracle might happen. As she suspected - *no service.*

Chapter Eight

Since beginning the trek, they'd forded several rivers. The river crossings were, to Aimee's way of thinking, the most arduous and frightening. Wagons got loose and floated away, people fell into the churning waters, but luck was on their side—none had drowned so far. Striding along, keeping pace with the wagons, her mind drifted, wondering about the other rivers, how many more to come and how many travelers would fall by the wayside. She stumbled, tripping over her long skirt. *One of these days, the skirt would grow magically shorter.*

Jake rode up, his agate blue eyes lighting with warmth as they found her. "Want to ride with me awhile? I won't be scouting ahead until later today and everything's peaceful for the moment."

Careful consideration of his offer took all of two seconds. She reached a hand up as he slipped his foot from the stirrup. Swinging her up, he settled her sidesaddle in front of him and tucked her full skirts beneath his knee. Leaning back, using his chest for support, she settled herself, pleased at the chance to ride for a change.

"You can nap if you want to. I'll keep you from falling." His lips tickled her ear, causing delicious tremors to spiral down her spine.

"I'm fine." She wiggled, finding a more comfortable position. "Just happy to ride for a change."

"You can ride in the wagon anytime you want. I'm packed pretty light." His warm breath fanned her cheek.

"And have everyone make fun of me? I don't *think* so." Not that she minded the teasing, but by now she had earned the right to a little respect.

"Just point out the ornery cuss, and I'll shoot him."

She giggled, snuggling a little closer. "Mostly it's the women, and I can't see you shooting an unarmed female."

"Just between you and me," he whispered, "given the chance, Mrs. Purdue would be first on my list."

Laughter burst from her lips. Mrs. Purdue was a whining mouse-faced shrew, whose poor husband suffered daily from her constant tirades. Every evening, without fail, Jake made sure their wagon was parked well away from her and her incessant complaining and bitching. Aimee pitied the poor souls who were stuck near her every night. The three Purdue girls, christened Faith, Hope, and Charity, were all under ten years old; solemn, shy, little girls with big soulful eyes, who followed her quite often during the day, walking along and chatting, their eyes widening when their mother yelled. The littlest one, Charity, would gather a handful of Aimee's skirt, holding on with one hand while sucking her thumb. A rag doll, named Martha, stuffed under her arm for safekeeping. The girls were starved for attention and looked to her for companionship.

Her eyes were drawn to Jake's hands gripping the reins, strong, capable hands that could be so gentle. Fascinated, she stared at his hands, swallowing the urge to touch them, worried about the growing attraction.

"You're pretty quiet for a change," he murmured.

"Just thinking."

"What about?"

Sighing, she shifted away. "Nothing important. Just daydreaming."

Turning to face him, she immediately realized her mistake. Her face was mere inches from his, and from the smoldering look in his eyes, it was too late to pull back. His lips molded to hers, licking and scorching, burning with heat. Dazed, she grabbed hold of his shirt, fearful of letting go, of losing herself in his embrace. The world tilted.

His husky voice brought her back to reality. "Might want to save this for later. Looks like we've drawn an audience."

Sure enough, besides the Purdue sisters, several other children had gathered, dancing around the horse, giggling and pointing.

"Oh, for God's sake!" Mortified, caught—by children—in such a compromising situation. "Mrs. Purdue will be all over me after she hears about this."

"We won't tell," Charity lisped. "Momma never listens to us anyway."

"Papa and Momma never kiss," added Hope. "She says a good woman only allows a man to touch her when she needs a baby. Momma doesn't kiss us either."

The three little girls nodded in unison.

"What a bunch of crap!" How could any mother stuff such nonsense down unsuspecting little girls?

"People marry because they want to be together, and that includes touching. Good women touch their husbands all the time. It's part of life." Sliding off the horse, she stumbled.

"Do you like Mr. Marshall to touch you?" Three pairs of questioning eyes gazed at her.

Jake leaned over the pommel, waiting for her response. "I'd like to hear the answer to that one myself."

"Well," she began, smoothing her blouse down as

she stalled for time. "That's a pretty personal question."

Feeling awkward and ridiculous, she groped for the right words, finding none. *Some child psychologist I'd make!* "I think this discussion is over, and we'd probably better not mention it to your mama."

Faith, Hope, and Charity nodded in agreement.

Faith turned to the other children. "And you'd better not tell either or I'll make you sorry."

The troupe of children nodded and crossed their hearts. The unwitting show would be kept a secret.

Aimee squirmed in embarrassment. "I think I'd better walk now."

Jake leaned down, whispering for her alone. "I'd have liked to hear your answer." Whirling the big gelding, he rode off, his laughter trailing behind.

She stomped off, the group of still giggling children following along. Reaching into her pocket, she drew out a book.

"Would anyone like to hear me read?"

"I would," squeaked Charity.

"Me, too," yelled another child.

"Good," she nodded. "I'll read while we walk. But someone will have to help me so I don't trip over something and fall."

Faith strode ahead of her. "I'll walk first and you stay behind me, and I'll let you know if something is in the way."

"Good plan!"

Opening the book, she began to read, feeling like the Pied Piper of Hamilton or Hamblen or wherever he came from.

Chapter Nine

They reached the Platte River. The captain declared the following day as a day of rest, not only for the tired emigrants, but also to give the animals some much needed rest and grazing time. The day of rest sent waves of joy rippling through the camp; laundry would be done, and baths would be taken in the slow moving river. Aimee, along with several others, made their way down to the bank where a group of women and younger children had converged. Taking turns keeping watch, they stripped down to their underclothes and waded in. The muddy water was freezing, but she wasn't about to pass up the opportunity for a bath, even if it was a dirty one. Romping and splashing along with everyone else, she ducked her head, washing and soaping to her heart's content.

Afterwards, she lay on a warm rock slab and sunned until her unmentionables—as the other women called them—dried out. It felt so good to be clean, even using muddy water. Reluctantly, she dressed and hurried to their campsite, gathering up the dirty laundry, a bar of soap and this century's answer to the washing machine—a wooden paddle. Maybe she could get a little instruction as to its possible use if one of the other women was doing laundry at the same time.

Ardis and Rose crouched on the bank, their skirts tied up around their waists, rubbing soap onto clothing and pounding the wet articles against large rocks. Seemed like a lot of hard work, but if that was the way it was done, she'd give it a try.

Ardis slanted an amused look in her direction. “Just make sure you rub the soap over the wet clothes first.”

Couldn't be that difficult. Tying up her skirt, she hunkered down near them and dipped in a pair of Jake's pants, almost losing them in the current. The soap bar slipped from her wet hands and started to float downriver. She jumped in, saved the soap, but got soaked in the process. Ardis and Rose stood on the bank, laughing until they cried.

Disgruntled, she crawled from the water, shivering in the cool air, but determined to get the job done, notwithstanding the unfavorable conditions. Holding the soap with a tighter grip, she rubbed it briskly over the pants and started slapping until every piece of dirty laundry had suffered the same energetic result.

Ardis nodded her approval. “You slap a mean paddle,” she said. “Couldn't have done better myself.”

“I've got a lot of anger and frustration built up.”

“Yep,” Ardis agreed. “It's a good way to keep sane sometimes.”

Rose shook out a wet shirt, smoothing the wrinkles. “I think it'd be wonderful to have a man to wash for.”

In unison, Ardis and Aimee snorted.

“Enjoy being young,” Ardis told the girl. “You've got a lot of years ahead of you to do that.”

Rose stiffened, lips pouting. “I'm almost fifteen. Plenty of girls are married by the time they're fifteen. You were,” she pointed out.

“Yeah, but I regretted it ever since. I'd of married your Pa anyway, but I should've waited awhile before getting hitched and then having you. Maybe if I'd been older, birthing you wouldn't have hurt me so bad, and I could've had other children.”

“Cripes!” Aimee gasped. “I just got married and

I'm twenty-one."

Rose's eyes fastened on her, their depths saying volumes. Her lips curled in a nasty grin. "Why, you're almost an old maid."

"Rose!" Ardis's face darkened. "No reason to shame Aimee. Lots of girls wait."

"I'm not the least shamed." She dipped another piece of clothing. "I wish I'd been older. Where I come from, a lot of people wait until their thirties and it's perfectly fine. I only married Jake so I could come on this trip." Instantly, she regretted her thoughtless choice of words. Ardis and Rose looked at her as if she had grown horns. Word traveled fast and Jake would, no doubt, be told what she'd just said.

"Uh…I didn't mean that," she stuttered. "I just meant that, um, Jake and I were so much in love, and we got married sooner than we planned so I could come with him."

Ardis nodded. "Wouldn't want to be left behind myself." As an afterthought, she added, "Jake's a fine-looking man. None better."

Privately, Aimee agreed with her. He was a fine-looking man. Added to that, he was honest, full of confidence, and people respected him. He was cleaner than most, taking time to wash every morning and night, which in itself was a huge plus in her book.

Her own attempts at personal hygiene met with serious drawbacks, but a night didn't go by that she didn't at least have a spit bath, and her hair was washed every three days.

Ardis mentioned one evening, after viewing her endeavors with ill-concealed skepticism, that she only washed her hair once a month, and Aimee's hair was going to suffer if she kept over-washing it. *Aimee was horrified!* Just thinking about letting her hair go for a month without washing had her head itching and crawly-feeling.

After that, she caught herself more than once staring at Ardis's hair, wondering if she would see live things wiggling around in it.

Chapter Ten

All along the arduous route, graves lined the trail. Aimee avoided looking at them as they passed the sad burial places. In some spots, whole families had died and warnings of cholera were posted. Sometimes the bodies had been dug up by wild animals and parts littered the trail. The sight grossed her out, and if she knew about them in advance, she crawled into the wagon and hid. While efforts were made to rebury the bodies, some felt it was a useless practice. Jake nevertheless ordered some of the teen-aged boys to take care of the reburials, which wasn't always popular. Aimee warned them about personal contact and using lye soap afterwards to wash up. That much she could offer as help.

Their train had their own mishaps as well. A young man died after a rifle accidentally discharged; something Jake mentioned happened all too often. Many of the emigrants had never handled a gun before and giving them a loaded gun was, in his opinion, "chancy" as he put it. A group of the more experienced males took it upon themselves to give lessons to the beginners, and that's when the accident occurred. The whole train gathered for the funeral. The grieving family's anguish was a hard thing to witness. Another lonely grave was added to the landscape and another sad entry to her journal. The incident left her depressed for days afterwards. She'd never met the victim, but losing his life so young was painful.

By her reckoning, today marked the thirtieth

day since she'd wed Jake. Anxious, stomach in knots, she waited until he left before clambering down from the wagon. He'd left without breakfast or even the comfort of a hot cup of coffee. Riddled with guilt, she fixed a quick plate and strode out to the stock area where he was busy rounding the animals up in preparation for the day's march. His look of surprise when he saw her added to her remorse. A warm smile lit his face when she handed him the plate.

"You can't hide from me." He grinned, dimples dancing. "The wagon's too small."

"I wasn't hiding," she said, defending herself. "I just overslept."

"You make a lot of noise when you sleep." His amazing blue eyes twinkled with humor.

She fidgeted for several seconds and then blurted. "Would it make any difference if I said I don't want to have sex with you?" She sounded angry even to herself.

His eyes sparkled. "We're not going to have sex."

"We're not?" she gasped, hopeful.

"No," his lips curved. "We're going to make love."

Disgusted that she'd been taken in, she groaned. "It's the same thing!"

"No, it isn't—and when we're finished, you'll know why."

Chin up, her eyes narrowed in fury, she glared at him. "I've been with a man before! I told you I had boyfriends."

A shadow passed over his face. "But did you enjoy it? Did he make you scream with passion or wet with wanting?"

"It's none of your business whether I enjoyed it or not. The simple truth is I'm not a virgin and that's what every man wants!"

"I guess being a virgin has its advantages, the first being the woman doesn't know when a man isn't doing it right." He grinned, adding with smug self-pride. "I'm not inexperienced."

"Ooooo," she sneered, "I can hardly wait."

Leaning close, he ran a finger over her breast, thumbing a nipple in the process. "You won't have to." His eyes smoldered. "I'll make sure you forget you were ever with another man. My lips and hands will be on every part of you. All you'll be able to think about will be me. I'll make you cry with need, and I won't stop until you beg me to."

She licked her now dry lips. *She'd forgotten the lip gloss.*

He exuded heat and passion, something she didn't want to feel. She responded as tension sparked between them. Her traitorous body reacted to the sensual images his words conveyed, heat pooling at the apex of her thighs. Her mind whispered he was, after all, her husband, and who would argue her right to sleep with him.

His mouth covered hers in a demanding kiss, licking and tasting, smothering her with his burgeoning desire.

He drew back. "Prepare yourself, wife."

Her fingers touched her lips, hot from his kiss.

"I don't want to do this!" she screeched.

"I didn't want to marry you," he retorted, "but I did."

Taking a deep, fortifying breath, she fought for control. Once again, he'd put her on the defensive and without a weapon. Whirling, she stomped back to the wagons, cussing him with every foul word she knew and some she didn't. *Why couldn't she have picked a man who was ugly and repulsive, and one who found her the same*?

Throughout the day, she worked on formulating a rough, but plausible plan. By the time he returned to the wagon that evening, she was hanging out her "rags," taking her time and rinsing out more than she could use in a month. Every few minutes, she would moan and grab her stomach, pretending pain.

He watched for awhile, then burst out laughing. “Your woman time ended last week, or did you think I didn’t notice.”

Great! Just great! Not only did her plan fail, but she looked like an idiot to boot.

“I was only rewashing them while we had a good supply of water. Is that too hard to understand?” Stalking away with haughty disdain, she went to the fire and began ladling up dinner.

“Oh, so you weren’t trying to fool me?”

Smiling with acerbic sweetness, she handed him a plate. “I have no idea what you mean.”

“I’m sure you don’t.” His eyes roamed over her. “But I’d hate to think you were trying to avoid me.”

“Me? Avoid you? Why would I do that? Do I appear like I’m avoiding you? I’m here. You’re here. We’re both here. So what’s your point?” She glared at him.

“No point,” he said. “Just looking forward to our wedding night.”

Her stomach hit rock bottom. “Do we really have to do this? I would really, really rather wait.”

“We already waited. Tonight’s the night. In fact, it’s time for bed.”

Dusk had fallen and night would soon be upon them. Grabbing her night things, she almost ran down to the small stream gurgling nearby.

She heated water and washed all over, taking as much time as she dared, even to shampooing her hair several times. Donning a clean pair of drawers over her bikini panties, and adding a chemise for additional protection, she searched through her baggage, selecting the most hideous of the high collared nightgowns Molly had been so generous in supplying. A voluminous gray flannel gown, drab and unattractive, added just the right touch. Pulling her hair back, she anchored it in one long braid, tying the end with a blue ribbon, her only concession to beauty. Satisfied she'd done her best—or at least worst—she peeked through the wagon flap. He sat by the fire, sipping a cup of coffee, seemingly lost in thought. Gathering up her courage, she climbed down and approached her nemesis.

Jake glanced up, his sparkling blue eyes glistening with amusement. "It'd take more than that to make you look bad."

"I wasn't trying to look bad," she lied. "This just happened to be the only clean nightie I had."

"And you figured it'd make me lose interest. You forgot one small item—even with your hair back and dressed in that rag, you're one of the most beautiful women I've ever seen and nothing's going to change that fact."

Her back stiffened. He wasn't going to bend one bit.

"I could care less what you think." She fiddled with her sleeve, almost panicked with nerves. "Let's just get this over with. I'm tired and it's late."

Jake tossed the remainder of his coffee into the fire and motioned for Aimee to stay put. The wagon rocked as he moved supplies around, banging and rattling until he was satisfied. *It was as good as he could make it.*

Drawing back the flap, he waved Aimee in. The interior was lit by a single candle, sputtering as it cast a soft glow on the intimate scene. He'd done his best to make it comfortable, heaping blankets over the supplies and containers of food, forming a soft cushion. She crawled in, a look of surprise on her face, and sat in the center of the bed, waiting for his next move. *She looked so tempting sitting there—dreamlike!*

The hastily contrived bedroom muted the noise of the camp to some extent, but in the stillness of the night, a fiddle played a lilting tune, while from another direction, a female voice crooned a soothing lullaby.

"Take off that damned ugly nightgown!" His voice sounded loud in the relative quiet of the small enclosure.

"I'll do no such thing!" she huffed, indignant. "Whatever you're planning, we can do it just as well without me being naked."

"Suit yourself." *She wasn't making this easy.* He reached over and began unbuttoning the collar of her gown.

She slapped his hands away. "I told you no!"

"Are you going to fight me all night?"

"Only if you continue to push me," she shrilled. "I told you I didn't want to do this, or did you plan to simply rape me."

Her words sucker punched him. He dropped his hands to his side and gazed at her, long and hard. The candle flickered off her tight features. Fear dilated her pupils until her eyes appeared almost black. Having her afraid of him wasn't what he wanted or what he expected from her. She'd shown a lot of sass and pride since the day they first met, qualities he most admired in her. Damn fool that he was, he wanted this night to be special—more than just sex. She might not like it, but he was her husband. Her unwanted husband.

"Tell me about yourself. Tell me who Aimee is or who she thinks she is."

Startled, she gaped at him. He eased down on the pallet, reclining on his side, head propped in his hand for support, watching her with concentrated interest. Confused, she stuttered, "Wha...What do you want to know?"

"How old are you? I don't even think I know that for certain." He took her hand, rubbing small circles with the pad of his thumb, gentling her. Against his large hands, hers looked small and delicate, the fingers long and slim—*hands of a lady.*

She coughed. "I'm twenty-one."

"You look younger. I'd have thought eighteen or so." He traced a blue-tinged vein on her wrist. "And your mother's name?"

"Liz. Elizabeth. Why do you want to know this stuff?"

"Just making conversation." He kissed her wrist, lips lingering for just a moment. "Learning about you."

"How old are you?"

He chuckled, amused by the turnabout. "I'm twenty-eight and in a month I'll be twenty-nine." He shifted, drawing closer. "Why were you in St. Louis? I'm pretty sure my first impressions of you are wrong."

"You wouldn't believe me if I told you."

"Try me," he prompted. "Never know what a person will believe until you try."

He released her hand, his exploring fingers working their way up her inner arm. She licked her lips. He leaned over and planted a soft kiss on the inner side of her elbow, blowing warm air on the spot. She shivered.

"Why are you doing that?" She jerked her arm back.

He rolled over, cradling his head on crossed arms. He ached to touch her, but she needed time to get used to him.

"When I was young, my father raised stallions for breeding. I remember two in particular. One was mean and vicious, and if a mare was in season, he'd scream for days, kicking the stalls and ripping off parts, and biting if anyone got too near. The mares were pretty beat up when he got done with them. Once, he almost stomped a man to death before the handlers pulled him off. We all decided he was the devil's spawn, and we weren't allowed near him, but I could hear him screaming clear up at the big house. The other stallion—now he was a gentleman, always gentle, nipping the mares and courting them, never scaring or hurting any. We never had any problems with that one."

"Oh, I get it," she snapped. "I'm the brood mare. So which stallion are you?"

"The gentleman, of course," he drawled, his lips curving. "Otherwise, I'd have bitten the back of your neck and forced you." He resumed his casual exploration, loosening the tight braid she had tied in her unruly hair. Red-gold curls sprang free. He stroked his fingers through the strands, gently massaging her scalp. Her eyes were softer now, less wary. She was responding, even if she was fighting it all the way.

He pushed her down on the improvised bed, pulled her stiff body close, and held her until she relaxed, secure within his unrelenting embrace. He ran a finger down the side of her elegant fine-boned face, tracing each feature, memorizing every line, and liking what he saw. He planted a light kiss at the corner of her mouth, just a touch. Her full lips trembled, her amber eyes glinted with unspoken words in the flickering light of the candle, hinting at forbidden secrets in their closed depths.

Inhaling, he tasted her scent, clean and smelling of something flowery, but underneath that, the heady smell of woman. Keeping his pace slow, he nuzzled the vee of her neck, planting feather-light kisses, felt the blood pounding in her veins, felt her breathing coming in short gasps. *He was making some progress, even though the going was slow.*

"Don't be afraid of me," his voice came low and guttural. "I want you to enjoy this." He wanted her to want him—with everything she had.

Emboldened by her subtle physical reactions, he

dipped his head and ran his tongue around the shell of her outer ear, causing her to jump. He waited for her to protest. She didn't. His groin throbbed, his control slipped. It took every bit of restraint he could muster to hold back.

Aimee's mind whirled, senses alive and stimulated. The rasp of Jake's beard on her sensitive skin kindled a spark of electrical currents zipping along her nerve endings. His hands, roughened by work, were at the same time, gentle and provocative.

She stared at the dark face poised above her, mesmerized by the glittering blue eyes and curve of his sensuous mouth. A two day's growth of beard covered his chin, adding a raffish appeal to his beautiful masculine features. Even here in this quiet place, he exuded confidence and power. She had so much to lose by succumbing to desire. She wasn't a virgin, but her experiences were few. She always believed sex was part of love. But sex could be just sex—couldn't it? People had sex all the time and then just walked away. But he wasn't treating her like she was just a sex object. He was—what was the word? Courting! He was courting her.

She fought against it, but some of her reticence melted away to be replaced by a whisper of desire. She felt dizzy, the enclosure far too warm. His hands continued their random exploration, cool air brushing her neck and shoulders as the ugly gown fell back under his determined onslaught.

He nipped at the corner of her mouth. Her lips parted, welcoming his kiss, tongues dueling with unbridled passion.

Her traitorous breasts peaked with need, aching for his touch. He nibbled, licking and nipping, slowly bringing every atom of her being to life, thumbing sensitized nipples on his downward journey, his mouth closing over one erect point, tongue tormenting her with light gentle strokes until she thought she would scream. Past experiences had never made her feel so sexy, or so desired, and nothing had prepared her for Jake.

"Can we get rid of the nightgown now?"

Suffused with fiery longings, she nodded, raising her arms to allow him to pull the confining clothing off. Her underwear followed. Her last defense went by the wayside. He hesitated, his fingers pulling at the elastic of her bikinis.

"What're these?"

"They're panties." She gasped, arching against his hand. "Be careful with them, they're the only pair I've got."

"Don't look good for much," he muttered.

"Forget about the panties," she moaned. "Pay attention to what you're doing."

He stripped off his trousers in one slick movement. Naked, pressed against his muscular form, she could feel him, thick and hard, and gloriously male.

He lifted up on his elbows, gazing at her with hungry fascination. "I want to see you."

Instinctively, she covered her bare breasts. He pushed her hands away, leaning down to suckle one pink tip. She moaned, grabbing handfuls of his hair.

"Never hide from me," he rasped. "I won't allow it."

Aimee writhed as his lips brushed across her sensitized belly, muscles contracting as she reacted to the hot sensations his mouth evoked. She gasped as he nuzzled her most intimate parts, whimpering with tortured need, crying out as his tongue stroked and teased. She moaned, jerking her knees together, face heating up. The intimate caress, shameless and intoxicating, was unlike any she'd ever experienced.

Jake raked Aimee with his gaze. The meager light of the candle flowed across her bare form, wrapping her in a golden halo. Her glazed eyes shone through narrowed lids, a light sheen of perspiration caused her skin to gleam like satin in the soft glow. Tonight, she was his—no matter what—and he was going to make sure she remembered every second.

"You're so beautiful," he groaned. "More beautiful than I could've imagined."

She reached out and touched him, stroking his whiskered cheek. "You're kind of pretty yourself."

"*Pretty*," he snorted. "Men aren't pretty."

"Some are," she breathed, her voice husky with passion. "You are."

Brazenly, she parted her legs, offering herself with sensuous invitation. "I think we were in the middle of something."

This was the passionate woman he'd known was hidden beneath the sassy exterior.

His lips curved. She was just about right where he wanted her. Cupping her breasts, he blew on them, teasing and suckling first one and then the other, enjoying the sensations as she squirmed beneath him. His lips devoured hers, his hands stroked her soft skin, memorizing every contour.

She moaned, rolling her hips against his now engorged member, the contact delicious and exciting. She reached down, her hands circling his swollen shaft, caressing his hard length and running small circles around the tip with her finger.

"You keep that up," he gasped, arching against her, "and this isn't going to last."

"We have time," she whispered. "All night."

He pushed forward, parting the silken folds, groaning as she closed around him, muscles pulsing as he slid in deeper, waiting for her tight casing to adjust, forcing himself to hold back.

She ran her hands up and down his thighs, raising to meet his thrusts. Her hands gripped his buttocks, holding tight and grinding against him, hissing in ecstasy as he plunged in over and over again, pulling her along in a tide of passion.

"Jake," she moaned, biting her lip, "I need—don't stop."

"What do you need?" he ground out. "Tell me what you want."

"I don't know," she wailed. "Just don't stop!"

His control slipped another notch, he wanted nothing more than to pound into her, driving into her until this gut-wrenching need ended. Sparks flew. The heat unbearable as sweat pooled between them. She writhed, screaming as she climaxed

He hurried to join her, catching her scream in his mouth, gasping as he came with surging force, pulsating in unison with the tremors of her sheath.

Relaxed, supporting his weight on trembling elbows, Jake kissed her, with lips both teasing and gentle.

"That was pretty good for a first time."

"Uh, huh," she panted in breathless gasps. "First for a lot of things."

Curious, he delved further. "What things?"

"Oh, you know." Her gaze fell away.

Shaking her, he pressed, knowing what the answer would be. "First for what?"

"If you must know," she huffed. "It was my first orgasm!"

Ego puffed and flying high, he smiled down at her. "I told you I'd make you scream."

Her lips curved, beguiling him with her allure. "You did, didn't you? More than once."

Rolling her on top, he stroked her thrusting breasts, leisurely thumbing small circles around the pink tips. She arched like a little cat, hissing with pleasure, rotating her hips against him, smiling as he grew hard again. He arched up. Reaching down, she wrapped a hand around him, stroking the glistening drop of moisture on the tip before positioning him against her and then eased down until he filled her completely, muscles convulsing as her body opened to accept him.

Jake groaned, chest heaving. "You're gonna kill me."

She leaned over, hands planted on either side of his face, her glorious long red gold curls tickling his cheeks. "You can't die from sex," she gasped, rocking against him.

He cupped her behind, increasing the tempo, bucking against her, growling in satisfaction as her muscles rippled, building to another climax.

"Scream for me," he groaned, his mouth moving possessively over her lips, tongue delving into her silken warmth, demanding a response.

Her fingers dug into his pec muscles, clenching and unclenching as she moved. Her nails raked his skin causing a brief spasm of pain. He could feel her heart pounding beneath his hands, frantic. She was almost there—and then she gasped, back arching, she reached the pinnacle and cried out.

He held back until her tremors eased, then let his control go, climaxing in one bright burst of light.

Later, he cuddled her closer, content to lie there and listen to her even breathing, wondering what her shifting temperament would be in the morning. Warm, he hoped.

Chapter Eleven

Deciding it was best for all if she didn't sleep with Jake again, Aimee retired early the following night. She could hear Jake's movements near the wagon, the jingle of his spurs, water splashing as he washed up. A few moments silence, and then the canvas flipped back. She yelped in surprise when he grabbed an ankle and dragged her out. Stubborn and determined, she fought and kicked all the way, refusing to go without a fight.

He held on, unbending and unyielding, forcing her to capitulate. "Quiet down or you'll have the whole camp over here," he growled low.

"Maybe that's what I want." Panting, she struggled to free herself.

"You never do anything the easy way, do you?"

She relaxed. "Why should I? At least you know I'm not here because I want to be."

"Seems to me you were pretty willing back in St. Louis, or did I misunderstand?" Dropping his arms, he stepped back. "Maybe you'd have rather stayed behind and taken your chances." He turned away, staring into the night.

Her mind replayed the incident down by the dock. The scary encounter with the hulking oaf still caused her to sweat, and most of the time, she avoided that revolting mental image. Jake had been her rescuer then and had cared for her since. Grudgingly, she acquiesced, admitting to herself that she needed him, at least for now.

"I wanted to come with you," she admitted. "I guess I'm still trying to adjust."

He whirled. "Adjust to *what*? What's so different that you have to adjust, as you put it?"

"You wouldn't understand." She had no way to explain. "It doesn't make sense, even to me."

"Try me! Or would you rather keep pretending and not admit what you really are?"

"What do you mean?"

His eyes burned with contempt. "That you're a whore, and I took you to wife."

The scathing words pierced her lightly held control.

Gasping in outrage, she lunged at him, slapping his face. "That's a lie! And if you ever say that to me again, you'll regret it!"

Jake rubbed his cheek, a small glimmer of respect shone in his eyes. "What are you then?"

She could barely speak, she was so angry. "I'm your wife, but that's impossible, because if it is, I must be crazy."

"Nothing crazy about it. We got married. I have the certificate to prove it."

"And that in itself is ridiculous. I can't be married to you because, in my reality, you don't exist."

"Now you *are* talking crazy." He threw up his hands. "I'm standing right here in front of you, big as day. I beginning to think maybe you did escape from Bedlam, maybe that's the answer to everything."

"Do you want to know the truth or not?"

He nodded. "I'd rather know than not—and don't lie to me."

"All rightee then. But you won't believe me, I can guarantee it." She took a deep breath and then exhaled. "I was born in the year 1987. I'd just finished my third year at a university in Seattle, Washington, and just before I met you, I was shopping with my younger sister, Sara, at Pike's

Street Market. I bought this locket from an antique store." She lifted the locket, showing him. "After I put it on, I fainted and when I woke up, I was laying in the mud in St. Louis, and you were there."

He snorted. "You really expect me to believe that story?"

"Believe what you like, but it's the truth." She stood her ground, keeping her voice calm and reasonable. "I can't prove it, but I can tell you some things that are going to happen soon—maybe that'll help convince you."

"Like what?"

She shut her eyes, thinking hard. "In 1848, January, I think, gold will be discovered at Sutter's Mill in California and thousands of men will flock there hoping to get in on the riches."

He snorted. "Gold seekers come west all the time."

"But very few of them will find gold. Gold will be discovered at Sutter's Mill in 1848." She raised her chin, daring him to contradict her. "There will be a great civil war starting in 1860 or 1861, I'm not exactly sure on the starting date, but it'll be between the Northern states and the Southern states and it'll start at Fort Sumter."

"Why would they go to war?" Curious now, he waited, his head cocked.

"The Southern states want to secede from the Union. They want to keep owning slaves and the North wants to stop slavery."

He stared into the darkness, rubbing his chin. "I've heard rumors."

"It'll be more than rumors in a few years." She warmed to her topic. "And the president will be Abraham Lincoln, and he'll be shot and killed at Ford's Theatre."

"Who wins the war?" His eyes shone with interest, fueled no doubt by her fervent recitation.

"The North does and even in 2008, people in the South still say stupid stuff like *the South will rise again*."

"And the year was 2008 when you were at the Market?" His voice was laced with skepticism.

She bobbed her head. "It was. I had driven down there in my car to go shopping."

"Car? You mean like a trolley or a train?"

"No." She frowned. "I mean like a car. Everybody has at least one, but more likely two in every family. Cars are powered by gasoline, although because of the greenhouse effect, we're trying to invent electric cars, and we have thousands of roadways all over the United States."

"This is all very interesting, but why should I believe you?"

Yes, why should he believe her? Aimee hardly believed it herself, and she was the one wandering around in la-la land.

"Trust me," she murmured, "I'm not making it up. I don't belong in this time, and I'm trying to go back. Maybe if I return to the place I was before this all happened, even if it's the wrong time, I might get home."

"Why don't you just wish on a star? Maybe that'll do it!" Disbelief was stamped all over his face.

"I said you wouldn't believe me." Frustrated, she glared at him, regretting her unwise decision in trying to explain anything to him.

"Just a minute." She whirled, climbing into the wagon. Searching through her discarded clothing, she found her cell phone.

"Look at this!" She waved the cell phone in his face.

Curious, he examined the small object. "What is it?"

"It's a cell phone. We use it in my time to call people."

"What do you call them?" His face registered confusion.

"We don't 'call' them anything. We call them on it. See,"—she pressed buttons—"it has pictures on it. Have you ever seen anything like this?"

He took the cell phone, studying the small picture of Sara. "Can't say that I have. Never seen a tintype with so many colors."

"It isn't a tintype. It's a photograph. It also connects with other cell phones, and I can talk to people over long distances."

"So make it work."

"I can't make it work. No one else has one in this time so I can't call anyone. I don't even know if the battery will hold out much longer. I'm afraid to even look at it much because I want the battery to last as long as possible."

"So you say this thing is from the future?"

"Yes. That's exactly what I'm saying. And so am I. I know it's hard to believe, but it's the truth!"

He yawned, weariness evident in his every movement. "That was a good story, but it's time to bed down. We've got an early start, and I can't stand here arguing with you anymore. Come to bed. I won't touch you unless you want me to, but I want you near me. We're getting into rougher territory, and if something happens, you need to be where I can protect you."

Opening her mouth to argue, she snapped it shut. The word *protect* had caught her attention. They'd glimpsed Indians in the distance, but so far none had ventured close to the train.

"Do we have to worry about Indians attacking?"

He held the tent flap open, waiting for her to enter. "A train this size is safe. Indians aren't stupid, but right now, I'm more worried about stampeding buffalo or lightning storms. You've never seen a storm until you've witnessed some of the ones that hit around here."

She glanced over her shoulder. A million twinkling stars lit the cloudless night sky. Beyond the soft glow of the campfire, darkness blanketed the unfamiliar landscape. Sharing his cramped little tent was sounding better all the time. Being brave was for idiots and adrenalin junkies. *She wasn't either of those.*

True to his word, Jake rolled to his side and was fast asleep in seconds, while she lay awake for a long time, thinking about home and family. Worry kept her from relaxing. Long past midnight, she was still awake, fretting over things she couldn't change.

Chapter Twelve

Aimee stayed near the wagon, prepared to leap under it in a moment's notice. They'd reached the great prairies, grasslands rolling into the distance for as far as the eye could see. Herds of buffalo were spotted by the outriders and from the top of a small hillock, she got her first glimpse. It was an amazing site, but one that left her jumpy and afraid.

"Stay close to the wagons," Jake warned. "If the buffalo stampede, they can run for miles over anything and everything in their path."

"Why don't we just go around?" Seemed like a perfect answer.

"Too many and the herds are huge. We could travel for days without seeing the end."

Stories were told around the campfires about unlucky travelers who were trampled to death when the buffalo got spooked. She'd listened carefully to every word, planning an escape route if and when such an event occurred. Mindful of the warnings, the emigrant train skirted the herds, careful to keep the noise down to a minimum. Shots rang out as some of the younger men took several of the huge animals down and meat would be plentiful for all.

"Aimee!" Ardis called. "Get a bucket. We're gathering buffalo chips."

She frowned. "Why in God's name would I do something like that?"

Laughing, Ardis explained. "No firewood out here. Buffalo chips work just as well. The chips smolder for a long time. Best thing out here for a cooking fire."

"You have *got* to be kidding." She couldn't believe they were actually going to gather buffalo poop. Ardis must be smoking weed. *But it was true.* Disgruntled and totally grossed out, she joined the group, flinching as she collected the nasty things. It was so yucky to pick up a recently deposited chip—which she did more than once—but by the end of the day, she had enough to keep the fire going well into the night.

She'd just finished fixing dinner when a rider from one of the forward trains brought news of cholera. Several unfortunates from his company had been stricken and two had perished already. Wracking her brain, she tried to remember the symptoms and prognosis of cholera, but all she could pull from her memory was something about bad water or human waste. She resolved to boil all the drinking water every day and keep it in a special keg.

The monotony of the trek was an ongoing thing. With nothing better to do besides walking, she spent time visiting with the other women and learning a few tricks of the trade.

"You can churn fresh butter by putting milk into a container and tying it onto the side of the wagon." Rose offered the scrap of information, puffed with importance. "The bumping and rocking works as well as hand churning."

Aimee grinned, glad not to have that chore. "Jake doesn't have a cow. Wasn't on his list of priorities."

"Our cow ain't putting out much milk, but maybe we can spare you a bit." Ardis wiped her brow. "Nothing better on biscuits than fresh butter."

The few times she'd helped one of the other ladies churn, she'd hated it. Maybe when they got to Oregon, she would just have a wagon go in circles all day and avoid that boring chore.

She'd just finished heating beans and baking biscuits when Jake rode up.

He eyed her quizzically. "Why don't you ever use the camp stove?"

"What camp stove?"

He dismounted, shoving back his hat. "The one in the wagon."

"I…there isn't one in there."

"Take another look. I bought a new one in Independence."

Humiliated, she discovered the small iron stove packed under the food supplies. She hauled it out, setting it near the fire. And all this time, she'd been struggling to cook over the campfire. *It really pissed her off!*

"You could've said something," she grumbled.

He laughed. "I thought you knew—you always seem to know everything."

She harrumphed, stalking to the McAfee's campsite. *He could eat alone—the big jerk!*

Ardis and Rose, and Ardis in particular, became her close friends, though she was careful not to disclose any information she didn't want disseminated throughout the camp. She hadn't forgotten the good-natured teasing she'd borne regarding her cooking skills. Ardis was a good woman, but she didn't know the meaning of the word confidential or how to keep her mouth shut. Rose, on the other hand, seldom spoke, her attention most often focused on Nolan and Nolan's whereabouts.

Right on cue, Rose piped up. "Have you seen Nolan this evening?"

Ardis's glance was sharp. "Don't get no ideas about that young man." Her voice was stern. "You ain't old enough yet."

Rose's mouth drew down in a pout. "I was just asking. Don't hurt to ask."

Aimee plunked down. "Seems like you spend a

lot of time mooning over Nolan." She arched her eyebrows. "Maybe you should spend more time with reading or sewing."

Rose scowled. "I get enough of that from Ma. Don't need it from you too."

"*Sorry!* I'll shut my mouth."

Rose's focus on Nolan might just be a problem. Aimee watched the young woman. She'd make it her personal crusade to try to interest Rose in something other than an early marriage. Even though the woman believed her incompetent.

Chapter Thirteen

Roiling black clouds blew in on winds so violent they had to tie the wagons down. The canvas coverings whipped and tore loose, flapping wildly in the powerful gusts. As the storm intensified, several wagons blew over, the contents spewing out and flying through the air. Aimee crouched beneath the wagon box, choking on airborne dust and debris, her eyes glued to the raging maelstrom in horrified fascination. Lightning bolts pelted the earth, even balling up and rolling along the wide expanse. Thunder boomed, shaking the heavens while the earth shuddered beneath its tumultuous pounding.

Teeth chattering in fright, she clutched the wheel spokes, praying for deliverance. Jake, with Nolan in tow, had hurried out with the rest of the men, bent on rounding up the scattering herd. Before he left, he'd hobbled the team and tied them on short leads. Now, the frenzied mules were braying in terror, attempting to kick free. One of the mules, Jack, she thought, reared back, snapping the lead to his halter. If she didn't do something soon, the mule would be gone, lost in the storm.

Bolstering her courage, she dashed out from cover, fighting to stand in the raging winds, and grabbed the halter. Tossing his head, stomping in fear, the mule literally lifted her off the ground and into the air. Hanging on for dear life, she fought with the terrified animal.

Ardis and Rose rushed from the cover of their wagon, seized the mule's halter and forced his head down. Grabbing his ears, Rose and Aimee held him while Ardis tied a length of cloth over the animal's face. "If he can't see," she screamed into the howling wind, "maybe he'll settle down."

The cloth did the trick. His big body trembling, the mule quieted, and they staked him back down, then dove for cover under the wagon.

Huddling together under a canvas tarp, they waited for the storm to pass. Mouth to Ardis's ear, Aimee yelled. "How long will this last?"

Ardis shook her head, screaming back. "Never seen anything like it before!"

Neither had she. Being a Seattle native, she had seen some pretty terrific storms roll in from the Pacific, but nothing like this! She hadn't seen any funnels yet, but this storm had all the makings of a tornado.

Following the winds, rain fell in torrents, soaking everything for miles around in mere minutes. Water pooled everywhere, drenching the earth and forming deep mud pockets almost as fast as the rain fell.

After what seemed like forever, the rain lessened and then stopped. Crawling from cover, chilled to the bone and dripping wet, the women surveyed the damage. Strewn across the landscape were bits and pieces of clothing, bedding, and household items. Jake's wagon had survived with only minor damage, as had Ardis's wagon. Not everyone fared so well. Ravaged by the ferocity of the storm, one family lost everything. Their wagon had been one of the first upended by the raging winds and now lay in shards. Stunned and overwrought, they wandered aimlessly, searching for their personal belongings. Aimee's heart went out to them. Theirs was a large family, including several very young children, and little, if anything, remained of their provisions and supplies. Their only alternative was to quit the train and go back home.

Others had suffered damage as well, but none so much as that family. It seemed it was God's intervention that kept them all alive.

Ardis and Rose, stalwart plucky women, hurried off to begin the thankless job of drying out their possessions. Unsure where to start, she followed their example, hauled out the bedding and clothing, wrung out each item and then draped it over the wagon box or nearby bushes. The other women and children had the same thoughts, and within minutes, the campsite looked like a huge outdoor laundry.

Jake rode up a few minutes later, looking concerned. "Sorry I didn't get back sooner, but I had to hunker down with the animals during the storm. You okay?"

She breathed a sigh of relief, refusing to admit even to herself she'd been worried. He looked hale and hearty, albeit somewhat worse for wear, and so covered with mud, she could barely make out his features.

"Wet, but otherwise fine, thank you very much. You need to have a serious talk with Jack, though." She laughed, almost hysterical. "I wouldn't be nearly as filthy if he hadn't been so darn stupid."

He looked over to the recalcitrant mule, the makeshift mask hanging from the animal's nose.

"What'd he do?"

"Just about everything! He tried to get loose, but we managed to tie him back up, and it wasn't easy, I can tell you." She drew herself up. "But we did it."

He grinned, showing approval. "I'll make a pioneer woman out of you yet."

"*I don't think so*" she sang. "This was a one-time deal and next time, I'll just shoot him. It'd be easier."

His amazing blue eyes twinkled. "Who'll pull the wagon if you do?"

Smirking, she batted her eyes. "Why, Jakey, I

suspect you'd have to do it."

"Why do you act like that?" He scowled.

"Because you're a man and you deserve it." Her reasoning was total female logic, and rightly so. Giggling, she strode off, lightheaded in the aftermath of extreme peril, warmed by his obvious concern, tickled by his evident displeasure.

He called to her retreating figure. "What's for supper?"

Snorting, she kept on walking, not bothering to look back. Did men ever think of anything besides their stomachs? *Oh, yeah, right—sex*!

****

Aimee tiptoed through the sticky black muck, cursing the disgusting sludge. There'd be no riding in the wagons today. They'd gotten a late start this morning, waiting for the ground to dry enough to allow passage. A light drizzling of rain had fallen off and on throughout the night, soaking the ground even more. Gray clouds still covered the sky, and it looked like more rain was in the offing. She skirted around a mud pocket, one of many littering the route. Over and over, the wagons mired down, and valuable time was lost harnessing extra teams to pull the wagons free. Every hand was drafted to help and even Aimee took her turn shoveling, cursing as huge blisters formed on her tender palms. The grueling labor was frustrating. Tension ran high, and by the end of the day, they had covered at most five miles.

The forward scouts located a passable campsite on higher ground, and the hapless travelers sighed with relief as the captain signaled for the train to halt for the night. Nolan unhitched the mules and led them off to graze with the rest of the stock, saying he would see her in the morning. Tired and discouraged, she threw a quick meal together, thinking of bed. Clouds of mosquitoes swarmed after the rains, drawn by the promise of warm blood. Miserably, she swatted yet another bloodsucker. *One down, four hundred million to go.*

Jake rode in and dismounted, taking the plate of cold food Aimee offered. She looked ready to drop, lines of fatigue marked her face as she went through the motions of cleaning. He'd kept an eye on her throughout the day, surprised by her willingness to pitch in and dig right alongside the others. A suspicious smear of blood marked his plate. Reaching out, he grabbed her hand, lifting it for inspection. Her palm looked like raw meat. Bloody blisters covered almost the entire underside.

"What the hell is this?" he growled.

Shrugging, unconcerned, her voice grated with weariness. "We all had to dig."

"Why didn't you wear gloves?"

Sighing, she pulled her hand back. "I didn't have any."

He forced her to sit while he examined her hands. How she'd been able to keep digging with her hands in that condition, he would never know.

"I have an extra pair in the wagon. You should have worn those."

A spark of anger flickered in those amber eyes, turning them almost golden in the waning light. "You might have said something. I didn't do this just to irritate you."

He rubbed her wrists, his thumbs moving in small circles, easing the tension in her hands. "Next time, ask."

She nodded, too drained to argue for once. She started to stand, but he pushed her back down, motioning her to stay. Filling a bowl with water, he collected some soap and began washing her hands, taking care to clean each oozing sore. The stinging pain caused by the caustic soap brought quick tears flooding her eyes, spilling onto cheeks covered with grime. He reached into the wagon and brought out a small leather pouch. Inside were several small jars and some clean rags. He opened one of the jars and applied a thick yellowish paste over most of her palms, covering everything with the clean rags.

"Keep this on for a few days. I'll put more on tomorrow. You'd best wear my gloves for a few days until these heal."

His mouth twisted with sympathy. "You look like a street urchin."

Rinsing out the cloth, he cleansed the muck from her petal-soft skin, electric sparks tingling his fingertips with each touch. Forcing himself to ignore the passion ignited by her nearness, he dipped his head, fearful she'd see in his eyes what his heart so often felt.

"I feel like a street urchin," she admitted, pushing back a lock of hair. "A very tired street urchin."

She cupped his hand to her face. "Thank you," she whispered, rubbing her cheek against his palm. "My hands feel better already."

He froze, barely able to breathe, his stomach clenching as desire rose up in growing waves. Of its own accord, his hand found the silken strands of her glorious hair, massaging her temple as she purred in delight, eyes closed to better enjoy.

Without regard to the consequences, he leaned forward, planting a searching kiss on her full sensuous lips, relishing the moment and her unguarded acceptance. Emboldened, he forced her mouth open, plundering the silken depth, tongues dueling in the age old dance of passion. Raging hunger swelled in his groin as he pulled her closer. Hesitating for a brief moment, her arms circled his neck, gasping aloud as her ruined hands made contact. He groaned, pulling away, nudging her back.

Startled, her eyes flew open, questioning and confused.

"You're in no condition for this," he stated, taking a deep breath to still his raw aching emotions. "Some other time when you really want *me*, not just comfort."

"Maybe I do want you," she whispered. "Maybe I need this."

Shaking his head, he stood up, moving away. "No. Right now you're tired and discouraged, and I'm just here. I don't want that. I want all of you, not just your body, but that quick mind as well."

"Why the sudden change? Most men would jump at the chance. What is it that makes you so different?"

He swiped a hand through his hair. "You have your secrets, I have mine. Maybe like you, someday I'll tell you mine, but not now, not like this."

Aimee felt her eyes watering. "I told you my secret, you just don't believe it."

It had been several days since she'd revealed her past life, but not once since that day had Jake questioned her, or even mentioned anything more about it. It was as if he chose to ignore what he considered to be ridiculous or impossible. His face settled into that closed I-have-nothing-to-say look, shutting her out again.

"Don't do that," she implored. "Don't look like that."

The stark planes of his face softened. "Do you have any idea how hard it is for me not to touch you? I look at you every day and all I want to do is jump on you and bury myself in your sweet warmth. You're my wife, but you don't want me as a husband."

"I don't want anyone as a husband, you included." The words were out before she had time to consider the ramifications, and judging by his face, he didn't take it very well.

He stiffened, his eyes emitting sparks. "I'm beginning to understand that more and more. I'm just the tool you're using to get what you want. Maybe calling you a *whore* was the right word." Grabbing his hat, he stalked off, his back rigid and unyielding.

Stunned, she watched him leave, realizing too late how unfeeling her words had sounded.

"Jake! I didn't mean it."

But he had already gone, disappearing into the night, leaving her alone, bereft of his company.

She crawled into the wagon, cursing herself for a fool. The condition of her hands made everything harder, even unbuttoning her dress caused painful prickles of agony. By the time she was ready for bed, several hours had slipped by, and he'd still not returned. Torn between remorse and anger, she fluctuated between making peace and letting him just stay wherever he was—and good riddance.

Grumbling, she made her decision, grabbed a shawl, and jumped out of the wagon, nearly falling face first as she hit the ground. Grimacing in pain, she pushed herself up, muttering oaths at the wagon, the mules, the rain, and everything in between. Full dark had fallen by now, eerie shadows and shapes danced in the meager light cast by the full moon. Coyotes howled in the distance and night-flying predators soared overhead, dark shadows outlined against the shining yellow orb. Bravery was not one of her high points, but unless she did something soon, he wouldn't come back tonight, and she couldn't bear that again. Pulling a heavy blanket from the wagon, she stepped into the dark, heading the direction he'd taken. In the distance, she could hear the stock milling about and settling down for the night, soothed by the haunting lullabies crooned by the drovers.

Picking her steps with care, she moved through the dark towards what she hoped would be his location. Blinded by the dark, she groped ahead, terrified by the void, wondering why she'd been so stupid as to venture out alone. Twigs snapped and, turning, she gasped as a form materialized in front of her.

"Where the hell do you think you're going?" Jake's voice came out of the black.

"You scared the crap out of me!" She sagged with relief. "I was trying to find you."

"Well, you found me," he growled. "So what?"

Gathering her courage, she took a deep breath. "I came to apologize. I didn't mean what I said." The words came soft and plaintive. "Come back to the wagon."

"I'm comfortable where I'm at. At least out here I don't have to deal with your mouth."

He was going to be difficult, but overcoming adversity was one of her strong points.

"Okay. Then we'll both stay out here." She shook out the blanket and busied herself making a bed. Settling down, she focused on his dark form. "Are you joining me or not?"

She could hear his sharp intake of breath and could feel his tension.

"Why?" The stark question asked so much.

Choosing her words with regard to her ability to twist each syllable, she fought to speak around the lump that grew in her throat. "Because you're my pillar in this mess I've found myself in and without you, I have nothing. I don't know what I'd do without you."

She waited, holding her breath, praying he would mellow out and forgive her. The minutes ticked by. She was beginning to feel ridiculous when he bent down and pulled the covers back.

"You could have picked a better spot." He

groaned, sounding grumpy—but at least talking.

"We could go back to the wagon. It's pretty comfortable in there, a little crowded, but comfortable."

"Maybe later," he said, taking her in his arms. "But we got some business to attend to right now."

Her breath caught. He forced her back, locking her arms overhead, his mouth devouring her lips. She had no defenses against his onslaught and wanted none. She writhed against him, held prisoner by his muscled physique, moaning with passion and unquenched desire. The nightgown was suddenly too confining, rasping her sensitive skin. Pushing the ugly gown up, he nuzzled her stomach, nipping and caressing while his hands cupped and massaged her breasts, sending shivers of delight dancing down her stomach. His mouth tasted her most sensitive spot, laving the bud with small teasing licks, lifting her higher towards that one bright climax. *She needed all of him.*

Frantic with need, she unhooked his trousers, groaning as he rolled aside. He divested himself of the item and then buried himself to the hilt in her warmth, moaning as her sheath clenched tightly around his engorged staff. Blood heating, senses tingling with desire, she clawed his back, dragging sharp nails down his backside, wrapping her legs around him and straining to take him deeper. He pummeled into her, his body crushing her against the hard ground, lips sucking at her earlobes, tongue delving into the delicate shell.

Past and future forgotten, this moment was theirs.

Hours later, Aimee groaned as he gathered her up and carried her back to the wagon. The contrived bed was much more comfortable, tighter quarters, but she didn't notice the cramped space since he was spooned around her.

On the edge of sleep, her lips curved in a slight smile, replaying the night. She could feel his body reacting to her nearness. She stirred, leaning back to plant a soft kiss on his cheek.

"Go to sleep," she yawned. "I need some rest."

She grinned as his roaming hands sampled her, then came to rest under her breasts as he relaxed, his body pressed against her backside. Although she didn't want to admit it, he was getting to her. Other than her father, she'd never met a man who cared for her as this man did. He might be a little rough around the edges, but that only served to make him more interesting. *Funny how her preferences had changed.* Impish thoughts danced through her mind, and she squirmed, rubbing her butt against him, testing his response. His shaft bulged, straining against her.

"I thought you wanted to sleep," he whispered low, his voice husky with desire.

"I did," she admitted. "But something caught my attention, and now I'm awake again."

Rolling beneath him, she cried out in abandon as he plunged in.

****

The camp was in an uproar when Aimee climbed out of their wagon the next morning. Sometime in the night, Indians made off with several head of cattle. Jake, along with a small group of men, rode out in pursuit, but after searching most of the day, found only scattered prints. The culprits' lead was just too good and their knowledge of the area made tracking almost impossible. This was the first time Indians had ventured into camp. The idea made Aimee ill at ease knowing they'd gotten in and out unscathed. The captain posted more guards at night and everyone was put on alert.

Jake indicated, from now on, they would have more contact with the tribes as they traveled farther into Indian territory. Most were pacified by receiving goods in payment for passage through their lands, and he, as well as the captain and several others, had purposely brought along lengths of cloth, beads, tobacco plugs and the like as gifts.

The threat of hostiles made everyone edgy, everyone with any sense that is. Not everyone on the wagon train had that level of intelligence. Booker, a small-brained moron lacking even the basics of education or manners, stated on several occasions he would love to get an Indian in his sights. She was outraged. The idea someone would shoot an Indian for no purpose whatsoever infuriated her. She avoided Booker, and if she had to come in contact with him, her mouth got the better of her. She amused herself by calling him horrific names in terms he wouldn't or couldn't understand.

"Excuse me." She intentionally bumped into him. Fluttering her eyelashes in mock surprise, she pasted a smile on her face. "Aren't you one of the Prurient Troglodytes from New York City?"

Booker halted, suspicion glinting from his malicious beady eyes. "Nah, I ain't. My kin are from the mountains of Kentucky," he growled, reminding her of a grouchy ill-mannered bear.

"Well, that's the answer then. But I swear," she gushed, "the resemblance is amazing!"

Booker preened, reminding her of a giant buzzard. "I get confused with a lot of folks. But if you want, you can call me anything you like." Ogling her with disgusting intensity, his eyes roamed over her breasts, ending with her crotch area.

"Why, thank you!" She clapped her hands together. "I certainly will."

Behind Booker, she could see Jake sneaking up. His lips twitched suspiciously. She grinned back, unrepentant at being caught in her latest escapade. He wasted no time grabbing her by the nape of the neck and hauling her off right in the middle of a soon-to-be wonderful tirade. When they were out of sight, he burst out laughing.

"One of these days, Booker is going to catch on, and then what'll you do?"

"You'll save me," she smiled, complacent in the knowledge. "You always do."

"I do, don't I?" Cupping her face, he kissed her so thoroughly her toes curled.

She sighed, dreamy. "You really know how to kiss." Her mind wandered. "Who taught you?" A prickle of jealousy shot through her.

His eyes twinkled. "It comes naturally."

She pushed him away, grinning. "I just bet it does. Seems to me practice might have a little something to do with it."

His eyes roamed over her, mischief lurking in their depths. "You're the first girl I ever kissed."

She groaned, but had to laugh. "Yeah, and I own some beach property in Nevada."

He tilted his head, questioning.

"Never mind!" She exhaled. "Someday you'll understand."

Chapter Fourteen

Aimee's excitement grew as they reached Fort Bridger. *Civilization, again, at last*! Her enthusiasm, however, was short lived. She'd envisioned something grander, but it fell flat beneath her expectations.

A subdued group met them with news. In one of the earlier trains, an over-zealous Indian-hater had sighted on a young Indian woman nursing her baby and killed her. The Indians were furious and demanded the fort turn the man over for their brand of punishment. Left with few options, they finally agreed, knowing the man was guilty and if they didn't turn him over, war was on the horizon. The Indians punished the man as they deemed fit and peace was restored. Without admitting it to anyone, Aimee felt the punishment was justified.

One good thing came from the incident. Booker's morbid interest in shooting Indians waned, to everyone's relief. Left with few pleasures, Aimee refused to stop harassing the scumbag, deciding he deserved every foul epithet she could conjure, even to the point of adding a few he *could* understand.

The fort personnel welcomed them with open arms. The emigrants decided to rest for a few days, allowing the animals some good grazing time and themselves the opportunity to restock their supplies. Any repairs to the wagons were also taken care of as it was a long stretch to the next fort or way station.

After investigating the meager shops lining the garrison walls, Aimee discovered a bathhouse that catered to everyone. Jake agreed to stand guard while she frolicked, delighting in her first real bath since they left Independence, in a tub complete with hot water. The bath took more of her small horde of coins, but afterwards, she decided it was worth every penny. Soaking for at least an hour, she lathered every square inch numerous times and shampooed her head until every single strand squeaked. Her husband guard ended her delicious sojourn by yelling that if she didn't hurry up, she was on her own.

Every item of clothing and bedding they owned was also washed and those that wouldn't be used for awhile, she wrapped in cloth and tied for safekeeping and cleanliness, much to everyone's amusement. No amount of teasing daunted her in her quest, they might be able to handle being dirty and smelly, but she wasn't about to languish in filth. She'd had enough of that already, and if a little planning and preparation was necessary, she was up to the task. *Momma would be so proud.*

On the evening before their departure, she strolled around the enclave, peeking into the shops for one last moment of shopping bliss. In a dusty corner of a small dry goods store, she found a new treasure, a battered and worn copy of *Pride and Prejudice.* Something to pass the long hours ahead. The shopkeeper was a tough character and recognized a soft sell when he saw one, but she finally acquired the book at a price she could pay and added it to her small library. Jake's lips twitched when he saw her purchase, but later suggested she read aloud.

The emigrants broke camp at first light, leaving the protection of the fort. Drovers whistled as they circled the herd, forcing the cattle to move, while the muleskinners cracked whips, shouting as they maneuvered their wagons into line. Aimee trailed behind with the other walkers as she had done on so many occasions before, the new book tucked into a pocket for reading later. As the train cleared the fort, they passed a nearby graveyard. The starkness of the setting and the newness of so many of the mounds caused her to shiver in the warm morning air, feeling as though they were dark portents of things to come. Sadness pervaded the site, dreams lost and left behind.

Children ran by, laughing and playing, unconcerned with the trials and tribulations of the journey. *Wasn't that long ago when she would have been running with them herself.*

Maybe she was just plain tired. There had been quite a lot to do while they were at the fort, restocking, cleaning, preserving, bartering for new stock—everyone had been busy. That had to be the reason for her morbid thoughts and feelings of depression. It really sucked, though, seeing the lonely graveyard. Silly to feel that way when so many graves lined the route. Maybe she was coming down with something. God only knew what diseases she had or would come in contact with. Sighing, she mentally shook off such thoughts. They weren't productive in any event.

Charity latched onto her skirts, thumb secure in her tiny mouth, and Martha, her doll, tucked in her armpit. Nothing had been done to clean the child, her long light brown hair hung in knotted curls, while dirty stains spotted her worn pinafore. Not that staying clean was easy, but at least her mother could have dressed her hair, she mused, finger-combing the tangles.

"Where are the other girls?"

Pulling the thumb from her mouth, Charity lisped. "They're chasing Matt." Matt being one of the other children, she supposed.

"Why aren't you playing with them?"

A shy smile lit her piquant face. "I want to hear

a story."

As usual, she had one of her books in a skirt pocket, waiting for the right moment, but right now she didn't feel like reading.

"How about we practice the ABC's?"

Charity's eyes dropped. "I don't know how."

"For goodness sakes. You don't know how to recite your ABC's?"

"Nope," Charity admitted, her little face downcast. "Momma said we don't need to learn them."

"What about the other girls? Do they know their ABC's?"

Charity shook her head no.

"You mean to tell me, you girls haven't gone to school?" *How totally ridiculous was that?* At the very least, Faith and Hope had to be school age.

"Momma said we don't need book learning."

Exasperated, she stalked along, Charity trailing behind. She cursed the worthless woman under her breath. Mrs. Purdue was fast becoming pond scum—no, lower than pond scum.

She stopped so abruptly, Charity bumped headlong into her. "How about I teach you the ABC's, and then we can start learning to read?"

"Momma won't let me." Charity sniffled against her skirt.

That comment raised her dander. "Well, how is she going to stop me if I just walk along and say them and you hear me and repeat them?"

"You mean like a game?"

"Yes, like a game. I'm the leader and you follow."

"Momma don't care if we play games!" Charity's eyes lit with excitement. "But we have to be quiet."

"Well, we don't have to be quiet if we don't walk near your Momma's wagon."

Charity danced along, singing a wordless tune, animated by the prospect of a new game.

"Why don't you run and find Faith and Hope and see if they want to play too?" Might as well teach all three. It would help pass the time.

Curls bouncing, Charity darted away, her little feet flying as she went in search of her sisters.

Aimee drew a deep breath, readying herself for the storm that was sure to hit as the children gathered. She grimaced. Being a child psychologist in this era was unheard of as far as she knew and teaching school might be the only alternative left if she couldn't get back. Having some experience before she arrived in Seattle certainly wouldn't hurt and teaching the girls would do a lot to alleviate the boredom, not only for her, but for them as well.

Within minutes, Charity returned, Faith and Hope in tow, along with Matt, who she recognized as the wagon master's son, and another child who introduced himself loudly as "Charlie Tuttle." Dark-haired Matt was solemn and quiet, whereas Charlie was talkative and precocious, his carrot red hair a perfect foil for his big blue eyes and freckled skin. Excited, they formed a circle around her, eager to begin.

"First off," she cautioned, "no matter what, we have to keep up with the wagons, so we walk and talk. Is that understood?"

Every head nodded "yes."

"Second, if we're going to play this game, everyone takes part, and we're quiet when it's not our turn. Is that understood again?"

"How do we know when it's our turn?" Charlie shouted.

"Have any of you been to school before?"

Matt raised his hand. "I have, Mrs. Marshall."

"Good, then you know when you want it to be your turn, you raise your hand. Everyone raise your hand." Five pairs of hands lifted.

"No, I meant just one hand each." Five hands

dropped.

"Okay, that's better. Now, when you know an answer or want to say something, you raise your hand. Do you understand?"

Charlie immediately raised his hand. "I want to say something."

"Somehow I knew that." She grimaced, imagining the worst. "Okay, Charlie, what do you want to say?"

"I want to say, er... I think...ummm, I forgot!"

This was going to be fun!

The remainder of their first lesson went well and by later in the day, they had progressed through the letter "C." Not wanting to push them too hard and lose their interest, she decided learning three letters per day would be enough along with the beginnings of addition. The children were bright and soaked up the lessons like little sponges. Gratified she had such a willing little class, she resolved to spend some time each evening coming up with an interesting lesson plan.

Later that evening, Matt's mother, Annabeth, approached her. "Matt said you were going to teach school."

Aimee coughed, surprised. "Well, not exactly school, just work on letters and numbers."

"I think it's wonderful," Annabeth exclaimed, a delighted smile creasing her face. "The children need some sort of schooling and anything at all is good."

"Well, I'm not exactly sure how much I can teach them, but at least I can teach them the basics."

Annabeth handed her a small chalkboard and some chalk. "Maybe this will help. You have my support, and if you need someone to keep the children in control, just let me know."

"Thanks, I might take you up on that. I just hope this is fine with the other mothers." She rolled her eyes towards the Purdue wagon.

Annabeth grinned. "I'll just make my husband have a word with her and that should take care of any problems. What about the other children? Can more join your group?"

Alarmed, she could only stutter in surprise. "H-how- how many others?"

"Probably twelve or so," Annabeth said, a cheerful smile accompanying the words. "Give or take a few who might be too young."

Stunned, she sat down, instantly regretting her impromptu decision to teach.

Annabeth patted her arm. "Now don't you worry, dear, all the mothers will help. We'll take turns and help you herd them. It'll be good for all of us."

"I don't suppose we could leave Mrs. Purdue out?"

Nodding, Annabeth laughed. "I suspect we could. I doubt she would help anyway. She barely does anything now. Such a terrible woman. I must go, my family awaits." Having said her piece, she strode away, humming to herself.

Yeah, you can hum, Aimee grumbled. Not you who's stuck with fifteen kids every day. It's for real, I'm the Pied Piper.

Chapter Fifteen

Summer came in full force. The heat increased, forcing them to find water each evening. Most of the emigrants carried some water, but the stock needed more if they were to keep going. Clouds of dust kicked up by the wagons and animals continued to be a big problem. Aimee fought to keep her charges near the lead wagons, thereby avoiding some of the throat-clogging dust, but even near the front, dust flew. No matter what the history books said, she considered the dust and bugs to be the most problematic. The children seemed content to follow her and, as time went by, more and more women joined the boisterous group.

As the train traveled deeper into Indian territory, Jake beefed up security, warning the walkers to stay close. One of the scouts sighted a small band of Indians following the train along a high ridge. So far, they had kept their distance, but she hadn't forgotten the earlier raid on the cattle. The rough terrain allowed for a vast number of hiding spots, and her inept ability at spotting anything was, in her view, a major hindrance. The children pointed out deer, rabbits, and other animals which, unless they moved, she would never have seen. An Indian could be standing right in front of her and she wouldn't notice.

Jake found a good campsite near a slow moving river. The wagons were corralled and the stock herded to the center for safekeeping. Nolan unhitched the team, watered the animals, and then waved goodnight, leaving Aimee with a few moments of peace before starting dinner. She sat down with a thump, her feet throbbing with pain from the ankles down. It had been a particularly tiring day. They'd traveled farther than normal, attempting to reach the river to avoid a dry camp. Sitting there, lost in thought, she wiped the day's accumulation of dust from her face, brushed at the dirt caking her skirt, wishing for a hot tub of water and a few hours alone. Heaving a sigh, she dragged herself up and started a fire. The usual fare, beans and biscuits, seemed almost too complicated to her now almost catatonic state of mind, but Jake would need food when he showed up.

She was feeling particularly put upon. Teaching had been a trial, the children tired and hot, attention wandering too often. Exasperated, she'd ended the session, shooing them off to find their mothers.

She counted the days. By her calculations, they still had at least three more months on the trail, dependent upon just about anything. Seattle loomed too far in the distance.

"Counting sheep." Jake's voice caused her to start.

"Just the days," she said, tired and discouraged. "Trying to keep track."

"You anxious to get rid of me?" His voice teased.

Her lips curved. "Would it do any good? You just seem to keep showing up."

He turned her around, facing away from him, and began massaging her shoulders and back, his strong hands finding every little kink and knotted muscle. She moaned in ecstasy. This was one of those "too good to be true" moments that only happened in her dreams.

"Sit down," he commanded. "I'll rub your legs too."

He didn't have to ask her twice. She found a

good spot, relaxing as he kneaded her calf muscles.

"You know, the one thing that could make this better would be having a bath first."

His hands stopped. "Do you want a bath?"

"Look at me and ask that again." She wiped at her dusty cheeks, self-conscious at his close scrutiny.

"You do look a little worse for wear. Do you want a bath?" he asked again.

She straightened up. "I don't suppose you have one hiding in your pocket?"

He chuckled. "No, but I have something almost as good."

Her interest piqued, she could barely contain her interest. "Well, spit it out, I don't have all day."

"I found a nice pool down by the river, pretty secluded. Grab your stuff, and we'll go swimming."

She jumped up and then froze. "What about dinner?"

"We'll eat when we get back. Pull it off the fire and let's go before the mosquitoes move in."

She raced around, her earlier weariness forgotten by the promise of a bath. Grabbing soap, towels, and clean clothes, she stuffed it all in a bag, ready in minutes.

Jake was astride his horse. He hauled her up behind him. The horse cantered off towards the river, following the river's bend until they found the spot. Surrounded by brush and small trees, the clear, quiet pool beckoned.

"Ever gone skinny dipping?" Wolfish, Jake grinned, teeth gleaming.

"No, but I'm planning on it," she quipped.

His eyes lit, smoldering beneath furrowed brows. "What happened to that lady you always insist you are?"

Struggling out of her clothing, she stood bare as the day she was born, unashamed as his hot eyes roved over her.

"Far as I know, even ladies don't have to bathe with their clothes on."

Giggling, she dove in and stroked quickly to the far side of the pool, rolling and laughing as she played. He followed suit, surfacing right next to her, water glistening off his broad shoulders.

"You swim pretty good for a lady."

"Swimming lessons from age three," she grinned, "down at the YMCA."

"The what?"

"YMCA. You know, Young Men's Christian Association, or something like that." Tired of treading water, she ducked under and swam away. The water in the pool was almost clear, exhilarating, cold, and wonderful. Back and forth she swam, warming up with the strenuous exercise. Relaxed and blissfully cool, she grabbed the bar of soap and proceeded to scrub. Jake came up behind her and took the soap, lathering her hair with firm fingers, while pressing light kisses on her bare shoulders.

His hands massaging her scalp was akin to paradise. "I didn't think men these days were so romantic," she murmured.

"I notice you keep saying 'these days'. What's that all about?"

Surprised, she vaguely recalled using that term on more than one occasion. "I've already told you."

The massage stopped. "That you're from the future. Yeah, I remember."

Her stomach contracted. "But you don't believe me!"

He moved away, avoiding her stare. "How would you feel if you were me? Would you believe me if I told you a story like that?"

He was right, she admitted to herself. If someone told her a whopper like she'd told him, she would probably think they were crazy or the pot bong had been used a little too much.

"No, probably not. All I ask is that you *try* to give me the benefit of the doubt."

"I am trying. But it's a little hard to take."

Taking the soap from her hand, he washed and then swam to the side and climbed out. The late evening sun caressed his masculine body with a warm glow. Mesmerized by the sight, she drank in the firm contours and musculature of his form. He looked like a Greek sculpture posing there in the waning light. He hadn't shaved today so perhaps a scruffy Greek sculpture, but a Greek sculpture all the same. All pretense aside, he was a beautiful man and quite well hung.

"Are you coming?" He reached out a hand, waving her near.

She swam one more lap, ducked under for one last rinse, and then reached up. He pulled her from the water with one easy tug, reaching for a towel to wrap around her.

She looked into his brilliant eyes, spellbound by the latent desire lurking in their crystalline depths.

A movement behind him caught her attention.

Booker stood there, a lascivious grin spread across his ugly face. She screeched and grabbed for her dress as Jake whirled, reaching at the same time for his gun.

"No reason to git excited," Booker smirked. "Jist enjoyin' the show."

"Move on," Jake growled. "Move on while you can."

Booker shrugged. "It's a free country. I can stand whar's I want to."

"I won't tell you again." Jake lifted the gun.

She slipped the dress on, covering up. Reaching out, she tugged at Jake's arm. "Let him go," she whispered. "He's a moron and not worth your time."

His attention didn't waver from Booker for even a second. "I'll handle this," he muttered. "Just stay behind me."

"Leave now," Jake demanded, "or you won't."

Snickering, the obscene Booker spat tobacco juice at them. "Today I will, but maybe not tomorrow. Best keep your woman close." He sauntered away, unconcerned that his back was exposed, daring Jake to make a move.

Jake growled in disgust. "One day I'll have to kill that bastard."

"No, you won't." She caressed his arm. "I'm thinking someone else will do it for you. It's only a matter of time."

He visibly relaxed. "Won't be too soon for me."

She stretched up, kissing his cheek. "By the way, did you notice you're still naked? Not that I care, but one of the other ladies might. Oh, and thanks for bringing me here. I loved every minute, and I feel so clean!"

Managing to look crestfallen, he reached for his trousers. "A kiss is all I get for my efforts?"

Watching him dress, fighting the urge to run her hands over every delicious inch, she laughed. "Oh, quit whining. Besides, it's early yet. Dinner first and then we'll discuss the matter further."

Jake's eyes fixated on her, eyebrows raised. "Is that an invitation?"

"Perhaps," she teased. "I don't have a headache yet."

"What's that supposed to mean?" He frowned as he adjusted his form-fitting leather pants.

"Oh, nothing. Just a saying we women use from time to time."

"Sounds like a 'maybe' to me." His frown deepened to a full-fledged scowl.

She giggled. "Relax, he-man. The invitation is still good. You haven't RSVP'd yet though."

"RSVP'd?"

"French for respond."

"I don't know how to speak French, other than a few choice words I learned down in the French quarter. I suppose that counts me out?"

Laughing now, she very nearly choked. "I swear, men are so transparent."

The hard planes of Jake's face relaxed, dimples dancing in his cheeks as he reacted to her laughter. "Why? Because we say what we mean?"

"Maybe you do, but most men don't."

"Who told you that?"

"It's from personal experience. Most of the men I know, except for my father, would rather embellish the truth or just plain lie."

"Maybe you just haven't met the right men."

Maybe not. So far, her experience with men had been high school boys and the jerks she met at college, nothing like the all-too-male specimen standing half-naked in front of her. He continued dressing, his wide shoulders and arms rippling with well-defined muscles. Her breath caught in her throat. The Greek god comparison resurfaced.

She was beginning to appreciate this guy, not only for his outward appearance, but also because he made her feel safe and cared for. Groaning silently, she cursed herself for a fool. It had been so easy to believe she wouldn't be tempted by his constant nearness and these unwanted emotions worried and frustrated her. *He just wasn't her type of guy*! Parting would be so much easier if she could divorce herself from such feelings. Disgusted, she gathered up the wet towels and soap and marched over to the horse, waiting for him to join her.

Jake sensed the subtle change in her mood. She'd never have the ability to mask her feelings; her face was too open by far. Right now, her generous lips were pressed together, as if preventing an outburst. He approached, wary of her new mood, debating on whether to question her or just let her be. Letting her be won out. She had a way of attacking so verbally sometimes, his stomach clenched in remembrance. Why one little female could affect him so was beyond his understanding. Not that he was afraid of her, but he didn't want to ruin his chances for later.

Most of the train had settled down by the time they got back. Jake fed and watered the horse and then staked him, allowing her some alone time.

When he returned, he stepped lightly, wondering what her mood would be. She dished up a plate of leftover beans and some dried meat, adding a slice of pan bread for good measure. He wolfed the food down and dished up seconds for both of them, his hand grazing hers for a brief second. Electricity sparked between them, igniting a slow burning ache.

Aimee stared at his face. Light from the campfire reflected in his narrowed gaze, intense and compelling, his face tight with need.

Unable to withstand her own mushrooming feelings, she stood up, reached out for his hand and drew him behind her. The wagon rocked as they climbed in. He dropped the oil cloth over the opening as she lay back on the makeshift pallet, lips trembling with anticipation.

His hands, reverent and gentle, unbuttoned the ugly dress. As if in a dream, she watched him through half-closed eyes, reveling in his nearness, as desire bloomed in one sudden rush. Grabbing his shirttails, she pulled the offending garment off, running fevered hands over his sleek chest muscles, angling his head down, and thrusting her tongue into his welcoming lips, kissing him passionately and possessively. Moaning with lusty need, she pushed his trousers down, rubbing against his now engorged shaft.

He pulled back. "You're so beautiful. Even if you are kinda ornery at times."

"Are you trying to compliment me or piss me off?" she gasped, her breath coming in little pants.

He chuckled, licking her inner ear, whispering. "Neither one. Just making conversation."

"Don't want conversation right now." Rolling her hips, she accepted his one deep thrust, gasping as she arched against him.

"What do you want?"

"You!" She hissed. "Only you."

Cupping her face in his hands, Jake pressed soft kisses along her jaw line and down her neck, fastening on a peaked nipple. He forced her legs further apart, opening her wider and deepening his thrusts. Moaning, she tensed, lifting her hips and bucking against him, drowning in need, her body responding so completely and quickly, she was stunned.

Sensing her near climax, his movements grew more frenzied, holding nothing back, dragging her along in a tide of swirling emotion, bright sparks flashed in her brain. Her limbs trembled, burning with scorching heat. She stiffened, straining upwards, and finally, bursting in one sizzling climax.

"I don't have a headache," Aimee squeaked, still quivering in the aftermath.

He chuckled, his lips moving against her skin. "I still don't understand that."

Grinning in the dark, she cuddled against him. "Maybe not tonight, but you will."

Chapter Sixteen

The brush was thicker here and the ground rough and rocky. Aimee decided instead of reading to the children today, a better plan would be to keep her eyes focused on the uneven terrain to avoid any missteps. There were a lot of things they could practice out loud while paying heed to the dangers of the trail.

"What are we going to do today?" Hope asked. The usual troupe of children clustered around Aimee, chaos reigning as they raised their voices in simultaneous questions, each battling for attention.

"Now what did I say about talking out of turn?" She admonished, brows drawn down, eyeing them sternly.

Charity pulled her thumb from her mouth. "You said raise your hand."

"Very good, Charity, and since you were the only one being quiet, you get to ask a question."

The little girl fidgeted, hopping from one foot to the other, her face a mask of determination as she searched for the perfect subject matter. The other children giggled and snickered, garnering another dark look from Aimee.

"When is recess?" Charity asked.

Aimee's lips quivered. Class had only started about ten minutes ago and they had yet to begin lessons.

"We'll walk for about an hour, and then you all can have some play time. Let's start by reciting our ABC's."

The hour passed, the mid-summer day heating

up. She let the children run. It would be too hot later and it was better to get their exercise now rather than end up with heat stroke. She plodded along, lost in thought, her mouth once again covered against the never-ending cloud of dust.

A child's scream rent the air. Aimee, along with the other women, ran towards the hysterical child. Several children grouped about a prone figure. Charlie Tuttle lay on the ground screaming as he clutched his leg, tears streamed down his freckled face.

"A snake bit me," he screamed. "A rattlesnake."

"It did! I saw it," Matt confirmed, his lips trembling. "It crawled over that way," he said, pointing into the brush.

Faith, Hope, and Charity grouped around Charlie, all three wailing in loud unison. "Charlie's going to die," Hope sobbed.

"No, he's not," Aimee snapped. "Just be quiet so we can think."

She pushed her way through the children, dropping down beside Charlie. Pushing the pant leg up, she gasped. Just above Charlie's boot top, two ugly indentations marked his calf muscle. The leg was already beginning to bruise and swell, reddened skin stretching over the purpling flesh.

"One of you," she shouted at the women, "wrap your hands around his leg just above the bite marks and hold tight while I check it out."

Annabeth hurried to help, grabbing his leg and holding on for dear life. "You need to cut the wounds and suck the poison out."

"No, we don't." She drew a deep breath, remembering her lessons. "That might spread the poison."

"I need a knife! Somebody get me a knife," she yelled.

Several ladies ran off towards the wagons. Matt

stepped forward, a well-honed pocket knife held out for her inspection.

"That'll do just fine. Thank you, Matt."

"Hold him down." She hacked several long strips of cloth from her petticoat. Carefully, she tied them above and below the bite marks as Charlie screeched in pain.

"I'm gonna die," he cried, fighting to get up. "I'm gonna die!"

Faith, Hope and Charity sobbed even louder.

"No-you-are-not!" *Not if I can help it.* She wrestled with the small boy.

"Hold him down. Try to keep him calm!" Several women immediately leaned on Charlie, preventing any further movement. "Ardis, take care of the girls, please!"

Rose raced up, holding a butcher knife. "It's all I could find."

"See if you can cut me some strong sticks."

"Sticks? What for?" Rose's face mirrored her confusion.

"Just do what I told you," she spat.

"Do you know what you're doing?" Annabeth asked, concerned. "This isn't the way snake bites are usually treated."

"I was a Girl Scout," she said, tying the rags in place.

Jake raced up, leaping off his horse, almost falling in his haste. "What happened?"

"Charlie got snake bit," Ardis was quick to explain, the sobbing girls held within the comfort of her arms.

Rose ran back with four sturdy sticks. Aimee ripped off more of her slip, improvising a leg brace, while Charlie's mother, Norma, stood near, keening and wringing her hands.

"We need to keep Charlie quiet and his leg lower than his body. The poison will enter his bloodstream a lot slower that way. Too bad we don't have some ice water."

Kneeling down, Norma hugged Charlie to her bosom, her face a mask of fear and grief. Snake bites were a serious matter. Charlie quieted somewhat but still sniffed, rubbing his nose against his mother's ample chest.

"We need to get Charlie into their wagon. He needs to be as quiet as possible for a few days, until the poison is out of his system and needs to drink lots of good, clean water."

Jake leaned over and hauled the child up, striding towards the wagons. Charlie's mother tripped alongside, intent on keeping the leg brace in place.

As they neared the wagons, Charlie's father, Red, raced towards them. Charlie was a small replica of his father, same red hair and freckles, but Red's blue eyes, usually snapping in his merry face, were now grim and fraught with worry.

"What happened," he choked out.

"I got bit by a snake," Charlie moaned.

Red staggered, his face paling.

"Is he going to be okay?" Red whispered, smoothing a huge work-roughened hand over Charlie's flushed face. "He's fevering up already."

"I did what I could," Aimee said, wondering why she felt the need to apologize. "We need to keep him quiet so the poison doesn't spread fast."

Anxious and worried, Red examined the wounds. "Did you suck the poison out?"

"She wouldn't," Norma cried. "She said it just made things worse."

"You have to suck the poison out," Red grabbed the child, ran to the wagon and climbed in.

Aimee raced after him, crying out. "No, no you don't. That's wrong. You'll just make things worse."

Reaching the wagon, she tried to climb in, but

Red shoved her back. "I'll take care of this. You get away."

Stunned, she fell back overwhelmed by the desperation in Red's face.

"You have to listen to me. Just keep him quiet and his leg lower than his body and the poison will enter his bloodstream slower."

Charlie's mother stepped in front of her. "We have the right to do what we think's best for our boy. You've done enough. Now leave us be."

Aimee could hear Charlie's childish voice crying inside the wagon, his father's softly soothing as he worked on the child.

"Please, don't do this." Tears washed her eyes and slid down her cheeks.

"We don't want your help." Norma whirled and climbed into the wagon as Charlie screamed in pain. "We'll do what should be done."

Frustrated, she plunked down on a nearby rock, praying they would see reason, but knowing they wouldn't. Determined, she stood up and climbed into the wagon. Red and his wife glared at her, but she refused to be intimidated. Red had a knife in hand, preparing to lance the wounds.

"Do you have some sort of oil?" She pushed passed Norma. "You need to coat the inside of your mouth to keep from ingesting any of the poison, and you need to wash the wounds first and make sure the knife is sterilized, otherwise Charlie faces the risk of a bad infection."

Red hesitated, indecision written on his face.

Norma reached for a small green bottle. "I have some olive oil. I use it on my hands. It's all I have."

"That'll work." She took the bottle, opened it and handed it to Red.

"If you are going to do this, rinse your mouth first. Do you have any open sores in your mouth?"

Red shook his head. He took the bottle, dumped

a good swallow in his mouth, and swished the liquid around, grimacing at the taste.

Aimee grabbed the wicked looking knife, reaching for a bar of lye soap.

"Do you have any boiled water?"

Norma nodded towards a small keg sitting at the back of the wagon. Aimee poured out a good portion, soaped the knife several times, and then poured more clean water over it. Satisfied that she had done the best she could under these conditions, she handed the knife back to Red.

She grabbed Red's arm. "Wash the area first. I hope to God you know what you're doing. But it's your choice."

Norma rushed to wash the area and then held Charlie down while Red cut the wounds. Charlie screamed with each slice, fighting his mother, tears streaming down his little face. Red bent over and sucked at the cuts, spitting several times into a wooden bucket nearby and then sat back, wiping at his lips.

Aimee handed him a cup of water. "Rinse your mouth out. Keep rinsing until you think your mouth is totally clean."

"Do you have any sort of antibiotic?" she asked the white-faced Norma, who stared back, uncomprehending.

"Some sort of…any kind of medicine to put on the cuts?"

"I have some goose grease." Norma reached for a small bucket.

"Ick! No, that won't do. Just wrap some clean cloths around the wound, but keep the ties I put on above and below, that will slow down whatever poison is left."

By now, Charlie's face was red and sweating, the fever already beginning to take its toll.

Aimee bunched up several blankets and put

them under Charlie's upper body, dropping the injured leg down so that it rested lower.

"Keep his leg down." Worry made her voice sound angry and forceful. "It has to be lower than the rest of his body. Promise me you'll do that."

Red and Norma nodded, holding to each other for comfort.

As she climbed from the wagon, she paused. "And keep him warm, he's likely in shock and that's another problem."

Jake stood by the wagon, staying close if she needed his help. Stone-faced, he glared at her. "I ask again. What the hell were you doing? You're not a doctor."

"I was a Girl Scout."

"A what?"

"A Girl Scout. I even got my merit badge for snake bite," she added, pride ringing in her voice. "Although when I got the badge, I used a snake bite kit so it was a little different. But I read all about what to do if you didn't have one available—and what they're doing is wrong. They're risking a bad infection along with everything else by cutting the marks."

"He's their son. They can do what they want."

"I know that! But Charlie has a better chance if they do what I told them."

He drew her away from the wagon, his face anguished as he stated low, "Charlie won't make it. People die all the time from snake bite."

She staggered, refusing to accept that the little boy was doomed.

"I won't believe that," she declared. She looked back at Red's wagon, "He can make it if the poison slows down going to his heart. They just have to keep him quiet and keep his leg down. It'll work!"

Red climbed down from the wagon, his head bent, tears washing his weathered face.

"How's he doing?"

Red shook his head. "His leg is swelling real big and he's getting hotter all the time. Norma is beside herself. I don't know what else to do."

"Nothing else you can do." Jake gripped Red's shoulder. "It's in God's hands now."

Red turned away. Grief held him powerless to talk any longer. Like a weary old man, he climbed back into the wagon box and slapped the reins, the wagon rolling forward.

Chapter Seventeen

Throughout the next few days, Charlie's fever raged. Aimee took turns with Norma, sponging the child and comforting him when the fever caused hallucinations.

Late one night, Norma's screaming woke Aimee. She ran to help. Charlie's body had stiffened up, thrashing and jerking, eyes rolled up and froth formed around lips tinged blue. His breathing came in short labored gasps, but he was breathing. She picked the boy up and waded into the nearby slow moving stream, ducking the child down until all but his face was under water. The water in the stream was cool, but not cold, and within minutes the convulsions ceased.

Struggling, she waded out, hampered by the child and her now wet nightgown. Norma took Charlie from her arms and wrapped him with a thick blanket, tears streaming down her face.

"I don't think he's going to make it." She wailed, choking on tears. "He just seems to get worse and worse."

Unable to find words to comfort her, she wrapped an arm around Norma and helped her carry Charlie back to their wagon. Red lifted the now sleeping child up, his lips pressed together, holding in his sorrow.

She turned to leave. "Call me if you need anything."

Norma nodded, worry etched on her despairing face.

Heavy of heart, Aimee dropped the wet

nightgown and crawled into the tent, into Jake's waiting arms.

Morning found her morose and despondent, positive Charlie had succumbed during the night and unwilling to hear the bad news. At breakfast, Jake avoided talking about the matter and only kissed her briefly before he rode off. She avoided contact with everyone, barely acknowledging Nolan's presence as he hitched up the mule team.

Staying close to the wagon, she steered clear of even the children, unable to face their questions, unable to bear Charlie's absence. Sick at heart, she only wanted to go home where things like this didn't happen, or if they did, modern medicine could cure almost everything. Even the dust was worse than usual this morning, adding to her upset and despair.

She managed to sidestep any contact with the others throughout the morning, but that respite ended at the noonday stop.

Ardis approached, her angular face concerned. "Where have you been? Everyone's looking for you."

Aimee's head dropped, her face hidden by the droopy bonnet. "I just couldn't face anyone today," she murmured, a sob catching in her throat. "I can't bear to hear whatever you're going to say to me."

"You don't want to hear that Charlie's better?" Ardis exclaimed. "Now that's the dangdest thing I ever heard!"

Shaking her head dumbly, Aimee froze, stunned, her mind refusing to accept Ardis's words.

Beaming, Ardis confirmed. "Charlie took a turn for the better last night. He even ate a little breakfast this morning. Color's good, too!"

She staggered as Ardis's words fully hit her. *Charlie was going to live!*

Ardis took her arm and led her to a large rock, pushing her down. "You look like you're going to pass out."

Dropping her head down between her knees, she gasped, "I feel like it. My heart almost stopped when you came up. I was sure you were going to tell me Charlie died last night."

"Why would I tell you that?" Ardis looked askance. "I went over to Norma's wagon earlier, and Charlie was sitting up in bed eating some broth. He looks pretty good. Still pale, but I suspect he will be up and running in no time. You know how children are."

Choking on emotion, tears rained down her cheeks. "I-I," she stuttered. "I'm so happy." She wailed aloud. "I just knew he was going to die and there wasn't anything I could do about it."

Ardis patted her arm. "Hush, now. We were all worried, but he's going to be fine, and Norma really appreciated all the times you sat with Charlie. She wants you to come over when you can so she can thank you."

Wiping her dripping nose on her sleeve, she blubbered. "She doesn't need to thank me. I'm just happy Charlie's okay."

Jake rode up, concern evident on his lean handsome face. "What happened?" He dismounted slowly, as if fearing her answer. "Is everything okay?"

"Charlie's going to live." She wailed again, almost hysterical now. "He's going to live!"

Jake and Ardis exchanged looks. She bawled even louder, releasing pent-up emotions which had threatened to strangle her over the past few days.

Dropping down, he took her into his arms. He rubbed her back and rocked, offering what consolation he could. After sniffling a few more times, she sat back and pushed the floppy bonnet out of her face.

"I need a hanky," she hiccupped, her voice gravelly from crying.

He pulled out a clean if worn handkerchief. “Not my best one, but I suspect it will do.”

She took the proffered bit of cloth, wiping her nose and eyes. Taking a cleansing breath, she exhaled and relaxed.

“I must look a mess.”

His lips curved. She dropped her head. She knew how she looked when she cried. Her complexion would be blotchy and pale, eyes bloodshot and watery, and nose red and swollen.

“So Charlie’s going to be okay,” he began.

Tears blurred her vision again.

“Whoa, now,” he burst out. “We’re already passed that.”

Her lips trembled. “I know,” she croaked. “But I’ve never prayed so hard in all my life. I just don’t think I could’ve stood it if Charlie’d died.”

She pulled the ugly bonnet from her head and stared into his glittering blue eyes. “I don’t think I like this time.”

“What time is that?” Ardis broke in confused.

“No time is perfect,” he whispered.

“What time?” Ardis exclaimed.

Her lips curved. “Time to fix something to eat.”

“Wha—” Rolling her eyes, Ardis turned to leave. “Sometimes you don’t make no sense a-tall.”

“I make perfect sense.” She laughed, sucking in a deep breath of air. “To me, anyway.”

Jake grinned, relief sparkling in his brilliant eyes. “Guess if you understand you, that’s all that matters,”

“I suspect you’re starving.” She pushed him away and bustled around, putting together a quick meal.

“Food isn’t what I’m hungry for.” Eyes gleaming, teeth bared in a wolfish smile, he stalked forward.

She swallowed, head tilted. “It’s only noon!”

“Does it matter?” He circled her, his eyes

roaming over her form. Visions of their nights together danced through her mind, too many days had passed since they'd last shared those moments. Too many wagons were gathered nearby.

"They'll hear us," she whispered, stimulated by the prospect of a noonday assignation.

"What's to hear?" He shrugged, his eyes glittering. "If you scream, I'll cover your mouth."

"What about Nolan?"

"I already told him I was going to spend the afternoon with you. He's helping his Pa."

Excited, she strolled toward the wagon, rolling her hips in invitation. "If you're sure there's time." She glanced over her shoulder, her invitation clear.

He practically ran after her, jumped into the wagon and hauled her up with one determined swoop. He dropped the canvas covers down, and his clever hands set about unfastening the numerous buttons of her bodice.

"Might have to eat dust all afternoon," he muttered low. "But if they leave soon, it'll cover any noise the wagon springs make."

"Good thinking." Ripping his shirt off, she busied herself stroking his broad chest. Her fingers twined in the soft black hair and traveled up to lock behind his neck, pulling his head down. Her lips seared his with a soul-burning kiss. His lips left hers to rain kisses down her neck and along the soft curve of her chin and down to her bosom, his hands stroking and caressing every bare inch.

"Damn these ribbons," he growled as he fought with the chemise.

****

Aimee strode across the moonlit camp enclosure, guided by the meager light emanating from the dying embers of several untended campfires. She'd sat with Charlie for several hours, reading to the little boy—and grateful for the opportunity.

Charlie'd finally drifted off to sleep and now it was her turn to find rest. She glanced around, hurrying faster, the enveloping darkness sinister and foreboding beyond the ring of wagons. A team of mules blocked her path, staked out for the night near a darkened wagon. She edged around the team and almost stepped on two prone figures locked together in a tight embrace. Startled, she backed off, stumbling in her haste to get away and knocked over a bucket of water before landing hard on her backside. Nolan's surprised face lifted up, allowing Aimee to catch a glimpse of his female companion.

It was Rose.

From the looks of things, the two of them had gone way past simple petting. Rose scrambled to cover her bare breasts, fumbling as she adjusted her skirts, gasping in stunned humiliation. Aimee pushed herself up, brushing dirt and debris from her dress.

"Don't tell Ma," Rose whispered, starting to cry. "She'll whip me for sure."

"I ought to whip you myself," Aimee hissed. "And you first," she snapped, glaring at Nolan. "What were you thinking? She's only fifteen!"

Aimee reached down, soundly pinching the sobbing Rose. "Shut up! Do you want the whole camp to hear you?"

Nolan adjusted his gaping trousers. "We're in love, and we're going to get married."

"I-don't-care," she snapped. "But if Ardis finds out, you're both in *so* much trouble."

"Don't tell on us," Rose pleaded, her face skewed with worry. "Pa'll shoot Nolan for sure and Ma'll help him."

"He should be shot!" Aimee whispered, furious. She had too much to deal with lately, and this stupid episode only compounded her feelings of frustration and anxiety.

"How far did this go?" she asked. "Is this the first time?"

Rose clutched her bodice, guilt strewn across her face. Looking to Nolan for courage, she mumbled, "No, but we're getting married anyway so it doesn't matter."

"It does matter! It matters to your mother and your father and a whole lot of good people who believe in decency and doing what's right." She flinched. *How often had she'd heard those same words from her parents*? Not only was she the Pied Piper, she had now become her parents.

"What are you going to do?" Rose's voice sounded plaintive.

Pacing back and forth, Aimee stopped just long enough to snip at the wayward Rose. "I told you to keep quiet! Just give me a minute to think."

"If we can catch the train up ahead," Nolan began. "There's a preacher with them, and he can marry us."

"Can she get married without her parents' consent?"

"I'm not a baby," Rose sniffed.

"You are a baby! And a really stupid one."

"No one asked for your opinion," Rose grumbled. "We're old enough to make up our own minds."

"We have to get married," Nolan murmured.

A niggling thought wormed its way into Aimee's tired and jumbled mind. "Are you pregnant?" she asked Rose, knowing beforehand what the answer would be.

Eyelashes fluttering, Rose turned away, shamefaced, refusing to answer.

Exhaling with disgust, Aimee strove for composure. "For God's sake, Rose! Do you have any brains at all?" *There it was again, her mother's words.*

Stepping between them, Nolan defended Rose.

"Don't yell at her. It was as much my fault as it was hers, maybe more my fault since I'm older than she is."

"I didn't say it was *just* her fault. It's both your fault!"

Taking Rose's trembling hand in his, Nolan faced Aimee. "We can't change what's done, but we can make things right."

"How do you plan to do that?"

"Like I said, there's a train up ahead with a preacher. We'll ride out tonight and get hitched, and join up by late afternoon tomorrow." Nolan, earnest and calm, set forth his strategy, and in so doing, convinced Aimee they'd been planning this for some time.

She drew a deep breath and then let it out. "What if something happens? What if you don't make it?"

"We will make it," Rose exclaimed, dramatically. "Nolan and I were meant to be together."

She wished she could slap the shit out of Rose. "You have no idea what's out there. You could be killed, and we'd never know what happened to you."

"I'll protect her with my life," Nolan cried. "I'd never let anything happen to my sweet Rose."

"Oh, puleeez," Aimee groaned. "Stop with the theatrics."

Chewing on her nail, she analyzed their few options.

"What about just telling your parents and facing the consequences? You'll end up married anyway and won't have to risk riding out. It's a safer plan."

"No, it isn't!" Rose blubbered. "Pa'll kill him, and then I'll be alone and with a baby on the way."

"You don't know that."

"I do so know it." Rose's chin lifted, stubborn as an ornery mule. "You don't understand how my pa thinks."

"No, I don't know how your pa thinks, but I do know how most fathers think, and I think he's going to make the right decision and let you two get married. Sure, he'll probably rant and rave and maybe even knock Nolan around a bit, and from my point of view, Nolan deserves a good thumping, but he's going to have to accept and let you two get married. The baby pretty much decided that."

"Will you talk to him?" Rose's voice trembled. "He'll listen to you."

Shoulders slumping, head shaking in silent denial, she fumed. *Why was she always the one to clean up the messes?* First for Sara, and now for Rose.

"I'll think about it tonight, but you have to promise me you'll wait until I decide what I'm going to do." She grabbed Rose's arm and gave her a good shake. "You promise?"

Nolan looked down at Rose, who nodded faintly. "We promise, but we don't want to wait too long. There'd be too many fingers counting months if we do."

"Just don't go off half-cocked and end up in more trouble than you are now. You know as well as I do what can happen if you aren't careful."

Nolan nodded. "Just don't take too long."

Aching, tired in every bone, and needing the comfort of Jake's arms, she stomped away, leaving the two misguided souls to their own devices. There was nothing more she could do this night, and in any event, she was too weary to even attempt to do anything else. Perhaps by morning, she would be more in control and more able to formulate a presentable plan to Rose's father. She hoped the two idiots had the good sense to listen to her advice and refrain from screwing up any further. Right now, she was almost too tired to care.

****

Jake threw back the covers, reaching for his pants. Aimee should have been back by now. Guards were posted, but that didn't mean she wasn't in trouble. *His woman could find more trouble than a passel of raccoons.* The tent flap pulled back, and her head poked in.

"Where were you for so long?" Jake whispered, his voice laced with concern. "I'd almost decided to come look for you."

She snuggled close, her cold body not deterring him from drawing her tight to him. "I was helping with Charlie and then on the way back, I almost stepped on Nolan and Rose."

"What were they doing out so late?"

"They weren't counting stars, I can tell you that."

Jake stiffened. "Are you saying what I think you're saying?"

"And then some," she admitted. "They were planning on taking off to find a preacher, but I convinced them to wait until I talked to her father. At least I hope I convinced them."

He rose up halfway, resting on his elbow. "Maybe I should talk to them."

She pushed him back down, snuggling close. "I don't know if they'd listen to you. I said about all there was to say anyway."

Cuddled in his arms, Aimee's eyes closed, her breathing stilled within minutes.

Jake lay there, reluctant to move, unwilling to do anything to dispel the closeness of the moment. Nolan deserved a good thrashing, but morning was soon enough to confront him at any rate. This wife of his was full of surprises. He never knew what she'd get into next. But her heart was in the right place. Yawning, contented, he drew Aimee closer and drifted off to sleep.

Chapter Eighteen

Nolan was late the next morning. The wagons were already forming up, and he still hadn't showed. A sick feeling grew in the pit of Aimee's stomach. Jake wandered over to Nolan's parents' wagon while she waited in trepidation, cursing the whole ugly situation.

Ardis hurried over, her careworn face worried and pale. "Have you seen Rose this morning? She was gone before I got up. I kept thinking she just went to the bushes or getting water, but I haven't seen her!"

Aimee shook her head, eyes downcast. "Not this morning. I saw her last night but not today."

Noticing for the first time that Jake's team was still unhitched, Ardis's eyes rounded in alarm. "Where's Nolan? Shouldn't he be here by now?"

"I hate to say this," she admitted, choosing her words, "but I think Nolan and Rose ran off." Just saying it out loud left her feeling as though she'd been punched.

Ardis staggered. "Ran off? Where would they run to?"

Damning the two for leaving her holding the bag, she couldn't answer with less than the truth. "I bumped into them last night. They talked about getting married, but they promised me they'd wait and talk to you and John before they did."

"You knew about this and you didn't tell me?" Ardis spat. "You should've woke me last night. Now it might be too late!"

"I know, it's my fault! I should have done

something last night. I just didn't think they'd go through with it. They promised me they'd wait."

Ardis paced back and forth, wringing her hands and keening.

Jake came back, his face grim. "Nolan's missing this morning. His parents said they saw him last night, but that's the last time they did."

"Rose is gone, too!" Ardis cried. "Something's happened to them. I just know it."

"Let's not get excited. Aimee said they were going to catch up to the forward train and get married. If everything goes well, they should be back by tonight."

Ardis stopped pacing. Her hands fisted, clenching and unclenching. Shaking like a leaf, tortured eyes glazed with pain, she ground out. "But what if they aren't?"

"Then me and some of the other scouts will ride out and find them."

"Maybe you should go after them now," Aimee interjected. "They can't be that far ahead. It would've been too dark to travel any great distance."

"We'll wait," he said. "No reason to run all over the place until we have a better idea of what's happening."

Ardis sobbed. "I have this terrible feeling I'll never see my baby again!"

Wrapping her arms around the anguished woman, Aimee felt tears sliding down her cheeks as well. "Don't say that," she whispered. "Rose and Nolan will come back." *They have to come back.* She'd never forgive herself otherwise.

Ardis pushed away, her face buried in a wrinkled blue hanky, shoulders heaving in grief. Without looking or speaking, she hurried away.

Swallowing convulsively, Aimee's heart constricted. *How much more would they have to endure?*

Jake hitched up the team, slapping the ornery mule, Jack, whenever he tried any of his tricks. The other mules shifted, restless, stomping and snorting, seemingly affected by the air of disquiet surrounding the travelers.

"Can you handle the team?" Jake asked, his eyes assessing her greenhorn abilities.

"Me!" she exclaimed. "You want me to drive the team? Are you nuts?"

He scanned the campsite. "I don't see anyone else here. Who do you think I was talking to?"

"I've never even touched the reins. How do you expect me to handle them without any experience?"

It wasn't like driving a car or leading a dog by a leash, for cripes sake! Sometimes, it was all Nolan could go to keep control of the animals. She couldn't do this.

"It won't be that hard today. I'll get you in line and all you have to do is just keep them moving. They'll follow the rest."

Her stomach started flip-flopping. "What about you? Why can't you do it?"

"I have to scout ahead. You can do it. It isn't that hard."

"I can't do it," she shrilled. "And if you make me, I'll never talk to you again."

"What am I supposed to do? I'm a scout, it's my job."

"How about one of Nolan's brothers? Couldn't one of them drive? Really, Jake, I have no idea what to do and if something scared the team, I couldn't handle it."

Shaking his head in disbelief, he snorted. "Well, I guess today's a good day to learn."

The last of the mules were hitched up, and the horse tied to the back of the wagon. He climbed in and motioned for her to step up. Dragging her feet, feeling like she was the proverbial sacrificial lamb, she scrambled up and settled herself next to him in the wagon box. He whistled, a piercing blast of sound, and snapped the reins. The mules leaned into their collars, falling in behind the other wagons.

Though she had ridden up front before, Aimee had never noticed before how far down the ground looked from up here. She reached into her pocket, pulled out a kerchief, and tied it over the lower part of her face as the dust kicked up. It would be worse than usual today, and because of their lateness getting started, they would eat dust all day long.

Jake handled the reins with very little conscious effort, his fingers loose and relaxed, keeping the mules in line and moving. He almost made it look easy, but she wasn't falling for that one. Nolan was an efficient muleskinner, but even he had problems with the team from time to time. Mules just weren't the most placid creatures on the face of the earth.

One of the outriders pulled up as he neared the wagon.

"You riding point today?" he yelled.

"Not today," Jake called. "I'm needed here for awhile, but maybe this afternoon." She caught his sideways glance. She stiffened, biting back a nasty comment.

"Maybe not 'til tomorrow," he amended. "Nolan's missing, and I don't have a driver. Wife here's a citified girl and doesn't know how to handle a team." Grinding her teeth in frustration, she glared at him, outraged that he would belittle her in public—again.

Wheeling his horse, the other man laughed as he cantered off. "Looks quiet today," he threw over his shoulder. "I'll yell if we need you."

She opened her mouth.

"Don't say it," Jake warned. "I wasn't making fun of you, just making conversation."

The wagon lurched abruptly, snapping her mouth shut, and almost causing her to fall off. He reached out at the last minute and grabbed her arm, hauling her back onto the wagon seat. Deciding to ignore him, she turned away, refusing to respond to his casual banter, silently punishing him for being the person he was.

By late afternoon, there was still no word from Nolan and Rose. Ardis kept a silent vigil, striding ahead of the emigrant train, her eyes fixated on the horizon. Refusing emotional support from anyone, nothing could dissuade her from the conviction that something had gone very wrong.

True to his word, Jake rode out that evening along with several handpicked scouts, hoping to catch the forward train before nightfall, and with luck, bring the wayward couple back. Left to her own devices, Aimee prowled the camp, stopping to visit with several family groups, but by their whispered words and sidelong looks, she had little doubt as to their feelings. Several emigrants openly voiced the opinion that blame for the young couple's disappearance rested on her shoulders. Had Aimee roused the camp, the couple wouldn't have had the opportunity to leave.

By nightfall, she'd suffered enough snide remarks and glares to last a lifetime. She retired to the wagon, and snuggled into her solitary bed, feeling sad and abandoned by her husband and few friends. *Hadn't she done what she could to stop Nolan and Rose from leaving?*

Miserable with guilt, she conceded she'd made a huge mistake, and a lot of people could suffer because of that inadvertent error. Exhaling in a long sigh, depressed and lonesome, she reaffirmed her self-image. She just wasn't cut out for this lifestyle. It wasn't what she'd planned on or worked towards. Her background dictated she was meant for the finer things in life, a home, a well-to-do husband, two and a half children—the American dream. If the unimaginable occurred and Nolan and Rose never came back, she alone would bear the brunt of the emigrants' blame, treated as a pariah for the remainder of the journey. Not a pleasant thought. Worrying about Jake didn't help either. He'd promised he'd be back before dawn, but what if something happened to him as well? One of his pistols was within easy reach, but even that gave her little comfort. Tossing and turning, jerking awake at every little sound, she spent a restless and nervous night, dragging herself out of bed long before dawn.

She busied herself fixing Jake a big breakfast of coffee, griddle cakes, and thick slices of cured bacon. Her weary body sagged, and she sat down to eat when Jake rode in, his face grim and foreboding. She set her plate aside, hunger wiped away by the expression on his pale face.

He dismounted, unsaddled the gelding, and staked it near the wagon, his movements slow and studied. *The news couldn't be good.* Her heart constricted, her stomach roiling in anguish, dreading what he would say, self-blame kept her from speaking.

Without a word, he strode to Ardis's campsite. Ardis flew out of the wagon, hope emanating from every action, only to drop to the ground wailing pitifully as Jake murmured to her. John ran from the front of the wagon, pulling Ardis into his arms, rocking her, and smoothing her gray-streaked hair with work-roughened hands, his face a mask of grief. More of the scouts cantered into the campsite, two blanket-wrapped forms tied across their pack horses.

Stunned, Aimee covered her face with her hands, tears leaking through her fingers. How she wished she could go back in time again and change this one awful moment. She prayed as hard as she could, hands locked around the locket for strength.

Sweat beaded on her brow. *Please! Please! Make everything right.* So forceful was her grip, the prongs punctured her hands. But she kept praying, promising God anything and everything. She'd be good if he'd just fix this. She pleaded, she wept, but nothing happened. God had forgotten her. Anger welled up. She threw the locket down, wishing she'd never seen the damn thing, wishing this nightmare would end.

Jake stayed with the stricken couple for some time, offering consolation and support until others took over the solemn task. Sick at heart, she stayed away, alternating between offering to help and hiding out, knowing full well they would resent her intrusion.

Jake sent several men out with picks and shovels and only then did he return to their campsite. Solemn, his face weary and sad, he relayed the heartbreaking details.

"They almost made it. They were just a few miles behind the forward train when they were ambushed. From the looks of things, Rose probably died right off." Dark emotions flickered across his face. He coughed. "Nolan suffered a mite more, took a pretty brutal beating before they killed him."

"*They*?" she interrupted, furious. "I'm assuming you mean Indians?"

He shook his head. "Don't think so. Think it was more likely bushwhackers or horse thieves. White men from what I could tell. Indians would've taken anything worth having, clothes, shoes, whatever. Whoever it was took their horses and gear, but that's about all. They were riding shod horses. We tracked them, but lost the trail once we got into the hills."

"I can't believe it," she cried. "Those kids only had the horses they were riding. They didn't have anything worth dying for."

"That's why we hang horse thieves. Horses can

be the fine line between living and dying out here."

"How am I ever going to face Ardis again?" Tears streamed down her face, torment wrenched her soul. "I should've done something more. I should've said something. Now it's too late."

Head down, he studied the ground, hands resting on his belt buckle. "Won't do any good to make yourself sick. What's done is done. Give Ardis some time to mourn. I don't think she blames you anymore than she blames herself for not seeing what was happening."

"Can you forgive me?" She choked, barely able to speak. "I need you to forgive me, too."

"Nothing to forgive. I didn't do anything either. We both should've done something."

He was right. They both should have, but *she* didn't. She stood there, numbed by the aftermath of spent emotions.

He broke the silence. "I could use some food if there's anything left. Sure smelled good when I rode in."

Roused to action, she rushed to serve him, praying the food wasn't ruined, grateful to have some direction.

"I hope it's still edible," she muttered, handing him a plate. "I couldn't sleep so I cooked it pretty early."

Jake wolfed down a good portion before speaking. "Best food I've had since yesterday."

Her lips twisted. "Probably the only food you've had."

Leaning over, he planted a firm kiss on her willing lips. "Forgot to do that when I rode in. Had other things on my mind."

Warmth spread, flooding her with the sheer joy of his presence. Watching him eat, she was amazed by her response to his merest touch, leaving little doubt as to her growing emotional attachment. Her brow furrowed with concern. She had no intention of remaining in this time. If the opportunity presented itself, she was out of here in a second. *It was what she wanted, wasn't it?*

She turned away, confused by conflicting emotions. Her life was in modern-day Seattle, with her family and friends, not here in this backward, unforgiving time. She wanted all the things her previous life had to offer—not this—not now.

Uneasy, Jake watched as the play of emotions crossed Aimee's face, confusion, consternation, frustration. He felt her withdrawal, felt the wall slamming down, shutting her away from him. Tossing the remains of his half-eaten food, he reached out, only to have her jerk away and stomp off, stiff and unbending. She was the most contrary woman he'd ever met. And the most interesting.

She was everything he ever wanted in a woman. He tensed up.

Jesus!

Where had that come from? What would he do if she left him? He didn't want to think about it. Better to leave her be until she wanted to talk. If nothing else, he'd learned that much over the past months.

****

Grief-stricken, the emigrants gathered to witness the burial. Aimee watched from a distance, choking with grief and self-recrimination. As if to share their sorrow, dark clouds rolled in and wind swept the rocky plain. Standing with bowed heads and crossed hands, shivering in the drizzling rain, she watched as the shrouded forms were lowered into a single makeshift grave.

The wagon master opened his Bible and read a few short stanzas, offering what words of comfort he could to the grief-stricken families. A final prayer was said, a chorus of "Amazing Grace" was sung by the flock of mourners, and then it was over.

Several strapping youths shoveled dirt over the bodies, hurrying to finish so the train could be on its way. The parents of the two fallen young people stood with bowed heads, hands clasped together, rain and tears dripping down their faces, until the last shovelful of dirt had been thrown. At the last moment, Ardis threw herself face down on the muddy mound, wailing in anguish, her hands digging into the damp earth. Tears spilled down Aimee's cheeks. Would Ardis ever forgive her? Could she ever forgive herself?

The train loaded up and moved out, the wagons driving over the grave, trying to eradicate any outward signs that it ever existed.

When Jake moved to follow, Aimee lashed out in anger, reaching for the reins. "No," she cried. "I won't let you. We aren't going to do this!"

His agate blue eyes gleamed with disapproval. "Do you remember the bodies we passed early on, the bones picked clean and scattered around? Do you want Nolan and Rose to end up that way?"

Images flashed across her mind, the starkness of the bleached bones, disturbed and forsaken. Her horror at the sight.

Dropping her head, she capitulated. "No! But it's just so hard to leave them, and driving over them like they were nothing. It isn't fair!" She wept, sobbing in sorrow, both for the two young people, and for herself.

Turning away, she closed her eyes, refusing to watch as the wagon rolled over the lonely grave of the ill-fated lovers. "I don't want to be here anymore."

"Too late to change your mind," he responded. "You could walk, but St. Louis is a long ways back."

She stiffened, lashing out. "I didn't mean that. I meant here,"—she waved her arm—"here in this time. I want to go home to my time where things make sense. I don't belong here."

Rolling his heavily-lashed, beautiful blue eyes, Jake grumbled. "Do you ever stop with the nonsense?"

Doubling up her fist, she punched him squarely on the arm. "It isn't nonsense. I was born in 1987 in Seattle, Washington. How many times do I have to tell you the same thing?"

Furious, she climbed down from the moving wagon and stalked away. *She hated him right now!* When she was far enough away and free from his eagle eyes, she bent over, wailing in grief.

Chapter Nineteen

From that moment on, trouble dogged the train. The full summer sun bore down with unrelenting force, wheels broke, animals perished, and cholera—the dreaded scourge of the emigrant trains—struck with full force.

They'd stopped at a small muddy watering hole the evening before. Human refuse from previous trains littered the campsite, reeking in the heat as flies swarmed in horrific numbers.

Kneeling beside the rank bug-infested sludge, Aimee shuddered in disgust as she filled a bucket, thanking heaven for Jake's insistence they boil and carry an extra barrel of water for just such an emergency. How the animals could endure drinking the miserable stuff was beyond her, but unless she wanted to share their drinking water with the animals, this would have to do.

Not all of the emigrants shared her concern. Laughing at her squeamishness, Faith, Hope, and Charity's mother hauled her lazy behind to the watering hole, scooped up the disgusting bilge and strained it through a length of muslin, then added it to their depleted water barrel.

Horrified, Aimee gathered up the little girls, along with the other children, admonishing them harshly not to drink from any water but Jake's. Though mystified by her forceful words, they promised, their rounded eyes questioning but silently accepting.

By mid-morning the following day, a third of the train had sickened. Muscle cramps, diarrhea, and vomiting were the first signs, and as the disease progressed, dehydration, ravenous thirst, cold skin, sunken eyes, and shock soon followed. Death was the ultimate end.

The disease struck almost every family as it rampaged throughout the camp. Those who were symptom-free worked long hours tending to the sick, sponging fevers, emptying slop buckets, and forcing liquids down fever-parched throats. With so many ailing, the wagon master called a halt, hoping against hope to save as many as possible.

Aimee woke to the sound of scratching on the tent.

"Miz Marshall," Faith's plaintive little voice whispered. "Can we come in?"

Rolling to the side, Jake flipped the tent flap back. The three little girls crawled in, crowding around Aimee for comfort, their little faces streaked with tears.

"Why are you out at this time of night?" Aimee whispered, cuddling the little girls close, knowing without having to be told that catastrophe had hit with full force.

"Momma's dead," Faith hiccupped, fresh tears streaking her face.

"And Papa left," Hope added sadly. "Momma's laying dead in the wagon, and Papa left us alone."

Charity sucked her thumb, clutching Martha, confused and frightened, needing some stability in her upside-down world.

Stunned, Aimee groped for something consoling to say.

"You'd better stay here with us," Jake murmured. "We'll figure things out in the morning." He patted each girl, giving them a kiss, his eyes speaking volumes. "We won't leave you."

She rearranged the girls in the crowded little tent, silently cursing their father for deserting them when they needed him so very much, cursing whatever trick of fate had cast her adrift on this perilous journey into the past, and cursing her inability to change anything.

Chapter Twenty

The girls became Aimee's constant companions, though more subdued than before. Jake had simply nodded when she mentioned they'd need somewhere to stay.

The girls rarely mentioned their parents, so it was with surprise when Faith opened up. "Did Ma go to Heaven?" Her little face was hidden by the brim of her bonnet.

"I suspect she did." Aimee wondered though. Mrs. Purdie wasn't the kindest of souls.

"I'm thinking she did." Hope confided. "Mama wasn't mean all the time."

"Am I going to Heaven?" Charity hugged Martha, her wide eyes fearful. "Is Mama gonna take me?"

Aimee stopped walking and grabbed Charity's shoulders. "Don't you worry about stuff like that right now. Someday when you're really old and ready to meet the angels, you'll go, but not before."

"Ma wasn't old, but she died." Faith kicked a rock, looking down. "She was fourteen when I was born. I heard her tell Charlie's mama."

Holy Shit! "Well, some women marry young. And your mama didn't die because she was old. She got sick, just like a lot of people. Sometimes things just happen. We don't want it to, but that's the way it is." Aimee drew a deep breath. Her religious training was skimpy at best.

"Maybe God just wanted you to be with me. Maybe that's why all this happened." She couldn't think of a better reason or one less hurtful.

"Will Pa ever come back?" Hope's voice was sad.

"I don't know, sweetie. But if he doesn't, Jake and I will always take care of you." She knew she shouldn't promise that, but these babies needed some comfort. Even if she wasn't around, she knew Jake would care for them. He wasn't the kind to leave them alone.

The days melded together, passage through the high deserts in mid-August was grueling and endless. Water was scarce and the wagon scouts, Jake included, labored long hours to find watering holes. A dry camp now was a harbinger of death to the already footsore and weary animals, and a growing line of carcasses littered the wayside as the travelers forged on.

Aimee trudged near Jake's wagon, the never-ending dust made even worse by the scorched earth and dry conditions. Even with the tiresome bonnet, her face grew red and blistered from the sun and, by now, her hands and lower arms were tanned as dark as a Hispanic. The long dresses and layers of underwear, even without the tortuous corset, grew increasingly more uncomfortable, hot and irritating. She longed for a bikini and a huge pool of cold water to dive into. Tempers were short and the days long.

As she feared, because of the incident with the two young lovers, she was treated as the proverbial pariah by the other members of the train, who blamed her for their premature deaths. Burdened by her own guilt and the overbearing contempt of the other emigrants, she stayed away, preferring to avoid their company. Jake was away much of the time, so she was often left to her own devices.

Even when he was in camp, which was for the most part very late, he was too exhausted to spend any time visiting. Though the little girls were always close, the other children steered clear of her as well, either by choice or through the demands of their parents. Starved for adult conversation and overwhelmed by the rigors of the trek, her desire to return home grew in leaps and bounds.

It had been a particularly arduous day, the terrain was sandy and many of the wagons had bogged down. One wagon broke a wheel and valuable time was lost repairing it. By the time they halted for the evening, the entire group was exhausted and miserable. It would be another dry camp and every spare drop of water would go to the animals. The girls had wandered over to Ardis's camp, looking for a treat.

Standing near the wagon, Aimee tugged the ugly bonnet off, sighing in relief as she unwound her mass of sweat-soaked hair. Clutching the locket to her breast, tired and disheartened, she mentally reviewed the events giving rise to this whole inexplicable incident. Try as she might, she could find no reasonable explanation as to why she ended up here. One minute she was on the streets of Seattle, and the next moment, she was landing on her head in St. Louis. *Maybe if she'd stayed put, she'd already be home.*

Holding the locket to her cheek, she closed her eyes, praying and beseeching God or the Fates to return her home. She stood there for some moments, her mother's face uppermost in her mind, heart laden with grief and loneliness. The locket grew warmer as energy seemed to pulse from the trinket. Surging heat waves rocketed through her hands, almost causing her to drop the delicate cameo. Gray mist, swirling layers of smoke, clouded her vision.

Through the haze, she could see Sara's form, reaching out as she had that morning, her face contorted with fear, tears streaking her young face, mouth gaping open in a silent scream. Aimee stretched towards her, trying to break through the barrier that held her prisoner, separated by time and space, straining to step through. Sara's mouth opened again, silently screaming, her arms reaching out to embrace her.

The vision began to dissipate. "*No,*" she cried out in anguish. "No! Sara, come back! Don't leave me!"

She heard Jake calling her, his muffled voice distant, as though through layers of cotton, but she paid him little heed—*she wanted to go home*! As she strained to step through, Sara's ghostly form faded and then vanished. Falling to her knees, she wailed, pounding the earth in her anger and frustration.

"What the hell was that?" Jake's voice croaked. The load of kindling he carried dropped to the ground. "I could see right through you," he growled, his eyes bright with disbelief. "I could see the wagon right through your body, like you were a spirit or something."

Sobbing and wailing, her arms wrapped her waist, rocking with mindless abandon as she vented her anguish, refusing to look at him.

Jake warily approached, knelt down, and reached out to touch her.

"I could see right through you," he whispered, his voice hoarse and shaken. "What was happening?"

She jerked away, slapping at his hand. "Did you see her? Did you see Sara?" She wiped at her face, rubbing her eyes. "I almost made it! She was right there, and I almost stepped through!"

Jake's mind whirled. What he'd seen had been unbelievable, but he'd seen it! Damned if he hadn't.

"I only saw you, nothing else." He briefly hesitated. "But I could see right through you! Damnedest thing I ever saw!"

She continued to sob, rocking and swaying in grief. "I could see her, just like she looked that morning. She was screaming and reaching towards me, but I couldn't reach her," Aimee wailed. "It was like a smoky hallway opened up and sucked me through. And just now, it happened again, only I couldn't step back through. I could just see Sara."

He pulled her close, holding on while she scratched and hit, fighting to break free. Exhausted, she leaned against him, tears still streaking her tormented face. Caressing her riotous mane of red gold hair, he murmured soothing words of comfort, while inside, he reeled with disbelief and denial.

When she could cry no more, she shoved him away.

"I hate this place," she spat. "And I hate you. I hate everyone, and I never want to talk to any of you again! I-want-to-go-home!"

For the first time since he laid eyes on her, Jake began to believe she might be telling the truth. He wasn't one to believe in what he couldn't touch or see, but he'd seen what he'd seen, and he was still shaken from the experience.

What bothered him even more was his utter helplessness. He'd been powerless to act. There was nothing he could have done if she'd faded totally away. The image left him edgy and confused.

"Tell me again," he demanded. "Tell me who you are and where you came from."

She hiccupped. "I already told you. My name is, or was, Aimee Russell, and I'm a student at the University of Seattle. My younger sister's name is Sara and my parents are David and Liz. I was born in 1987, in Seattle, Washington, and I've lived there all my life—until now that is."

Jake shook his head, clearing his thoughts. "And if that part is true, how did you get here?"

Eyes red from the storm of tears, she reached for the locket she always wore. Holding it out with shaking hands, she stared at him. "I was shopping with Sara, and I bought this locket. After I put it on, it started to itch and I got dizzy, and then Sara started screaming and the next thing I knew, I landed on my head in St. Louis, and there you were, laughing at me."

His lips tightened. What he'd seen didn't make sense. People just didn't turn into ghosts. "Do you realize how really hard it is for me to believe that? But I saw what I saw," he added. "I could see right through you."

Her hands stroked the locket. "I think it has something to do with this."

Her amber eyes pleaded, willing him to understand. "Both times it happened to me, I was touching or wearing the locket. When I first came here, I'd just purchased it and put it on. I have no idea why—just I feel like the locket is the key."

He took the piece of jewelry. "Maybe you'd better not wear it until we can figure out what's going on."

"But if I don't, how will I get back?"

Jake stood up, fighting the hurt he felt inside. "And you're so all fired up about going home?"

"Of course," she gasped. "It's the only reason I'm on this Godforsaken trip."

He stared into the distance, wondering why he was surprised by her admission. "I knew you only married me to get home, but I had no idea home was in some future place I'll never see. A part of me always believed you might change your mind and stay with me. Now I know it isn't going to happen. I can't fight what I can't see."

"I never meant to hurt you," she apologized, sounding sad. "But if there's even a small chance I can go home, I'm going to try. I don't belong here. I belong with my family, and I want that life. This"—she waved her arms—"this isn't what I want out of life. It isn't what I've worked for. Do you understand?"

"I understand that the first chance you get, you're leaving me." With that, he stalked away, not looking back, not even once. He felt like he'd been kicked in the gut, and he needed time.

Aimee dragged herself to her feet, feeling so much older than her twenty-two years. Surprised, she counted the months. Her birthday had come and gone. She was twenty-two, but right now, she felt like eighty. Brushing futilely at the dirt caking her dress, she finally gave up and went in search of the little girls, worried now that they hadn't checked in. The girls took turns staying with her and then with Ardis, who seemed to draw comfort from their visits.

Sure enough, after a quick search of the campsite, the little girls were found grouped around Ardis, their faces washed and hair combed, while Ardis read them a bedtime story.

Reluctant to intrude, Aimee ventured near, holding her breath in anticipation of Ardis's probable reception. It had been well over a month since Rose's death, and Ardis hadn't spoken a single word to her since.

"And that's the end," Ardis closed the book. "Now it's off to bed with the lot of you." Giving each little girl a kiss and a big hug, she shooed them off. The girls scampered to the wagon and squealing with glee, fought each other to climb in.

Fighting not to feel the small spurt of jealousy, she cleared her throat. "Are they staying with you tonight?"

Ardis turned, catching sight of her. "They can if they want," she said. "Makes no matter to me one way or the other, but they're already bedded down. Seems silly to drag them out again."

She nodded, turning to leave, then stopped. "I am so very sorry, Ardis," she whispered. "I know you won't ever forgive me—I can't forgive myself, but I wanted you to know that if I could, I would have taken Rose's place." Tears streaming down her face again, she hurried away.

Jake didn't return that night, nor did she see

him the next morning. One of Nolan's younger brothers arrived early to drive the wagon, but like everyone else, he avoided speaking to her unless absolutely necessary.

A respite from the hot and dry conditions came when they camped along the banks of the Snake River, in what Aimee believed in modern times would be southern Idaho. Fort Hall loomed nearer and the emigrants looked forward to arriving soon.

The river beckoned. Gathering the little girls together, Aimee led her little group to the banks, far enough downriver to avoid prying eyes. Charlie and Matt joined them as soon as they were out of sight of the train, keeping a sharp lookout for their parents.

Sadly, she understood their concern. Being caught in her company was a quick trip to the rushes for a strong cane and undeserved—to her thinking—punishment. With a lot to catch up on, Charlie's mouth was in high gear, asking questions and filling her in on his family's latest gossip. Somber Matt held back, letting Charlie take center stage.

"My ma said you were trouble," Charlie blurted. "She said you don't love Mr. Marshall at all. You're just using him."

Aimee halted the small group, glaring at Charlie. "Your mother is wrong," she stated, frowning for emphasis. "Of course I love Mr. Marshall, and I'm not just using him. Why would I do that?"

He shrugged.

"Don't ever say that again to Miz Marshall," Hope scolded, pinching him.

Charity pulled her thumb out of her mouth long enough to deliver a swift kick to Charlie's knee. "You're mean," she sniffed, popping her thumb back in.

Charlie shrieked, jumping around and rubbing

his bruised knee. "That was my sore knee, you idjit!"

"Next time, just shut up," Matt interjected.

"Okay, children," Aimee said firmly. "Stop the fussing and let's go cool off."

Waving the group on, she trudged forward. The incident with the young couple still surrounded her like a brooding miasma. If the whole train thought as Charlie's mom did, it was no wonder they weren't talking to her. She'd never be more than just an outsider. *Wonder what they'd think if they knew for sure she was just using Jake?*

He was respected and admired by everyone, except perhaps Booker, but he didn't count anyway. Unbidden, thoughts of Booker sent chills of disgust running up her spine. He'd been more of a pain than normal, perhaps seeing Jake's standoffish attitude with her as an opening for his revolting attention. He was always there, leering, and, if the situation permitted, brushing up against her while his hands made contact with usually her breasts or behind if he could manage it. He made her *so* sick, she could just puke. She'd considered bringing these incidents to Jake's attention, but secretly worried he would feel she was getting what she deserved. That alone kept her from seeking him out.

"My pa said we should be careful. There's a lot of killer Injuns around here." Matt drew himself up. "They're hiding out there. Pa said so."

She halted, nervous now, scanning the landscape. "Has anyone reported seeing Indians lately?"

Matt nodded. "My pa saw some a couple of days back but they were too far away to make out which tribe."

"My pa said they would scalp us!" Charlie chortled. "Then leave us for the buzzards to pick our bones dry."

"You pa has a vivid imagination," Aimee

retorted. Glancing anxiously around, she rethought her desire for a swim. “Maybe we should go back.”

“I don’t want my bones picked dry,” Charity wailed. “What does ‘picked dry’ mean?”

Charlie’s inadvertent comments sent the little girls into a noisy uproar, until Aimee clapped her hands, drawing their attention.

“No one is going to scalp us or pick our bones dry,” she said. “And thank you, Charlie, for that visual. We’ll all benefit from your colorful comments.”

“Charlie’s an idjit,” Faith declared, nose in the air. “He’s just trying to scare us anyway.”

“Am not!” Charlie yelled.

“Are too!” Faith cried.

“Am not!”

“Are too!”

“Okay, guys.” Aimee threw up her hands in exasperation. “Stop or we’re going back. I need some quiet time here. From now on, if I do this,” she said, making a T with her hands, “it means time out and you have to be quiet and not move, or no more fun time. Understand?”

The noise ceased, unanimous nods of comprehension showing they understood. She was betting on the fact the promised dip in the river was too good to pass up and none of them wanted to go back.

Still concerned about Charlie’s inadvertent comment, her eyes narrowed. Scanning the terrain, she looked for signs of trouble, but saw nothing that caused immediate concern.

“We’ll go for a short swim, but if anyone sees anything, holler and we’ll run back. Okay?”

A chorus of “yeses” followed.

“Okay, but no more fighting! Agreed?” She pointed a finger at each child as she voiced her stern demand.

Subdued, the small group reached the river and tumbled down the high bank. A huge tree leaned out over a slow moving pool, shallow enough that Aimee could see the bottom through the murky water. Reeds lined the banks and cattails grew in abundance from the river bottom. Secluded from prying eyes, it was a perfect swimming hole.

"Okay, now, here's the rules. Stay close and no going out into the deep parts. Everyone understand?"

Five heads nodded.

"And if I have to tell you more than once, the swimming's over."

Again, the five heads nodded.

"Take your shoes off and put them where they won't get wet."

Charlie found a small rock overhang far enough back from the river to hide their shoes, so he said, from robbers and bad men. All five pairs of shoes were deposited into the secret place, and amid squeals of delight, the five charged into the water, jumping and splashing and whooping with joy.

Aimee waded in, wiggling her toes in the mud and watching small minnows dart away. The water felt wonderful! Her mind wandered to the earlier swimming excursion with Jake. They had been so close, and she'd been almost happy. Sighing, she sat down in the water, allowing the cooling waters to soothe her troubled mind.

The children waded into the cattails, chasing frogs and stopping to examine each and every creature. Faith squealed and Aimee jumped when a small water snake zipped by, escaping from the rambunctious intruders. Keeping one eye on the children, who by now were attempting to make fishing poles from willows, she slipped off her dress, washed it, and spread it across a large rock to dry. Clad only in her long drawers and chemise, she rolled and kicked, enjoying the sensation of freedom from the constraining clothes. Deciding it was time to end the excursion, she started to wade out, only to be stopped by Booker's voice.

"Now ain't that a sight fer sore eyes," he snickered, his mouth twisted in what she could only imagine he believed was sexy. "I kin see your titties sticking out."

Standing above her on the bank, he had a clear view of her scantily covered form. She imagined he could see every curve outlined by the wet and now clinging undergarments. From his comments, Booker was unaware or unconcerned that the children might be close, or perhaps by now the children were downriver far enough to be hidden from view.

"Go away you perverted miscreant." She splashed water at him. "Or I'll have Jake pay you a nice little visit—*real soon*." She slid back into the water, covering her breasts with her arms.

Booker squatted down, chewing on a blade of grass. "I've been watchin' and it don't seem like Jake pays you any mind a-tall these days." His thick lips twisted in a sneer. "Maybe I could take his place."

"Maybe you'd better leave." Aimee scowled, tightening her lips. "I wouldn't want Jake to hurt you too much when he finds out about this little incident."

Cackling like a turkey buzzard, Booker stood up, tossing the blade of grass. "He ain't coming here. Last I see'd him, he was following tracks. Said they's Injuns."

From the corner of her eye, she could see the children, stone-faced as they listened to the heated conversation. Tough little Matt started forward, but froze as her hands formed a quick T. The little group stood silently in place watching her every move.

"What's that yore doin'?" The tone of Booker's

voice became menacing. "You puttin' some kind of hex on me?"

"Yes, Booker." She bared her teeth, snarling. "That's exactly what I'm doing. I'm hexing you. In the morning, you'll look down and your balls'll be gone. Now won't that be a sight for sore eyes." She smirked, mimicking his earlier remark.

Booker's eyes rounded. Sputtering, he let loose a string of curses. Aimee could only hope the children couldn't hear. "Whar I come from, we tar and feather the likes a you."

"I'm surprised you survived." Her voice dripped with sarcasm. "I would have thought you'd have been one of the first. Now go away!"

Submerged to her neck, the coolness of the water was becoming uncomfortable. She could only hope the big lout would leave her in peace—and soon.

"Maybe it's time I taught you a lesson," he growled, starting down the bank.

"I always knew you had shit for brains, Booker, but I just never realized before how bad it really was."

Booker had only taken a few steps when he stopped, stumbled, his face contorted in pain. So sudden was the impact, her mind refused to accept what her eyes beheld. An arrow protruded from both sides of Booker's neck. Blood gushed down his shirt front. He clawed at the projectile. Almost in slow motion, he fell forward, landing face down on the bank. Excited yelps and whoops sounded from beyond the high bank along with the thunder of galloping horses.

Backpedaling, slipping and sliding in her haste to reach the children, her mind numbed with fear. Frantic, she gathered the children, forcing them deeper into the dark water beneath the low spreading tree where the cattails grew the thickest, shushing them with her finger to her lips. Stoic Matt covered Charlie's mouth with his hand, and Faith followed suit with Charity. Careful not to move too fast, Aimee parted the cattails, barely breathing, and watched in horrified disbelief as five painted savages on horseback flew down the steep bank, laughing and hollering with unsuppressed hilarity. Dismounting, they circled Booker, clubbing and stabbing the still body, laughing as each blow landed with a solid thunk. Though she hated Booker, she hoped for his sake he was already dead. Cursing her stupidity, her breath caught as she realized her dress was still there, spread out in the open, clear as day. If they knew anything about the white man's mode of dress, they would know someone else was in the vicinity.

The Indians divested Booker's body of his gun and ammunition, and then stripped the body of every last vestige of clothing. The boots were a good-natured bone of contention among the group until an older individual pushed the others away and pulled the boots on, stomping and prancing for the group's amusement. Her stomach lurched as one fierce individual drew his knife and began sawing at Booker's scalp. Unable to watch the gory spectacle, she closed her eyes and prayed. Thanks to God, the children stayed silent, shocked and unmoving among the reeds. When she felt sufficient time had passed, she opened her eyes, prepared for the worst.

Stepping over to her dress, a single warrior, bigger and brawnier than the rest, pulled it from the rock and eyed it curiously, muttering something unintelligible to the others, and drawing their undivided attention. He stepped around, checking the ground near the dress, looking for something. Without a doubt in her mind, she knew they were looking for tracks. Perhaps their own stomping and swaggering obscured any footprints she and the children might have left, but she feared it wasn't so. Standing there, his dark face devoid of emotion, the big Indian looked out over the water, his piercing black eyes scanning the water. At one point, he appeared to stare right at Aimee, and when he looked away, she almost fainted with relief.

Where was Jake or the other men? If they didn't show up soon, she and the children were in some serious trouble—like they weren't anyway.

Charity whimpered. Aimee gasped, praying the noise of the river had covered the small sound. Reaching down, her fingers fumbled on the river bottom, searching for a rock or a stick or anything she could use as a weapon. She latched onto a large stone. She worked it free, stirring the water as little as possible. It was a paltry weapon, but the best she could find. Fearful and unmoving, she waited, hoping against hope the savages would just ride off and leave them alone.

The big Indian stood up and for a second time looked in their direction, his eyes narrowed in concentration. Holding the dress up, he studied it, looking again at the body of Booker. The other Indians waited, watching as he examined the dress. He chattered something to the others, then moved to the edge of the river.

Aimee's heart stopped as waves of dizziness washed over her. She and the children were going to die because of her continuing stupidity. How many times had Mom told her to think things through before she acted? *Please God!* If only she'd ever paid attention to what Mom said, maybe she wouldn't be here in this cold river trying to protect the children with nothing but a stupid rock. *Jake,* she desperately prayed, *where are you?*

The big one pulled out a large wicked-looking knife and waded into the water, slipping and falling as the others hooted. He righted himself and then came on, focused on their hiding place. She clenched her teeth, fighting to suppress the wail of fear threatening to burst from her lips. She couldn't prevail against this fierce looking monster, and if she didn't, what would happen to the children? With little time left, she backed the children deeper into the rushes, a finger to her lips, motioning them to stay still, and then moved forward. If they found her, perhaps they'd believe she was the only one there and the children would survive. Frightened tears spilled down her cheeks as she forced her way through the cattails, the rock gripped in her fist.

His eyes widened when he caught sight of her in the dark shadows beneath the tree. Now was her chance to draw them away from the children.

Splashing and crying out, making sure she was seen, she struggled through the reeds, away from the children and into the deeper water. She was a good swimmer and with just a little luck, she might get away. Hooting and hollering from the bank, the remaining four Indians yelled encouragement to her attacker.

Her nemesis lunged, diving into the current, covering more ground than she had anticipated. He was mere yards away as she dove, swimming underwater, out into the stronger river current. As she resurfaced, standing on tiptoe, he grabbed a handful of hair, yanking her back, his eyes glinting in amused contempt. Unthinking, her teeth chattering in terror, she brought her fist up and struck him hard in the temple, the rock contacting with a loud crack. Blood spurted from the wound, spewing in dark red gouts across the water. His demeanor abruptly changed. Face twisting in anger, his hands circled her neck, throttling her and preventing escape.

Choking and gasping, she fought him, nails digging into his wrists and arms, and failing that, scratching at his face, trying to blind him, twisting and turning in the cold watery depths. His hands were like vises as he forced her head under water, holding her there, viciously cruel.

Exhausted and unable to fight any longer, she relaxed, hands floating out and eyes pleading for mercy when no mercy would be given. Loss of oxygen caused waves of blackness to assail her. *She didn't want to die!* It would be too unfair. She never wanted to be here in the first place. *She just wanted to go home*! But there was no time left. Seen through the dirty water above her, the Indian's dark, hate-filled face was the last thing she'd see before leaving this life.

His head jerked as his eyes glazed. A small round hole appeared in the center of his forehead.

Mercifully, his hands let go, and falling backwards into the water, he sank from sight. Aimee bobbed to the surface, gasping as she sucked in large drafts of life-giving air, struggling to tread water and fighting to find footing in the swift flowing river. Screams and bloodcurdling yells echoed from the banks while the sound of gunfire blasted the water's edge.

Chaos reigned as the Indians scattered, hampered by their bucking and plunging horses. A rider splashed into the river and then she was lifted into Jake's strong arms, his eyes burning with unsuppressed emotion.

"How many times am I going to have to rescue you?" he ground out.

Shaking, she buried her nose in his shirt, unable to form a coherent response, finding the solace she needed in his solid comforting warmth. The steady thump of his heart beneath her ear was a soothing reminder she still lived. His arms enfolded her, securely wrapping her within his protection. Rubbing her cheek against his chest, Aimee shuddered as the events of the past few moments swirled through her tortured brain.

She could still feel the Indian's huge vise-like hands clamped in a stranglehold around her neck, and her overwhelming fear as she struggled to escape. She reached up and probed the painful swelling around her throat. Her eyes filled with moisture. The raw bruising would eventually disappear, but the image of his hideous, contorted face and hate-filled eyes glaring at her through the murky water was implanted on her mind for all eternity.

Jake forced her chin up, planting a soft kiss on her trembling lips. "I don't ever want to see what I just saw again," he growled. "Took about ten years off my life."

"I lost about twenty." Her voice sounded croaky and weak. "Thank you."

"You're welcome. But if you ever do that again, I'll kick your butt from here to Oregon."

"If I ever do that again,"—she coughed—"I'll happily lean over and let you."

A gleam of mischief twinkled in his incredible blue eyes. "Is that an offer?"

She pressed her lips together to keep from grinning. In the midst of the worst nightmare she'd ever endured, and possibly traumatized for life, Jake had the propensity to make her laugh. "It's a promise." She glanced at the river bank. "I guess you know they killed Booker."

Jake frowned. "Saved me the trouble. His time was coming. What was he doing down here anyway?"

"He was following me. Seemed to think since you were ignoring me, he'd take over." Though it pained her, she forced the words out.

Jake's eyes narrowed. "He did, did he?"

"Yes, he did. And he wasn't taking no for an answer."

"Maybe a quick death was too easy," he growled. "I could've made it last a little longer."

She cuddled closer, content to lie in his embrace, secretly pleased with his reaction. "Why? All you've done *is* ignore me, just like Booker said."

"I wasn't ignoring you. I was mad at you. There's a difference."

"But the end result is you wouldn't talk to me."

Jake pressed another quick kiss on her lips. "How many times do I have to tell you not to run around in your drawers?"

She gasped. Several of the men were busy loading up Booker's body and disposing of the dead Indians. Their movements halted as they shamelessly eavesdropped on the conversation. Flushing, she cowered against Jake, mortified by their frank perusal. Sliding off his horse, she reached for the now ruined dress, pulling it over her head and brushing at the dirt and creases.

"Miz Marshall!" Charlie's voice quavered. "Can we move yet?"

"*Crap*!" she exclaimed, guilt-stricken at having forgotten the children. "Of course you can," she croaked.

The youngsters rushed from the dark recesses below the tree, burying their faces in her skirts.

"Miz Marshall saved us," Charlie's voice quaked. "She hid us from those mean Injuns."

A chorus of childish voices piped agreement.

Charity popped her thumb out. "Miz Marshall was gonna be killed and her bones picked dry."

"She told us to hide and not move," Hope chirped. "We were really scared."

Kneeling down, hugging them close, Aimee was overwhelmed with pride. "But you did exactly what I told you to do, and we're all okay. Aren't we?"

Five heads nodded 'yes'.

Her eyes lifted to Jake. "They were all very

brave and kept very quiet."

"Charlie wouldn't shut up so I had to hold his mouth shut." Matt shoved at his friend.

"I woulda shut up," Charlie yelled. "You didn't hafta smother me!"

"Charlie's an idjit," Faith huffed.

"He's gonna get his bones picked dry," Charity added.

Jake burst out laughing, his eyes alight with humor.

"Okay, kids." Aimee threw up her hands. "Enough's enough. Everyone - quiet!"

A horse carrying Matt's father flew over the bank. Throwing himself off the horse, he ran to the group and pulled Matt into his arms, checking the child for injuries.

Squirming free, Matt looked up at his father. "Miz Marshall hid us and then let the Indians see her and when she tried to swim away, she almost drowned."

Mr. Markham stared hard at Aimee, focusing on the red bruising around her neck. "My thanks to you," he said, sounding so much like Matt, she grinned in spite of herself.

"You're welcome," she croaked out, coughing.

Mr. Markham frowned at the small boy. "You were told to stay near the wagons."

Digging his toe into the mud, Matt hung his head. "I know," he admitted, miserable. "I'll get a switch." Dragging his feet, he turned towards the nearby reeds.

Aimee reached towards Mr. Markham, silently pleading. The child deserved better than a whipping this day.

His mouth quirked, eyes twinkling. "I guess we can forget the switch today, but there better not be a next time." Matt whooped in relief, running to hug his father again.

"Next time he'll die and his bones'll be picked dry," Charity added again.

Groaning, Aimee pounced on Charlie. "Never," she threatened, pointing to Charity, "never say that again in front of her."

"She's an idjit." Charlie smirked. "Just like her sisters."

Howling in outrage, the three little girls jumped in, pummeling Charlie and landing several good punches before Jake stopped the fight.

"How do you do this?" he complained, pulling the children apart. "I'd be in Bedlam if I had to be around this every day."

She laughed. "Correct me if I'm wrong, but isn't it you who thinks I escaped from Bedlam anyway?"

"If you did," he chuckled, struggling with the children, "I can understand why."

"Still want to be a father?" she commented, grinning.

"Maybe—maybe not." He laughed, grabbing Charlie by the nape of his neck. "Let me think a little harder about it."

Feeling a small tug of guilt, Aimee turned away, gathering up the children's shoes from their hidey hole and handing out pairs to the children. Hopefully, a baby wasn't something she would have to contend with right now, even though Jake had made it very clear a child of his own was what he wanted from their relationship.

A wave of sadness washed over her. Beside the fact he was extremely handsome and possessed a body most women could only dream about, Jake was a good man, and a woman in this time would be proud to have him as a husband. His plans to homestead in Oregon and be a farmer didn't appeal to her one bit.

She wasn't interested in being a farmer's wife even if she never made it home. She didn't belong in this time, and she didn't want to be here. He deserved better than that. He deserved a woman who loved him. Someone who planned to have a life with him. A lump grew in her already sore throat. Why would the thought of leaving him make her so sad?

"A penny for your thoughts," Jake's voice intruded.

Shaking her head, Aimee led the children up the river bank. "They aren't worth even that."

Chapter Twenty-One

That night, after the fire had been banked and the little girls settled down in the wagon, Aimee crawled into the tent, exhausted by the events of the day. Alone and afraid, she left the candle burning, her eyes glued to the tent flap, praying Jake would come. He'd absented himself after supper, explaining he wanted to make one last check of the perimeter, assuring himself extra guards had been posted. Though more approachable than he'd been during the past few weeks, he still seemed somewhat reticent after their return to camp. Tense and edgy, she waited in nervous expectation. Shadows flickered on the tent walls and every sound seemed magnified in the small tent, adding to her misery.

She was just beginning to relax when he opened the tent flap, hesitating before he entered. Naked from the waist up, his unbuttoned trousers rode low on trim hips, while droplets of water glistened on his smooth tanned skin. His questioning eyes caught the glow of the small candle glinting in his shadowed face.

Heart full to bursting, she rolled to the side, making room, all the while drinking in the sight of his strong features and beautiful masculine form. Somehow, along the way, he had become so important, so central to her existence. Her stomach and thighs clenched in anticipation, responding with primal need, craving his touch. Breathless, eyes narrowed, she waited, reacting mindlessly to the stimulus of his rock-hard muscles, bunching beneath supple skin as he closed the tent flap.

Stretching out beside her, Jake reached out with one work-roughened hand, cupping her face. His eyes clouded, full of questions as he gazed at her. He leaned forward, his lips teasing and tasting, tongue probing her willing mouth.

Inhaling, she could smell the soap he'd used, overlaying his own spicy male scent, heady and erotic, and so sexually stimulating. Moaning, she writhed against him, her hands stroking his hard pecs and washboard stomach. She pushed the offending trousers further down, wanting nothing between them, relishing skin to skin contact. Her hands played, tickling and caressing, encircling his swollen shaft and guiding him to her center. Briefly he held back, then sank into her warmth, grinding against her.

"I've missed you," she whispered.

He held back, stroking hair from her face. "All you had to do was make the first move. I would've liked that."

She arched up, pulling him in deeper. "I am making the first move," she giggled, breathless and hot. "Time you made the second one."

He growled, capturing her lips, his tongue moving in unison with his frenzied thrusts. She gasped, her sheath pulsing in time to his movements. She spiraled up. Stars exploded.

****

The attitude of the emigrants changed after that. Word about Aimee's selfless efforts to save the children spread, and as the days progressed, more and more of the emigrants stopped by their wagon, chitchatting and offering thanks. Charlie's mother was effusive in her gratitude, even offering to help teach if the need arose. She received their appreciation with a grain of salt, never forgetting that she was, after all, only an outsider. School resumed and life returned to a semblance of normalcy. Leading her little parade of children, never far from the lumbering wagons, she kept up a parade of good cheer, quizzing them on their schoolwork, turning the lessons into games, forgetting for awhile her life was other than it should have been. When reality did poke its head up, she forced it down. Sadness and depression lay along that path, and she needed to stay focused and alert, not only for herself, but for the children as well.

It was with a great amount of surprise that Ardis joined their little group one morning, holding Charity's hand and helping her with answers. Aimee welcomed her with guarded pleasure and then resumed lessons, hoping she would make the first move towards reconciliation. The lines of pain and sorrow ravaging her face softened as Ardis gazed at the little girls. She appeared to draw comfort from their nearness, and they in turn had someone besides Aimee to lean on. Though suffering slight pangs of jealousy, she nevertheless realized if she did manage somehow to return home, the little girls would need a whole family and Jake certainly wasn't set up to care for three homeless little females.

Charlie grimaced, spitting a wad of phlegm. "I'm gonna die of thirst if we don't get a drink of water soon."

"And then the buzzards will pick your bones dry." Charity was always quick with that little adage.

Aimee threw up her hands in amused frustration. "Charity, if I hear that one more time, I'll gladly lie down and let the buzzards pick my bones."

"Hear that!" Charlie chortled. "Buzzards are gonna pick Miz Marshall's bones!"

"*ARRRGGGGHHHHH*," Aimee screeched. "Enough is enough!" Though not yet noon, the children's attention span was practically nonexistent. Not that she could blame them. It was already hotter than hell, and they still had a lot of ground to cover before the day ended. Deciding school was over, she shooed the children toward the wagons.

Ardis fell into step beside her. "I never did tell you that I don't blame you for what happened to Rose."

Aimee almost choked on the sudden lump in her throat, as tears spilled unchecked down her face. "I'm…I'm so sorry, Ardis. I never meant for anyone to get hurt."

Ardis patted her arm. "I know you didn't," she commented, lines of pain fanning out from her eyes. "Sometimes things just happen. Rose was a headstrong girl, and if she decided to do something, she did it."

Her mind whirled, seeking the right words to say. "I wish it had been me," she whispered. "Rose had so much to live for."

Ardis nodded, her voice achingly poignant. "She was the only child I had. There won't be any others."

Breathing became difficult as pain grew in her chest. "It's so unfair," she cried. "This life is so harsh and unforgiving. There isn't room for even small mistakes. I wish I'd never come on this Godforsaken trip."

Ardis halted, her anguished face a mixture of emotions. "You aren't much older than Rose was—just a girl. I can understand how hard it is being apart from your family, but Jake's a good man, a good husband, and he needs you, and if you're smart and treat him good, you won't ever have to do without. There aren't many better 'n him."

Aimee drew a deep breath, steadying herself. "Th-thank you,' she stammered. "Thank you for talking to me again. You're pretty much the only friend I have, other than Jake, and he doesn't count."

Nodding, Ardis's lips twisted in a brief smile. "Not easy out here and these folks are a pretty close group. They don't like change."

"And I don't exactly fit in." Aimee chuckled. "I'm the outsider, and I've already made more than my share of mistakes."

Ardis hugged her. "You'll do. Just don't let us scare you. 'Sides, I heard talk that we're more than halfway there."

"Thank the good Lord." Aimee laughed, relieved.

"Amen to that," Ardis agreed.

****

Standing unseen behind a nearby cottonwood, Jake silently watched his mysterious and perplexing bride. Enchanted, his lips curved. Her bright laughter tinkled on the breeze, her wondrous red gold hair glinting in the sun's rays. He'd never before kissed lips so sweet nor touched skin so soft, except maybe for his sister's baby. In truth, he admitted, he'd never met a woman more beautiful or desirable. Watching her, an ache grew in the pit of his stomach. She seemed more relaxed and happier than she'd been for some time. The emigrants hadn't been kind in their treatment, and in all honesty, neither had he. Shifting uncomfortably, he acknowledged his own culpability. Though he'd tried to pretend otherwise, Aimee was always on his mind, no matter where or what he was doing.

The image of her dissolving right in front of him left him rattled and bewildered, and it galled him to know there was nothing he could've done to stop it. He'd never been confused about anything in his life, but he was at a loss to understand who she was or where she came from. She said she was from some place called Seattle, but there were no white men in the area where this Seattle place was supposed to be, just Indians.

It was as plain as the nose on her face she was used to the finer things in life. She was book educated when most women were hard pressed to even write their names, but she'd had to learn even the most mundane tasks women knew by the time they were five years old. That she'd been raised a lady was obvious, and it was even more obvious she wasn't meant to be the wife of a farmer.

Jake grimaced, rubbing his boot in the dirt, wondering what she'd say if she knew he loved her. He'd never meant to feel anything for her, it'd just happened. So here he was, hiding like a damn lovesick fool, watching the only woman he'd ever really wanted, knowing full well that given the chance, she'd leave him.

Chapter Twenty-Two

Aimee's stomach fluttered with excitement. The feeling lasted only as long as it took to get her first good look of Fort Hall. She didn't know what she'd expected—maybe something like one of those old shows she'd seen on TV—but certainly not this. The fort was nothing more than a few adobe blockhouses surrounded by a cottonwood stockade, nothing nearly as grand as her imagination had conjured.

Owned and maintained by the Hudson Bay Company as a fur trading post, it was a major way station along the Oregon Trail. Primitive dwellings outside the stockade evidenced the flourishing fur trade with the nearby Indian tribes. She had no idea which tribes were represented, but Jake later informed her that a motley collection of Shoshone-Bannock were generally present.

She shivered involuntarily as they passed through the Indian encampment, avoiding eye contact with the savage individuals lining the roadway leading into the fort. Indian children ran by, laughing and pointing, while older, more intimidating individuals stared at the procession of wagons, their dark, impassive eyes a vivid reminder of the incident a few weeks before. Jake rode near their wagon, keeping a running conversation to ease her anxiety. It was only after the last wagon pulled through the stockade gate she was able to breathe in other than short gasps. The oppressive visuals of the drowning incident were still too fresh in her memory.

The fort personnel welcomed them with open

arms. The next several days, Jake made the rounds replacing fresh stock for animals too travel-worn to continue, buying supplies, and repairing the wagons and equipment. To Aimee's surprise, Jack, the most cantankerous of all the team, was in the best condition and not traded off. Most, if not all, of the men were engaged in similar activities, leaving the women and children to fend for themselves, which they did with alacrity. The very first day, the wagon master's wife discovered the fort had a good-sized bathhouse. For a small amount of coinage a hot bath was available. Aimee did a quick review of her meager finances, dismayed by the depressing results.

While most of the women rushed off to tend to their ablutions, Aimee wandered around the fort, negotiating around the smattering of Indians either loitering on the walkways or heatedly involved in trading. She couldn't help her uneasy feelings. Their presence was disturbing. Several of the younger females eyed her hair with more than passing interest, which did little to alleviate her anxiety.

One young Indian woman even had the temerity to actually reach up and yank on an errant lock of hair, causing Aimee to jump in surprise and yelp in pain. Fixing the young woman with the fiercest glare she could summon, she stalked off, head high, nose in the air. She might be frightened, but she'd be damned if she'd let that little twit know. Behind her, the female's companions laughed, no doubt amused by her hasty retreat.

The incident caused her bladder to react. Stepping into a small shop, she hesitated before approaching the small grubby man behind the counter. "Excuse me," she began, shifting from foot to foot, "but do you have a bath...er...an outhouse I could use?"

The man smiled, revealing crusty green teeth in

his foot-long dirty beard. "Out back," he gestured. "Shet the door on your way out. Don't want critters in there messing things up."

She nodded, thanked him, and headed in the direction he indicated. Sure enough, out back was a beat-up old outhouse, leaning precariously to the left, the sickening smell of feces wafting in the air. Covering her mouth and nose, she pulled the bolt back and leaned in for a better look.

"*Holy God!*" Gagging, she backed up. The inside reeked with years of use and no sanitation. Shit lined the wooden seat and even from the doorway, she could see the hole was near to overflowing. Slamming the wooden door in disgust, she stomped away. She'd used outhouses before, but never one so revolting. She'd wet her drawers before she'd step foot in that piss hole. Like the "critters" would make any difference if they did get in.

Several hours later, Jake returned to the wagon, finding her depressed and alone.

"Why aren't you palavering about with the other ladies?"

Morose and glum, she explained. "It costs money to have a bath, and I don't have that much left."

Heaving an exaggerated sigh, eyes rolling, Jake reached into the wagon and drew out a leather packet, and handed her a small amount of money.

"Go have a bath! Take your time and relax for awhile." He grinned, his eyes sparkling with mischief. "I like my women clean!"

She took the money, amazed he would part with his hard-earned money for something as inconsequential as a mere bath. "Women?" she asked archly, after she recovered sufficiently. "Are you inferring that you have more than *one* woman?"

Unabashed, Jake chuckled. "I haven't always been married. I was a single man at one time." Reaching over, he pulled her bonnet string, his hand lingering for just a moment.

Favoring him with a cheeky grin, Aimee bundled up clean clothing, a treasured bar of soap, and bathing needs. She sauntered off, the small horde of money clutched in her fist. "Just remember you're married now," she called over her shoulder. "I might have to hurt you if you don't."

Deep in thought, Jake watched her depart, noting the way her slim hips swayed beneath the shapeless brown dress. Didn't matter what she had on, she always looked beautiful. His body reacted. His groin grew hot. Damn fool that he was, he couldn't even look at her and not get hard.

As he watched, she almost ran to the bathhouse, her step light and joyful. Even from here, he could feel her excitement. Seemed pretty silly to be so set on a bath, but if it made her happy, it was money well spent. He rubbed his chin, thinking back. She'd been less snappy the past weeks, softer, easier to be around. He didn't know the why of it, but he wouldn't look a gift horse in the mouth.

Maybe she was beginning to care for him. Maybe she wouldn't leave. But what if she couldn't control what happened? What if one day she just went up in smoke? What would he do then? He hated even considering that possibility. Just thinking about losing her caused a pain to grow in his chest. Unconsciously, he massaged the sore spot, wondering how he'd ended up like most every other male he knew—tied down and happy about it.

****

Amid the laughter and chatter of the emigrant women, Aimee's fondest wish—at least for the moment—came true. Several female attendants, she guessed them to be part Indian by their lighter skin and white man's attire, filled a huge tub with hot water and then left the bathhouse. Standing there, gazing at the tub in abject delight, she willed the moment to last. *Another real bath!* A real honest-to-God real bath. Undressing quickly, she eased in, sinking down until only her head remained above water. Soaping several times, savoring the delicious sensations, she was unwilling to relinquish the tub too soon. It had been a month at least since she'd felt so well scrubbed, not since the last bath, and she was reluctant to let it end. When the water had cooled and her skin wrinkled, she dragged herself out, wrapping in a large drying cloth and wringing the excess water from her squeaky clean hair.

Her lips curved in amusement. Several mothers were busy scrubbing small children in the now dirty water, leaving Aimee to wonder if they were cleaner before or after the bath, but it was a common practice and no one seemed concerned. She, at any rate, had been the first in her bathwater and unless someone else stepped forward, the only one. The bathhouse was emptying fast, women and children hurrying out to cook dinner and do evening chores.

Not wanting to be left alone in the silent bathhouse, Aimee hurried to dress then followed the dwindling crowd out into the evening air. Jake paced in front of the bathhouse, a look of annoyed concern marring his features.

"I was beginning to think you floated away or something," he growled.

"I was bathing," she stated primly, "with your money."

Jake grinned, his white teeth flashing. "You smell like jasmine or honeysuckle," he said, sniffing the air.

"I smell *clean*," she laughed. "I'd forgotten what really clean smelled like." Her eyes roamed over his dusty form. "If you get in there right now, my tub is still filled up and you can bathe, too."

He peeked in the door. "Are all the women gone now?"

She nodded, grinning. "Your manhood's safe."

"Wasn't my manhood I was worrying about. Just didn't want to cause a stampede."

"A stampede? In or out?"

Roguish and all male, Jake grinned, waggling his eyebrows.

Groaning aloud, she burst out laughing. "Do all men think alike?"

"What'd you mean?" he asked, feigning innocence. "I was just being considerate of the womenfolk."

"Go get your bath," she giggled. "I'll stand guard."

His eyes measured her, warm lights sparkling in the blue depths. "Tub's big enough for two."

She tossed her head. "I've already had my bath—remember?"

Jake's too sensuous lips widened. "Might be the last one you get for awhile," he reminded her. "Might be you'd want to share," his voice lowered, suggesting there was more to the offer.

Her lungs expanded as titillating images danced through her now stimulated mind. The offer was tempting, and he was so sexily male posing there, his voice husky with desire.

"I-Don't-Think-So," she said, reluctantly. "But I might be interested in company later."

"I'll hold you to that, though we might want to go to the dance for awhile."

"A dance? Tonight?" she gasped, thrilled by the prospect of some real fun.

He nodded. "There's always a dance the first night a train arrives. Kind of expected."

"You'd better believe we're going!" *A chance to relax and enjoy life, and dance with a handsome man!* What could be better?

Whirling around, she almost ran in her haste to get back to their wagon. "I need to get ready. I'm going to wear my wedding dress," she called, her feet flying.

****

Jake returned to the wagon, shaking his head and grinning over Aimee's excitement about the dance. The woman could be so cussed confusing and ornery at times, but not always. He found her red faced and perspiring, struggling with a corset when he climbed into the wagon. Clad only in her chemise and under-drawers, the corset hung around her slim hips while she tried to lace it up. Frustrated, she ripped it away, stomping it into the wagon bed.

Breathing heavy with exertion, she glared at him. "I'm never wearing that thing again!"

He swallowed, entranced. Red gold hair curled in riotous disarray around her elfin face and down gently sloping shoulders, slanted golden eyes flashed. She'd never looked so beguiling or so sensuous. His hand lifted, tracing the soft contours of her face and down her throat. He itched to bury his face in the sweet-smelling valley nestled between her swelling breasts.

His lips curved. "I thought you'd already decided that."

"Well, I had," she admitted, pouting. "But then I decided to dress up extra special, and since women these days wear them, I was going to give it another try."

"Women these days?"

"You know what I mean." She grinned, wrinkling her nose. "Women in the 1800's, not my time. *Crikey!* The only comparable thing women wear in my time are bustiers. Sort of like this—but made to be sexy. Pushes boobs up for cleavage."

"Boobs?"

"You know," she said, her face pinking. "Breasts!"

"Maybe you should just forget about it and

relax." His hand explored, tracing the soft curve of her cheek. "Maybe we should just forget about the dance."

Her eyes flashed golden sparks. "Not on your life," she almost shrieked. "We haven't had any fun for ages, and I'm not missing it."

Her staunch determination tickled him. He wouldn't let her miss the dance. She'd worked hard and complained little. She deserved some fun. He shifted. His groin wasn't cooperating. Seemed to have a mind of its own. *Maybe later.*

"I kinda thought you'd feel that way." Turning her around, he pulled the corset in place and began lacing it up, amid her yelps and groans of protest.

"I bet a man invented these things," she grumbled, lifting her hair with one hand while hanging onto the wagon box with the other. "No woman in her right mind would deliberately make something so gosh-darned uncomfortable."

Her nearness and the smell of clean woman assaulted his senses. Curls clung to the nape of her neck, just asking to be nuzzled, which he did, pressing soft kisses along her neck and shoulder.

She twisted, glaring at him, her eyes dropping to the bulge in the front of his breeches. "I'm going to the dance, so forget whatever you're thinking—or planning."

He laughed, pushing her facedown onto the narrow cot, while lifting her voluminous petticoats at the same time.

Pulling her drawers down, he stroked the soft flesh of her inner thighs, rubbing circles on her willing flesh.

She bucked against his hand, moaning soft little sighs as his fingers found her most sensitive spot, massaging and caressing. He slipped a finger into her pulsing sheath. Warm moisture filled his palm. She rolled over, her slanted amber eyes narrowed in passion. "Maybe we still have a few minutes." She gasped, pulling his head down and capturing his impatient lips. "Maybe more than a few."

He broke free and dropped to his knees. His hands skimmed her silken thighs, his lips burned a hot trail as he moved closer to her core. He nuzzled the soft down, nipping and teasing as she writhed. His tongue laved her most sensitive spot. She tasted like honey and lust. Her slim hips jerked, and she whimpered, burying her hands in his hair, opening herself to his fiery assault. His heart thundered in his chest, his groin throbbed. The aching need to possess her was destroying his tightly held control.

Her hands convulsed, and he felt a brief spasm of pain as she pulled at his hair. Jake rose up, leaning on his elbows, rubbing against her, using his hard length to tempt and seduce. Aimee moaned as his tongue swept her mouth, hot and hungry. Her hands worked the buttons of his trousers, freeing his engorged shaft. He wanted her—as he'd never wanted another. He pounded into her, fast and furious, holding back just enough, catching her scream as she climaxed, then exploding in one blinding white flash.

****

Aimee breathed in the smells of the night, enjoying the moment. Jake offered his arm, and she accepted, giving it a soft squeeze. He leaned over and planted a light kiss on her hand, his blue eyes twinkling with warmth and humor. She sighed. He looked very handsome tonight, freshly shaved and groomed. He made her proud to be with him. With a slight bow, he led her towards the dancing, a smile lighting his face.

Fiddle music permeated the night air. The dance was in full swing by the time they arrived. The little girls were grouped around Ardis, eyes shining in the light of the campfire. Ardis nodded a welcome, her feet tapping to the strains of a Virginia Reel. Pushing the girls towards Aimee, Ardis pulled John, from the line of males guarding the liberally spiked punch bowl, and dragged him out into the crush of dancers. Hugging each of the girls, planting a kiss on their brows, Aimee settled herself down in Ardis's now vacated chair, laughing as couples whirled by, the women's skirts flying. The mood of the crowd was lighthearted, a far cry from the worries of the journey. Relaxed and replete, she was enjoying the respite from all cares.

Jake wandered over to the punch bowl, joining the line of married and unmarried males, his eyes centered on Aimee. She was so beautiful, sometimes it made his heart ache. Admittedly, he was a lovesick fool. Prickly as a cactus at times, all it took was one of her smiles to turn him inside out. He watched her as he had so many times before, wanting to possess her, knowing she would never let that happen. The flickering light of the fire cast dancing shadows on her finely boned features, enhancing the soft curves of her lips and cheeks, now laughing as she clapped her hands to the music. The sight of her sitting there would be burned in his mind forever. He turned away, a pain growing in his chest. How much longer would he have with her?

A female form materialized in front of him. Groaning, knowing he couldn't escape, he pasted a smile on his face as the young woman, Janie, he guessed, cornered him. The female was sneakier than a weasel and twice as fast. He couldn't count the times he'd run the other direction when he saw her coming. It was fast becoming a joke around the camp that if you could outrun the woman, you could outrun anything. Gritting his teeth, he listened, an unwilling captive to her inane chatter, wishing he could somehow escape.

From the corner of her eye, Aimee noticed a

young, bland-faced woman approach Jake, giggling like a village idiot as she drew him into the circle of dancers. Though she had never spent much time with her, Aimee knew the young woman to be Charlie's cousin, Jenny, and Ardis had mentioned more than once the woman was crazy man-hungry.

Smiling, Jake swept the young woman into his arms, moving through the dancers and disappearing from view. Aimee's lips tightened, her eyes narrowed. *How dare she?* Jake belonged to her, didn't he? Jealousy reared its nasty little head. As they whirled by, she glared at the pasty-faced blonde, visualizing the woman's bald head after she got through with it. Besides being plain and obviously stupid, the blonde's screechy voice could be heard babbling nonstop over the strains of the music.

"Aren't the dancers just wonderful!" Faith exclaimed, clapping her hands and nearly jumping with glee. "Watch Mr. Marshall. He's the best dancer ever." Envious and hopeful, she eyed the swaying couples. "I wish I could dance."

"I heard Jenny say she was going to marry Mr. Marshall," Hope mentioned. "But Mr. Marshall's your husband, isn't he?"

Aimee nodded, lip curling.

"Jenny's an idjit," Charity lisped.

"She likes Mr. Marshall," Hope explained. "I seen her a lot of times talking to him. I even saw her touch his arm once."

Aimee had heard enough.

"You girls stay right here." Drawing a deep breath, she stood up, forcing her way through the crush of dancing couples. Tapping harder than necessary on the woman's bony shoulder, Aimee bared her teeth in a semblance of a smile.

"I'm cutting in." She pushed herself between them.

Jenny backed away, smiling like a moron. "Thank you for dancing with me. I felt like we were floating! It was so romantic!" she gushed.

"Yeah, romantic," Aimee added dryly. "I was under-whelmed."

Jake's lips pressed together, his blue eyes sparkling with ill-suppressed humor.

"I believe the first dance was supposed to be mine." She elbowed him, arching her brows.

Drawing her into the circle of dancers, he breathed a sigh of relief. "It *was* supposed to be. I got caught before I'd even got a drink." His face darkened.

"That's what you get for enticing unsuspecting females!"

Shuddering slightly, he shook his head. "I wasn't enticing her. And I think she was expecting more than I plan to give. She's got it in her head somehow that I'm interested in her."

"And what gave her that idea?"

"Not me! I can vouch for that!" Jake guided her away from the gawking, lovelorn Jenny, into the shadows. "All I've done since we started on this trip is side-step her. It's like having a dog tailing me, sniffing around and waiting to pounce."

"Most men would be thrilled by the attention."

"Most men aren't me," he stated, his voice warm and compelling. "Most men don't have you."

She stumbled, alarmed by his unguarded response. Her mother's face surfaced in her mind, sad and worried. Righting herself, she pushed away.

"I…I can't promise you forever," she stuttered. "I can only promise today."

Jake's glittering blue eyes grew cheerless and cold. "I wasn't asking for forever." He stepped away. "You don't give an inch, do you?"

"I didn't mean it that way," she cried. "I only meant that I don't know what's going to happen. I can't promise that someday I won't just disappear like I did before. I had no control then and if it happens again, I won't be able to stop it. I do know I want to see my parents and my sister again, but I don't know if that'll ever happen. Can't you understand?"

His eyes probed hers, searching for the truth. Lips trembling, she returned his gaze, unafraid of what he would find, needing him to understand. Jake pulled her unresisting form into his arms, ravaging her lips.

"I guess it'll have to do."

The fiddlers began a slow, stately waltz. Jake glided into the path of the dancers, leading her with an expertise even modern men would find hard to duplicate. Dreamlike, she followed, dancing under the stars with the man she loved. Yes, she admitted, she did love him. Right or wrong, she loved him, even if it was only for the moment. Nothing would change that. Nestling against him, she closed her eyes, content just to be with him. No one could promise forever—least of all her.

Chapter Twenty-Three

Aimee hated the river crossings the most, but passage through the mountains came as a close second. Over the course of the journey, several emigrants drowned in river crossings and more than one emigrant had died or suffered severe injuries traversing the treacherous mountain passes. It was with trepidation she looked towards crossing more mountain ranges before trip's end in the Willamette Valley.

More and more, her thoughts turned to that eventual ending. She was uncomfortably aware that, by now, Jake thought she had given up her dream to go home and was wholehearted planning for their future. To his way of thinking, their relationship had come full circle and without question she was staying.

She didn't have the heart to dissuade him, but when the time came, she was going on, with or without him. After all, she stubbornly reasoned, the only reason she was on this horrible journey was to reach Seattle, even though Seattle had yet to come into being. If she remembered right, the first white settlers to the region stepped foot on Seattle's soil in 1851, four years from now. Somehow, no matter how long in the future, she would stand on what would be Pike's Street and, if things went according to her hopes, she would transport home, back where she belonged.

Try as she might, whenever she thought about the future, her soul wept. Whatever the ultimate result, she would lose someone she treasured. Jake was still new to the picture, but he was fast becoming so dear. That in its self caused her no small measure of anxiety. How could one man have become so important to her in the short time they'd been acquainted? One who was so vastly different from any of her previous men? It made no sense, but then this whole messed up reality made no sense.

Walking along, face covered against the never-ending dust, Aimee's mind wandered. Perhaps, she mused, she could convince Jake to go with her. But how would he handle life in the future, if that was even remotely possible? His education ended in the eighth grade, and even he admitted—somewhat shamefaced—that he'd quit school the first chance he'd got and headed West. As to his employment opportunities, he didn't have a career choice that would carry over into her time. There wasn't much call for wagontrain scouts in 2008 and a good farming operation was too expensive for a lone entrepreneur. Failing those two choices, sitting in an office taking orders from some idiot who thought he or she had all the answers wasn't an option. Jake was his own man, and his life was here. Sadly, she admitted, he just wouldn't fit into her hoped-for future. On the other hand, she'd had some success at fitting in and adjusting, but not because she wanted to, but because she'd had to. Jake was another matter. He would be miserable in her reality.

She kicked at a dirt clod, peevish and frustrated by her inability to discover a workable solution. Time was her enemy and unless she came up with an answer soon, losing Jake was predestined. As if by cue, he rode up, expertly handling the side-stomping and frisky gelding.

Reaching down, he hauled her up, settling her sidesaddle in front of him. "Thought you might enjoy riding for a change."

"Oh, no," was her flippant reply. "I'm just happy

to be on this Godforsaken trip, walking my legs off and eating enough dirt to cover Kansas."

Jake burst out laughing, white teeth gleaming in his dusty face. "Makes two of us," he grinned. "But at least I get to ride most of the time."

"Most of the men do," she grumbled. "Seems like it's the women and children who get stuck walking all the time."

"You can ride anytime you want," he reminded her. "My teams can pull the extra weight."

"I'm so glad your *teams* are able to handle my added tonnage." Using her kerchief, she wiped at the dust and sweat caking her forehead.

"You look a whole lot better," Jake chuckled. "Now the dirt's smeared all over your face."

Uncorking his canteen, Jake poured water over a somewhat dirt-free handkerchief, and matter-of-factly sponged her face. Her eyes fastened on his all-to-familiar features, sparkling agate blue eyes, firm sensuous lips, strong chin, memorizing every line and nuance as he wiped the dust away. *He was so damn sexy*!

Clearing her dry throat, she asked. "Jake, have you ever considered doing anything else besides farming when we reach Oregon?"

Jake's lips thinned, one dark eyebrow cocked. "No. Why?"

Eyeing him sidewise, she hedged, resigning herself to silence. "No reason, just wondering. Doesn't really matter."

"Must be a reason," he prompted, "or you wouldn't have said anything."

She stiffened, pushing away from his chest. "I *said* I was just wondering."

His eyes bored into her. "I know you well enough by now that you don't just *wonder*. So be a good girl and tell me what's bothering you."

The horse took that moment to stumble.

Startled, she clutched the saddle horn, feeling herself slip backwards, feet flailing skyward. Eyes twinkling, Jake watched her undignified maneuverings, clearly amused.

Her butt slid precariously as she peeked at the ground below. Nothing but hard ground and spindly vegetation to break her fall if she tumbled.

"You could help me," she snapped, sweaty hands slipping.

"Looks like you're doing all right to me."

"Oh, yeah, sure!" she snarled, as one hand broke free.

Eyes twinkling, Jake prodded. "Tell me."

"Are you going to let me fall?" she screeched.

Jake caught her under one arm as the other hand slipped off the saddle horn. "Serve you right if I did," he chuckled, dangling her under his arm like an unwanted sack of potatoes. From this position, she would now land facedown if he dropped her.

"Put. Me. Down." she spat, struggling to right herself. "Now!"

"Only if you tell me why you asked about farming." Adding insult to injury, he jiggled her thrashing form as if to give emphasis to his request.

Pissed off and feeling nasty, Aimee dug her fingernails into his upper thigh, digging with glee until he yelped, dropping her to the ground. Her landing was ungraceful, but unhurt, she rolled over, smirking at his disgruntled expression. *Success was sweet!*

Jake glared at her, rubbing his injured leg. "Sometimes, woman," he growled, "you'd try the patience of a saint."

"Since you're not a saint," she grinned, "it doesn't matter." She flicked a hand at him and strode jauntily towards the wagons. Let him stew for a change.

Chapter Twenty-Four

Aimee wiped a hand across her face. Sweat ran in rivulets down her temples and dripped on her bosom.

She groaned, almost crawling as she struggled up the steep terrain. On all sides, emigrants young and old were following suit. Higher up, the girls shouted encouragement, laughing as they cheered her on.

Jake whistled, waving his arm. He was just one of a large group of men who were lined up at lead ropes, helping to haul the wagons up. The overworked and underweight mules labored hard, often stopping and refusing to go on until they were forced to by their handlers. It was a long and demanding process. She was thankful the only thing she had to drag up the mountain was her own body.

A loud crack rent the air followed by screams and cries of alarm. She glanced up just in time to see a wagon careening down the hillside right toward her. For a brief moment, she froze, panic-stricken, hypnotized by the oncoming menace. Adrenaline surged and instinct hurtled her sideways, landing with a thump on the rocky slope. She heard Jake calling her name.

Strong arms lifted her up. "Are you hurt?" Jake smoothed her hair, his face a mask of concern. He prodded her arms and legs, checking for injuries. Several others rushed over.

She wiggled free, brushing the dust from her skirts. "Just my pride."

"Scared the hell out of me," he growled. He

motioned with his arm. "Stay on the north slope. If you're up there, you're out of the way if another one breaks free. Happens all the time, and if you're in the way, you'll be crushed."

The loose wagon had rolled down a high incline and smashed onto the rocks below. No one was injured but the luckless family lost almost everything. Salvaging what they could, they packed up their mules and proceeded on foot, still determined to make it to Oregon City.

Aimee's heart went out to them, wishing she had some way to ease their loss, but her own possessions were too limited to provide any help. The other emigrants chipped in as they could, keeping in mind they still had some distance to travel over some pretty rough country. At night, the wagonless family slept in a makeshift tent, using borrowed blankets scavenged from the more fortunate travelers. Nights cooled down as the first blush of fall covered the mountains. The autumn colors were striking, and but for the worries of the trail, Aimee would have enjoyed the beauty of her surroundings.

The days dragged. She seldom saw Jake during the day. He and the other scouts were always on the trial, pushing the train as hard as possible. When she did see him, he was worn out by the grueling pace. Complications met them at every turn. The train barely got over one hurdle, only to encounter four more. It didn't take a genius to figure out that they needed to get through the mountains before the first snows of winter blanketed the countryside. Even she felt the threat of impending weather and grew increasingly uneasy as the weather grew colder.

The wagons rolled into Fort Walla Walla. Aimee walked beside the wagon, thankful to be this much closer to home. Jake rode up, his face grim.

"Been some trouble with one of the trains last

winter." He swung down, his spurs jingling. "Donner Party got caught in the mountains and word is they were eating bodies to survive."

Aimee grimaced. She knew the story. Her fanciful mind conjured up visions of the unfortunate group and their stories of survival.

"Do you think any of the emigrants would view me as a possible food source if we faced the same situation. I am an outsider you know."

"I doubt it. Too tough." His eyes warmed. "I might be tempted to *eat* you, but I'd make sure you enjoyed it."

Her face grew warm, her imagination ran wild. How like Jake to turn the tables and make it sexual. Not that it was a bad thing. She wasn't sorry Booker was gone, though. *He just might be willing to sacrifice her for a full stomach.* Totally grossed out by her own sick inventions, she shook off such thoughts and instead focused on getting through this last leg of the trip. She, like the others, watched the skies for any telltale signs of approaching storms, praying for an Indian summer. So far, the weather held.

Perhaps because she was conscious that her time with Jake was limited, she made a concerted effort to be pleasant and receptive. He seemed not to notice, but on more than one occasion, she caught him staring at her, a quizzical expression on his face.

The camp retired early for some much needed rest. Aimee and the little girls had been visiting Ardis, and when they returned, Jake was drinking coffee and gazing into the fire. Tossing the contents away, he faced her, his chiseled face grim.

"Maybe the little girls would like to stay with Ardis tonight." The tone of his voice left little room for argument.

Surprised, she bundled them up, hurrying the

now tired and whiney little girls over to Ardis, who welcomed them with open arms. Satisfied, they were in good hands, she rushed back, puzzled by his attitude.

As she entered their campsite, she hesitated, waiting for him to begin.

"I want to know why you wondered about farming."

She stiffened, nervous, searching for a quick answer. "I told you it was nothing. I was just curious. Is that what's been bothering you?"

"Quit skirting the subject," he growled. "I want to know."

"Why? It's not like whatever I say is going to make any difference."

"Maybe not to you, but it might to me."

Fascinated, she watched the play of emotions flitting across his open face; anger, sadness, hurt and, lastly, resignation. He wasn't going to accept her half-hearted excuses, and she owed him the truth.

Taking a deep breath, she hoped she could make him understand. "I'm not staying in the Willamette when we get there."

"And when were you going to tell me?"

She couldn't look at him, it was too painful. "I-I would've told you before I left."

He snorted, dropping his head. "I guess that's supposed to make it okay."

Her heart ached. She wanted to cry. "No! It doesn't make it okay, but it's the only reason I came along. I need to go home. I don't belong here. I've told you that a hundred times."

His eyes, bleak and despairing, measured her. "And it doesn't matter that your leaving will tear me apart?"

She sobbed, covering her face. "Of course it matters! It's breaking my heart, and I've tried to figure out a way for us to be together. But I don't belong in your world, and you wouldn't fit into mine."

He yanked her to him. "You belong with me," he snapped. "No matter how you got here, you belong with me!"

Struggling against his hard chest, she fought to free herself. "No! I don't belong here, and I don't want to be here. I belong in the future with my family—in Seattle."

He released her, stepping back, his face a storm cloud of passionate denial. "There is no Seattle! There's nothing where you say this place is. I know. I've been there. It's just mountains and trees and Indians."

"There will be someday," she said. "I won't give up trying to go home."

Realization dawned on his face. "That's why you wondered about the farming. You thought I'd give up my dream for yours." Shaking his head, he turned away. "Your dream's just that—a dream. At least I have a chance of succeeding."

"I have a chance as well." Defiant, her chin rose. "I won't give up. I can't give up." She glared at him. "How would you feel if you were in my place? Would you calmly accept and do nothing? Or would you keep trying?"

He turned away, the minutes ticking by as she waited, not daring to breath. Finally, hands on hips, he faced her. "I would keep trying," he admitted. "However long it took."

Having said his piece, he grabbed his hat, leapt on the gelding and rode off into the fast approaching night. Stricken with despair, she watched him ride away, wondering if she would ever see him again, and knowing that there was nothing she could or would do to change the outcome.

Jake didn't return that night, nor did he seek

her bed in the ensuing days. He ate his meals in silence and would immediately leave. During the day, she caught sight of him now and again, riding in the distance or helping drive stock, and at night, he found other sleeping arrangements. The little girls, although confused and upset by his continued absence and Aimee's gloomy outlook, were her lifesavers. Charity even offered her dolly Martha in an effort to cheer her.

"You can hold Martha," she lisped, around her thumb. "But I have to hold onto her arm so she won't fall down."

"She doesn't want your stupid doll," Faith sniffed. "She wants Mr. Marshall."

Aimee's mouth dropped, surprised that Faith was so discerning for such a young girl.

"Why isn't Mr. Marshall talking to you?" Hope's lips trembled. "We miss him."

Tears sprang unbidden into her eyes. Surreptitiously wiping them away with her kerchief, she tried to explain. "Mr. Marshall and I have different ideas about things, and we disagreed on something important."

"So just say you're sorry," Charity stated. Faith and Hope nodded in agreement.

"It isn't that simple."

Hope's fingers smoothed her pinafore. "Why not?"

"Yeah, why not?" Faith joined in. "Mama always told us to say we're sorry when we did something wrong."

"It's not like I did anything wrong. It's just we don't agree on an important issue."

Charity endeavored to stay in the conversation. "What's *important issue* mean?"

"It means I want to do something, and he doesn't want me to do it."

"But he's a man," Faith piped up. "Women are

supposed to obey men."

Aimee rolled her eyes, disgusted. "No. Women aren't supposed to obey men. That's silly and archaic."

"What's *archaic* mean?" Charity chimed in again.

"It means old fashioned and stupid."

"Then Mr. Marshall's an idjit," Charity reasoned. The other girls nodded wisely.

What happened to the conversation? "No, Mr. Marshall isn't an idjit—or idiot as it's correctly pronounced. He just doesn't agree with what I am going to do."

"What're you going to do?" Hope asked.

"She's leaving! I heard her asking the other ladies," Faith cried.

Aimee knelt in front of the girl. "Faith! Have you been spying on me?"

Shamefaced, the miserable little girl nodded her head. "I get scared sometimes that you'll go away too, so I follow you and make sure you don't leave us."

Choking on emotion, tears slipping down her cheeks, she gathered the little girls close. "Let's not worry about that now. You just need to know how much I love each one of you."

"Are you going to leave us?" Charity's baby blue eyes begged for reassurance.

"Not today and not for awhile. But if I do leave, I'll make sure you have someone special to love you. I promise." It wasn't enough, but it was all she could find to say.

"Nobody else will love us," Hope cried out. "Everybody leaves us."

Tears erupted from all three little girls. Their heartbreak was so unnerving, she cried right along with them, burying her face against Charity's bib.

"What's going on?" Jake's deep voice broke

through their wailing.

Aimee stiffened, lifting her head to gaze at him.

"I was just explaining to the girls why we aren't talking."

His sparkling deep blue eyes lit on each female, his full sensuous lips quirked in amusement. "And that made all of you cry?"

Charity stepped forward, lower lip sticking out. "You and Miz Marshall are idjits, and we're mad at you." The other girls nodded.

Swinging down from the gelding, he loosely held the reins.

"Yes," his warm eyes searched out Aimee's. "We *are* idiots, and I came to say I'm sorry to Mrs. Marshall and ask her forgiveness."

"*Oh, Jake,*" she cried, throwing herself on him. "I'm sorry too! I just don't know what to do."

"We'll take it one day at a time," he said, hugging her. "If that's all we can do, that's how it'll be."

"There has to be a solution!" She searched his face. "We just have to find it."

His firm lips found hers, poignantly gentle. "For however long," he whispered.

Chapter Twenty-Five

Seen from the summit of the Blues, Mt. Hood soared majestically in the distance. Even from so far away, it was a welcome sight for the travel-weary emigrants. A time for silent reflection, the emigrants took a few minutes from the trail, drinking in the miraculous spectacle of the snow-covered peak floating above the low-lying clouds.

Standing alongside everyone else, Aimee and the girls gazed in awe, filled with wonderment and overwhelming relief. The end of the long and arduous trek was at hand. Matt and Charlie ran up, chattering about the mountain. Aimee was as excited as they were, clapping her hands and laughing—and then she got a good look at Charlie. His eyes were horribly bloodshot, small sores ringed his weepy sockets.

"Charlie, what the heck's wrong with your eyes?" If the child had pinkeye, the girls wouldn't be playing with him for some time.

He shrugged, sheepish, face flaming beneath the spattering of freckles. "Matt said if I stood on a big rock and rubbed lye soap in my eyes, I'd be able to see all the way to Oregon City."

"And you believed him?" Aghast that Charlie could be so gullible or that serious Matt would be so devious.

Matt grinned. "Charlie'd believe anything. He's easy pickings for the master." Strutting with pride, Matt's words spurred the hapless Charlie.

"You take that back," Charlie shrilled, "or I'll punch you right in the nose."

Smirking, Matt offered Charlie his chin. "Go ahead, bean brain, take your best shot."

Aimee turned away, lips pressed together, struggling to keep from laughing out loud.

Charlie swung at Matt, tripping and stumbling in the process. Snickering, Matt kicked dirt at him, further riling the already red-faced Charlie. Charlie threw a lucky punch and down they went in a flurry of angry little boys.

"Charlie's an idjit," Charity interposed. "Idjit! Idjit! Idjit!"

"Charity!" Aimee gasped, hurrying to intercede. "That isn't nice."

Stepping among the battling twosome, she grabbed each by the nape, holding on tight to the squirming little males. "Now, stop it! Both of you! Now, or I'll tell your parents."

"He started it," Charlie fumed. "I just wanted to see how far we still had to go."

"You're so dumb," Matt yelled. "Even my papa's mules are smarter 'n you."

She shook them, banging their heads. "I said stop, and I meant it! Do you realize you could've permanently injured Charlie?" she asked the wiggling Matt.

"Yeah!" Charlie said, aiming a kick at Matt. "You coulda blinded me for good. Then what sorta scout would I be?"

Matt smirked. "You won't be any sorta scout anyway. Your pa's a farmer and that's all you'll ever be."

"Won't!"

"Will to!"

"Okay, guys!" She snapped, seriously considering throwing them off the nearest cliff. "I said stop—and that means now!"

"Boys are so dumb," commented Faith. Hope nodded sagely.

"They're just idjits," Charity added.

Rolling her eyes and heaving an exaggerated sigh, she shook the boys one more time for good measure. "One more word from any of you," she snarled, "and you'll all be in big trouble. Do you understand me?"

Five heads bobbed.

"Now, everyone, say you're sorry! And Matt, you tell Charlie you're very sorry for causing him to get hurt. Understand?"

Morose and guilt-stricken, Matt nodded, lower lip protruding. "Sorry," he gulped. "I didn't think it'd hurt so much."

Four voices piped "Sorry" in unison. Bolstered by the apology, Charlie aimed a punch at Matt, who turned and ran—with Charlie hot on his tail.

"And I wanted to be a child psychologist." Aimee slapped her forehead.

"What's a child sicomagist?" Charity chirped.

Aimee scowled. "Psy-chol-o-gist! It's someone who thinks they understand children. Obviously, I don't."

"Don't what." Jake had come up behind her, catching part of the conversation.

She looked up. "I don't understand children, and I don't know why I'm even bothering."

Dimples flashed in Jake's cheeks, deep blue eyes sparkling. "Must be because you're a glutton for punishment."

"That is the truest statement I've ever heard," she agreed. "Otherwise, I wouldn't be on this trip, pretending I'm a teacher."

"I think you're doing just fine." He murmured for her alone, his heated gaze sending chills running up her spine. "Leastways, the mothers seem to think so."

"They do?" She smiled, her world brightened by his comment. "About time someone noticed my good qualities."

"Hasn't been a day that I didn't notice your *good* qualities," he whispered in that husky voice she loved so much. "But I like your bad ones even better."

Her eyes narrowed. "Now you sound like a bad phone sex hotline."

"Phone sex?"

"Forget it!" She took a deep breath and exhaled. "You wouldn't understand anyway."

"I understand the 'sex' part," he chuckled, eyebrows lifted.

Noticing the little girls' fixated interest in the adult conversation, she hissed. "Shut up! Do you want to scar them for life?"

Grinning, unrepentant, Jake shrugged. "I haven't said anything life-threatening."

Grabbing him by the arm, she dragged him out of sight and hearing range. "They're little girls, and they shouldn't be subjected to such conversation." She sniffed. "We are, after all, supposed to be good examples."

Unexpectedly, he planted a kiss on her upturned mouth, lips hot and searching. Whimpering, she turned into the caress, forgetting for the moment what she was saying and not giving a damn.

Lifting his head, he smiled, rogue that he was. "I wondered how long it'd take to get you alone."

Senses swirling, she gasped. "A simple 'we need to talk' would have sufficed."

"But this is so much better, and I'm so good at what I do!" His lips curved. "Here's where you're supposed to express admiration for my many good qualities."

"You're so full of it," she groaned in disgust. "Why is that?"

"I'm a man."

Yeah, she agreed, *it's a man thing, no matter*

where or when.

"Well, get over yourself, you aren't that good." Secretly, she admitted, he was, but that didn't mean she had to let him know. It was hard not to admire him. He was such a perfect male. *Now where'd that come from!*

Pinning her against a tree, hands roaming, he rocked against her. "Tell me you crave me," he whispered. "Tell me I'm the one you dream about."

His hand slipped beneath her bodice, massaging her breast. His fingers caressed her nipple to a taut peak. She gripped his shoulders, moaning.

"I didn't know you were into nooners," she gasped.

"Nooners?"

"You know, sex at noon."

"People don't have sex during the day in your time?"

Mind whirling, she struggled for breath. "We just call sex at noon 'nooners.'"

"Sounds silly to me," he growled against her mouth.

Faith's trilling voice broke into their play. "Miz Marshall! The wagons are leaving!"

He groaned, pulling away. "This being a father's hard at times."

She glanced at his trousers. "That's not the only hard thing." She grinned, patting the front.

"Better put this away for later." He adjusted the obvious bulge, taking his time, his smoldering gaze centered on her face.

She giggled, titillated by the prospect. "You really do sound like a phone sex operator!"

"Is that a good thing?"

"Umm, not really. At least, not from my viewpoint. There're those who think 1-900 numbers are pretty handy at times."

He threw up his hands. "I have no idea what you

are talking about, other than it doesn't sound good."

"Miz Marshall," Faith screamed again. "The wagons are leaving."

Aimee sighed. Jake was right, being a parent was hard work.

Chapter Twenty-Six

Oregon City loomed in the distance, journey's end for the greater number of emigrants. Talk around the campfires revealed several families would continue on, with Portland as their ultimate destination. Aimee carried that bit of information for days, chewing it over, secretly making plans.

Portland put her closer to home and sometime in the future, settlers would step onto the shores of what would become Seattle. Ships ran regular schedules up and down the coastal waters, and if she could reach Portland, chances are she could eventually go home. Indecision preyed on her mind. Continuing on meant leaving Jake, and she wasn't sure if she was capable of or even wanted to do that. It also meant giving up the little girls, and they'd suffered so much loss already. She wasn't certain they could handle being left again, little Charity couldn't. Mulling over the situation tied her insides in knots, causing her to be short and oftentimes downright ornery.

Matt's parents were with the group who would continue. Mr. Markham planned on joining up with a partner who'd come out several years before and opened a lumber mill on the Willamette River. The business was thriving, and Matt's family looked forward to being a part of such a lucrative endeavor.

Aimee cornered Mrs. Markham one afternoon, questioning her about their destination and offering her traveling money if they would agree to her company. Mrs. Markham hesitated accepting the money, disapproval written on every line of her face.

"Does Jake know you're leaving?" she asked, her eyes narrowed with concern.

Aimee looked away, uncomfortable under her knowing scrutiny. "He knows I don't plan to stay."

"That isn't what I asked you."

"Jake and I married for convenience. I paid him to bring me. I needed to come West to find my family, and he needed the money for his farm." She choked on the words. The excuse sounded lame even to her.

"Lots of people have marriages of convenience, and they're very successful. Very few couples marry for love. From watching you and Jake, I would've guessed yours was a love match."

"Hardly. I only met him the day before we were married."

From her expression, Mrs. Markham hadn't expected that answer. "I-I didn't realize."

"It isn't something we talk about. Jake never really wanted me. I sort of forced myself on him."

Mrs. Markham scowled.

"But I'm paying him for letting me travel with him," she hurried to add. "He was sure that unless we were married, your husband wouldn't allow me to come along."

Mrs. Markham nodded. "That's the way of the world. If it was up to me, I'd give women the same rights as men." She grinned, her look conspiratorial. "I'm a suffragette at heart, but don't mention you know to Mr. Markham, he's such a stickler for propriety."

"My lips are sealed," Aimee chuckled. "Though I have to admit, I'm impressed."

"Lots of women feel the same way I do. Back in Philadelphia, I joined a group led by Lucretia Mott. Mr. Markham had a fit when he found out. She's a Quaker you know. He tried to stop me from attending the meetings, but I told him if he did, I'd start wearing bloomers and smoke a pipe. He never said another word."

Aimee laughed out loud. Who would have thought the prim Mrs. Markham was really a rebel. From outward appearances, she was the epitome of nineteenth century womanhood.

Mrs. Markham turned to go, stopping abruptly. "If you're really sure you want to go, the rafts leave on Monday morning. If you're not there, we'll leave without you. If you decide to go, you can pay me then."

"If I'm not there, I've decided to stay." Aimee felt like a leaden weight had settled on her chest, even breathing caused intense pain. Her lips trembled and tears threatened. She only had a few days to make up her mind.

The girls were fixing dinner by the time she returned. Faith had bread warming in the small oven and Hope had the beans simmering over the fire. Charity was rounding up plates and silverware. They looked up as she entered the camp, welcoming smiles spread on three little faces. She bit her lip to keep from weeping. They had become so precious to her. Ardis would care for them if she left, but they would feel so betrayed, betrayed by another adult who promised to care for them. Wiping her eyes, she gathered the girls close, covering them with kisses, hugging them to her heart.

"You know I love you, don't you?"

Three little solemn faces nodded.

"And you know I always will?"

Again, they nodded.

"Why are you crying," Charity lisped. "Are you hurt?"

"No, sweetie, I'm not hurt, just sad."

Faith touched Aimee's face. "Why are you sad?"

"Nothing for you girls to worry about. Just silly stuff."

"You always tell us not to worry about silly stuff," Hope observed. "So don't think about it."

"You're right!" She stood up, rubbing her hands. "I won't until I have to."

Jake'd be back soon and hungry. If she didn't cheer up, he'd know something was wrong. She didn't want to get into such a conversation with him right now. Better to wait until she knew for sure one way or the other what she was going to do. Wiping her face and composing herself, she jumped into making dinner, resolved that it would be the best dinner he'd have for a long time.

The ensuing days passed too swiftly for her comfort. Jake rode out each morning, either to the land office or the homestead, intent on getting the basics of a cabin up before the first winter storms hit the valley. Each night, he returned to their camp, bone tired but anxious to update her and the little girls on his progress. Several of the emigrants had banded together in a communal effort to build shelters as fast as possible. His cabin was third on the list, and he hoped to have that finished within a month's time. Aimee responded to his cheerful updates, uneasy and still uncertain what she was going to do, made harder by the fact that the little girls had begun calling her "Mama Aimee" and Jake "Papa Jake." He returned their love, no question in his mind about whether or not he would take responsibility for them. The little girls showered them with love, all the love they had in their lonely little hearts.

Her relationship with Jake only intensified. Perhaps the possibility of imminent loss added weight to her feelings. No matter how late he returned, how tired he was, or his mood, she sought him out, unwilling to waste even one night of their remaining time together. He, like all men, didn't question her unrequited passion, and welcomed her advances with open arms, finding new ways to please and taking her to heights of sexual gratification never before dreamed about. He was the perfect lover.

On the morning the Markham's were to depart, Jake rose before dawn as was his usual practice, washed up, ate breakfast, and saddled up the gelding. Aimee could barely speak, the lump in her throat threatened strangulation and tears were just below the surface. Jake cupped her face, privy to her changing moods.

"Are you okay?" he asked, stroking her cheek, his eyes worried.

Swallowing was painful. She forced back tears. "I'm fine. Just a headache, nothing I can't handle."

He leaned down and kissed the corner of her mouth. "Rest today. Take the girls to Ardis and have a day to yourself. You've been working pretty hard lately." His beautiful blue eyes shone with concern and love. *Yes—with love, the real kind, the forever kind.*

"I love you," she choked. "Don't forget that!"

Tilting his head, he gazed at her, questioning. "What's wrong? You've been pretty quiet the last few days."

She threw herself at him, wrapping her arms around him. "Nothing." She took a deep breath. "Just overwhelmed by everything." Tears washed her cheeks. Crying was the last thing she wanted to do.

Jake's lips claimed hers, searing and hot with need. Pressed against him, she could feel his burgeoning desire, hard and probing against her belly. Running her hands down his back, she reveled in his muscular physique, made even stronger by the rigors of the last while.

Teeth gleaming white in the early morning light, he grinned. "I can be a little late this morning if you want."

Sighing, she rubbed her hands over his chest. "Not that I'm not interested, but the girls are stirring."

Three little disheveled heads poked out of the wagon flap, eyes squinting in the bright morning.

"I can throw them away," he offered, waggling his eyebrows.

She pushed him back. 'You can't throw little girls away," she huffed.

"How about I just loan them out for awhile?" Out of the girls' view, his large hand massaged her breast

"You're impossible," she growled, surreptitiously stroking the bulge in his trouser front. "I think I could use this," she murmured, pressing closer. Warmth flooded her.

His heated blue eyes narrowed with lust. "Unless you want to shock the girls, we either need to go someplace else or send them somewhere."

She gave him a quick kiss. "Just keep that thought until I see you again."

Jake frowned, suspicion glimmering in his eyes. "Are you trying to tell me something?"

She turned away, unwilling to look at him, knowing that if she did, the truth would come out. "Just don't forget I love you," she said, sadness constricting her voice. "Just remember it, no matter what."

"Maybe I should stay with you today." He sounded uncertain.

She pulled his face down, kissing him one last time. "No! You need to go. I'll be fine. Almost my woman time. You know how I am when that happens."

He nodded, his face showing relief. "Just do what I said. Take the girls to Ardis and spend the day relaxing. You'll feel better."

No, I won't. She was leaving, and the future was so uncertain, and he would never, ever understand why she left him and the girls.

She watched him walk away, admiring the way his tight butt and long legs filled up the leather pants, spurs clanking as he walked. Swinging onto the gelding, he turned to her and smiled. "I love you, too." Tilting his hat, he spurred the horse and cantered off, turning once to wave from the distance.

The little girls scrambled down from the wagon, shivering in the chilly morning air. She busied herself combing tangled locks of hair, washing little faces, and dressing them in clean clothes. After they had been fed and breakfast cleared away, she lined them up, checking each carefully.

"I'm going to take you over to Ardis's wagon this morning, and you're going to stay with her today. Tonight, Jake will bring you back and you're to mind him and be very good girls. Do you understand?"

Three little heads nodded.

"Where will you be?" Faith asked, forehead wrinkling with concern.

"I'm going to find my mama and papa," she explained. "So I have to leave for awhile." She hated telling the lie, but couldn't leave them without hope.

"When will you be back?" Charity's little face scowled.

"I'm not sure," she said, careful not to say too much. "But Jake is here, and he won't let anything happen to you. You know that, don't you?"

"Are you going to die?" Charity asked.

"No, silly!" She laughed. "I'm just going to find my family."

"Then you'll be back!" Hope's face brightened.

"I'll be home!" She couldn't bear to hurt them. "Just be my good girls and remember I love you."

She rushed to prepare a lunch box, adding special things she knew they liked. She flew around, gathering up her few belongings, and wrapping up the lone diamond earring in a small leather pouch. When all was ready, she led the little girls to Ardis's wagon. Ardis welcomed the girls, nodding in understanding as Aimee told the lie about needing the day to herself.

"We'll be fine. Won't we, girls?" Ardis ushered them to the fire. "We'll go for a walk down by the river later today and see if we can find some frogs or snakes."

"Ick," Faith sniffed. "I hate snakes."

Hope and Charity chimed in. "Me, too!"

"I hate frogs!"

Heart breaking, Aimee hugged them one last time. "I love you so much," she whispered. "You be good girls, you hear me?"

Nodding, they hugged her back, planting wet kisses on her now damp cheeks.

Ardis eyed her, suspicion rampant in that look. Unable to bear the pain any longer, she ran from the camp, stopping by the wagon long enough to grab her things. She placed the earring and a brief note where Jake would be sure to find them.

Running towards the Markham's camp, she barely made it in time. The wagon had already been loaded onto the raft, and they had just begun to untie the ropes. Seven other wagons were also on similar rafts and several were already floating down the river. Mrs. Markham waved a welcome.

"I was beginning to think you'd changed your mind."

Shaking her head, Aimee stepped onto the raft, panting and breathless from the wild dash here. Opening her pack, she handed Mrs. Markham the money she'd squirreled away.

"We'll work out what you owe later." Mrs. Markham pushed the money back. "I think I owe you something for Matt's schooling and perhaps you could continue that for awhile."

Aimee nodded mutely, the lump in her throat made conversation impossible. Nervous and sad, she held onto the tied-down wagon as the raft pulled away from the bank, swirling and dipping as the men fought to gain control, using long poles to push the raft further into the river until it floated free in the deeper waters. She watched the bank recede in the distance, part of her hoping against hope Jake would dash up and take her away, like some hero in a romance novel. But he never came. She wondered what the outcome would have been if he'd known his child rested beneath her heart.

Several hours later, she was heaving over the side, the motion of the raft and early pregnancy having taken their toll. Weak and dizzy, she leaned against a wagon wheel, waiting for the next purge to begin.

Mrs. Markham held her hand, wiping her forehead with a wet rag, offering what comfort she could. "How far along are you?" Her knowing comment made lying impossible.

Hanging her head, shamefaced, Aimee admitted. "I think two months, maybe less." She tossed her head. "I don't know. I didn't pay that much attention!" Stomach heaving again, she had just enough time to make it to the raft's edge before she spewed.

"Maybe you should've stayed with Jake." Mrs. Markham shrewd eyes missed nothing.

Wiping her mouth, grimacing at the foul taste, Aimee dropped down onto the deck again. "If Jake'd known I was expecting, he'd never have let me go, and I need to find my family."

"Is your family in Portland?"

"No," she admitted. "They're farther up the Oregon coast." For want of a better explanation, this was the best she could do. "I'm just not sure where."

"How did you get separated from your family?"

"It's a long story."

"Maybe it would've been better to stay in Oregon City and send inquiries asking if anyone knows of their whereabouts."

"That wouldn't work. It's just too hard to explain, and if I told you, you'd think I'm crazy or something."

Mrs. Markham laughed delightedly, eyes twinkling with amusement. "People say I'm crazy all the time, Mr. Markham foremost. I don't make rash judgments."

"Believe me," Aimee moaned, stomach rolling again. "There's no other explanation." Rushing to the raft's edge, she hung there, gagging as her stomach cramped once again. By now, all that came up was clear liquid, but even that was disgusting.

Faced with her uncertain future, Aimee curled up in misery, crying for Jake.

Chapter Twenty-Seven

The trip from Oregon City took only a few miserable days. Portland, dubbed Stumptown by the locals, was a hodgepodge of roughhewn log edifices lining muddy causeways, hacked out from the dense forests which surrounded it on three sides. Situated near the convergence of the Columbia and Willamette Rivers, Portland was a thriving frontier community, complete with a log cabin boarding house, sawmill, and two churches. From first glance, Aimee estimated the population to be approximately five hundred hardy souls, give or take a few hundred.

Still suffering from morning sickness lasting the entire day, it was a relief to be on solid ground again. Saying her sad goodbyes to the Markhams, she procured lodging at the only available boarding house. The presence of a single young female caused the proprietor some concern, but anticipating his reluctance, she'd come prepared. Explaining her husband would be joining her within the week, she allayed any concerns the gruff innkeeper had and settled in, desperately needing time to recuperate from the rigors of the raft trip. Alone, sick, and sad, depression threatened to overwhelm her. Adding to her already gloomy outlook, rain fell in blinding sheets, drenching the already soggy ground, and even small trips outdoors were rendered almost impossible. From the small window in the bleak little room, she found herself watching every dark-haired man who passed by, hoping against hope Jake had followed. Time and time again, her fanciful dreaming met with disillusionment.

Two days and many disappointments later, Aimee forced herself to accept the fact he wasn't coming. She'd deserted him and the girls, and he would never forgive her. It was time to move on, whether she was prepared to or not. Focusing on her ultimate goal, she took care to consider every alternative, her immediate plan to find transportation across the Columbia and, after that, winter in Vancouver. At least Vancouver was one step closer to home.

Money was a huge problem, but selling more of her small horde of jewelry proved easier than anticipated. Even here in this uncivilized territory, fancy embellishments were sought after and worn with great pride. Now, after some heated bargaining, only two of her cherished rings remained; the bracelets and gold chain had been sold for a mere pittance, but enough to sustain her for a little while. Once she reached Vancouver, she'd better come up with some sort of employment fast or the winter was going to be a harsh one.

Though suspicious, the innkeeper helped her secure transport across the Columbia, assuring her the captain of the ferry was an honorable man. The ferry ran twice a week across the Columbia, and the cost was reasonable, so she assumed. Arriving at the docks early on the third morning of her stay, she viewed the conveyance with misgivings. The boat, though sturdy, had seen better times. The crew, a seedy mishmash of Europeans and leather-clad half-breeds, stopped working and stared with open lust. The captain, a rotund, no-neck, greasy, gap-toothed caricature of a man, growled a churlish welcome as she stepped onto the boat. Aimee shivered. *Maybe this wasn't such a good idea.*

The captain viewed her presence with dubious misgiving. "Whar's your man?"

Composure slipping, she replied as haughty as any queen. "My man will be joining me within the week." She hesitated, adding for color. "He had last minute business to attend to. We decided I would go on alone and find suitable accommodations."

"Your man must be new to this country," he smirked, while picking his rather bulbous nose. "Otherwise, he wouldn't leave you unprotected."

"I can assure you," she sniffed, "that I am perfectly capable of caring for myself."

Flicking his finger, the captain attempted to dislodge the adhesive booger, shaking his hand several times until it flipped into the water. Aimee's stomach rolled, praying his aim was true.

"Guess it's no skin off my nose," he muttered.

"Or in it either," she quipped, gagging.

"Not one to stick my nose in where it's not wanted," he said not unkindly. His dirty paw reached into his loose trousers and began scratching his balls. At the same time, he hacked a wad of phlegm and spat it into the wind. "But you best be wary. This country's no place for a lone female."

Unable to stomach looking at him any longer, she turned away. "I told you I'm not alone. My husband will be joining me within the week."

"Is there a problem?" A male voice asked.

"Nossir," the captain replied, doffing his scruffy cap. Fawning at the newcomer, he half-bowed, a sickly smile pasted on his rough features.

"Then let's be off." The voice, imperious and over-bearing, grated on Aimee's ears.

The captain scuttled away, barking orders to the crew. Uneasy and edgy, eyes averted from the new arrival, the crew scurried to comply, and within minutes the boat pulled from the docks.

Curious, Aimee turned, studying the newcomer. The gentleman, in his mid to late thirties, was somewhat attractive in a GQ sort of way. Tipping his hat, baring his head, the gentleman's dark blonde hair lay flat against his skull, heavily pomaded with what she suspected was Makassar Oil. A small neatly trimmed mustache capped red, too-full lips, parted in a predatory semblance of a smile. Reeking of insincerity, the phony smile never touched his cold gray eyes. Her internal warning signals zipped off the scale.

Mr. GQ introduced himself. "Roland Spencer at your service." Gallant as only the sleazy can be, he offered her his arm. "And you are?"

She hesitated, torn between civility and rudeness, opting for the former. "Aimee Marshall. Mrs. Jake Marshall."

His thick lips twisted in a fake smile. "Ahh! A married lady. My bad luck continues."

"*Happily* married."

His eyes roamed over her slender form, inspecting her feminine attributes a little too close, rather like she was under a microscope. *There was one in every crowd.*

"Perhaps you'd allow me to escort you to the main cabin. It's warmer there and out of the wind."

Shaking her head, she stepped back. "I paid for a seat on the deck. I couldn't afford inside."

"As my guest," his lips widened, shark's teeth gleaming.

Her chin went up as she smiled, the prim and proper lady. "Though I appreciate your offer, I'd better stay here."

He might be smooth as silk, but she knew a snake in the grass when she saw one.

"What kind of gentleman would I be if I allowed a *married* woman to linger in the cold?"

A small shiver ran up her spine, reminding her that it was chilly, or maybe it was just his slimy presence.

"I appreciate your offer. Really, I do. But I'd

rather sit out here and enjoy the scenery." Wrapping her shawl closer, she started towards some wooden benches lining the deck.

His face darkened. "Oh, but I insist!"

Roland offered his arm once again, the command obvious. Aimee looked to the crew, abjectly certain not a single scurvy soul would lift a finger to intercede.

Erring on the side of caution, she allowed him to draw her along, responding to his questions with inconsequential bits of nothing. As they strolled, crew members scampered out of their way, furtively eyeing her companion.

He paused, facing the distant shoreline. "My father owns almost all of Vancouver," he stated, waving to the distant shore. "I'm sure you've heard of him."

"As a matter of fact, I haven't." Pulling her hand free, she brushed back her windblown tresses. "You must be very proud."

"Are you planning on relocating to Vancouver?"

Divulging her life story wasn't part of her plan, but she had contrived some pretty snappy comebacks if needed. "We haven't decided for sure where we'll end up. My husband's interests are quite varied."

Brushing an imaginary piece of lint from his otherwise spotless jacket, Roland gazed at her. "I manage most of my father's businesses, including the saloon and store. We'll cross paths from time to time. I guarantee it."

She sat down. "From recent experience, I gather women aren't allowed in saloons, at least the *good* women aren't, but I'm sure I'll visit the store from time to time."

Fastidious to a fault, he brushed the bench with a handkerchief, seating himself almost on top of her.

"It's dangerous out here for unprotected females.

I'm surprised your husband allowed you to travel alone."

"Thanks for the warning, but I won't be alone for long." Loneliness settled on her heart. Would she ever see Jake again?

He leaned back, reclining against the cabin wall, hands clasped around his knee. "And where is this husband? Or is that just a story for unwanted suitors?"

Aimee glanced away. "He's coming over later," she murmured. "I came ahead to find suitable lodging."

He slid even closer. "There's only one decent place to stay in Vancouver, and my family owns it."

My luck. She edged farther down the bench. "You own the hotel, too?"

He shrugged. "That and pretty much everything else. My father came out here before the influx of emigrants. He realized even then the possibilities for advancement. We've been adding to our properties every since."

"How very interesting." *Not!*

Examining his well-groomed fingernails, he mentioned, almost as an afterthought. "I'm thought of as quite a catch around here."

Her stomach lurched. "I'm sure you are," she responded wryly. "Why hasn't some desperate female dragged you to the altar yet?"

Placing a sweaty palm on her forearm, Roland leaned close. "I'm waiting for the right woman."

The weather had taken a turn for the worse, the sky grew dark, storm clouds rushed in, and wind whipped the boat with gale force. The boat tipped in the fast-building waves and combined with the smell of alcohol and tobacco on Roland's breath, nausea hit hard. Her stomach lurched again.

Gulping spasmodically, she stood up, reeling on the rocking boat. "Could you excuse me for a moment?"

He nodded, looking concerned. *But not for me.*

Staggering to the boat's railing, bumping and weaving around stacks of cargo lashed to the boat's deck, Aimee grabbed the railing and leaned over, emptying her stomach into the churning river.

A young boatsman approached and held her steady as she heaved. "Sometimes the water can get pretty rough," he muttered.

"Get away from her, you filthy scum!" Roland stalked towards them.

Shocked, Aimee could only stare at the young man, humiliated by Roland's unwarranted outburst. The young boatsman, concern and sympathy lurking in the depths of his dark brown eyes, dropped his hand, tugged his forelock, and slunk away.

Weak and sick, she leaned against the railing, holding on as the boat bucked and swayed.

"What was that for?" she gasped, outraged. "He was just trying to help."

"He's trash, and trash has no business touching respectable women!"

"Whose law is that?" This respectable woman thing was really beginning to bug her.

He glared at her, his lips curling with distaste. "Do you want him touching you?"

Better him than you! Wiping her mouth, she grimaced. "At the moment, I couldn't care less." Bending over the rail, holding on for dear life, she let loose again, gagging and retching into the frothy wind-swept waters.

Roland moved away. "I'll leave you to your misery."

I bet you will. It's a perfect plan. Toss my cookies the rest of the way and he'll leave me alone.

Crouching against the railing, self-pitying tears leaked from her closed lids. What she wouldn't do to see Mom right now! Or Dad—or Sara! But most of all, she wanted Jake, wrapping her in his warm embrace.

The captain approached, covered against the storm in a frayed and dirty rain slicker. "P'raps you'd better step into the cabin. This storm looks to be a bad 'un."

Hacking a wad of yellow phlegm onto the deck, he wiped his mouth with the back of his hand and then reached for her. Aimee choked, her gag reflex working overtime.

Helping her to her feet, the captain led her into the cabin, where she collapsed, falling into a nearby chair. Roland sat at a table sipping a hot drink, but stood up and sauntered to the other side of the cabin as they entered, far enough away to avoid contact.

Reaching behind a bench, the captain pulled out a slop bucket and set it nearby.

The boat continued to rock and sway. Moaning, she prayed for an early demise. She'd never been seasick a day in her life, but then she'd never been pregnant before either.

"How much farther?" she croaked.

"Not much. We're heading into the wind, so the going's slower."

He turned to leave. "Yell at Cookie if ya want anything. Tell him I said to get ya whatever."

She nodded, thankful for his kindness. The cabin, stark and bare, was nevertheless warm and dry. A small coal brazier stood against the wall, its sooty black stovepipe venting out the ceiling. Pulling her chair nearer, Aimee reveled in the blasts of heat emanating from the small stove. Cookie, she presumed by his dirty white apron, entered the cabin and thumped a cup of hot tea down in front of her.

She reached for her small hoard of coins.

"No reason for that," Cookie grumbled. "This one's on the house."

She took a tentative sip. It tasted wonderful. The boat's motion had eased, and her nausea subsided somewhat.

****

Jake stood on the dock, cursing himself for a fool. In the distance, he could see Aimee's burnished red-gold curls blowing in the wind, her hand resting on the forearm of a male escort. *Hadn't taken her long to hook up with another man.* He ground his teeth in rage and imagined the worst. Was their wedding and the long trek just a ploy so she could end up with the man on the boat? His gut clenched. Had Aimee turned and looked back, she'd have seen him standing there, but he was too late to stop her, even if she'd wanted him to.

On the day she'd disappeared, he'd waited until well after dark before seeking her out, convinced she was just running late. Ardis and the girls were adamant she'd gone into Oregon City, but other than that small bit of information, no one else had anything to offer. The following morning, he'd set out, making it halfway to Portland before driving rain hit the Willamette. Mud and fallen debris clogged the rutty trail, and travel had been impossible until the rains abated. By the time he arrived in Portland, and forced the surly innkeeper to divulge her whereabouts, the ferry had already departed. So here he stood, watching his Aimee with another man, leaving him as she'd always said she would. Pain and anguish welled up in a strangling flood of emotion.

Furious now, he headed for the nearest saloon and the biggest shot of whiskey he could find, intent on drowning his sorrows. The waterfront was a hodgepodge of seedy rundown bars, populated by the lower dregs of Portland's humanity; just the environment he needed right now. Entering the first establishment he came to, he stomped in and headed straight for the counter. Skimpily-clad, aging whores from the nearby bawdyhouse leaned against scratched and dented slats masquerading as the bar. They eyed him with greed intermixed with unconcealed lust, brazenly flaunting sagging and unappealing body parts as they vied for his attention. Disgusted, he pushed them aside and slapped money down.

Hours later, sloppy drunk and nasty, he picked a fight with the biggest mountain of muscle he could find, waking up the next morning in jail, head pounding, stomach rolling, and mouth tasting like shit. Wincing, he rolled off the cot and staggered to his feet. Weaving across the treacherous floor, he flopped back down on the hard cot, willing his bleary eyes to focus. A deputy unlocked the cell and motioned him out.

"You can leave after you pay the fine."

Leaning against the wall for support, Jake edged his way past the deputy, tripping, and then falling into the outer room.

"Rube said you attacked him for no reason," the deputy commented, helping him to stand, then laughed. "Rube wouldn't be my first choice to pick a fight with."

"Is Rube the other half?" Jake croaked.

Nodding, the deputy grinned.

Rubbing his jaw, he flinched as his fingers found a number of painful abrasions. Aching over almost the entire length of his body, he figured Rube'd worked him over pretty good.

"How's Rube this morning?" he rumbled.

"Oh, Rube's fine, never better. Nothing he likes more'n a good fight."

"So I didn't hurt his hands much with my face?"

The deputy hee-hawed. "Nope. He said it was kinda like taking candy from a baby. You was so drunk, one of the bawds coulda took ya."

Jake nodded. “What do I owe you for the party?”

The deputy pulled out a list from the desk, examining it cursorily. “The bartender said you broke the place up pretty good, but it wasn’t much to begin with, and one of the bawds said you didn’t pay her, but she always says that, and then there’s the fee for drunk and disorderly. I’m thinking fifteen dollars orta do it.”

Groaning and unsteady, he paid the fine and collected his gear, shuffling out the door and stumbling to the stable. The roan gelding nickered in greeting, munching on a bale of hay, his coat glistening from a fresh grooming.

A stable boy ran up, face alight with interest, taking note of Jake’s bruised and beaten face.

“I hear ole Rube dang near beat you to death,” he chortled. “Nobody picks a fight with ole Rube. He’s meaner a grizzly in mating season.”

“Wish I’d have known that yesterday,” Jake growled. “Might have saved me a night in jail and a passel of aches.” *Probably not.* Nothing would’ve stopped him from picking a fight last night, and his cussed orneriness would have demanded the meanest critter in town. Served him right.

Aimee’s perfect features rose up in his mind, his gut clenching in response.

“You okay, mister?” the kid asked.

No, he wasn’t. He felt Aimee’s loss with every ounce of his being. He wasn’t what she wanted and never would be. That was pretty obvious by the outward appearance of her male friend. He heaved a sigh of regret. Time to put that all behind and take care of his responsibilities. He was a father now. Fate had gifted him with that. The little girls’d been almost hysterical when he left, thinking he was deserting them along with everyone else. They deserved better. Saddling up the roan, he mounted, willing himself to leave, knowing he could never forget her.

Flipping the kid a coin, he reined the gelding toward Oregon City, pushing the horse hard, trying to deny the ache that made breathing almost impossible.

Chapter Twenty-Eight

Vancouver was a bustling sprawling frontier town, easily the most populated of any township along these coastal waters. Dockworkers swarmed the banks, looking for work or hustling to unload the voluminous number of boats moored at the docks. Aimee followed the line of debarking passengers, avoiding Roland like the plague.

The young boatsman who'd aided her earlier, stopped working as she neared. He muttered softly, "The Spencers don't own everything. There's a boarding house, O'Malley's. Not as fancy as some, but clean. It's just off Main Street, past the church and up the hill. Tell Maudie I sent you."

She nodded, thanking him under her breath. Lodging in anything owned or managed by Roland was pure idiocy. His type expected favors for any supposed help he might offer.

Lugging the awkward valise, she started up the boardwalk, halting as Roland blocked the path.

"Let me carry that for you." His smile was as solicitous as a viper.

"No. No. It's very light. I can handle it." Pulling the valise free from his clutching fingers, she made to step around him.

His attitude changed for the worse. "I insist."

Her lips tightened. Some guys just can't take a hint. "No. Thank. You." Hoping he'd get the hint and buzz off, she started up the walkway.

Roland hurried to overtake her. "You'll need a place to stay and our hotel is the best in town."

"I already have a room." It wasn't going to be

easy shaking this irritating piece of crap.

His demeanor darkened. "You didn't mention that earlier."

"I didn't see any reason to mention it. I don't know enough about you to give out my personal information."

Clearly nonplussed, he nonetheless tried again. "I can't let you stay someplace where you won't be safe," he said, baring his teeth.

A crowd of onlookers gathered, curiosity fired by their interchange.

Aimee's tolerance dropped to zero. Enunciating clearly and audibly for everyone's benefit, she let him have it. "Mr. Spencer. I'm tired and nauseated, and you're adding to the *nausea* part. So freakin' buzz off—*now*."

His face flushed, and he grabbed her arm, forcing her to face him. "You'd do well to stay on good terms with me," he hissed.

"You'd do well to get lost," she hissed back, jerking her arm free.

Facing the growing crowd, she became the frightened virgin. "Will anyone come to my aid?" she pleaded, using her best southern accent. Throwing a forearm across her face, she pretended to swoon. "This person is threatening my very being. Why, I'm almost faint with fear." *Scarlett O'Hara would be so proud.*

A burly seaman stepped from the crowd. "This man bother'n you, ma'am?"

Dropping her arm, she slanted a quick peek at her would-be savior. He certainly looked like he could do some major damage.

Dropping her arm, batting her eyelashes, she drawled. "Why, yes, kind sir, he is."

Roland's eyes narrowed. "Do you know who I am?"

Shrugging, the big sailor scowled. "You're the

fella what's bother'n this here little lady."

"If you want to work in this town again," Roland snapped, "walk away."

Grinning, the big sailor raised ham-sized fists. "I don't work in this town, never have, never will. Leave the lady alone."

The crowd cheered him on, shouting words of encouragement. It was patently obvious neither Roland nor his family were popular hereabouts. Aimee banked on that supposition.

"I think you'd better leave," she said, waving at the crowd. "We've had enough of you."

Undermined by the crowd's support of the sailor, Roland snarled, spewing venom at the unfortunate bystanders while stalking away. She grinned, full of good cheer. From her vantage point, he moved like he had a big stick up his butt.

The onlookers roared their approval, laughing and clapping each other on the shoulders as though they themselves had stepped forward.

The burly seaman grinned, showing gaps in his yellowed teeth. "He won't be bother'n ya anymores, Missy."

Patting his huge arm, she breathed a sigh of relief. "At least not today."

"If he bothers ya again, you just come git Davie."

Another man sang out, "Everyone to Mae's. Drinks are on me."

Boisterously, the crowd surged away, uplifted by the promise of free whiskey and the spectacle of a member of the Spencer family getting his comeuppance.

Davie bobbed his head. "Ya wants to come with us?" He asked, full of hope.

"I'd love to," she replied as gracious as she could. "But I need to rest. It's been a very long day."

Davie nodded, disappointed. "Well, if ya change your mind, come on down."

"I certainly will."

Lumbering away, the huge seaman joined the crowd of revelers, disappearing into their midst.

Standing alone, she viewed her new surroundings with trepidation. If the boardinghouse was full, what other options would she have? And how long before she had to endure Roland again? She grimaced. Might just have to bone up on her karate skills.

After several stops along the way asking for directions, Aimee made it to the boardinghouse. Displayed prominently over the door, O'Malley's was a poignant reminder of the one in St. Louis where she'd spent those first days with Jake. This one, though more rustic in appearance, was, by contrast, freshly painted.

A short buxom woman scurried to the desk in answer to Aimee's hesitant call.

"I was told you might have a room available."

The woman nodded.

"Can you tell me how much?"

The woman nodded again.

Aimee waited several minutes for her response. "Well, how much?"

The woman blinked, as if startled. "You mean for yourself?"

Looking behind her, Aimee lifted her shoulders. "Is anyone with me?"

The woman peered behind her. "Don't see anyone."

"Then I must be alone." *Duh!*

The woman's eyes narrowed. "I don't allow floozies in my place."

Here we go again! "I'm not a floozy. I'm a married woman. Aimee Marshall. *Mrs.* Jake Marshall." Funny how that sounded so comforting.

"How long you planning to stay?"

"I'm not certain yet. At least for a few days. Can

you accommodate a stay that long?"

The woman nodded. "Dollar a day, bed and breakfast included. Extra fifty cents a day for midday meal and supper. You want bath water, there's a washroom out back. You're welcome to use it, but let me know in advance so I can keep the male boarders out." She glanced at Aimee. "Lessen you don't care?"

"Well, of course I care." *Sheesh!* The woman was seriously aggravating.

"Name's Maudie," the short tormentor mumbled, handing Aimee a feather quill to sign the register. After several misstarts and blobbed ink, Aimee succeeded.

"Your room's the first on the left at the top of the stairs. Yell if you need anything."

Having said her piece, Maudie bustled back to wherever she'd come from, her mind on other matters besides a new boarder.

Exhausted and in need of sleep, Aimee struggled up the stairs, dragging the heavy valise behind her. She hadn't realized what a blessing wheeled luggage was.

The room was small. A single cot and a wavy mirror above a small washstand were the only pieces of furniture. Some attempt had been made to make the room appear more cheerful; a bright patterned wedding ring quilt covered the small cot, and a large rag rug covered most of the wood floor. Everything was spotless and neat. Several hooks on the wall offered the only means of storing clothing, but knowing her funds were limited, she didn't plan on unpacking as yet. Tomorrow, she would ask around and see if she could drum up some sort of job, maybe even find someplace to sell the last of her treasured pieces of jewelry.

Dragging herself to bed, stomach growling, she threw herself down, reluctant to part with more of her hoard of coins for something to eat. Lying in the cold uncomfortable cot, missing Jake's warmth, tears spilled down her cheeks. *What possessed her to leave him and travel here alone, and why did she think Vancouver was going to change anything*?

Her hand wrapped around the locket. Somehow it was the focal point of everything. She just needed to figure out how to solve the puzzle. Focusing her mind, she wished with everything she had to go home, visualizing her parents and Sara, imagining herself surrounded by their company. But, no matter how hard she tried, Jake's image kept stepping into her fantasy and ruining her concentration. Dejected and alone, she wept for all the losses she'd endured—those that came unbidden and those she'd unwittingly caused.

Chapter Twenty-Nine

Maudie thumped a bowl of gravy on the table, along with homemade sourdough biscuits and slabs of bacon. Large mugs of coffee followed, and milk was offered as an alternative. Aimee opted for the milk, knowing the little person she carried needed the vitamins and calcium. Several other boarders shared the table with her, two single men and a married couple. None of them offered conversation, their interest solely on the food before them, which they consumed with amazing speed. She'd just taken a few bites when they finished and left the table, leaving her to eat alone. The food was good, nothing fancy, but wholesome and tasty. She'd just finished her third biscuit when Maudie came back in and began clearing up.

Aimee cleared her throat. "I don't suppose you know anyone who might need to hire extra help, do you?"

Maudie stopped and glared at her. "You saying you can't pay?"

"No, nothing like that," she stammered. "I have money, but if I'm to remain here, I'll need to find work."

"I thought you were married." Maudie frowned, her disapproval obvious.

"I was, er, I am." The lie came easier each time. "My husband is joining me in the spring, and he'll be sending money from time to time, but until he does, I need to find work."

"I can't afford any help," Maudie huffed, her eyes flashing.

"No, I didn't mean here. I meant like one of the stores or the church or maybe the school. I do have some education. I could teach perhaps."

Her face skewed in concentration, Maudie suggested, "You might try Reverend James over at the church. He'd know if anyone's looking for help. Best I can tell you." She scurried off, back to her hidey hole.

Brushing crumbs from her skirt, she longed for a cup of coffee, but decided coffee was something she'd better learn to live without until the baby came. Not that coffee was a bad thing, but without a modern obstetrician, she'd better watch what she ate and drank, and coffee was a stimulant, ergo, not good for the baby. She pressed her hands against her still flat stomach, imagining how she'd look by Christmas and wondering what was in store for her until spring. Her prospects didn't look good and unless she found work, they could get even worse.

Pushing away from the table, she stood up, determination giving her impetus. Sitting here moping wasn't doing any good.

Several shops and numerous disappointments later, she felt the first twinges of frustration. *She'd never had trouble finding a job before.* Word about the incident involving Roland had traveled fast and most of the shops she visited were either owned by the Spencers or the Spencers did enough business in them to preclude hiring her. One shopkeeper even had the temerity to actually run her out of the store, making it very clear that Roland Spencer had issued a specific warning where she was concerned—that she wasn't welcome. *Damn Roland Spencer!* What stupid trick of fate had placed her on the same boat with that lowlife scumbag?

The other possible options along the main thoroughfare were several taverns and saloons, and unless her circumstances dictated otherwise, she wouldn't choose to work in any of them. Not that they'd hire a pregnant woman in any event.

Maudie had mentioned visiting Reverend James, and it looked like that was her next best choice. If luck was with her, the church wasn't a Spencer holding. Sighing in resignation, she marched on. The church stood on a small hill overlooking Main Street, solid and respectable. Small posies still bloomed along the white picket fence surrounding the church, but autumn was taking its toll on the gardens. She was puffing by the time she rapped at the door to the living quarters. The door swung open posthaste, and the Reverend and his wife stood before her.

Reverend James was an amiable, if somewhat absentminded, white-haired old gentleman who greeted her, his smile open and warm. His wife, white-haired as well and sporting wire-framed spectacles, was even more affable, offering tea and cakes, while quizzing Aimee about who she was, why she was here, and where her husband was. She gave them the same story, adding into the scenario her encounter the day before with Roland Spencer. Horrified, their eyes rounded with concern, they warned her about the hazards of being crosswise with the Spencers and their ilk, and offering what limited information they could on job opportunities. She stood up and thanked them for their kindness.

As she turned to go, Reverend James raised a hand. "I believe the school is looking for a new schoolmistress. I don't know much about what they expect, but I can make an inquiry for you."

Aimee brightened. "I'm well educated and working with children was a huge part of that education. I taught several of the children along the trail from St. Louis, and I think I'd make a passably good teacher."

"What level have you reached?" Reverend James

asked.

"College. I'd have graduated in two more years."

"You've been to college?" Reverend James asked in disbelief.

"Er," she thought frantically, chewing her lip. "Finishing school, I meant finishing school. It's in the east. Connecticut." *Another lame story.* She needed to sit down and write it all out so could tell the same story twice.

Reverend James nodded his approval. "I see."

"Is the school owned by the Spencers?"

Mrs. James interjected, a sweet smile on her lips. "Good heavens, no. The school's under the church's direction. Reverend James sits on the board."

Reverend James beamed at his wife. "Well said." He paused. "I believe the position is only for the primer level, but I could be wrong. Would you like me to check into it for you?"

Would she! "Anything you can do would be *very* appreciated."

Reverend James took her hand, patting it. "I'll check first thing tomorrow. Where can I reach you after I've talked to them?"

"I'm staying at O'Malley's for the present." She smiled, grateful for their kindness and stepped into the sunshine. *Things were looking up!*

Chapter Thirty

Not wanting to let any opportunities pass by, Aimee continued her search for employment. One shopkeeper offered her a few hours each day as the cashier, but the pay was pathetic and the shopkeeper spent too much time ogling her body parts through lust-filled eyes, his face flushed beet red as though in the throws of an orgasm. Sickened by his flagrant sexual hunger, she stalked out, vowing never to step foot in the place again. *Jake, why did I ever leave you?* Agate blue eyes and a flashing smile haunted her every step.

Late in the afternoon on the following day, Reverend and Mrs. James came calling.

Reverend James cleared his throat. "The news is good. Barnard Olson, the schoolmaster, has agreed to an interview. Would you be available tomorrow at ten a.m.?"

"Would I? Of course!" Ecstatic, she hugged the old couple, thrilled by the news. Maudie, ungracious and sour, served tea, shuffling back and forth from the kitchen area. After the old couple departed, Maudie hung around, sneaking glances at Aimee while she cleaned. Finally, she thumped a kettle down on the table.

"I don't have any book learning," she burst out.

Aimee waited, giving her the chance to elaborate.

Maudie continued. "My pa said book learning was a waste of time. Women don't need any."

"Your pa was wrong." How glad she was she grew up in a time where women were granted the same privileges as the men.

"My pa was a good man," Maudie said defensively. "He worked hard up until the day he died."

"I'm sure he was a good man. I didn't say he wasn't."

Mollified, Maudie relaxed. "I always wanted to read, but never had the chance to learn."

"Are you asking if I'd teach you?" Amazing as it seemed, that was what she was getting from this strange conversation.

Maudie's face betrayed her uncertainty. "I can pay, maybe take some off your rent and throw in supper besides."

This sounded good. "How much?"

She thought for a moment. "How about seventy-five cents a day, including breakfast and supper?"

Aimee pretended to mull over the offer. "Make it sixty-five cents and supper, but I want Sunday off. Agreed?"

Maudie frowned, visibly working out the numbers. Finally, she nodded. "Can we start now?"

Chapter Thirty-One

Early the next morning, Aimee dressed with care in a plain black wool skirt and white tailored blouse, gritting her teeth as Maudie grudgingly laced her into the hated corset, muttering under her breath about uppity Eastern women. Aimee's attempts to fasten her unruly mop of curling hair into a severe, old lady teacher-type bun met with limited success. Errant strands kept coming loose and falling into ringlets about her face. Frustrated, she gave up, opting for femininity over straight-laced prude. As a finishing touch, she draped the locket about her neck, cupping it and performing a routine moment of intense wishful concentration. Nothing happened—*again*. Studying herself in the cloudy mirror, she was pleased with the result.

The interview went far better than expected. After quizzing her about math, reading, history, and English language, Schoolmaster Olson informed her she could begin her new teaching position next week. He touched lightly on the anticipated curriculum, pointing out that she'd be expected to teach the younger girls manners and deportment. *Manners and deportment!* She almost laughed in his face, but managed to contain her incredulity under a guise of cheerful interest.

"What level of deportment must the girls attain?" she asked in her best schoolteacher voice.

"We're not as strict here as the East, but we expect the girls to have a modicum of drawing room etiquette."

She nodded her understanding, smiling like one

of those stupid yellow happy faces, blank and idiotic. "And I'm sure you have the necessary teaching materials?"

His eyebrows drew together in confusion. "Every schoolmistress knows the basics of manners and deportment. That's all I expect, just the basics."

Nodding again in feigned agreement, she hoped she exuded an aura of competence and knowledge.

"I'll certainly see they have the basics." *Pray God, Mrs. James could help with this one.*

"You're starting wage has been approved by the Board and is well within the range for starting schoolmistresses."

"And that is?"

"Fifteen dollars a month and found."

Fifteen dollars! How could she live on fifteen dollars? And what the heck was found?

Her expression mirrored her confusion.

Schoolmaster Olson smiled. "Fifteen dollars plus your room and board. Mrs. James indicated you're staying at O'Malley's. Just let Maudie know I'll be paying your lodging, unless you prefer to stay elsewhere."

Heaving a sigh of relief, she relaxed. "No. Please. I'm totally content at O'Malley's. Thank you!"

"I do have one question for you. Reverend James indicates your husband will be joining you in the spring. Do you intend to stay in the area? We like to think our teachers will stay on for some time."

"My husband is a man of varied interests," she began, concocting the next phase of her lie. "But I'm sure we'll be here for at least a few years." *She was getting really good at improvising.*

Pleased, Schoolmaster Olson stood up, extending his hand. "Welcome to Vancouver." He literally beamed. "We look forward to good things from you."

Elated, she headed back to the boarding house, almost dancing in her excitement. Exuberant and happy, she drew the attention of more than one passing male. Her mind ran wild, planning and scheming for the future. So intent on telling Maudie the good news, she failed to notice the blocked pathway and ran headlong into Roland. He stiffened, shoving her back.

"Watch where you're going," he snarled, gray eyes pools of smoldering malice.

"*Eat shit!*" Aimee snarled back, smoothing her now rumpled blouse, glaring at him.

Roland's face flushed, adding to his unattractiveness, thick lips tightening in fury.

"I could make things very uncomfortable for you here," he growled, his voice laced with venom.

"I'm sure you could try. It's what I would expect from a lowlife scumbag like you," she spat over her shoulder, hurrying on. Geez, the guy was seriously disturbed.

Maudie's eyes lit with pleasure, lips almost smiling as she joyfully relayed the morning's events.

"Since the school board is paying for my lodging," Aimee began, "we won't tell them about our arrangement."

Maudie's face fell, disappointment dripping from every pore. "Does that mean you won't teach me to read?" She muttered, looking at the floor.

"No. No." She hastened to assure her. "That's not what I was trying to say. This way, you can still get the dollar per day for room and breakfast. But in exchange for teaching you to read, will you be willing to provide lunch *and* supper?"

Like rays of sunshine breaking through storm clouds, Maudie's face brightened. "It's a deal," she exclaimed, pumping Aimee's hand with gusto. "When do we start?"

Life took on a comfortable if unexciting routine.

During the day, she taught school to a rambunctious classroom of six through eleven-year-old girls. Evenings were spent working with Maudie, whom she discovered was an apt pupil, learning the alphabet in a few short lessons and already recognizing small words. Her nights were spent in lonely solitude, heart aching for Jake and her family, wondering if she'd ever see any of them again. Her fevered dreams were always of Jake, waking up at night, drenched in sweat, breasts tingling in response. As the baby grew and hormones raged out of control, her nighttime imaginings only intensified. She ached for Jake's caresses.

When she had some time to herself, Aimee explored Vancouver, taking in the sights amid long walks. Walking was, after all, good for her condition, or so she'd heard.

Strolling along the street, Aimee nodded and smiled at now familiar faces—faces that had begun to accept her. Reverend James sat outside a small dry goods store reading a well-worn newspaper. Newspapers that were months old, brought in by the visiting ships, were snatched up almost immediately and read with enthusiasm. The populace thirsted for information about life in the East, and the homes and family left behind. Every battered well-used paper had something new to impart.

Reverend James carefully folded the newspaper and secured it under his arm. He harrumphed, clearing his throat. "It's good to see you, my dear." His spectacles slipped down his nose, balancing on the tip. "Cold today. Going to get colder. How are things at school? The children misbehaving?"

"No. No. Everything's fine. I have a fine group of girls, and they're progressing well." She hoped she sounded convincing.

"I've heard good things," he nodded. "We seemed to have chosen well."

"We did indeed." Mrs. James stepped out of the shop, laden with packages. "I've chosen the perfect material for the new curtains. It's the most wonderful blue."

Reverend James' brows drew together. "I was saying to Mrs. Marshall that the school board is pleased with their decision to hire her."

Mrs. James giggled, a high-pitched girlish sound. "Silly me. I thought you were remarking on my purchases." Her head tilted, her eyes sparkled with curiosity. "Where is that young man?"

"What man?"

Mrs. James looked perplexed. "Why—your husband, of course."

Aimee almost groaned at her own stupidity. "Oh. Yeah. Him." She coughed, covering her face, thinking fast. "Excuse me. My mind was elsewhere." She hated lying to this sweet old couple. "I received a post just recently, in fact. He's been delayed—again. I had hoped to see him before now, but it isn't to be. I miss him, of course, but his business comes first."

Reverend James nodded. "We men must do what we must do to provide."

Mrs. James hugged his arm. "You do indeed." Mrs. James clasped Aimee's hand. "You must come to dinner soon. Company helps ease loneliness."

Aimee breathed a sigh of relief. They'd accepted her excuse. "I will. I promise." She looked at the sky. "Goodness. It's getting late, and I still need to prepare tomorrow's lessons."

"We won't hold you then." Reverend James pushed his spectacles up. "Will we, my dear?"

Mrs. James laughed. "Most certainly not. The children must be taught. Come to dinner soon—and bring that young man with you." She pulled on the Reverend's arm, dragging him behind her.

Aimee's heart constricted. She wished it were possible. *Jake*, she whispered, *I miss you so much.*

Chapter Thirty-Two

Cold winds blew down the Columbia Gorge as winter settled on the Pacific Northwest. Rain and sleet turned to snow, blanketing the countryside in a thin layer of white. Aimee's first wages were spent buying warmer clothing and a heavy sheepskin coat, and with some of the remaining money, she bought soft lawn material to sew baby clothes during the long winter evenings. Her stomach had started to bulge, but it would be some months before she showed too much. She guesstimated she was three and a half months into her pregnancy, the nausea had finally ceased and her energy level was up. How she wished she had Mom's shoulder to lean on.

After some subtle prodding, Maudie informed her there was a practicing doctor in town, but Aimee was reluctant to approach him. God only knew what kind of backward medicine he practiced and how trustworthy could he be? She needed her job, and she really didn't know how her pregnancy would be viewed by the good people of Vancouver. She'd seen pregnant women from time to time, but never unchaperoned and for only short periods of time.

One evening, after Aimee finished Maudie's lesson and they were having a cup of tea, the older woman stared across the table at her.

"I happened across some material in your room while dusting today."

Aimee took a sip of tea, stalling.

"When's the baby due?"

Rendered speechless, Aimee froze.

"You know," Maudie prompted, "the one you

think I don't know about."

Crumbling, Aimee stroked her stomach. "Late May or early June, I can't be sure."

"Do you for sure have a husband?" Maudie gazed at her, watching her reaction.

"Of course I do," Aimee exclaimed, insulted. "His name's Jake, and we were married last April, just before we headed west."

"Why isn't he here with you? And don't lie this time. I know what you told me, but what's the real reason?"

She sighed in resignation. She wouldn't be able to keep the secret much longer anyway. "If anyone finds out, I'll lose my job and then we'd both lose. Do you understand?

Maudie nodded. "I won't say nuthin."

"Anything. Double negative," Aimee corrected.

"Anything." For reasons unknown to her, she believed this gruff little woman. Lying was a hard thing for her to do, and finally, there was someone she could be honest with.

"I guess because I wanted to find my family, and he had other dreams. That's about the gist of it."

"I can't believe any man'd just let you go. I see'd the way men look at you."

"Seen," Aimee corrected. "I didn't give him a chance to stop me," she admitted, ashamed. "I just up and left him. I don't even know for sure where he is. Last I knew he was in Oregon City."

"Does he know about the baby?"

"No," she whispered. Her heart ached at the admission.

"Don't you think it's about time you told him? Some men like the idea of having a son."

"It could be a girl." She scowled. "Girls do get born once in awhile."

"Maybe you should write him a letter. Don't take that long for a letter to reach Oregon City."

"Doesn't. Don't is the incorrect usage."

Maudie scowled, slamming her mug on the table. "Would you quit teachin' and just talk for a change?"

Startled by her vehemence, Aimee set her cup down as well. "I'm sorry. I'm so used to correcting the children, I just don't realize I'm doing it."

"Well, I ain't one of your children."

Her mouth opened and then snapped shut, warned by Maudie's granite look. "I won't do it again, unless we're working."

"So when you going to write him a letter?'

When would she indeed? She'd been thinking about it a lot, but couldn't find the right words to begin.

Maudie bustled out of the kitchen, returning with paper, quill pen, and inkwell, slapping them down.

"No time like the present!"

"I don't know what to say." She felt like crying. "I usually say the wrong things where he's concerned, and it just makes things worse."

"Tell him about the baby," Maudie prompted, wriggling the pen. "He's got a right to know."

She reached for the paper, smoothing it as she wracked her beleaguered brain. How did one write to a guy she dumped without so much as a simple goodbye? Would he read the letter if he even received it? And if he did, would it matter to him?

Maudie rapped on the table. "Write something!"

"I'm thinking," Aimee snapped. "Give me a minute!"

Taking up the pen, she daubed it in the inkwell and then began scratching.

Dear Jake, She dropped the pen. What to say next?

"You need to write more'n that," Maudie grumbled, cranky. "I can't read, but I know it's not enough."

"For Pete's sake. I can't think with you yapping at me."

Exasperated, lips pursed with annoyance, Maudie huffed in disgust as she stomped to the stove and yanked the oven door down, scowling all the while.

"You shoulda never left him to begin with."

"I know that." She drew in a deep breath and then exhaled. "Don't think I don't."

Stomach knotting in anxiety, hands cramping, she picked up the pen, trying to focus her wayward thoughts. The words were long in coming, but as she wrote, her fingers began to fly across the page, setting down a heartfelt apology for leaving and begging his forgiveness and, as a final note, telling him about the baby. She longed to tell him how much she ached for him, more so every day, and that her restless dreaming was only of him, but she refrained from adding those details, stating simply that she missed him. The letter left so many things unsaid but, with a flourish, she signed her name.

"Now you gonna send that thing?" Maudie asked, her brows arched.

Aimee groaned. "Yes, I'll send the damn thing—tomorrow."

Maudie smiled her approval. "Takes some time to get there, but you might have an answer by Thanksgiving."

"Or not," Aimee replied. Her own reaction in the same circumstances wouldn't be pretty. "He might just tear it up and stomp on it. I would."

Maudie finished buttering the light brown loaves of fresh baked bread and then wrapped them in clean flour sacks.

"He doesn't sound like the type to do that sort of thing."

"Probably not," she agreed, albeit reluctantly.

"He's a nicer person than I am."

Snorting, Maudie chuckled. "Good thing, too. You're an ornery little cuss."

Propping her chin on her hands, she watched as the industrious Maudie scrubbed the kitchen, doing more with limited effort than she could have done with twice the time and energy.

"Why aren't you married?" Aimee asked. "You would make someone a wonderful wife."

"Was married once," was Maudie's gruff reply. "He died along with my two boys. Smallpox."

Oh my God! Get the foot out of my mouth and shut me up!

"I am so sorry!" She could feel her face heating up. "I didn't know."

"How could you?" Maudie wiped a quick hand across her face, but not before Aimee spotted a tear sliding down her weathered cheek. "It was more'n ten years ago." She paused, as if gathering her thoughts. "They were all I had."

Aimee rounded the table, hugging Maudie, full of remorse, mentally bashing herself for causing her newfound friend pain.

"I don't know when to shut up," she whispered her apology. "Forgive me."

"Nothing to forgive." Maudie blew her nose, snuffling into her handkerchief. "Thinking about your little un's got me remembering."

"Maybe you can teach me how to be a mother." Aimee threw out the suggestion. "I don't have anyone else to look to."

Smiling shyly, Maudie nodded, pleased. "I was a good ma, but God saw fit to take them."

Aimee's heart ached anew. Smallpox was almost eradicated in her world. Not that people didn't die from other diseases, but smallpox wasn't on the list of the ten most dangerous maladies.

"You're not too old to have more children some

day."

Maudie choked, face flushing in embarrassment. "Turn thirty-four near Christmastime. Too old to think about having more babies!"

Shocked, Aimee remained silent, praying her face didn't betray her thoughts. She'd assumed Maudie was so much older. "Where I come from, older women have babies all the time." *Lord, give me brains!*

"I'd like another baby," Maudie replied, looking wistful. "But who's gonna marry an old workhorse like me. I don't have time for courting."

"We'll just have to see about that." Her mind was already working. "My friends don't call me a matchmaker for nothing."

"Anything," Maudie echoed.

"Nothing," Aimee corrected. "Nothing is perfectly fine in this instance."

"Go to bed," Maudie grumbled. "You're making my head hurt."

****

Jake leaned on the ship's rail, gazing out over the vast expanse of the Pacific. His thoughts were troubled, and for the first time in his life, he was at a loss as to who or what he was. He'd never questioned himself or his plans before, but nothing seemed to fit now. *That's what Aimee's leaving did to him.*

The cabin door opened and John McAfee stepped out. Jake acknowledged him with a curt nod.

"How're the girls?"

John leaned over the rail, spitting a stream of tobacco, wiping his mouth with the back of his hand. "Sleeping. Took me some time to get 'em settled. That little one don't want to stay down for more'n five minutes."

Jake's lips twisted. "No—she doesn't. But there's a whole lot of new stuff to see and I can't say as I blame her."

A pod of whales surfaced, their blowholes shooting arcs of water. Fascinated, he watched them play, rolling and diving, only to resurface and call to each other. He'd heard the sailors talking about the singing of the whales, but this was the first he'd ever heard them. It was an eerie sound, like a lost soul calling for deliverance.

A big wave rocked the packet ship, and he tightened his grip. He wasn't meant for the sea. He was a landlubber, and so much water made him ill at ease.

"How much longer till we get there." John made a face. "I don't like it out here. Don't seem natural."

"I know the feeling." Jake turned, leaning against the railing. He eyed his friend. "Why'd you come with us?"

"Nothing to keep me in Oregon. Oregon was Ardis's dream mostly. I sorta went along to make her happy. Losing her and Rose took the heart out of me. Just couldn't face staying there no more."

"Well, me and the girls'd be lost without you." Jake slapped John on the shoulder. "Maybe we'll find a new start for all of us in California."

"If'n we don't drown on the way," John grumbled. "Seems like we could've just took the wagon down there."

"Would've taken too long, and I've got some ideas once we land."

John shivered in the chill, his weathered face grumpy. "What're we gonna do for a stake when we get where we're going?"

Jake fingered the small pouch he kept in his pocket. *His payment for her passage west.* "I've got some stuff to sell when we get there. I expect we'll be fine for awhile."

John grumbled. "Don't look to me. I sold purt' near everything I had to come with you."

"I told you—we'll be fine. I still have some left

from the money I made scouting. We won't live fancy, but we'll be fine."

"You okay?" John muttered. "Seems like you don't talk much anymore."

Some day he would. If his heart ever quit aching. Betrayal was a hard lump to swallow. He grimaced, cussing himself. Even now, given the chance, he'd take her back and be glad of it. He stared into the distance. *Where is she?*

Chapter Thirty-Three

Thanksgiving passed uneventfully. Maudie spent several days preparing a lavish feast, but in the end, only Aimee and a few boarders shared the sumptuous meal. It was a sad and lonely event for her. In the past, Thanksgiving had always been a boisterous event at the Reynolds's household, relatives swarmed in large numbers, loaded with home-baked goods and the latest family gossip. Maudie had outdone herself, but Aimee didn't feel much like thanking anyone for anything. On top of that, still nothing from Jake.

Word came from Vancouver's upper society that the older Spencer had passed away and rumors were rife with speculation as to who would inherit. Roland was the prime candidate, since he was the only surviving heir, but there were those who inferred that Roland and his father hadn't been on the best of terms. Imagining Roland in complete control caused Aimee no small amount of anxiety.

"That'll make it bad for everyone," Maudie said. "That Roland's a bad 'un."

"You aren't telling me anything I didn't already know."

"I heard once," Maudie rushed on as though Aimee hadn't spoken, "that he near beat a whore to death down at Lena's place. I don't cotton to whores, but they don't deserve to die that-a-way. Ain't the first time I heard that neither."

Just what she needed to know! "Has he ever been accused of attacking a *respectable* woman?"

"Not that I know of, but I wouldn't put anything

past him." Maudie's lips thinned in anger as she gazed at Aimee. "You just watch your back."

****

November gave way to December, and by now, the pregnancy was showing. Maudie lent her several aprons, reminiscent of a little girl's pinafore, which did a satisfactory job of disguising her growing figure. Notwithstanding the added pounds, Aimee bloomed with health, skin clear and glowing, and eyes bright and sparkling. Without the guidance of a modern obstetrician, she haunted the marketplace, buying a variety of fresh vegetables, fruits, and nutmeats she guessed the baby's system would need for healthy growth. Maudie's eyes twinkled in amusement each time she came back laden with foodstuffs, laughing as she stored them for future use. Milk was a staple of her diet. She forced herself to drink at least two glasses with every meal, whether she wanted to or not.

As the winter season advanced, gusting winds from the river gorge whistled around the boardinghouse and only the heat from the cast iron oven kept the cold drafts at bay. The barren little room on the upper floor, devoid of warmth or companionship, held little interest for Aimee. Most nights, she retreated to the cozy little kitchen, sitting at the freshly scrubbed table, sewing, reading aloud or listening as Maudie practiced the alphabet.

The woman studied hard and was soon reading at the first grade level, sounding out words and whooping with delight as she figured out each new one. From the gruff little woman of Aimee's first encounter, Maudie had blossomed into a staunch friend and confidant.

Though not her first career choice, teaching was a satisfying and uplifting experience. The children as a whole were well-mannered and eager to learn. The problematic area of manners and deportment was easily taken care of. A quick trip to the church, several subtle hints later, and Mrs. James, the Reverend's wife, fell into Aimee's clever scheme, delighted by the opportunity to be a "substitute teacher." Stopping by on Tuesday and Thursday afternoons for several hours, Mrs. James instructed the young ladies on the finer points of pouring tea, delicately dabbing lips with fine lawn napkins, performing well-executed curtsies, and the art of using a fan, everything a Victorian lady should know. Aimee gave Mrs. James full rein and studied right along with the girls. You never knew when a flirtatious fan just might come in handy.

The life she was now forced to lead might be considered mundane by modern standards, but she found some measure of contentment in her routine activities. The only hazard appeared to be Roland, and sidestepping Roland and his cronies wasn't always successful, but she kept her eyes open and watchful, moving across the street if she spied him in the distance and keeping to the shadows if she chanced to be alone. As always, the locket was her constant companion, brief moments of every day spent in concentrated wishful thinking.

In the weeks before Christmas, Maudie convinced her to write another letter to Jake. She filled it with details of her life in Vancouver, the teaching position, Maudie, and the growing baby. Filled with hope, she posted the letter and began the long process of waiting.

Chapter Thirty-Four

Even in this backwoods part of the world, Christmas was a time of rejoicing. Maudie found a small spindly tree and the two of them spent several hours decorating with strings of pretty yarn, popcorn, and numerous handmade decorations she'd squirreled away. When the decorating was complete, the little tree glowed with holiday spirit. Aimee pretended to herself the tree belonged to her and Jake, and he would be there Christmas morning. It was a silly daydream, but one that gave her comfort.

Reverend James and his wife, glowing with good cheer, delivered an invitation for Christmas dinner. After services on Christmas morning, the church was sponsoring a potluck social, followed by dancing, and the whole community was invited.

Chuckling with glee, Maudie jumped into food preparation, deciding on a roast leg of lamb with all the trimmings. Mouth-watering aromas wafted through the boardinghouse, adding spice to the Yuletide preparations. Fresh baked pies, breads, and several varieties of cookies soon lined the kitchen shelves.

Aimee's own holiday preparations included using some of her hard-earned coins to purchase a delicate, lace-edged blue-flowered blouse for Maudie, out of character for the plain Jane little woman, but perfect.

Word hit the settlement of a massacre at the Whitman Mission. Stunned, the populace waited in trepidation for more Indian attacks, grieving for the murdered missionaries. Troops were mustered and sent out to hunt down the perpetrators and subdue the tribes. She prayed for the Indians, knowing it was all a mistake and the Indians would be the ones to suffer for a long time.

Christmas day 1847 dawned crisp, clear, and cold. Breakfast was a casual affair, with only Aimee and Maudie in residence at the boardinghouse. The rest of the boarders had either gone home for the holidays or moved on. Nervous about her choice of a gift, she presented Maudie with the carefully wrapped package, holding her breath as Maudie, choked with emotion, untied the ribbon.

"No one's gave me a present since my Zeke died." Tears glistened in her faded blue eyes.

"Well, open it! Sheesh, I'd have had it torn open long before now."

Maudie folded back the tissue paper and lifted the blouse out, gasping in admiration. "Why! It's too pretty for the likes of me."

"No, it isn't," Aimee grinned, hugging her. "You're going to look just beautiful."

Maudie snorted in derision, clasping the top to her bosom, rubbing the soft material against her cheek. "I had a pretty shirt once a long time ago. Wore it when Zeke and me got hitched."

"Go put it on." Aimee pushed her towards the bedroom. "You can wear it to the social today. I'm betting there'll be plenty of beaus just waiting to pull you onto the dance floor."

Face pinking, Maudie clucked in embarrassed humor. "Now that'll be something."

Reaching behind the tree, she pulled out a package wrapped in a colorful length of cloth. "This is for you," she murmured, face red and voice gruff. "Not so nice as what you gave me, but I worked hard on them."

Thrilled to receive any sort of present this year, Aimee held the package for several seconds, feeling all warm and fuzzy inside.

"Open the dad-blamed thing!"

Aimee frowned in mock anger. "I'm savoring the moment."

"You're what?"

Laughing, she clarified. "Savoring the moment. It means I'm taking time to enjoy my feelings."

"Well, enjoy them some other time. Open the dratted thing or I'm taking it back."

"You will not." Aimee hugged the package to her chest, protecting it. "You gave it to me and it's mine!"

Taking her time, untying each ribbon with careful fingers, she opened the package. Inside were at least a dozen soft flannel baby gowns. Maudie had even taken the time to crochet around the necklines and sleeves. Several tiny bonnets were also inside. The wrapping itself was a quilted baby blanket. Tears sprang into Aimee's eyes as she examined each little piece, ooohing and ahhhing in amazement as she lifted them.

"When did you find the time to make all these?"

Maudie dipped her head. "I don't sleep much anymore. I worked on them every night 'til I got 'em done." She rubbed a little sleeve between her fingers. "I forgot how soft a baby feels," she added, eyes glinting with sadness.

Aimee wrapped her arms around the older woman, planting a kiss on her cheek. "Well, they're just beautiful, and I love every one of them. Now! Go get ready! We've got a party to go to!"

Urging Maudie to hurry up and change, she rushed upstairs, grabbed her heavy coat, and since it was a special occasion, she swiped on a layer of lip gloss. She studied the small plastic tube ruefully. *A couple more times and it'd be totally gone.* Then what would she do? Rub goose grease on her lips? Yuck!

As they entered the church, Aimee's stomach

plummeted, heart aching with sorrow. This would be the first Christmas without family to share all the joy and excitement so a part of the season. She scanned the room with misgiving. Maybe she'd made a big mistake coming here. She felt out of place. A stranger. Observing her melancholy expression, Maudie waved her forward, her expression urging Aimee to smile. Inhaling a deep, cleansing breath, she forced herself to relax, pasting a smile on her face.

Reverend James and his wife had decked the church hall with boughs of holly, a huge pine tree, little decorative angels, and a beautifully stirring nativity scene. Mrs. James took their coats, eyeing the apron she wore beneath.

Aimee hastened to explain. "Since my husband's not here, I won't be dancing and someone needs to watch the food table."

Mrs. James's face brightened. "Yes," she agreed, her relief obvious. "That's the proper and neighborly thing to do!" She glanced coyly at Reverend James. "Since I won't be at the table all the time, maybe we can take a swing around the dance floor."

Reverend James coughed, glasses sliding precariously down his large nose. "Why, er, yes, my dear." He stammered. "That's exactly what we'll do." Pushing his glasses back into place, he beamed at his wife.

Mrs. James leaned over, eyes twinkling as she whispered. "He's not fond of dancing, you know, but once in awhile, I can force him onto the dance floor."

Several other couples entered the church, allowing a cold draft of air to blast through the open door. Shivering in the icy breeze, Aimee and Maudie took the moment to slip away from the drafty hallway and find a seat, while Reverend and Mrs. James made their welcomes to the newcomers. The meeting room was full by the time they entered, but the good-natured parishioners slid closer together, allowing those still standing to take a seat. Aimee ended up between Maudie and a huge lumberjack smelling of pine and the great outdoors.

Reverend James took the stand and began speaking. His words resounded with the love of family and friends, praying for the Whitmans, caring for each other, and remembering that God forgives all. Lastly, he wished them all good tidings and great joy, and ended the service by leading them in several Christmas carols. Aimee's lumberjack podmate sang with great gusto in a clear baritone, drowning out the off-pitch and tone-deaf would-be vocalists surrounding them on every side.

After the service, the parishioners pushed the benches out of the way and carried in makeshift tables which were soon covered with food of every kind and nature. A small troupe of musicians warmed up in the corner, while the partygoers formed a line to the tables, now groaning under the weight of hundreds of tempting delicacies. Aimee'd just settled down to eat when a hush fell over the gathering. She glanced up, startled by the sudden silence. Casting a pall on the now silent throng, Roland strode into the room, smiling with insolent glee, and followed by three of his goons.

Arrogant as always, he scanned the room, sneering in contempt as he strode to Reverend James's table.

"I didn't get my invitation this year." He smirked, tapping on the table. "But I figured I'd come anyway."

Reverend James choked, wiping his mouth with his hand. "I didn't think you'd want to be here so soon after your father's death."

Roland's sharp laugh sounded more like a bark. His lip curled. "Maybe you just didn't want me here."

Reverend James stood up, his manifest

graciousness unaffected by Roland's ill manners.

"You and your friends are welcome here, Mr. Spencer, as is everyone."

Roland sneered, thick lips twisted. Strolling around the hall, bully boys hot on his tail, he perused the partygoers, stopping every so often to scrutinize a wary individual before moving on. As he drew nearer, Aimee dipped her head, staring at the plate in front of her, trying to avoid a confrontation,

Roland's footsteps slowed and then halted. Like a blast of cold arctic air, she could feel Roland's eyes boring into her, dark and menacing.

"Ah! The new schoolmistress!" His phony, semi-enthusiastic greeting echoed in the long hall.

She raised her head, heart pounding. "Mr. Spencer. How *nice* to see you."

Roland puffed up, looking like nothing more than a giant vulture. "I see you haven't forgotten me." His arrogance was only overshadowed by his egotistical self-conceit.

"How could I," she murmured in her sweetest voice. "When you've been such a *gentleman* at our every meeting."

Nudging her hard in the ribs, Maudie hissed, "Don't rile him!"

Roland leaned forward, mere inches from Aimee's face. "Listen to her," he nodded at Maudie. "Don't rile me," he said low. "You wouldn't like it."

"I don't suspect I would," she retorted, chin lifting. "But I don't like you to begin with so what's your point?"

A flicker of surprise flitted across Roland's countenance. Lips thinning in fury, he frowned.

"I think we need some music." Snapping his fingers at the musicians, he motioned for them to begin.

The hapless ensemble, tense and confused, hesitated, looking to Reverend James for guidance.

Stiff with indignation, Reverend James nodded, chin quivering with disapproval. Sweeping up their instruments, the nervous musicians began playing. The strains of a lively polka swept through the hall, a cheerful spark in the now gloomy atmosphere.

Roland reached down, grabbed Aimee's wrist, and pulled her onto the dance floor, while the crowd of onlookers watched in trepidation.

"I think this is my dance."

Twisting her hand and trying to break free, she glared, furious. "You're hurting me."

"All you have to do is quit fighting the inevitable and dance with me."

"I-Don't-Think-So." She twisted, struggling ineffectively against his greater strength.

"Oh, but I do," he muttered, pulling her resisting figure closer. "I know this is my dance."

Reverend James, acting on impulse, started forward only to be stopped by Roland's goons, their hands resting with dangerous intent on menacing-looking sidearms.

"Mrs. Marshall prefers not to dance without her husband in attendance," Reverend James protested.

Aimee had to give the reverend his due. He was trying, though little good it would do her, she reflected, since no one else was stepping forward.

"Tell the reverend to sit down," Roland whispered, "or I'll make this so much worse."

God, how she wished she had a .357 Magnum right now.

She stood as tall as her small frame would allow. "It's okay, Reverend James," she stated, forcing a casualness she didn't feel into her voice. "If this scumbag wants to dance with me, I'll force myself to endure his slimy touch."

Gasps of horror flew from every side.

Condescending, as though she were a queen and he a mere peon, she stepped forward. Little did he know that if she had anything to do with it, she was going to make this the most embarrassing and ill-advised experience he'd ever encountered.

Roland scowled, pulling her hard against him and spinning recklessly around the dance floor. She tensed up, stiffening like a wooden doll, dragging her feet, and stomping on his toes at every opportunity. She even managed to tread solidly on his instep several times, garnering numerous harsh and overly vulgar comments from her now disgruntled partner. *I must be doing a good job, judging by the titters and outright laughter coming from the audience.*

The faster Roland swirled, the clumsier she became, tripping and stumbling, wholly intent on making him appear like an utter fool. Flustered and perspiring, Roland stopped, shoving her away in disgust. Wiping a hand across his sweaty forehead, he glared venomously at the snickering spectators who did little to cover their amusement, delighted by the chance to witness Roland's comeuppance.

"You'll regret this," Roland hissed, his hot breath fanning her face.

"I already regret it. I regretted it the minute you walked in the door." Aimee grinned, sticking her nose in the air, further goading the already furious Roland.

Raising a hand, Roland froze momentarily, eyes flicking away.

He's going to hit me! Incredulous, she gawked at the upraised hand.

A growing number of angry townspeople stepped onto the dance floor, far more than Roland's goons could handle.

At the same time, Reverend James's voice lashed out. "Do you really think these good citizens will allow you to hit this young woman?"

Aimee took the opportunity to sucker punch Roland, so to speak. She kneed him hard in the nuts, just like the self-defense instructor coached, and followed up with a hard right to his temple. Roland bent over with a "*whoof*" and then yelped in pain as she nailed him. She brushed her hands together, grinning in satisfaction. *That'll teach this creep a thing or two!*

Maudie rushed forward, fists clenched in fury as she stepped in front of Aimee. "If you touch her," she screeched at Roland's bent-over form, "I'll kill you."

The temper of the crowd grew increasingly belligerent. Roland's goons, realizing they were outnumbered and outgunned, turned tail and ran, leaving Roland to face the mob alone.

"You forget who owns this town," he blustered, grimacing in pain as he shuffled towards the door, cradling his balls. "There wouldn't be a town if it weren't for my family."

A voice came from the crowd. "Yeah, we know about your family, and this town's better off without any of you."

Heads bobbed in agreement.

"You own a store because we let you," Roland screamed at the speaker.

"I own a store because I worked hard to get one," the speaker retorted. "I don't owe your family anything."

"Me neither," another man called.

"Or me," said another.

"Hang him," an older gentleman cried, shaking his bony fists. "His family killed my brother and his wife."

The crowd drew closer, circling Roland like a pack of wolves, and he the sacrificial lamb. Face blanching white, mouth working soundlessly, he scrambled to find an avenue of escape. His courage, dependent upon the strength of his paid muscle, evaporated in the wake of their desertion.

Reverend James lifted a restraining hand.

"*Please, everyone settle down!*"

He glared at Roland, his eyes flashing behind his round spectacles. "I think you'd better leave while you have the chance, and if you cause trouble for *any* of these good people, we won't hesitate to act."

The crowd parted, reluctant to open a narrow pathway to the church exit. Eyes darting with nervous anticipation, Roland inched sideways.

"You won't get away with this," he spat one last time before dashing out.

Aimee laughed. She could still see the yellow streak flashing on his rapidly disappearing backside. Grateful, she clasped Reverend James's hand.

"Thank you," she said, shaking inside.

Straightening his waistcoat and pushing his spectacles back into place, Reverend James coughed, clearing his throat. "My pleasure, young woman, though I suspect he got the worse end of the situation. But we aren't so uncivilized that we can ignore such brutish behavior."

Mrs. James slipped her arm through the crook of Reverend James's elbow, chattering inanely. "My goodness, no! I can't believe he actually thought he could accost you in front of the whole town! I'm so distressed! We're all distressed! Do you feel faint? That was so very exciting! Are you hurt?"

Laughing to herself, Aimee suspected that even though Mrs. James's hair was white, she might have been blonde in her younger years. Everything pointed in that direction, albeit in a kind and goodhearted way.

"I'm fine. My hand's a little sore, but I'm just happy he's gone, and for good, I hope."

"Good show! Remind me never to cross you." Reverend James beamed. "Then let's get this celebration going again. We've wasted enough time on the likes of him."

Maudie wrapped an arm around her. “Roland won’t let this pass,” she whispered darkly. “You shamed him in front of the whole town.”

“I don’t give a crap,” she hissed, uncaring if her words were overheard. “He deserved it, and I hope he sings soprano for a long time.”

The band struck up a perky Schottische and couples rushed out, laughing as they partnered up and stepped into the music. Aimee edged over to the food table, tapping her foot to the rhythm and humming to the melody long remembered from middle school PE classes. As she watched the couples, aching loneliness welled up, threatening to ruin the moment. Even Maudie had found a partner, smiling shyly into the face of a brawny, grinning farmer. *That new blouse was just the ticket.*

The pace of the music changed, blending into a haunting waltz.

Jake’s face rose unbidden in her mind, his sexy bedroom eyes shining with—was it just her imagination—love? The music flowed around her as she swayed to the lilting strains. If she pretended really hard, she could almost feel Jake’s arms wrapping her with possession as they did the night they danced beneath the stars months ago. She’d been so stupid to leave him, and she’d be lucky if he ever forgave her. She stifled a sob. An older lady, noticing her despondency, handed her a cup of punch, clucking with sympathy.

“It’s hard being alone,” she commiserated. “But I’m sure one of my sons would be pleased to dance with you, if you’d like.”

Oh, great! Now she looked like a weepy wallflower.

“No! No, that’s okay. I’m just thinking about my husband and missing him so much.” Never in her life had she said a truer thing. If he was here right now, she’d never let him go.

"I was so astonished the way you stood up to Mr. Spencer! I doubt anyone has ever done that before. It's about time, too," she exclaimed. "I've wanted to do the same thing myself a hundred times. I just never had your courage."

"He could cause a lot of trouble for a lot of people," Aimee ruefully admitted.

The woman patted Aimee's hand. "We won't worry about that until the time comes. Don't be so glum. It's Christmas, and we're having a party. Name's Myra, by the way."

A young man stepped near her. "Ma. Jeremy said you needed me."

"I don't need you. This young woman needs you." Myra pointed to Aimee.

Mortified, she stood speechless, mouth gaping open in surprise.

"Dance with her," Myra demanded. "She looks like she could use some fun."

The young man smiled, pleased by his mother's suggestion.

"I'm not much at dancing," he laughed. "But I won't pass up the chance to dance with a pretty woman."

Aimee's mouth slammed shut. "I don't know if I should be dancing," she began, searching for the right words. "I'm pre—er, I'm in the family way."

Myra laughed. "Been that way a time or two myself. Don't you worry about that. Look over yonder." She pointed to a large woman across the hall. "That's Mazie Dell. She's ready to drop at any minute and she's dancing."

Aimee flushed. "Well," she decided, taking note of Mazie's advanced pregnancy, "If Mazie Dell can dance, I guess I can, too!"

The rest of the afternoon and evening passed in a blur, good food, good companions, and lots of good cheer. By the time Aimee and Maudie departed the church, it was late, and they were both near to exhaustion, but happy and content. Maudie's dance partner would be heading to California in the morning, but even that couldn't dampen Maudie's spirits.

The new blouse and the dancing brought a sparkle to her eyes and color to her cheeks. She looked almost pretty and younger than Aimee's first impressions. They bundled up and began the short trek back to the boardinghouse. The night was full dark, the sky lit by a thousand twinkling stars stretching into infinity.

"I wonder where Jake is," Aimee whispered, faced uplifted. "I wonder if I'll ever see him again."

"You will," Maudie hugged her. "I kin feel it."

"Oh, now you're psychic," she chuckled.

"A what?"

"A psychic. It's a person who can feel other people's emotions."

"Don't everyone!"

"Doesn't," Aimee corrected unconsciously.

"Here we go again," Maudie grumped. "We ain't doing schoolwork now so quit nagging at me."

"I wasn't nagging," she protested, realizing for the first time the crowd of partygoers had thinned, dissipating until she and Maudie were walking alone, and only the glow of a few flickering lamps cast any light on the darkened street.

A shiver ran up her spine. Unwelcome thoughts of the earlier encounter with Roland sprang up. They should've brought a lantern or asked one of the males to accompany them home. Too many dark shadows and hiding places lined the street, and Roland wasn't the type to ignore the horrendous insult she'd dealt him. It was too quiet. Not even a dog barked or a cat meowed.

"This would be the perfect spot for an ambush."

Maudie glanced around, wide eyes shining in

the moon's light. "Seems like something Roland would do!"

"Maybe we should run," she suggested, eyeing the shadows.

"Run where?" Maudie asked.

"Home, you ding dong!"

Keeping to the center of the street, they held hands, ready to bolt at the slightest provocation. Music tinkled from the saloons and bawdy houses down by the river, lending an added sense of macabre to the already eerie scenario. *The boardinghouse seemed so far away*!

"Wish I had my scattergun handy," Maudie whispered. "Not many people brave enough to step in front of one of those."

"I don't doubt it." Aimee giggled. "I can still see Roland running out the door, yellow streak flashing." She paused, adding as an afterthought. "Jake would've killed him."

"I wish that husband of yours was here right now!"

"Me, too," she admitted. "More than you know."

A loud crash from a dark side street drew their startled attention. Breathless, filled with anxiety, they edged past the entrance to the narrow lane and, throwing caution to the wind, sprinted for the boardinghouse. Aimee's heart thudded in her chest, knees shook with exertion as they crashed through the door, slamming it behind, and throwing the bolt.

"You shouldn't be running, being pregnant and all," Maudie gasped, leaning against the door. "I shouldn't be running, cuz I'm old."

"You aren't old,' Aimee panted. "And I used to run before I got pregnant, so it's okay."

"Where'd you run to?"

"Wha—I didn't run anywhere. I did it for exercise."

Maudie slanted an amused look at her. "You ran

around—*for exercise*?"

"Exactly! People do it all the time."

"People must be sorta weird where you come from." Maudie chuckled, limping to the kitchen, rubbing her backside.

"People are a lot weirder here," Aimee grumbled. "At least I knew who to trust and who not to trust."

Maudie came back into the parlor, a shotgun held firmly in her grasp. Arching her eyebrows, she bluntly explained. "Just in case."

"You don't really think he'd try anything, do you?" *Surely, Roland wasn't that stupid. But then, maybe he was.*

"I think Roland would do just about anything he wanted, and, right now, he don't like you too much."

"For that I am forever grateful." The possibility that Roland *might* like her was even scarier than having him for an enemy.

Maudie wrapped a woolen shawl around her shoulders and sat down, the gun held crosswise in her lap. "You go on up to bed. I'm gonna sit here for awhile. Just in case."

"I'll sit with you."

"Nope." Maudie scowled. "You need your rest, and I don't sleep much anyways. I'll be fine. If'n I need you, I'll holler."

Rather than arguing with the obdurate Maudie, she nodded, lit a candle, and climbed up the steep stairway. It had been a long day, and she was close to collapsing. The bleak little room, cold and uninviting, was nonetheless welcome. At least she had a place she could call her own in this improbable reality.

****

Jake tucked wool blankets around the little girls, and then blew out the single candle, content to sit by the small stove and savor a cup of coffee. Wind whipped the sides of the tent, drafts of cold air seeped in.

"Ain't no place for children," John complained. "I daren't let em out of my sight for even a few minutes."

Jake sighed, knowing he was right. "Just a few more months and then we'll have enough. The ore's showing more promise every day. Heard tell the assayer is paying top dollar for an ounce."

John's eyes darkened. "I'm feeling like a nursemaid. Got a little girl tied to my tail every minute of the day. I can't even use the outhouse that one's not knocking on the door." He grumbled. "Hate to admit it, but I kinda like having 'em around."

"You're better at it than I am." Jake poured another cup. "Not that I don't love them. I do. Like they're my own, but I've never had any experience taking care of little girls."

"Nothing to it," John chuckled. "Give 'em lots of love and a plate of food. The rest is just gravy on the potatoes."

Jake sat back, staring into the open grate of the stove, his heart heavy. Aimee was a constant ache in his gut. He missed everything about her—her sass, the way she tossed her head, her smile, the soft sounds she made in her sleep. His dreams were always of her, waking up angry and even more alone.

He brushed his hair back, inhaling. He didn't even know if she was still in this time. Maybe by now she'd found a way home. The idea filled him with even deeper sorrow. If she'd made it home, there was no way they'd ever be together again. He knew in his heart she belonged to him—but how could he convince her of that. He'd tried everything when they were together and it hadn't worked. Why did he think he could change that? He didn't know, but he was going to try.

"You fussin' over Aimee again?" John's eyes

were full of sympathy. "Woman hurt you bad."

Yes, she had, but there were the good times, too. "I'm going after her when we're finished here." He glanced at John. "I have to."

John nodded. "Figured as much. Can't say I blame you. She's a fine looking woman." He grinned. "You up to taming that little filly?"

Jake smiled, remembering. "And then some."

Chapter Thirty-Five

Aimee and Maudie planned a small celebration for New Year's Eve, just the two of them, keeping the festivities to dinner and a glass of the homemade wine Mrs. James had given as a Christmas gift. Aimee sampled a small glass, grimacing at the sour bouquet and bitter aftertaste. Kind of reminded her of the cheap wines served up at the college bashes.

They were in the kitchen, cleaning up and planning to retire when shots rang out, shattering a window in the front parlor. Maudie blew out the lantern and pulled a stunned Aimee to the floor.

"You in there!" Roland's voice screamed. "Come out, come out!"

Catcalling and whistling, Roland and his goons opened fire, breaking several more windows and spraying glass everywhere.

"He waited longer than I expected him to," Maudie whispered. Belly-crawling below the window, she hesitated a few moments before jumping up and hauling down the scattergun resting over the kitchen door. Flipping open the chamber, she checked it quickly, nodding in grim satisfaction before snapping it shut.

"Pays to keep 'em loaded."

"You got an extra one of those?" Aimee hissed. "I've never shot one before, but I'm a quick learner."

Maudie settled herself, complacently patting the shotgun. "You just stay put. If they come through anywheres, I've got a bead on 'em."

Aimee crouched, head down, covering the back of her neck, and screeching as the next volley of gunfire hit the boardinghouse. No sooner had the gunshots subsided than Roland and his drunken goons circled the house, banging the walls, laughing and yelling obscenities.

Frightened at first, her blood began to boil. “If I ever get my hands on him again,” she growled, “I’ll strangle him.”

“Get in line.” Maudie hissed back. “Just look at the mess he’s making of my place. Take me months to clean it up.”

The assault lasted for at least a half hour, and then, without warning, the noise ceased. Tense and jumpy, they waited for the barrage to begin again, but when nothing further happened, Maudie stood and peeked out the kitchen window.

“Don’t see anything,” she whispered. “Looks like they left.”

“I don’t trust them for a second.” Aimee crawled over to her and sat down. “Probably just regrouping.”

The seconds ticked by and still nothing. Maudie crept into the parlor, stopping at every shattered window to sneak a quick look.

“Don’t see anything,” she muttered. Aimee crawled in behind her, cussing as she cut her hand on a sliver of broken glass.

Maudie chuckled. “They didn’t teach you that in boarding school.”

“You’d be surprised what I learned in school.”

Blasts of cold air blew in through the ruined windows, dropping the temperature to the point there was very little difference inside the boardinghouse and the outside. A tentative knock sounded at the door.

“You ladies okay in there?” a deep voice asked.

Maudie crouched by the door. “Who’s out there?”

“It’s me. Andy.”

Breathing a sigh of relief, Maudie unbolted the

door, allowing a male form to slip in.

"Heard the ruckus and hot-footed it over here." Andy, their guest, was the young half-breed from the ferry boat who'd directed her to Maudie's place.

"Did you see anyone out there?" Aimee peered out a small window.

"Saw somebody running as we got close, but couldn't really see who it was."

"Are there more of you out there?"

He nodded. "We were heading out to the village to visit our people when we heard the shooting."

Maudie opened the door, calling out. "The rest of you better come on in. No sense standing out there."

Five other men stepped in. From their dark complexions, four were full Indian and the fifth was considerably lighter skinned like Andy, another half-breed.

Matter-of-fact Maudie headed to the storeroom. "Better get some blankets over these windows or we'll freeze to death."

"What if they come back?" Aimee asked.

"If they do, we'll deal with it then. But right now, I'm cold and unless you want to spend the night freezing, I suspect we'd better fix things up."

Even with the help of Andy and his friends, it took the better part of three hours to clean up the mess and tack blankets and old boards over the broken windows. Andy and his friends took the cold food proffered by Maudie and then slipped into the night, heading home.

Exhausted, but triumphant, Aimee and Maudie sat down for a quick cup of tea before retiring. Maudie suggested, and Aimee readily accepted, the offer to spend the night in Maudie's room. Warmed by the kitchen stove, the room was comfortable and pleasant, a far cry from her austere room above. *Not like she'd ever made any attempt to make it more homey.* She just never thought she'd be here for so long.

"I'm going to the sheriff in the morning." Maudie's voice broke the silence.

"Do you think he'll do anything?"

"He'd better," Maudie growled. "Now that old man Spencer is dead, I doubt he'll cover for Roland anymore. Too many people are up in arms about Roland's doings."

"I'll go with you," she offered, sleep just a step away. "The more people griping about his behavior, the more chance the sheriff'll pay attention."

"He'll pay attention, or he'll wish he had," Maudie voice was stern. "Roland'd better plan on paying for this mess, or I'll fix him good."

Aimee rose up from her snug little nest. "Don't do anything crazy. We can fix things, but we can't heal you if you're dead."

Maudie chuckled. "Go to sleep. You're botherin' me."

****

Early the next morning, before they'd even finished breakfast, a noisy commotion rumbled from the front porch. Eyeballing Aimee owlishly, Maudie scurried to the door, peeking out. Reverend James stood on the stoop, his face drawn with concern.

"We heard the ruckus last night, but didn't realize it was coming from your place." He apologized, his face contrite. "You know I would have dashed over here if I'd known you were in trouble."

Opening the door wider, Maudie motioned him in. Aimee stared at the flood of males who followed close on his heels. From the oldest to the youngest, each man carried tools and equipment and even lengths of saw-cut board.

"We're here to fix the mess," one old man piped up, waving a hammer. "Roland's jist about gone far enough."

Heads bobbed in agreement. Without further

comment, the men were soon hammering and sawing, patching bullet holes and repainting the outside of the boardinghouse. By mid-afternoon, most of the garbage had been cleared away and the windows re-paned. By evening, the work was completed and the men left, heading towards home.

Standing on the porch admiring their work, Maudie was visibly impressed. "Land sakes!" she exclaimed. "Can you believe it? It looks better 'n ever."

"Let's just hope Roland doesn't decide to visit us again real soon," Aimee commented, knowing it was a distinct possibility.

"If'n that skunk does," Maudie scowled, pulling a lethal looking pistol from a pocket in her apron. "I'll be ready for him."

"Maybe I should carry one, too." Aimee hitched her skirt. "If you don't hit him, maybe I'll get lucky."

"You just leave that part to me. Ain't no reason for you to put yourself in danger. Pretty soon, you ain't gonna be able to move very easy, and we might have to hide."

"Isn't." Aimee corrected.

"Isn't. Ain't. What's the difference?" Maudie growled. "I swear. Do you ever quit?"

"No, I don't!" Aimee chuckled. "That's why you love me."

Maudie grinned. "I guess it's a reason."

Chapter Thirty-Six

Maudie left late in the afternoon to shop for groceries, leaving Aimee to fend for herself and enjoy some well-deserved alone time. Sitting by the kitchen stove, she cupped the locket to her cheek, daydreaming about Mom, Dad, Sara, and lastly, her darling Jake. Over the last few months, she'd posted three more letters, but still no word. Either the letters had been lost in transit or he was refusing to answer. She couldn't blame him if he was, but her heart ached for him. Very soon, a new little life would come into the world and that little life needed a father.

Too many bittersweet memories welled up, washing her in waves of loneliness and despair. Her self-control died. Wailing, gnashing her teeth, she rocked back and forth, face buried against the locket.

Life was so unfair! She'd been a good person, or so she thought, so why was she being punished? Why did she have to lose everything and end up in this Godforsaken place? Whatever sins she'd committed in her short life weren't so great that she had to atone for all eternity. God couldn't be that cruel! Grief-stricken, she gave vent to all the pent-up emotions buried for so long. So great was her pain, she at first didn't notice feeling dizzy and disoriented. Mind spinning, she opened tear-blurred eyes, gasping as she focused. A fleeting image, the mere blink of an eye, flashed across her vision, a startled woman danced in front of her, fading as quickly as it began. *The woman was dressed in modern clothing!* Of that, she was sure!

She'd somehow opened the veil between the present and the future again, and she hadn't been ready. Screaming, she stood up, stepping towards the void, groping blindly for the veiled abyss.

"For God's sake," Maudie exclaimed as she stepped into the room, slapping her forehead and collapsing into a nearby chair. "I must be tireder'n I thought."

"Wha—" Confused and upset, she turned, peering at the baffled Maudie.

"I coulda sworn I saw right through you." Maudie struggled to catch her breath. "Maybe I need spectacles or something."

"You *saw* through me?"

Maudie nodded, face coloring. "Told you I was getting old. Now I'm seein' things."

Uncertain how to respond, and knowing Maudie would never understand or believe, she shifted, uncomfortable.

"It's probably just the light in here." She wiped her face, struggling for composure. "You just came in from outside and your eyes haven't had time to adjust."

Maudie brightened. "I suspect that's the reason, and I've worked pretty hard today. I'm bone tired, and being tired does strange things to a body."

"Exactly." She heaved a sigh, relieved by Maudie's cheerful determination to brush the incident aside.

"Why're you cryin'?"

Self-conscious, Aimee coughed. "Just feeling sorry for myself. You know how it is when you're expecting."

Nodding in understanding, Maudie said, "I cried all the time."

A rush of warm liquid ran down Aimee's inner thighs, pooling on the floor. Petrified, she lifted her skirts, looking down. A small puddle of bloody liquid stained the wood floor.

Fear gripped her in a rising tide. “I’m bleeding! It’s too soon! The baby isn’t due for another two months at least!”

“Let’s get you to bed.” Maudie wrapped a supporting arm around her and half-carried her to bed.

“I’m going to lose the baby! I just know it!” Aimee sobbed. “I shouldn’t have held the locket.”

“No locket caused this. Quit your silliness,” Maudie crooned, smoothing her brow. “Nothing you did brought this on. All that fuss with Roland what’s did it.”

She held out the piece of jewelry, teeth chattering. “No! You don’t understand! I was wishing I could go home, and I was holding this locket!”

Dropping the locket on the bedside table, Aimee glared at the offending necklace.

Maudie clucked, helping her to sit, padding her unmentionables with a soft towel. “Don’t you worry about that. Just relax, and I’ll go for the doctor. Do you think you’ll be okay until I get back?”

She clutched Maudie’s arm. “You need to hurry! I can’t lose the baby, too!” Frightened tears streamed down her face. This baby was all she had—all she had left of Jake!

****

Jake stopped shoveling. For the second time today, he was hit with gut-wrenching nausea. Stomach clenching, he struggled to breathe. *Aimee was hurting!* He could feel her pain knifing through him. Sadness and grief gripped him so hard, his heart constricted.

“What’s the matter?” John eyed him. “You look sick, kinda pale green.”

He waited for the painful sensation to subside. Facing north, he inhaled, senses tingling. Aimee’s heart-shaped face rose up in his tortured brain, her slanted amber eyes glistening with tears, lips trembling. *She was calling to him!* God knows he'd felt her enough times over the past months. Why he even cared, he didn't know—but he did!

Wiping a hand across his face, he swallowed. "We've got enough. I'm not shoveling another load. Time to go back."

John shrugged, nodding. "Told you that a few weeks ago."

Throwing the shovel aside in disgust, Jake stalked from the creek bed—cold, wet and angry.

"Get your things," he growled. "We're leaving today."

****

Grabbing a shawl, Maudie flew out, slamming the door in her haste.

Forcing herself to lie still and relax, Aimee focused on staying calm and slowing her breathing down. In and out, in and out, she counted the breaths, praying the doctor would soon arrive. Time after time, she glanced at the locket, afraid to touch it again.

After what seemed like forever, Maudie ran in—alone.

"Doc wasn't there. I left a message for him to come soon's he can. How you feelin'?

Other than the show of blood and her uncontrolled histrionics, she felt quite well. "Not bad. Just scared. Do you think I'm losing the baby?"

Maudie shrugged. "Other women bleed sometimes and doesn't mean nuthin. Could be just the way it is for you."

Matter-of-fact Maudie pulled the padding aside.

"Looks like it's stopped," she commented. "You feeling any cramping or anything?"

Shaking her head, Aimee rubbed her enlarged stomach. "You stay put, little one," she crooned. "Not time for you yet."

"That baby will come when he's ready, whether we like it or not."

"It's too soon," she protested, her voice sharp. "He needs to grow more."

Maudie finished her examination and covered her with a warm blanket. "You just rest 'til the doc gets here."

Aimee grasped Maudie's hand. "Do you think I'm being punished for leaving Jake?"

"Don't you be silly. God doesn't hurt people that way." She snuffled into a hanky. "I confess I cussed at God when my boys and my man died, but wasn't God's fault they got sick." She patted Aimee's arm. "You relax and let things settle down. That baby's going to be fine."

They spent a long, tense night, waiting for the doc to arrive or something more to happen. The bleeding subsided, and the baby continued to move, kicking and shifting. It wasn't until early the next morning that the doctor arrived, long after the excitement passed, apologizing for his tardiness.

"Had to ride up to the logging camp. Fella broke an arm and needed it set."

Sparse graying hair askew, his bewhiskered face concerned, he scurried about, doing little if anything. When his cursory exam was finished, he gathered up his bag, preparing to leave.

"Looks like you've got everything under control." He smiled, showing square yellowed teeth. "Stay off your feet for a couple of days, and I'll check in later this week."

"What do I owe you?" Maudie asked dryly, eyeing Aimee.

"How about inviting me to dinner some evening?" Brushing back his hair, he coughed. "Can't remember the last time I had a piece of that homemade pie of yours."

Unless Aimee was mistaken, the doctor was interested in Maudie. Pretty weird and kind of disgusting.

Maudie ushered the doctor to the door, lips pursed together. Reaching into her pocket, she pulled out some coins and handed them to the doctor.

"We'll discuss that another time," she murmured, glancing sideways at Aimee, eyebrows arched. "When she's feeling better."

Aimee caught on, moaned and gasped. *She loved acting!* "I doubt I'll feel better until after the baby's born."

"Well," the doctor coughed again, patting Maudie's shoulder. "I'll drop by soon enough."

Pushing him out the door, she pasted a humorless smile on her face. "I'll send for you when we need you."

Covering her face with the blanket, Aimee smothered the giggles threatening to burst free. Wouldn't do to alienate the only doctor in the country. Ears perked, listening to their muted conversation, she waited until she felt certain the good doctor had vacated the premises and then burst out laughing.

"Better be laughing at something other than me," Maudie called from the outer room.

"I wasn't laughing at you," she chuckled. "I was laughing at your beau."

The floorboards bounced as Maudie stormed in. "He ain't no beau of mine. He might like to be, but he ain't."

"I don't know," she giggled. "He seemed pretty smitten to me."

Maudie's lips quirked, eyes dancing. "Don't matter what he feels. What matters is how I feel, and I don't feel nuthin for him. Never have. Never will."

Aimee tapped her lips. "Maybe we should invite him for tea sometime."

Maudie growled low, eyes narrowed. "If'n you do, you can entertain him. I won't be here."

Pretending to mull over the situation, Aimee waited for Maudie's reaction. "I don't know… He might just be the ticket. Where I come from, everyone wants to marry doctors. They make the most money."

"I don't need to marry anyone, specially him, and I make my own money."

Maudie busied herself straightening the bedding and fluffing the pillows.

"He seems to like you."

"Don't care whether he likes me or not. Haven't met anyone since my man died that I'd give a lick for."

"No one?" A surge of pity for the stalwart Maudie rushed through her.

"No one! Though, lately, I've kinda felt like I wouldn't mind having another man to do for," Maudie admitted, her face flushing.

Aimee smiled, her imagination running wild. *Matchmaking was such fun*!

Relegated to bed, she had little to do besides plan and scheme, and every single male became a prospective suitor for Maudie. The bleeding stopped, and within a week, she was back on her feet and back to routine, keeping her eyes open for a new man for Maudie.

Winter gave way to the first buds of spring. Flocks of birds flew overhead, heading to unknown northern destinations. Ice flows on the river broke up and activity at the docks increased in leaps and bounds.

Though she loved the springtime, Aimee viewed the increased activity with some misgivings. Spring meant the advent of the baby's birth, and following that, she'd be unable to work for some months while she healed and the baby grew stronger. Added to those concerns, what would she do with the baby while she was teaching? Mr. and Mrs. James and the School Board were gracious in their approval to allow her to continue teaching for as long as possible, judicially reminding her that there was no one else to take over her duties, and therefore, not to worry about being replaced. School took much of her time, and by day's end, she had little energy left for anything, let alone a new baby.

Roland disappeared from Vancouver and the surrounding countryside, much to everyone's relief. Story was a rather large group visited his establishment one night, roughed him and his cohorts up then made it very clear he was no longer welcome. The incident concluded when they tied Roland to a galloping horse headed west. No one seemed to know how far the horse ran or if Roland managed to stay on or whether he'd even survived. Aimee secretly hoped he hadn't.

As time passed, her advanced pregnancy caused Aimee no small amount of inconvenience. The stairwell at Maudie's being first on the list. Maudie watched her duck-walk up and down the stairs with great amusement, offering to change rooms until the baby's birth. As her pregnancy progressed, the baby's movements grew stronger and more regular.

In secret, she worried about continuing to wear the locket. What would happen to the baby if she transported home? Would the baby go with her or be left behind, or worse, would transporting cause the baby harm? The earlier incident still gripped her with fear. She couldn't bear to think of hurting the baby in any way. Without Jake, this little person was the only real family she had. Maudie continued to be her best friend and moral support, but this baby meant more than life.

Late at night, sitting in a rocking chair by the stove, she'd rub gentle circles on her belly while crooning lullabies. Maudie thought she was being silly, but modern medicine believed babies not only heard, but responded to sounds outside the womb, and so she sang songs remembered from childhood, heart bleeding with sadness as her mother's ghostly voice sang along with her.

With much soul-searching and many tears, she wrapped the locket in a soft cloth and put it away, never to be worn again. The choice had been made. Her life was here with Jake and the baby, God willing, and when the baby was strong enough, she was going husband hunting and Jake'd better be ready.

Chapter Thirty-Seven

Sara Elizabeth came into the world with very little fuss or bother. When Maudie placed the baby in her arms, Aimee's heart melted into a puddle of love so intense, she trembled. The baby's perfectly shaped little head was covered with black silky little curls. Long dark eyelashes surrounded her baby eyes and a tiny Cupid's bow mouth wailed in anger, small fists pumping at the unfriendly world. Kissing the soft little bundle, tears of joy streamed down Aimee's face.

"Do you think Jake'll mind?"

"Mind what?" Maudie frowned.

"That she's a girl, not a boy. Men always want boys."

"I think if he cares, he ain't worth having." Maudie patted the baby's cheek with pride. "Who wouldn't love this little darling?"

"Soon's you're up to it, we'll go find out." Maudie kissed Sara Elizabeth's tiny cheek.

"What do you mean 'we'?"

"I ain't been away from this boardinghouse since I opened it. Reverend's son said he'd watch it for awhile, until we get back."

Amazed that Maudie would even consider such a thing, Aimee's mouth fell open, stuttering in surprise. "Wh-why're you going with me?"

Maudie arched her eyebrows. "You think I'd let you and the baby wander off alone? Somebody's got to take care of you."

"You've been taking care of me since I got here," Aimee grinned. "Why is that?"

Face pinking, Maudie gazed at Aimee and the baby. “I don’t have any family and I sorta feel like you and the baby are mine.” She turned away, surreptitiously wiping her eyes.

A lump formed in Aimee’s throat. “We are,” she croaked. “I never had a big sister, just my little sister, Sara, and I always wanted one. You kinda fit the picture I had.”

Maudie blew her nose. “Too many years I grieved for my man and sons. Time I started living again.”

“So you think taking a vacation with me is a start?”

“Vacation? Never heard of it. But if you think I’m letting you wander all over tarnation alone, you best think again. ’Specially with my baby. You ain’t going nowhere that I ain’t along.”

Aimee opened her mouth, language corrections running rampant in her mind.

“Bah!” Maudie snorted, striding out of the room, her boisterous laughter echoing behind.

Aimee nestled the baby closer, studying the little face. Except for her feminine delicacy, Sara Elizabeth was the picture of Jake. She stroked the baby curls, contented and daydreaming of the future, a future where Jake joyously accepted her back, thrilled with a baby daughter.

Reality surfaced with a resounding thump. First thing was to find him and the best place to look was back in Oregon City. That’s where he’d homesteaded and that’s where she supposed he’d be. A small part of her wondered uneasily why he hadn’t come for her. Vancouver wasn’t that far away, and she’d sent all those letters. If he wanted her, why hadn’t he jumped the first boat and been here demanding she return, showering her with love and devotion?

Aimee sighed. It would be interesting to see what the future brought.

Chapter Thirty-Eight

Elated, Aimee tiptoed across the muddy street, ferry tickets clutched in her fist, lips curved in a triumphant smile. In five days, Maudie, Sara Elizabeth, and she would be on the ferry heading toward Portland. The baby was a healthy three-month-old, and she had healed. There wasn't any reason to put off searching for Jake any longer. Earlier that morning, Maudie'd handed her some money and told her to buy the tickets, saying it was time for the baby to meet her father.

She'd taken the money, worried about the outcome, but now that the tickets were actually in hand, she felt as though a load was off her chest. There was no going back. The tickets were purchased, and soon they would be on their way. So engrossed was she in her excitement and planning the venture, she didn't at first notice the scruffy dirty individual who stepped from a nearby saloon, blocking her path.

When she attempted to step around him, he grabbed her arm, his fetid breath engulfing her in a stinking miasma.

"Where you going, whore?"

Startled, Aimee attempted to pull her arm free from the disgusting creep, but he held on, grasping her in a vise-like grip. Her eyes flew to his face, a face covered by a dirty stringy beard and equally dirty mustache. Long greasy hair touched his skin-clad shoulders. He looked like a mountain man and reeked of animal.

"Let go of me," she shrieked. "Or I'll holler so

loud, the sheriff and every deputy in town will hear me."

"By the time any of them get here, I'll be gone and you'll be dead."

Something about his voice caused her to freeze. He grinned, showing dirty broken teeth.

"You recognize me, now," Roland growled. "This is what you did to me!"

"I didn't do anything to you," she spat, trying to dislodge his greasy paw. "You did this to yourself, and I think you got pretty much what you deserved."

"Maybe so, maybe not. But you're going to get what you deserve. If it hadn't been for you, I'd own this town by now."

She continued to struggle, held against his stinking body, forced to endure his filthy presence.

"Let go of me—now!" Furious, she pummeled his chest.

Roland stepped back and slapped her soundly across the face, the force of the blow snapping her head back and causing her to trip and roll into the muddy street. A rush of tears streamed down her smarting cheek. *God, that hurt!*

Cowering, she waited for the next blow. Roland moved closer, hands clenched, smirking as he lifted a foot, preparing to kick. Several men started towards him, angry disbelief blanketing their features.

"I wouldn't do that," a male voice barked. "Right now, you might live to see tomorrow, but if you kick her, you won't."

Roland hesitated, sneering at the interloper. "Mind your own business. This whore deserves what she gets."

"She is my business," Jake said, stepping towards Roland. "And I'll kill you if you touch her again."

"Try it," Roland laughed, uncaring. "My men are right inside, and you aren't man enough to take me and them too."

Cupping her smarting cheek, Aimee watched the heated interchange, too amazed by Jake's sudden appearance to utter a single word.

Jake smiled, lips thinning as he threw the first punch. Roland doubled over, gasping as the blow connected with his solar plexus. Jake followed with a well-timed uppercut, connecting solidly with Roland's chin and flipping him over backwards.

A number of equally filthy and disgusting individuals stepped from the saloon, only to be waylaid by the gawking townspeople, guns drawn and ready, halting the miscreants in their tracks.

Raining blows on the fallen man, Jake beat Roland with angry purpose, deliberately and brutally pummeling him with every ounce of hardened muscle. Roland was ill-prepared for Jake's ferocious attack, no doubt relying on his bully boys to handle actual physical encounters. The vicious bully quickly turned into a cowardly, groveling lump of flesh.

"Please," he choked, raising his hands in supplication. "No more."

"If you ever hit a woman again," Jake ground out, striking him again, "you won't live to see the sunrise."

Roland rolled to his side, moaning and whimpering in pain and humiliation. Face bruised and discolored, he struggled to his knees, and started to crawl away. Jake landed a hard kick on the seat of Roland's pants, causing him to fall face down in the mud again.

Hooting and laughing, the bystanders cheered Jake on, shouting words of encouragement, at the same time taunting the unfortunate Roland.

Hand resting on his low-slung holster, face dark and forbidding, Jake watched Roland's progress as the wretched scoundrel crept away. Satisfied the situation was at end, Jake turned, reached down, and smoothed back Aimee's hair, freed by Roland's blow.

"Can't you ever stay out of trouble?" He scowled.

She opened her mouth to speak, grimacing as pain knifed through her jaw. He helped her to her feet, brushing mud and dirt from her now ruined skirt and shirt. Self-conscious, she pushed his hands away, wanting nothing more than to fling herself on him, burying herself in his arms.

Instead, she reverted to form. "About time you got here," she grumbled, rubbing her cheek.

Jake glared, his brilliant blue eyes chips of ice in his smoldering gaze.

"I didn't think you wanted me around," he growled. "I wasn't the one who left."

The chips of ice thawed slightly, and Aimee glimpsed a flash of pain in their aquamarine depths. Unable to find a snappy comeback, discomfited by his obvious anger, her eyes slowly perused his much loved form. Tall, handsome, and rugged, she'd forgotten what a hunky male he was.

It had been too long since she'd fed the baby and her traitorous breasts reacted, dripping milk and staining her blouse even more, but he didn't notice the added moisture. She needed the right moment to tell him about Sara Elizabeth.

Grim and uncompromising, Jake glared at her. "We've got some talking to do."

Aimee straightened up, standing to her full height, chin up, meeting his gaze. "Of-of course," she stuttered. " I..."

A movement behind him distracted her. Choking, Aimee gasped in fright. Poised behind Jake, pistol cocked and pointing at his unsuspecting back, Roland grinned, his malevolent intent obvious.

She screamed a warning. Jake whirled, whipped out his gun, and fired in one smooth motion. A small neat hole bloomed in the center of Roland's forehead, followed by gunfire blaring from the growing crowd. Riddled by bullets, Roland's knees buckled, the pistol falling from his hand as he slowly crumpled, flopping face down, dead before he hit the ground.

Shivering and shaken, Aimee covered her face, horrified by the gory spectacle and Jake's near demise.

"Get this piece of shit off the street," Jake barked, waving at the body.

Several sturdy young men stepped out of the crowd and hurried over, nodding at Jake, eyes alight with respect. Callously, they dragged Roland's remains towards the undertaker's hut.

The crowd grew, drawn by the sound of gunfire.

Uncomfortable under their scrutiny, Jake snapped at Aimee. "Where's your place?"

"Wha—" Aimee murmured.

"I asked you where you live."

Aimee inclined her head up the hill. Jake grabbed her arm, hustling her off the street and onto the boardwalk. Shopkeepers and strollers gaped as he dragged her along the walkway.

"You need some help, Missy?" One of the bystanders asked, eyeing the sidearm displayed so blatantly on Jake's hip.

"I'm her husband," Jake growled. Smiling, the man moved away.

"You're walking too fast," Aimee grumbled, "and you're ripping my arm out of the socket."

"I should rip your head off," he snarled. Glancing around, he pulled her behind him. "Which direction?"

The boardinghouse was just a few blocks farther up the hill.

"There," she motioned. "That's where I live."

Maudie was standing in the parlor as they burst in. Startled, on instinct, she drew the gun from her pocket, pointing it at Jake.

"Let her go," she ground out, cocking the pistol.

"Maudie! Stop!" Aimee shrieked. "This is Jake!"

The gun stayed pointed as Maudie assessed Aimee's words. The gun dropped a mite. "*This* is Jake?"

"Yes," Aimee grinned. "This is Jake!"

"'Bout time you got here," Maudie grumbled. "What kind of man leaves his woman alone for so long?"

Jake's lips tightened. "I don't know who you are or why you think I left Aimee, unless she said I did, and if she did, then besides everything else, she's a damn liar, too."

Maudie tilted her head, studying Jake. "He's as pretty as you said he was," she commented. "Meaner, too."

Aimee flinched under Jake's curious perusal.

"Maudie, can you take care of things for a little bit longer. Jake and I need to talk."

"For a little bit longer, but you need—"

"I *know* what I need to do, but can you keep things under control for just a little while?"

Lips pursed in disapproval, Maudie nodded. "I can try but it won't last for long."

Aimee grasped Jake's hand, pulling him up the stairs to her barren little room, shutting the door, anxious to hear him speak. His scent teased her senses, reminding her of all those hot nights on the trail, made even hotter by his loving. Her breasts tingled again, stimulated and aching with need.

"I have something to say," he began, hesitating as he readied his thoughts.

All those post-delivery hormones raged unchecked as her body reacted to his husky voice, stomach clenching as moisture pooled at the apex of her thighs. She reached up, smoothing her hands along his shoulders and lightly caressing his pecs, delighting in the play of muscles. Jake stiffened, catching her hands and holding them against his chest.

"I said I have something to say," he growled.

"Me, too!" Aimee giggled, nibbling at the vee of his neck, licking and nuzzling. "But I think actions speak better than words."

Ripping his shirt open, she rubbed the soft hairs of his chest, teasing his flat nipples.

"That was a brand new shirt," he groaned.

"I'll buy you a new one," she whispered, hands working at his belt.

Shuddering, Jake caught her mouth, devouring her lips like a starving man, drowning her in a sea of passionate longing, tongues dancing and stroking.

"You shouldn't have left me," he murmured. "I've been crazy without you."

She pushed him backwards onto the narrow bed, kneeling in front of him and pulling off his boots and the form-fitting leather pants. His engorged shaft sprang free, huge and ready. Smiling, Aimee tongued the small opening at the tip, eliciting a tortured gasp from Jake. Bolder now, she laved the pulsing member as Jake writhed in ecstasy. She stroked, licked, and caressed her way up his muscular body, taking her time, remembering every curve and nuance of his beautiful male body. Jake cupped her face, kissing her with brutal force.

"You belong to me!"

She laughed against his lips. "I know," she chuckled. "Just like you belong to me."

He tore the muddy shirt from her, his fingers beginning to work at the laces of her chemise, stroking her breasts through the soft material.

"You're breasts are bigger," he muttered, confused.

He remembered!

Capturing his greedy hands, she lay against his

chest, wrapping his arms around her as she wiggled. Easily distracted, Jake flipped up the skirt and numerous petticoats, guiding her towards his heavy length. Aimee arched up, positioning herself and then eased down. A few seconds of after-baby discomfort, and he was filling her up. Her sheath muscles clenched pulling him in. She gasped as Jake's large hands clutched her buttocks, thrilled as he bucked against her, pressing deeper, opening her wider to his loving frenzy.

She rolled to her side, arching a leg over him, her movements in tune with his rhythmic passion, matching his thrusts as he plunged in again and again. She pulled his head down, mouths clashing and tongues dancing. She moaned, her hands caressing his sleek torso, her fingers tracing the taut muscles. He felt so good. He pushed her back, reaching down and thumbing her hot spot, lifting her even higher towards that one bright explosion.

The bed creaked, bumping against the wall and floor as he drove punishingly into her, erasing all those months of pain and loneliness. Come heaven or hell, she would never let him go again!

She wailed, stiffening as she came, bright lights exploded in her brain. Riding her hard and fast, Jake groaned as he came, shuddering and sweating as he climaxed.

Lips joined, they relaxed, breaths slowing and hearts pumping less thunderously.

Cuddling her close, Jake planted a kiss on her forehead, grinning with all too familiar arrogance. "Couldn't keep your hands off me, could you?"

Pinching him hard, she laughed. "I was just trying to show you how happy I was to see you."

"You did a good job. I'm pretty happy myself right now."

He lay there for a few minutes, looking so relaxed and content.

"I need to say something to you." He rolled away, sitting up. "When you left me, I was just going to let you go. But I couldn't forget you, so I made a decision. I want to be with you for however long we have and if one day you just up and disappear, I'll accept that. What I won't accept is being without you. You're in my heart, and you're there to stay."

Aimee sighed, lips trembling. "I'm not going anywhere."

"I know I'm not the man you want. But maybe I can learn."

He'd misunderstood! "You are the man I want. I was coming to find you. That's where I was earlier. I was buying tickets to Portland." She paused, asking testily. "Why didn't you answer any of my letters?"

He turned, face hopeful. "I never received any letters."

"I sent six letters to you over the past months, but I never received even one little note back." Her lips curved in a pout.

"Where'd you send them to?"

"Oregon City, of course. Where else would I send them?"

Jake stroked her arm, kissing the inside of her elbow. "I wasn't there. You never thought I listened or believed you, but after you left, John, me, and the girls left Oregon City and went to California. We got in on the gold rush—"

"John? John who?"

"John McAfee, from the wagon train."

"Ardis's husband? Where's Ardis?"

Jake grimaced. "Ardis caught the ague after you left and died. Several others did too. John didn't have anything left to hold him, so he went with us. He's taking a liking to the girls, and we all traveled here together."

"You mean John and the girls are here?"

He nodded. "They're over at the hotel. I wanted

a little time alone with you to talk."

Aimee jumped up. "We need to go over there and get them."

Pulling her back down, Jake kissed her, his tongue plunging. "We need to finish talking and then we'll get them."

She froze. She had some talking to do, too, and unless she was mistaken, Jake wasn't going to take it very well.

"Now," Jake said, "just keep your mouth shut while I finish saying what I have to say."

Lips compressed, crossing her heart, Aimee nodded.

Jake's eyes softened. "I always listened to everything you told me, even when I didn't believe any of it. But after you left, John, me and the girls went to Sutter's Mill and got in on the gold rush." He paused, adding dramatically. "We're rich, not filthy rich, but we're rich." He grinned, triumphant.

She opened her mouth to speak, but he glowered.

"On the way back up here, I stopped and talked to a group of investors planning on logging up north and bought in, so when this Seattle place opens up, we'll move there, and we'll just take it one day at a time. I'd rather have whatever time I can with you than none at all." Painful hope shadowed his eyes.

Aimee swallowed, heart full to bursting. "If I can help it, I'm not going anywhere. I had just bought tickets to Portland, and I was coming to find you when all this stuff happened earlier." She opened a drawer in the bedside table and pointed to a small, carefully wrapped packet. "I've always felt the locket had something to do with all of this, and when I decided you were my future, I took it off. I haven't worn it since and I won't. I'll keep it safe and hand it down to our descendants so they can give it to me when the time is right." Tears washed her eyes. "I always thought I could go home, but now I know I'm where I'm supposed to be."

Maudie rapped at the bedroom door. "You'd better be decent in there cuz I'm coming in."

Throwing open the door, she marched in, a small bundle held in her arms. Jake, cussed, throwing a quilt across his bare butt. Striding with determined purpose to the bed, Maudie thrust the small, squirming, angry-faced little baby girl into Jake's surprised arms.

"This baby's starving and a sugar tit ain't doing the trick anymore. Needs to be fed."

Aimee reached over, smoothing the baby's soft black curls. "It's way past time. Thanks for helping." She took the squalling baby from Jake's arms, cuddling the baby close as Sara Elizabeth nuzzled at her breast.

Dumfounded, Jake watched in amazement. "You ran off knowing full well you carried my son?" His blue eyes flashed dangerously.

"He's not your son," Aimee replied.

Jake's face fired red.

"He's your daughter." Aimee grinned, kissing the baby's tiny cheek. "Sara Elizabeth, meet your daddy."

"And if you have a problem with a baby girl," Maudie interjected, her eyes sparkling, "you can just get yourself up and get outta here—now!"

Reverently caressing one tiny hand, Jake murmured, "I never said I didn't want a baby girl. I just said some day I wanted a son." Leaning down he kissed his baby, pride and love shining from his agate blue eyes.

"There's just one problem with her," he began.

"There's nothing wrong with this baby," Maudie snapped, indignant.

Jake glared at her. "Do you women ever give a man the chance to finish a sentence? I was going to say, before I was interrupted, that there's just one problem with her." He grinned. "She doesn't have her mother's beautiful hair."

Aimee touched his face, loving him with every ounce of her being, looking forward to the future and life with the man of her dreams, her soul mate. Life was good, she was home.

Epilogue

It was late afternoon as Sara closed Aimee's journal. "That's the end of the story. That's all there is."

Dad looked like he held his breath. Mom cried openly, tears streaming down her face.

"We need to talk to the old lady," her mom choked. "I need some answers."

Her dad stood, helping Mom to stand. "I need some answers myself."

Dazed, Sara hesitated, caught in the past, held there by Aimee's story—a story of a life long passed, existing only in the well-worn book.

"This is crazy. We can't let ourselves believe this stuff. It's crazy." Dad shoved the chair. "If we believe it, then Aimee's gone forever!"

"Why?" Sara asked, her eyes brimming. "What else are we supposed to believe? That Aimee was kidnapped and murdered? I don't want to think that. This is so much better."

Mom nodded. "Better to believe she found another life than to believe the other. I couldn't bear that. At least this is something I can hold onto. If nothing else, she was happy."

A woman appeared. "Follow me, she's ready to tell you more."

Sara jumped to her feet and followed. Her parents trailed behind. They entered the bedroom and waited. A middle-aged woman leaned over the bed, murmuring to the old woman. She stood and turned.

"That's her," Sara gasped. "That's the woman

who sold Aimee the locket."

The old woman's thin reedy voice came from the depths of the bed. "My nephew's wife, Ellen." The woman nodded at the introduction.

The old lady spoke, her voice trembling and weak. "We only rented the shop for a month. Ellen opened it on my orders, or I should say on Aimee's orders." She coughed. "Lift me up so I can talk better."

Ellen busied herself rearranging pillows and helping the old woman to sit.

"I never really believed all of this," Ellen offered, contrite. "But when your daughter came up missing, it really threw me for a loop."

Mom stalked to the bed. "If you knew this was going to happen, why did you allow it?"

"It was what Aimee wanted. She set out all her wishes and instructions to the letter down on paper, and they've been handed down until me." The old woman's fingers plucked at the coverlet. "I hoped I'd be the one to give the book to you, but if not, I had told Ellen everything."

The old woman waved at the corner. "Sara, go open that trunk and tell me what you see."

Sara rushed across the room, kneeled beside the old box and lifted the lid, bracing it against the wall. Lifting out a tissue-wrapped package, she looked at the old woman.

"Open it up," the old woman smiled. "Tell me what you see."

Gently, Sara untied the strings and stared. Inside was Aimee's favorite outfit, old and worn, the lace yellowed with age. "It's the clothes Aimee wore the day she disappeared." Tears streamed down her face.

"There's more in there," the old lady explained. "She saved everything she had the day she disappeared. There are diaries in there, too. She kept one all the time. It was her way of making you part of her life. I've read them a million times. You're welcome to read them any time."

"Where is she?" The whispered words sounded as though Mom could barely form them.

Pity radiated from the old woman. "She's at Lake View Cemetery, near the huge oak tree in the back right corner." A fit of coughing wracked her.

Dad stared at the old lady and the woman, Ellen. "I still can't believe any of this."

The old woman smiled, pointing to a beribboned packet on the nightstand. "Aimee knew you'd be the hardest to convince. She left documents allowing you to exhume her body and take DNA samples. I never knew what DNA was until just the last few years, but Aimee left that option to you if you choose to take it." Her eyes closed in exhaustion, breaths laborious and fast.

"She's very tired," Ellen explained. "But she wanted to stay awake until after you'd read Aimee's book."

"I can die happy," the old woman's eyes flew open. "This was the day I've looked forward to since I was twelve-years-old."

"I want to go to the cemetery," Mom said, her grief-stricken eyes pleaded with Dad, heartbreaking in their intensity.

Dropping his head, nodding, he turned to go.

Sara rushed behind. They had one more stop to make before day's end.

Lake View Cemetery sat atop Capitol Hill. The gates were still open but a sign indicated the gates would soon close. They wound their way to the back corner as the old woman had indicated. An elderly caretaker, attacking weeds, stood up when they approached.

"Need some help finding someone?" he asked, his voice cheerful in the quiet.

"Yes," Sara answered. "We're looking for the grave of Aimee Reynolds Marshall."

"That one!" The old man's eyes lit. "She's one of our interesting ones. People visit her all the time. Follow me, she's right over here."

Wanting, but not wanting to see, she followed, steps lagging with trepidation.

"Right here," the old man cackled. "Whoever carved the inscription must have been tippling a little too much that day."

He pointed to a beautiful, carved pink granite headstone standing guard over a well-tended grave. "You need anything more, you just yell."

A huge oak tree, its limbs draped in protective folds, stood in glorious tribute to the grave beneath. Lilies grew in profusion around the base of the tree and along the fence, scenting the air with their exotic perfume.

Sara read the inscription, "Loving wife and mother, Aimee Reynolds Marshall. Born May 15, 1987, died October 6, 1910."

The lower right-hand corner of the headstone was embellished with an intricate design of converging lines and tiny squares, reminding her of Aimee's puzzle boxes. She studied the detailed carving, remembering the ease with which Aimee opened each one. *What if...* Excitement held her motionless. *It couldn't be—could it?*

She reached down, twisted the design, and grunted as the time-worn embellishment stuck. Another hard tug and the lines moved. Incredibly, a hidden door slid open, revealing a small concealed alcove. She reached in and pulled out a packet tied with a blue ribbon.

Shaking with nervous tension, Sara fingered the packet. "Can I open it?"

Dad nodded, his face anguished.

The ribbon was old, and after several attempts,

the knot loosened. Inside was a picture of a stately old couple, hands intertwined, and signed across the bottom as "Jacob and Aimee Marshall, July 14, 1896." Aimee's favorite ring was also there, along with a folded piece of paper. The brittle paper cracked as Sara unfolded it. She began reading.

My Dear Ones,

If you are reading this, Sara has not forgotten. Good for you, Sara!

Sara, I'm so sorry we didn't have the opportunity to share our lives as only sisters can share. I wasn't there to comfort you when you lost your first love, or to help you dress for your first prom. Having you as my baby sister was one of life's greatest gifts.

Mom, being without your love, wisdom, and guidance hurt so much, but I found you again in my daughter, Sara Elizabeth. She is you in so many ways, creative, fun, oftentimes forgetful, but oh, so dear. You would have loved all my children, my adopted daughters, Faith, Hope, and Charity, and my children with Jake: Sara Elizabeth, Jake Jr., David, and lastly, little Benjamin. Each is so special in so many ways.

Dad, believing will be the hardest for you. Your mathematical mind won't be able to accept such an abstract reality. I have left instructions to make believing easier. You were so many good things to me and I treasure my memories. I know you would have liked Jake, he reminds me of you; stable, protective, kind, and loving.

My children, my grandchildren, and even my great-grandchildren have played at my feet, and I have loved every one so very much. God sent me back to Jake and though I tried so very hard to come home, it wasn't meant to be. Weep no more for me, my dear ones. Though I missed you every day of my life, I found my heart's desire with Jake.

Love doesn't die, that I know for certain and if

we never meet again in this life, I know we will in the next—or even the next! I love you.

Aimee

As they stood over the grave, a gentle breeze sprang up. Warmth spread over Sara's grief-stricken heart as Aimee's laughter whispered on the wind. She could see her shining smile and feel her nearness.

Sara gasped, her heart thumping. "Dad, did you hear that?"

The wind whispered one last time, "*Goodbye.*"

A word about the author...

Offbeat is a perfect word when describing me. For many years I taught, performed as well as choreographed mideastern dance. I am a dreamer and an avid reader of fiction, a sometimes gardener and an inept crafter. I love to travel, always returning to my beautiful Idaho where I reside with my husband and best friend, Jack, my children and extended family, Jared, Travis, Zachary, and Tannis, two huge cats and a toy poodle. Currently, my books include *Fiona* and *Riley's Journey* (both Faery Rose), *Heart of the Sorcerer* (a Faery Miniature Rose), and this one, *Aimee's Locket* (Cactus Rose).

Visit P.L. at
www.myspace.com/mrsplparker or
www.plparker.com

Contact P.L. at plparker@plparker.com

www.ingramcontent.com/pod-product-compliance
Lightning Source LLC
Chambersburg PA
CBHW070203260626
47160CB00002B/432

* 9 7 8 1 6 0 1 5 4 6 8 3 8 *